Praise for Eileen Brady

Dr. Kate Vet Mysteries

"A pleasing mélange of mystery and pet lore."

—*Kirkus Reviews*

"Along with the intricately plotted mystery, Brady, herself a veterinarian, treats readers to useful information about organizing air travel with a pet, the proper diet for iguanas, and the sweet nature of properly raised and cared for pit bulls. Refreshingly well-adjusted Kate is a competent and compassionate protagonist cozy fans will want to see a lot more of. Pet lovers will adore this."

—*Publishers Weekly*

"A good, well-written cozy—the kind you can curl up on the couch with on Friday night and put it down on Sunday morning. Readers who are not familiar with Eileen Brady's work will become big fans."

—*New York Journal of Books*

Also by Eileen Brady

Dr. Kate Vet Mysteries
Saddled with Murder
Last but Not Leashed

Kate Turner, DVM Mysteries
Muzzled
Unleashed
Chained
Penned

MURDERS of
a FEATHER

MURDERS of a FEATHER

A DR. KATE VET MYSTERY

EILEEN BRADY

Poisoned Pen
PRESS

Published by Poisoned Pen Press, an imprint of Sourcebooks
P.O. Box 4410, Naperville, Illinois 60567-4410
(630) 961-3900
sourcebooks.com

Printed and bound in the United States of America.
KP 10 9 8 7 6 5 4 3 2 1

To all my readers, a heartfelt thank you. And to my newest and youngest, our lovely Claire Kathleen, welcome to the world.

"If men had wings and bore black feathers, few of them would be clever enough to be crows."

—Henry Ward Beecher

"Cats are inquisitive but hate to admit it."

—Mason Cooley

"Sometimes, your pet picks you."

—Julie Wenzel

Chapter One

"CUPID'S WAITING FOR YOU, DR. KATE," MARI, MY VETERI-nary technician, said.

"Do you have to rub it in?" I asked. It was the last half of January, and Valentine's Day loomed next month. I'd resigned myself to spending it alone with my dog, hiding out on my couch eating a frozen dinner for one.

Mari shook her head of black, glossy curls. "No, I mean Cupid is waiting for you in exam room two."

"Cupid is my patient?"

"Yep. But there aren't any arrows left in his quiver."

———

"Go potty, Cupid. Go potty."

"This looks like fun." Cindy, our receptionist, leaned against the treatment room door staring at the two of us, as crisp as we were wrinkled. Crowded with banks of cages, stainless-steel work tables, microscopes, and counters covered with diagnostic machines, this area was the heart of the Oak Falls Animal Hospital.

On a leash next to me trotted a slim Doberman pincher interested in anything but taking a leak. He'd come in for a suspected bladder infection. We needed a urine sample, but so far we had been unsuccessful. Mari, dressed in gray scrubs, followed the patient with a stainless-steel bowl, ready to catch a sample at the first sign of a leg lift, or a squat, as I marched him across the room. We'd been playing follow-the-leader throughout our lunch hour begging him to go.

"You're welcome to try," I told Cindy. "It's snowing outside, and his owner said this tough Dobie hates getting his feet wet." We'd been at this for fifteen minutes, and I was ready to put Cupid back in his run.

"No thank you," Cindy answered. "You couldn't get them to agree to a catheterized sample?"

"No such luck," Mari chimed in. "Wait…"

We all stared at the handsome black-and-tan dog as he paused, then lifted his leg and aimed for the end corner of the stainless-steel cages—a favorite spot for our male doggie patients.

Slick as a snake, Mari intervened. Cupid piddled his stream into the sanitized bowl, a direct hit. "Straight shot," she commented, "and more than enough. Hooray!"

Cupid looked up, flexed his back legs like he was digging up dirt a couple of times and probably wondered what all the fuss was about.

"Tell the owner he can pick him up anytime," I said, while opening the dog run door. "We'll have preliminary results in about thirty minutes. The culture and sensitivity will take the lab five to ten days."

"Will do." Cindy started to leave then stopped. "I'm going to miss you guys while I'm gone, but not enough to stay here."

Mari and I exchanged glances. Cindy was leaving for a week's vacation, spending the time relaxing on a warm Florida beach with her hubby and extended family. I hoped things would run smoothly while she was gone. Oak Falls Animal Hospital booked both clinic and house call appointments, keeping me super busy. I wondered about a stranger stepping into Cindy's sneakers for the week.

"Think positive," Mari commented when I confessed my fears to her. "It's only seven days and seven nights. It will be over before you know it."

Of course she was right. Cindy had proven herself a wonderful office manager, juggler of appointments, and fountain of good advice. Her job came with plenty of stress. Pleasing the public was tiring. I couldn't blame her for wanting to get away from the Hudson Valley during the winter. So far we'd had sun, snow, ice, sleet, rain, and golf ball-sized hailstones thrown at us by Mother Nature in the brief new year. Currently, a blast of arctic air that arrived late the previous night forced most residents to huddle inside.

Once caught up on my clinic notes, I moseyed over to my office and sat down in front of the computer. The cubbyhole-sized room, painted a restful cream color, was my retreat. In a corner lay the temperamental hospital cat, Mr. Katt, slumbering on his bed. He'd deposited his squeaky toy on my chair. I tossed it to him, but he didn't bother to acknowledge it.

The screensaver scrolled through several photos of gorgeous places I hadn't been. Sunbathing by the ocean sounded wonderful.

My train of thought was interrupted when I saw a stray potato chip wedged against the *V* on my keyboard. I absent-mindedly popped it in my mouth.

Since I had no hubby and no boyfriend and no prospects, I wondered again what kind of Valentine's Day I would have when Mari called out, "Dr. Kate. Do you need a fecal sample, too?"

That could only mean one thing. While I was musing about Valentine's Day, my Cupid had taken a dump.

———————————

Our busy morning passed quickly, but during lunchtime Cindy cautioned us about the afternoon schedule.

"Packed with house calls," she told us. "Plus I booked two drop-offs who needed to be seen."

A drop-off appointment meant the owner left their pet with us, and we basically saw them when we could, sometimes at the end of the day. That ensured they received veterinary care even when we technically didn't have any available appointments. I tried not to let any of my patients be without my help if humanly possible. This meant many late nights for my staff and me.

"I hope the house call appointments have plowed their driveways," I called out to Cindy's back.

Your next appointment is here, Mari texted me. Meet you in exam room one.

After powering down my computer I stood up, then ran the pet hair roller that had a treasured spot on my desk across my coat. Although Cupid was a shorthaired Dobie, he shed an amazing amount of black-and-tan fur on my white doctor's coat.

I didn't think that was what they meant by being "touched by Cupid."

Quickly checking in the employee bathroom that I looked presentable, I dipped both hands in water and slicked down my straight blond hair, some of which had escaped a tight ponytail. Nothing could be done about the pale makeup-free face that stared back at me. My friends sometimes told me I looked a little like a young Meryl Streep. Today I resembled a tired version of Meryl Streep who had recently crawled out from under a log.

With a sigh I swiped my lips with ChapStick, slipped my stethoscope around my neck, and walked toward the exam rooms.

Pausing outside exam room one, I took a breath before knocking and entering. Mari stood next to the stainless-steel exam table, her back obscuring the view of my patient. When she stepped away, I caught a glimpse of my second surprise of the day.

"So who is this cutie?" I asked. I normally didn't see pigs, but Cindy must have felt sorry for this client, who also brought his dog to us.

"It's Porky, our mini potbellied pig." The man who spoke rested his hand on the young piglet's gray-and-white back. "He just turned twelve weeks old."

So, you know how some people resemble their pets? The owner's nose had a definite upturn at the end. His bright blue eyes stared into mine, as though he knew what I was thinking and dared me to say anything.

"How long have you had him?" I asked. From where I

stood, there was no ambiguity as to Porky's gender. I slipped on a pair of exam gloves as we spoke.

"The wife and I got him as a baby. He's good as gold. House-trained, smart as can be—but he's got this lump here." With his forefinger he indicated the middle of Porky's belly. "My buddy said to put a quarter over it and duct tape it."

Now I'm as big a fan of duct tape as everyone else, but in this instance it wouldn't do any good. I immediately knew what was wrong. Porky had an umbilical hernia. Pressing gently I palpated to feel if any loops of intestine had slid into the swelling. Hernias aren't uncommon in pigs. This was a moderate one so far, caused by a deficit or weakness in the abdominal wall. Since Porky had not been neutered, I also checked for an inguinal hernia. His immature porcine package felt totally normal.

As I explained an umbilical hernia to the client, I also said there was only one option to fix the problem: surgery. As the piglet got bigger and put on weight this hernia would continue to swell. A neuter was also in order so their well-behaved baby wouldn't develop nasty hormonal behavior accompanied by very stinky urine.

"Plenty of people with pet pigs told me he had to be neutered. That's what I figured," the owner said. "We're okay with that. The wife and I love this little guy."

I also had a fondness for these happy, intelligent creatures. In fact, I'd spent several summers working at a rescue farm during vet school and assisted at piglet hernia repairs with my large-animal vet professor. Because of Porky's small size, I was comfortable doing the surgery, but I preferred to refer him to the nearby large-animal practice.

"Mari, can you have Cindy call the Hudson Valley Animal Clinic and Equine Center and find out when they can see Porky?" If they were half as busy as we were, it might be a month or longer.

While I waited for an answer I continued my exam, taking a moment to scratch the piglet on his snout. His coarse-hair coat was even and healthy, his lungs and heart normal. Porky poked his nose under my hand like a cat wanting to be petted again.

"He does that to me all the time," the owner said.

As I chatted about the proper feeding and husbandry of potbellied pigs, Mari interrupted. "Sorry, Dr. Kate. They've got one doctor out on maternity leave and a second doc who broke his wrist skiing. They won't have any openings for elective surgery for another three months."

"I'm not sure this guy can wait that long," I said. My palpations had revealed quite an opening in the abdominal wall. "Let me make some phone calls," I told the owner while absentmindedly stroking the piggy. "Worst case scenario, we can do it here."

"Thanks, Dr. Kate. You don't know how much this means to us."

The owner was wrong. I did have an inkling of how much he loved Porky and Porky loved him.

When he leaned over to pick up his pet he got a big wet porcine kiss.

Which was one more kiss than I'd had in a while.

Chapter Two

THE RUMBLE OF THE HOSPITAL F-150 TRUCK DOWN-shifting made me miss the last part of Mari's discussion of her Valentine's Day plans as we drove toward our final house call of the afternoon. She and her partner had reservations for dinner at an Italian restaurant, then arranged to meet up with friends for karaoke at the Red Lion Pub.

"You have to book early or you're out of luck," she reminded me. "Why don't you come along? We'd love to have you join us."

Being a third wheel was not my idea of fun, so I fibbed a little. "I've got a friend from school who might be in the neighborhood, but thanks for the offer."

We bounced over a rut in the road. Our seat hinges squeaked in protest.

Mari looked up from the office laptop and asked, "Who is that?"

Pinned to the wall I blurted out my old lab partner's name. "Danny Malone. He's just a friend, so don't get excited." I knew my staff wanted to see me happy. Maybe this would tide them over until the Ides of March, but I doubted it.

Before Mari could follow with a million questions I said, "Which pet are we looking at today?" It was Friday, and we were on our way to Maple Grove Farm, a rescue facility run by a retired NYC power couple. I'd seen several of their animals over the last few months.

"Ahh. Let me see. It looks like we're checking out some puppies, born to one of those puppy mill dogs they rescued. We're set to do first exams and vaccines, and one of the puppies is limping."

Puppy mill females were of use to breeders only as long as they could have puppies. The females are forced to have litter after litter until they are basically worn out. Here at the Maple Grove Farm, they gave happy lifetime homes to animals that desperately needed rescuing.

"Ashley and her husband do such needed work," I said, slowing down as we approached their driveway. The clank of our chains jangled harshly as we crossed over a spot of cleared asphalt. Pine branches weighed down with recent snow slapped the side of the truck. The new scratches would join all the other scratches. A sharp turn, and we were ready to climb the small hill leading to the farm. Quite a menagerie lived here, including goats, horses, donkeys, and a mule. On the small-animal side were multiple dogs, cats, assorted hamsters, and other pocket pets.

The tires dug into the snow, moving farther up the rise with minimum sliding and slipping, before breaking through to the fields above. Mari texted Ashley Kaminsky to let her know we were here. As we passed the barn I noticed a mobile veterinary truck parked outside.

"Who's that?" I asked, pulling up to the farmhouse and parking parallel to the front walkway.

Mari craned her neck and read "Hudson Valley Animal Clinic and Equine Center."

"Good," I said, digging out my medical bag from the back

seat. "Maybe after we're done, I can ask them about Porky the piglet."

Mari opened the passenger side door and secured the laptop computer into a carrying case. "Look out. We've got quite a welcoming committee today."

Sure enough, a pack of dogs woofed and wagged their tails, running to the truck to greet us. Standing on the wide wraparound porch, Ashley waved a greeting, one foot sporting a black orthopedic device. I waved back, sure that my words of greeting would be inaudible, as I waited for the barking to tamp down. The renovated farmhouse combined country charm with modern efficiency. Running a rescue farm had been the couple's longtime dream.

A deep woof next to me begged for attention. The vocalist turned out to be a shaggy shepherd mix named Tommy who stood by my side, his bushy tail swinging. He'd been treated for a terrible ear infection not long ago and had stayed at the hospital with us for a few days. Even in discomfort he'd been a cheerful, cooperative patient. Now, cured of a persistent mixed bacterial and yeast infection deep in the ear canal, he wriggled and wagged his greeting.

I bent down to say hi, softly petting his head and sneaking a quick peek into his thick, floppy ears. No funky smell was a good sign.

Meanwhile, Mari called the pooches to follow her up the stairs. With a whirl of energy, some sprinted ahead, while others preferred the gradual graded ramp built for the older and three-legged dogs. All were happy and enjoying their second chance at life, thanks to this well-run rescue farm.

My assistant and the dogs disappeared inside. A self-proclaimed dog person, Mari was in her element.

"Come on in," Ashley called out on her way to the kitchen. I brushed my boots off on the doormat then left them in the mudroom. A pair of loafers stashed in my backpack provided me with clean shoes. Once shod, I joined the crowd in the kitchen.

"Coffee?" our client asked. Although Ashley was worth a small fortune and had the money to wear designer clothes, she preferred well-worn jeans and a baggy sweatshirt.

"Thanks, for the offer. Maybe a quick one? How many puppies do we have to examine?"

"Only five survived. The mommy dog escaped while in heat and those dreadful puppy farm owners weren't happy about it. They dumped her on the side of a road, but someone saw them and brought her to our rescue. She's the sweetest golden retriever, considering all she's been through." Ashley made a move off the chair. "Let me get you that coffee."

Mari jumped up. "Wait. I'll pour. I see you still have your orthopedic boot on. You need to take it easy." The couple had created a fancy espresso/coffee/tea bar at the end of the gray-and-white granite countertop. Stainless-steel appliances shone next to their cobalt blue French enamel stove.

Ashley made a noise of disgust, focusing on the black shiny device clamped onto her lower leg.

"I hate this thing. Both my husband and my doctor have confined me to the house for ten days until my ankle begins to heal properly. Last week I tripped over something going out to the barn and reinjured it. That's the third or fourth time. I am unbelievably clumsy."

"Do you have someone helping you?" I asked. Besides feeding all the animals, there were stalls to muck out and medications to be given, not to mention checking on the livestock in the barn.

Ashley nodded, her shoulder-length hair bobbing. "I've got our farm manager full-time, and my neighbor's oldest daughter is coming over after school to help with the horses. On the weekends the volunteers take over."

"Well, if there's anything we can do, let us know," I said. "By the way, what are the large-animal vets doing here?"

"We just acquired twin goat rescues, and of course they're both pregnant. I asked the large-animal vets to come out and do ultrasounds, so I don't have any unpleasant surprises." She laughed at that, as if she didn't have enough surprises in her life. "They're also getting wellness checks."

Coffee cup drained, I felt the blast of caffeine energy. "Mari, have you got the vaccines with you?"

She held up our refrigerated traveling case. "Ready when you are, Doc. Ashley, can you point the way?"

"Straight down that hallway. They're in the back room on the right with the door that says 'Beware of Puppies,'" Ashley told us. "I played with them this morning," she added. "Mommy dog is over here taking a break." She pointed to a white-faced golden retriever with wavy hair, who obviously had been nursing for a while.

"Okay. We're going in."

Like the rest of the downstairs, all the farmhouse floors that looked like wide wooden planks were actually tile. During renovation Ashley made sure all the surfaces were pet cleanup friendly. Several cats strolled along with us, unconcerned by the dogs milling around.

When we opened the door, a symphony of high-pitched puppy yips forced me to use hand signals to communicate with my veterinary assistant.

The large room had been cordoned off into two spaces by temporary fencing, for ease of cleaning. Five playful puppies scrambled over each other as they ran to get petted. Each pup had a different-colored collar, making identification easier. In this case it wasn't necessary.

Each puppy looked completely different from its sibling. Truly a mixed bouquet of cuteness.

"Superfecundation at its finest," I commented as Mari put our supplies on a small table. In front of me the furry babies, some with ears that were up, some with floppy ears, and others with curled-up tails stared at me. The rainbow array of coat colors made me smile. Only one resembled their golden retriever mom.

"Super what?"

"Superfecundation. It happens when a dog in heat has had several boyfriends at the same time, to say it politely. These puppies all have the same mom, but there could well be multiple different daddies."

"So that's what they call it. Yep. A friend of mine's female Dalmatian jumped a fence when she was in heat after they bred her to a champion Dalmatian stud. She delivered seven spotted puppies and one that was dark brown and long-haired. The owner had DNA tests done so she could verify which ones were pure Dalmatians."

"So, obviously the brown one wasn't."

"Right. But neither were five of the spotted ones. She ended up with only two pure-blooded Dalmatians out of the entire litter."

"Bummer for her. But we don't have to worry about any of that with these cutie-pies. Who's first?"

Mari handed me a gray short-haired male with a broad head. "Maybe some pit bull in this one?"

"Time will tell." The little guy licked my face as I tried to listen to his heart. I had to hand it to Ashley. The entire litter was very socialized, friendly, and healthy. After I gave the pups their first set of shots, we stayed for about twenty minutes, making sure none of them showed any rare allergic reaction to their vaccines. My spirits definitely lifted with this full-immersion puppy therapy. It's impossible to be down when surrounded by puppies.

By the time we got up off the floor, both Mari and I had a dusting of puppy fuzz and debris on our scrub pants.

"Had your fill of puppy breath?" I asked my friend.

"Never," she answered with a big grin.

As we walked down the hallway toward the kitchen, I said, "While you get the puppy kits and exam paperwork ready, I'm going to take a quick trip to the barn and see if the large-animal doc needs any help. I'll text you when I'm done."

"No worries," Mari answered, plucking a clump of hair from her scrub top. "I'll check in with Cindy. I hope we're finished for the day."

We updated Ashley on each of her puppies, then I excused myself. "I'm going to head out to your barn and see if that large-animal vet needs any help. Any idea who is working out there?"

Ashley thought for a moment. "I'm pretty sure it's Dr. Mike. His wife just had twins. If he looks tired, then he's the one," she laughed.

"Okay. I'll be back soon."

I took my jacket off the mudroom coatrack, placed my shoes in the backpack, and slipped into my green rubber boots. Now outfitted, I left for the barn. I was very familiar with it, having helped Ashley gentle a wild mustang adoptee last month.

Out in the corral I said hi to two horses, including Lobo the mustang. A donkey and a few sheep meandered over, looking for the apple treats I always carried in my coat pocket.

"Later, guys." Above me the sky darkened, intensifying the cold. I left the animals pulling hay out of the hayrack and opened the barn door. "Hello," I called.

"Over here," came a somewhat muffled voice. "Just in time."

Sitting in the hay in one of the large pens wearing a wrinkled white coat over a sweater was a brown-haired man with straw on his shoulder. The large-animal vet, I assumed. A very pregnant nanny goat was tethered in front of him.

He looked up at me, his glasses sliding down his nose.

"Hey. I'm Dr. Turner. Oak Falls Animal Hospital. I'm doing a puppy wellness house call and thought I'd drop in and see if you needed any help."

He started to answer when the mother goat gave a grunt,

and out popped a sleek, wet goat head. I noticed movement in the hay nearby. Two more kids lay curled up together, slick and new.

In the far corner stood a portable ultrasound machine, safely stowed in its case.

I gingerly knelt down, checking first for any piles of goat yuck lying around. "How many?" I asked.

"We've got a trifecta here," he laughed. "Those two were already out when I got here. Let's see." He pushed his glasses back onto his nose. "Lost a contact and waiting for a replacement. These glasses are a pain." The goat bleated again, so he started talking to her in a calm deep voice. "You're almost finished, mommy. Just one more to go."

She must have listened because the baby's head moved forward.

"Do you assist at this point?" I asked. "My large-animal professor didn't recommend intervening unless absolutely necessary."

"Good advice." He leaned nearer the nanny goat. "I visually check for tears or inertia, or anything unusual. Otherwise, goats rarely need any help."

As he slid closer, the mom made another goaty noise and the baby slid out, feet with tiny black hooves neatly tucked up. In an instant we were dodging slime.

The vet's arms and hands—clear up to and over the elbow—were covered by his work gloves. I wasn't as prepared. I scuttled behind him and stood up.

"Looks like you're good here." I heard the baby goats begin to bleat.

"Thanks, Dr. Turner," he said. His grin was warm and friendly. The mother goat moved toward her babies, tossing hay in the air that landed on the large-animal veterinarian's head.

"Call me Kate," I told him.

"Mike," he answered. "Say, if you're going back to the house, tell Ms. Kaminsky I'll text her a full report with pictures in a few minutes. I want to finish checking out this little guy and clean up a bit before using my cell phone."

He held up both hands covered with various liquids, a big smile on his face. "Can't beat bringing a little one into the world."

"Agreed. I loved working in the cow barns in school," I confessed, "so this is a fun change of pace for me. These days I'm mostly small animals and pocket pets."

Three rambunctious baby goats interrupted our conversation butting his hands looking to nurse. He gently guided them to the mom feeding station.

"Nice meeting you," I told him. "Got to run."

"Thanks. See you around," he said before turning back to his goat patients.

I stopped at the barn door, almost forgetting my ulterior motive. "Oh. How's your elective surgery schedule? I've got an umbilical hernia and neuter in a mini potbellied piglet that's about twelve weeks old I'm trying to send to your surgeons."

His eyes squinted at the hanging light above my head. In the harsh light he looked to be in his early thirties.

"Call the office and check, but from what I hear, we're booking elective surgery out almost three months."

"This piggie may not be able to wait," I answered. "There is a large deficit in the abdominal wall, and he's got about a two-inch umbilical swelling already." A stray hen wandered over and pecked at my boot.

"If you need some help, call me," Mike said. "Hey. I've got a deal for you. I'll come over and assist in exchange for you seeing a bunch of barn cats at my client's stable. I'll text my cell number to your office. It's easier to get ahold of me by text these days."

"Deal. I hear you've got a lot on your plate at the moment, so I appreciate that generous offer. Get some rest and enjoy your new babies." I opened the barn door and went out through the corral to the main house.

———

"You've got baby goats," I told Ashley. "One of your females gave birth to three little ones. All healthy that I could see. Dwarf Nubians, right?" The kitchen felt unbearably warm after being outside.

"Right."

"Well, I'd love to run out and see them," Mari said, "but Cindy squeezed in another house call, so we've got to get going." She dodged a tiny dog while retrieving her coat.

"Who was out there? Dr. Mike?" Ashley asked. "He's the vet who came last time."

"Yes. He's going to text you about the second goat and the kid details when he finishes up," I said. "Now, please take care of that ankle. No tromping around in the mud and ice."

She bent down and scooted her finger around the top margin of the boot brace. "This thing is starting to itch."

"Don't scratch. You can get infected sores that way."

Reluctantly she pulled her fingers out and placed both hands on her kitchen table. "I've accepted that I'm house-bound for another week. Believe me, I've learned my lesson in a painful way."

"Stay there," I told her. "We'll see ourselves out." I hoisted my backpack and separate medical bag over my shoulder. "By the way, your orthopedic doctor can recommend something to calm that itch."

Mari moved ahead of me, our computer and other gear stowed in lightweight waterproof bags. We carefully snuck out the door leaving the dog pack inside.

Standing on the porch steps, I took another look at the red-painted barn in this beautiful rural setting, thinking about my decision to focus on small-animal medicine. Did my one hundred fifty thousand-plus dollars of student debt influence my choice? All I knew was it had been fun helping out in the barn today.

"You coming?" Mari asked, walking around the truck to the passenger side. Bits of frozen snow crunched under her high boots.

"On my way."

We climbed into the front seat of the old truck and began carefully maneuvering down the driveway. I downshifted, preparing for the steepest part of the slope before it evened out by the mailbox and the main road.

"Did you take pictures of the baby goats?" Mari asked. She was a sucker for baby animals, no matter the species.

"Nope. Sorry. It got busy and messy."

"What's the large-animal vet like?" she asked, opening up the laptop and scrolling through several pages.

"Nice." We were at the base of the driveway, waiting for an opening into traffic. As on most country roads, it seemed you could go for fifteen minutes without anyone passing, but when you needed to pull out into traffic, there was always a mess of cars and trucks zipping by.

"His name is Dr. Mike. I didn't get his last name. I guess he's the one with twins at home."

"He's lucky he doesn't have triplets," Mari commented. "Talk about needing a village."

I could only nod in agreement. For a while I took care of four dogs in my small studio apartment attached to the animal hospital. It felt like running a boarding facility, between the special diets, personalities, and trying to get them all to pee at the same time. And those were dogs, not children. At this point in my life, I couldn't imagine juggling work and family. So far, I'd been unsuccessful at maintaining a career and a relationship. No surprise that Valentine's Day was going to be a no-show for me again.

After a truck stacked with refuse for the dump rumbled by, I eased onto the road and drove toward our next appointment.

Mari chatted away while I concentrated on driving. Light snowflakes danced across our windshield. On either side of the country road rose hills of snow pushed high by the plows. It had snowed on and off for the last three days. Dirty with sand and grit, the piles on the side of the road would be melting soon when February turned into March. I was dreaming about bright yellow daffodils when I saw a red-jacketed person in the road, waving their hands.

"Hold on," I told Mari as I came to a sudden stop, hoping the person in front of me would get out of the way. As the truck slid to a halt, chains digging in, the ski-jacketed person scrambled over a shoulder of snow.

"What the heck?" Mari began to roll down her window.

We could see now it was a fellow in his thirties with a frenzied expression on his face. As I waited for him to approach, I noticed a tire trail off to the right across a field of white. Stranded about sixty feet away in a snowbank was an SUV, hood pointing down into a hidden gully. Was this guy doing the equivalent of off-road skiing with his truck?

"Hey," Mari said as the guy approached the passenger side window. "Is something wrong?"

The man's dark eyes darted, as he tried to explain, snowflakes frozen to his eyelashes. "There's a body in the woods," he gasped.

Chapter Three

"WHAT DID YOU SAY?" SAID MARI. BORN IN OAK FALLS, she knew every square meter of the local countryside.

"There's a body in the woods," he repeated loudly as if we hadn't heard him. "You've got to call the police. My stupid phone is out of charge." Out of frustration he slammed his gloved hand on our hood.

I put the truck into park. "A body? Where is it?"

"There." He pointed toward the distant tree line at the end of the snow-covered field.

"How far past your truck?" Mari asked. "There's only one trail on this side that I know about."

Instead of answering, he yelled, "Hurry up. Call them. What are you waiting for? Call the police now!"

Before he finished his sentence, Mari had her cell phone up to her ear, describing to the person on the other line exactly where we were. After a moment I heard her say, "Okay. We'll wait up there at the top of the hill."

"Get in," I told the stranger.

My assistant opened her door and motioned to the back seat. "Show us where it is. The police will be here as soon as they can."

When he crawled into our truck, he stumbled on some supplies bagged up in the back. At the sight of the syringes and vials of medications, he said, "Hey. What is this?"

I cranked the wheel to the right, following the break in

the snowbank and began maneuvering the truck over the barely visible tire tracks. Mari lowered her window and took pictures with her phone. "We're from Oak Falls Animal Hospital," I told him. "I'm a veterinarian and this is my technician."

"It's a human body," he said in an annoyed voice. "A human body, not some stupid animal. I wouldn't even have bothered to flag you down if I'd known. What good are you two girls at a time like this?"

Downshifting hard, I easily maneuvered our old F-150 with chains on the tires past his new SUV, stuck in the snow.

"Humans are animals," I reminded him. "But you've got a point. Some people are way more stupid than others."

Once we approached the tree line, I used the imprints in the snow as a map. We went as far as we could before I turned around, parking with the hood facing the road below. Once the police arrived, space for parking would get crowded. I could hear Mari snapping pictures all the way up the hill.

"Okay," I told the guy, who'd said his name was Bruce, taking a moment to secure my muffler around my neck. "Show us where you found the body."

We jumped down into the two-foot-high snow. I made sure to lock the truck behind us. You never knew if someone might be after the veterinary tranquilizers and other drugs we carried, and I wasn't about to find out. While Bruce scrambled out the passenger side door, I slipped the pepper spray my Gramps insisted I carry out of my backpack and placed it in my coat pocket. An icy gust of wind forced me to jam my knitted hat over my forehead. Something about Bruce felt off.

"It's over there," he said, pointing to an obvious trail that led into the woods. Mari went ahead with Bruce in the middle, while I lingered at the back of the line. An imprint in the snow led past a dirty splatter, witness that someone had lost the contents of their stomach.

"This yours?" I yelled to Bruce.

He turned his face to me and nodded.

After taking more photos for the police, I trudged along behind him until we reached a plateau and the trail entrance.

"Hey, I don't want to see that again," he said, stopping dead under a blackened pine. The heavy canopy of trees here meant the ground leading into the woods had only a sprinkling of snow over a thick mat of leaves and pine needles.

"Okay. You can wait for the police. Did you check for any signs of life?" I asked.

"Hell, no," he said. "The guy looked frozen solid."

Before I could ask any more questions, I heard Mari call, "Dr. Kate. Over here."

Bruce's face turned a gray patchy color, which I hoped didn't mean a repeat vomit performance.

"Alright. Stay here," I told him. "When the police arrive, explain that we went down the trail to the body. Even with a low charge, your phone should be able to call 911 if you need to."

"Okay." He'd pulled out his cell and lifted his gloved hand up searching for a signal. His curses at his cell phone carrier and the general world faded behind me as I headed into the woods.

Riddled with hidden tree roots, the path required concentration. Walking became slow and deliberate. Parts of this makeshift trail felt more like moving through a twisted tunnel than a pleasant stroll in the woods. Why would anyone voluntarily be traveling on this in winter?

I caught a glimpse of the bright blue of Mari's coat in the distance. She seemed to be bending over something. Mari had EMT training and knew from experience not to contaminate a crime scene—if this was a crime scene. I stopped to catch my breath. More likely the person succumbed to a heart attack or stroke. It wouldn't be the first time someone had underestimated the stress to the body of trudging through the snow.

Eventually the rough pathway opened, and I saw Mari in a small clearing. Here the snow looked undisturbed. I quickly noticed only one set of tracks other than Mari's. Those must have been left by Bruce. To document what I saw, I took more photos.

"Hey," I said, not going any closer. A person in bright ski clothes lay facedown in the snow. There were no indications that they tried to get up or move once they fell.

"He's gone," Mari said. "The body is stiff from cold or rigor mortis. No pulse. A case for the coroner now." It was impossible to tell who the victim was, but I guessed from the colors and cut of the outdoor wear that the body was male.

She carefully walked back in her boot tracks. We both turned our heads as sirens sounded in the far distance.

"In the summertime, this is a popular area to picnic and hang out," Mari said. She gestured off to the left. "There's a small lake just behind that cluster of trees whose water stays pretty cool, even in August. We locals have been known to go skinny-dipping there."

Following her gaze, I saw only more snow. Sunlight broke through the clouds, glaring off the relentless white landscape. Then, a sharp jolt of electric pink caught my eye. "Mari, there's something on the ground, just past the broken limb way over there."

"I see it," she said and began making her way through the virgin snow.

"Wait," I called to her, trying to catch up. Mari wore high, heavy boots. My shorter rubber boots couldn't compete. I trudged behind her, trying to walk in her tracks as snow slipped over the tops of my boots then melted from body heat. Icy droplets trickled down my legs and into my socks.

She strode way ahead of me. Mari had a lifetime of winter experiences on her side. Suddenly she disappeared into another pine grove, only visible as brief flashes of bright color among the dark branches.

Trying to keep out of the deep snow, I detoured through piles of debris and rotting leaves collecting under a large stand of pines. Caught under a dead tree limb lay a half-buried neon-pink hair scrunchie. After documenting it with another photo, I left it for the forensic team.

I'd reached Mari when I heard her cry out, "Oh, no!"

We met at the edge of a frozen pond. Spiky remnants of reeds stood stiff and brown, icy droplets glistening up and down the brown leaves like tiny silver beads. The wind had swept most of the lake's smooth surface clear of snow.

Mari pointed to the frozen water below.

Under the ice, a lovely face peered up at us, blank eyes clouded by the cold. Pale blond hair had floated around her head in long strands before freezing in place. Both hands were splayed out flat against the hard ice, as though trying to escape. Her blue lips were parted. Bubbles, captured under the icy surface, held her last breath or cry for help.

When I glanced at Mari, I saw hot tears winding a pathway down her cheeks.

———

When the Oak Falls Police Department arrived, they found Bruce and us waiting together next to the tree line. This would be a recovery operation, not a rescue. I replayed in my mind Mari's and my movements, so we could account for our footsteps in the snow. Did the woman fall into the pond first, leaving her companion to panic and perish in the snow?

My assistant leaned against a tree trunk, uncharacteristically silent.

We watched as emergency vehicles and several police cars left the main road and detoured one by one to avoid Bruce's SUV and our truck tire tracks in the snow. One officer remained parked at the bottom of the hill to discourage onlookers. Another officer set up caution light markers and detour signs. The EMT crew parked close to our truck, making an informal line, their brightly colored lights reflected in the snow.

Things escalated rapidly after Chief of Police Bobby

Garcia came on the scene. Another detective interrogated Bruce separately, while the chief spoke briefly to us. He persuaded the argumentative Bruce to hand over the keys to his stranded SUV, which would be towed to the police station. From experience, I figured at the police station this Good Samaritan would endure another lengthy conversation with more detectives.

Someone walked past carrying a chain saw. Mari turned her head away.

EMTs trudged behind with stretchers. Each of the locals nodded at Mari. A medical examiner carrying a black bag, his title boldly printed on his work vest, walked by, cell phone to his ear. Just another body for him in a workday filled with bodies.

When Chief Garcia returned he said, "We've verified your house call at Maple Hill Farm and the time you left. Mari, when you made your 911 call, were you still on the main road?" His voice sounded gentler than usual.

"Yes," she answered. "I even took a picture of Bruce standing on the shoulder of the road hailing us down. After he got into the truck, I documented our trip up the hill past his SUV."

It came as no surprise to me that Mari and I both recorded everything with our phone cameras. We often did the same thing at work. The time stamp and date proved handy while working a case.

She scrolled through her photos and videos and handed the chief her phone. The shadowy patches under Bobby's eyes made him look tired and older than he was. Anyone who underestimated him, however, made a big mistake.

"It's clear from this snapshot that when you arrived only one pair of tire tracks was visible."

Thinking back, I agreed with him. "The ground underneath our tires felt pretty compacted, as if other people had driven up the hill before the last snowstorm."

He made an indeterminate sound then asked, "Mari, you left Bruce standing at the tree line, then continued up the path. Dr. Kate followed. Correct?"

"Correct," she said. "There were obvious footprints leading up to the first body, most likely from Bruce, but none going toward the lake."

Replaying that short walk in the woods, I realized I wasn't sure if the body lying on the ground in the red jacket was a man or a woman.

"And what made you continue to Lover's Lake? There was no indication anyone else was still here." He pulled a small notebook from his jacket pocket.

Mari stayed silent.

"I saw something pink in the distance," I explained, "and pointed it out to Mari. It turned out to be a hair scrunchie. Someone either lost it or tossed it into that grove of trees."

The chief jotted something down in his notebook. Did that hair tie belong to the victim? The memory of long, flowing hair frozen in the ice made me wonder.

"I didn't see it until Dr. Kate pointed it out to me," Mari added. "That made me wonder if there might be another victim out there. The lake..."

Her voice faded.

"Did anyone take pictures?" The chief asked.

I opened my phone to recent photos. "I've got a photo of the scrunchie."

Mari looked at the police chief. For the first time I heard a note of stress in her voice. "I took one from the oak trees pointing out to the lake. Bobby, there were no prints on the ground, no animal tracks, no anything."

He shifted his weight before he asked, "What made you look in the lake?"

"You know why. It's a lake. Accidents happen all the time."

I'd rarely seen my assistant this agitated, but the chief simply nodded and said, "Okay. You two can leave, but expect a call in the next few days. Someone from my office will need official copies of those photos from both of you."

As I turned to go, I noticed Mari tug on the chief's sleeve and say quietly, "Thanks, Bobby. This brought back bad memories."

Their eyes locked briefly, and the chief muttered, "Yeah. Bad memories for both of us."

With her head down, Mari traced her own footsteps walking in the direction of our truck, quickly passing me without a word. In silence we stood on either side of the hospital truck, surrounded by movement and flashing lights. I unlocked the doors using the remote and Mari climbed inside.

When I glanced over my shoulder, Chief Garcia stared back at me, a frown on his face.

Chapter Four

WE SAT TOGETHER IN THE FRONT SEAT OF THE TRUCK, BUT for all intents and purposes, Mari wasn't there. After receiving only one-word answers to my questions, I decided to concentrate on the road. These were the last days Cindy was working before her vacation began, and despite this excitement, I was sure she had plenty to go over with us.

As soon as I turned into the Oak Falls Animal Hospital parking lot, Cindy opened the front door. She gestured for me to stop, something quite unusual since I normally parked at the back entrance of the hospital. To my surprise, Mari jumped out of the passenger side seat, slammed the door, and ran over to Cindy—who gave her a big hug and ushered her inside.

Something was up.

Assuming I was on my own for now, I parked the truck and hauled our equipment in through the back door. A trio of crows, perched near the hospital dumpster, cawed away at me. They must have figured they'd found a good place to forage while waiting for spring. Once inside the hospital, I assumed someone would tell me what was going on. After stowing all our gear, I made my way toward the employee lounge.

"We're in here," Cindy's voice called out from behind the door.

As soon as I entered, she said, "I made you some hot chocolate. Come, join us."

Mari sat at the far end of the employee lunch table, an identical hot chocolate in front of her. "Hey," she said.

"I rescheduled that last appointment, so you're both finished for today." Cindy indicated that I should sit opposite Mari. On the table lay a file folder full of papers. I knew that on Sunday she and her husband and their kids were driving down to Newark Airport for their early morning flight to Miami. She'd made these reservations over six months ago.

"We can finish closing up if you have to leave," I told her. Cindy liked to do things her way, acknowledging she was a bit of a control freak. Personally, I enjoyed her organizational skills. It made work so much easier to have someone else obsessing over every detail.

"Kate," Mari said, barely looking at me, "I need to explain something."

Midsip, I braced for hearing something I maybe didn't want to know.

Cindy walked over and put a protective arm around my assistant's shoulder. "Do you want me to tell her?" Our receptionist's face read concern.

"No, I can do this." Mari turned to face me, Cindy close by, supporting her by her very presence.

I hadn't a clue what was going on.

"When I was ten years old," Mari began, "my older sister and I snuck out to a lake near our house to go ice skating. We'd received new skates for Christmas. It was a perfect winter day, bright and sunny for a change. We left our stuff onshore and started skating toward the middle of the lake. That's when it happened. The ice cracked and my sister fell in. I tried to grab her hand and pull her out, but I wasn't strong enough. As she went under she pulled me in too."

Mari's voice shook as she explained what happened next. Their screams were heard by a man onshore walking his dog. A local, he rushed out to help. By carefully sprawling across the ice, he pulled Mari out.

"It was so cold," she said. "Colder than anything you can imagine. Colder than the moon. He kept yelling for help, but no one came."

"The stranger was Bobby Garcia," Cindy added.

Surprised, I looked up at Cindy, a question in my eyes. Things began to fall into place. Mari and now Chief of Police Bobby Garcia. Mari and Bobby.

"Bobby called 911, gave Mari his coat, then went back to help Mari's sister, Marjorie. The ice continued to splinter underneath his weight. He took his belt off and tossed it to Marjorie, but it kept skittering away from her sliding across the ice."

Cindy paused, allowing Mari to finish the story.

"He threw it again and again, but my sister couldn't hold on. I can still see her fingertips, trying to grasp on to the jagged edge of the ice. By the time the police and EMTs arrived. Marjorie had slipped under."

My friend looked terribly sad. Today she relived a horrific trauma.

"The emergency crew brought me a blanket and a hot drink. I refused to leave my sister," Mari said. "I watched when they finally pulled her out of the water. They tried CPR but it was too late."

Mari stared straight ahead.

"Seeing that poor woman today brought all of it back to me."

"Take a sip of hot chocolate," Cindy advised her. "It happened a long time ago."

There was nothing left to say. Cindy and Mari sat huddled together while my hot chocolate turned cold.

Chapter Five

WHILE WE TALKED ABOUT HOSPITAL SCHEDULES, CINDY'S temporary replacement, and the Florida tan we insisted Cindy come back with, Mari had slowly returned to her normal self, even laughing before walking out the front door with our receptionist. After they left, I locked up the hospital, checking all the windows before turning on the alarm system.

Getting to my apartment from the animal hospital was easy. I lived in the converted garage attached to the building. All I had to do was walk through the connecting door by the laundry room. It wasn't much. One large room with a bathroom and kitchen, but my place came free with the job.

Necessity had landed me in the Hudson Valley from New York City. When I answered Doc Anderson's ad for a relief vet, it was the prospect of free housing that interested me the most. Paying down my student loans faster would give me more freedom. After this, I wouldn't have to take just any job offered to me.

The position here in Oak Falls was quite different from the ones my vet school classmates had. Doc Anderson, who'd been practicing for over forty years, had decided at the last moment to join his sister, a breast cancer survivor, on a world cruise. They'd be gone a year, and I'd be running the medical side of the practice. He ran an old-fashioned one-person show, combining office visits and house calls, something I'd rarely experienced. I enjoyed it and counted my coworkers, Cindy and Mari, as friends.

Which is why today had such an effect on me. How well do you really know the people around you? How can you know the sorrow hidden under a carefree surface?

———

That night, I tossed and twisted under the covers, half in and half out of a horrible dream. I stood at the lake's edge looking down. Trapped under the ice was a person whose blond hair cascaded around her shoulders. She was alive! Slim hands beat against the ice. I tried to help, picking up a heavy stick and beating the ice as hard as I could. A thin layer of snow-flakes hid her face from view.

On my hands and knees, I wiped the light dusting of snow away, then woke up, heart pounding. The person under the ice trying to escape was me.

———

The next morning, I dragged myself into the animal hospital, groggy from lack of sleep. Mari was already there, sitting in the employee lounge. She appeared happy and upbeat and definitely more awake than I was.

"Sorry about yesterday," she said. "I'm not sure why it affected me so strongly."

"Completely understandable," I said as I spilled coffee and bent down to mop it up with a paper towel.

"I hope my story didn't make everything worse for you," she asked. "Such a gruesome scene. What do you think happened?"

Still a bit shaky, I collapsed into one of our sagging armchairs and took a few sips of coffee before I answered. "Best I can come up with is they were hiking, for some reason, and she fell into the lake. He may have suffered a heart attack trying to get help." It wasn't a great guess, but it was all I had.

The coffee began to work its magic. My appetite kicked in. I remembered I'd stashed a granola bar over by the employee fridge.

Mari stared at me before asking, "Where was their car or truck?"

"Whose car?" My brain fog disappeared as the importance of her question kicked in. "Oh, you've got a point there. We might have it backward. Perhaps they started somewhere else nearby and were going to hike back from the lake to their vehicle."

"A vehicle that no one has found."

Before I knew it, Mari began presenting multiple alternative scenarios of what happened. A friend dropped them off. They were going to call an Uber. Thieves stole their car. She'd obviously put some thought into it.

Barely up to speed, I simply nodded or grunted in agreement.

When she ran out of ideas, Mari said, "We'll find out when Cindy gets back."

That was a true statement. Cindy's brother-in-law was Bobby Garcia. Bobby wouldn't and couldn't supply any case details, but Cindy's sister had the inside track with her husband—and the sisters talked, all the time and incessantly. The chief of police of necessity was careful what information he shared with his chatty wife.

I suspected he deliberately leaked certain information through his spouse.

"Maybe you're right. Someone dropped them off on the trail," I suggested, "and was scheduled to pick them up at a specific time."

"Then why weren't they reported missing?"

I ventured that opinion because during the time I'd been working and living in the Hudson Valley, I'd noticed a rather cavalier attitude in the residents regarding the winter. People periodically froze to death up here. Going to get firewood and tripping. Warming up their cars in the garage and dying from carbon monoxide poisoning. Strolling in town wearing shorts and a T-shirt.

With the cobwebs cleared by coffee, I said, "If you figure it out, let me know. I'll be in my office checking lab results."

———

It didn't take too long before my staff updated me on the frozen bodies we'd found.

Cindy arrived bubbling like a teakettle with information. "Don't quote me, but the couple you found were engaged to be married. Alicia Ramsey and José Florez. José's got a big gunshot wound in his chest, which you must not have seen because he fell facedown. The snow froze the blood seeping from the wound. They aren't sure about Alicia's cause of death yet. They're waiting on some tests. The coroner suspects José committed suicide, after killing his fiancée."

"So it's a murder-suicide?" I asked.

"Terrible," Mari added, coming into the office and sitting down in front of my desk. Mr. Katt lay curled up on the other chair. "Why can't couples work things out? There's never any reason to kill someone."

"Agreed."

What could have happened? Did Alicia threaten to break off the engagement? Had José pushed her into the lake on an impulse, and then shot himself when he was unable to save her? The phrase "I can't live without her" reverberated in my mind. How many times had we read or heard that? The majority of times, it simply wasn't true. In my experience, a few weeks or months of painful separation passed, and then everyone moved on—the passion of the moment forgotten. Like swapping out an old sweater for a new blazer.

"Change of subject," Cindy said, ready to discuss the truly important decision of the day. "Let's pick the color of our spring uniforms before I leave."

"Oh, no," I groaned.

You might think this was an easy decision. You would be wrong.

Medical scrubs come in a dizzying array of fabrics, cuts, styles, and colors. Cindy, with her high school cheerleader body impeccably preserved, looked good in anything. Mari and I, on the other hand, had much more to consider. Our jobs required bending, kneeling, twisting, and holding on to our furry patients. We needed a certain roominess and give in our fabric. Not to mention a forgiving color.

"Pink?" suggested Cindy, in a temporary fit of insanity.

"No and no," Mari immediately countered.

"Veto that," I added. "How about black?"

"For springtime?" Cindy's tone implied I moonlighted as a terrorist.

"What about blue?" Mari suggested, taking the middle road.

Cindy clapped her hands. "Robin's egg blue. That would be nice."

Thinking of the size of my ass in baby blue, I vetoed that idea too.

"Maybe yellow. What does it matter to you, Kate?" Cindy asked, throwing sensitivity to the wind. "You just put a white coat over your scrubs."

"Yeah," Mari added. "We'll be the ones walking around looking like giant pencil erasers."

"I'll let you two decide," I said, figuring it was the most diplomatic thing to say. I really didn't care. Fashion is the last thing on my mind when I am working.

"Let's take this up again when I get back," Cindy said. "I'll leave you with the scrubs catalog and see what you come up with." She didn't sound too confident in our decision-making abilities. "Think pastels."

The idea of the staff walking around in a spring yellow, like Big Bird, gave me the shivers. I didn't see why veterinary uniforms had to be "fun." It was different in the human medical profession, I supposed, but our animals didn't care what we wore. It was how we handled them when they needed us that was far more important.

Maybe green?

After our Saturday morning half day of work, I kicked back, spending time with my King Charles spaniel rescue, Buddy. We sat on the sofa, as usual, me with my glass of white wine, listening to his snores. I was catching up on some veterinary journals and watching HGTV when my cell phone rang. Caller ID let me know the most important man in my life was calling, my Gramps.

After my mom and little brother were killed by a drunk driver, all I did was fight with my dad, and for good reason. Soon after the funerals, it became apparent that my surgeon dad had been cheating on my mom, and his surgical nurse/ girlfriend was pregnant. I couldn't deal with it, and my father didn't want to deal with me. Gramps took me in, despite my anger and teenage attitude. He was the reason for my successful graduation from high school, college, and veterinary school.

"Hey, Gramps," I said, "how are you?" He'd recently moved from his multistory brownstone in Brooklyn to an independent senior living facility. The COPD from his days as a firefighter had taken its toll on his lungs, making stairs difficult.

"Hi, Katie. What's this I read about a murder-suicide in your part of the woods?"

Busted, I thought. *Now, how to explain things without upsetting him?*

I stalled for time. "Do you mean the suspected murder-suicide?"

"Are you saying there is more than one?"

I sipped my wine. "Ah, no."

"A man dead in the snow. A woman in a lake trapped under the ice. The *Post* published quite a picture. They're calling her an ice princess." His voice ended with a mild, gravely cough, the result of smoke inhalation from a huge fire he'd help put out—the one where he went back in to save two children.

I didn't know if the *Post* had published Mari's and my names. I decided to try the role of objective observer.

"Really? They're that interested in what happens up here in the Hudson Valley?"

"Anything for a story," he said. "What's new with you? And Mari?"

Something jingled in the back of my consciousness. *He knows. There's no escape.*

"Busted. What do you want to know?"

He laughed. "How the heck did you come across two bodies?"

I explained about Bruce flagging us down, but I didn't include the trauma Mari relived at the scene, remembering the death of her sister. If Mari wanted to share those details, she would. As I explained discovering the first body and how the pink scrunchie led to the second body, he interrupted.

"Was the woman shot, too?"

"I honestly don't know. The coroner has clamped a lid on that sort of information."

"What about Cindy? Doesn't she have a direct line from the chief of police through her sister?"

"Cindy's getting ready to go on her annual family vacation to Florida. She hasn't been very forthcoming," I added.

In the background, I heard someone asking a question. I couldn't catch the words but the voice was female.

"Do you have guests?" I asked, being as diplomatic as possible. I found out the hard way that my Gramps is very popular with the ladies at his independent living facility. Which means Gramps enjoys a more active social life than I do.

He cleared his throat. "A friend stopped by for cocktails."

I found this so funny, because my Gramps was a drinking-beer-straight-from-the-bottle kind of guy for years until he recently started watching Internet videos. Now he made Negronis, Manhattans, and all sorts of fancy alcoholic drinks. Plus, he'd turned into a sort of card shark, playing poker for cash a few nights a week with his buddies.

"Katie," he said, "please tell me you're not going to get involved in this investigation."

Gramps was the only person left on our planet who called me Katie.

"Of course not. I've got too much to do," I reminded him. "And besides, it's a murder-suicide. There's nothing to investigate."

There was quite a pause before he commented, "Let's hope so. Prove me wrong, Katie, and stay out of this. I don't want to worry about you."

"There's nothing to worry about, Gramps," I repeated. "Except which house this couple is going to pick on *House Hunters*."

He laughed again. "I'll go with house number two, and I don't even know which episode you're watching."

"No way," I answered. "This one is a no-brainer. They just got engaged and have to have the house finished before the wedding."

"So, no stress. Let me know how that turns out," he joked. "Compromise is the name of the game."

After we hung up, I watched the program till the end. Before the final reveal segment, the couple fought about everything. At one point, I thought they were going to call off the engagement. The practical thing would be to choose house number one, which had more square footage, needed less work, and sported a nifty oversized three-car garage.

Of course, they picked house number two, the fixer-upper. I was lucky Gramps hadn't insisted on betting on it.

Chapter Six

OVERNIGHT, A THIN LAYER OF SNOW FELL, DUSTING THE
hospital parking lot. Buddy shook his feet after his morning
walk, leaving drops of water on the floor. I felt some trep-
idation as I opened the door between my apartment and
the animal hospital that Monday. Today was the first day of
a week without our longtime receptionist, Cindy. Frankly,
both Mari and I relied on her to keep us on schedule and
current with our clients and patients. Cindy combined
enthusiasm with razor-sharp efficiency. What would it be
like working with her substitute?

Voices came from the employee lounge. I recognized
Mari's, of course. The other, deeper voice must belong to
Babs Fields, our temporary office manager.

Armed with a second cup of coffee, I decided to join
them.

They seemed to be having an animated conversation
until I realized it was more of an animated argument. Babs
didn't appear that perturbed, but Mari's face was red, never
a good sign.

"Good morning, ladies," I said. That fell flat. Walking
over to our new receptionist, I stuck out my hand. "You must
be Babs. I'm Dr. Kate Turner." I mustered up a friendly smile
despite the glower on Mari's face.

Maybe it was unfair to make comparisons, but I couldn't
help noticing whereas Cindy always looked camera ready

and fresh no matter what time of the day it was, Babs didn't. She wore an old gray sweater over her scrub shirt that was loaded down with pins that said, "Take it slowww" and "Not the Boss," and "Don't argue or I'm out of here." Her short gray hair stuck up at the back of her head, and behind thick glasses her pale eyes appeared gigantic.

"Dr. Kate," Mari began with unnecessary formality, "Babs is uncomfortable adding additional appointments to the schedule." The stiff frown on my technician's face was in danger of becoming permanent.

"I'm sure we can work this out," I began, taking another sip of coffee to strengthen my resolve. "If one of my patients is sick and needs me, Babs, I will find the time to see them."

Our temporary receptionist said, "Hummph."

That didn't sound encouraging.

"Cindy always checks with me or Mari before squeezing them into the schedule." I punctuated this statement with another big friendly smile. Slightly forced.

"Hummmph." Babs didn't seem convinced. "A schedule is a schedule. That's why it's called a schedule."

After mulling over that circuitous statement, I found no good response. "Well, it's almost time to start morning appointments. Cindy told us you are familiar with our veterinary software program?"

"Yes. After I retired from Allendale Animal Hospital and moved up here, I've made myself available for part-time work at various animal hospitals in this area and across the river in Rhinebeck. I've worked here before with Doc Anderson."

My ears picked up a chiming noise. "Did you unlock our

front door?" I asked Babs. "Because I think someone's at the receptionist desk."

"I'll go with you," Mari volunteered. "We can go through today's appointments while Dr. Kate checks the overnight lab results."

As they disappeared down the hall, I noted this first morning felt a little bit rocky. Over the years I'd worked with many different veterinary employees, some more proficient than others. Cindy would only be gone for one week.

How badly could things get messed up in seven days?

———

Our first patient of the day was a silver-gray Weimaraner dog, well muscled with a shiny coat. Mari normally does a brief triage for me, taking the vitals and a history, but Babs must have detained her. I was asking the owner if he planned on neutering his dog when Mari opened the exam room door. She immediately went over to our patient, who was wagging his tail, and gave him a pat.

"You were saying…?"

"He's neutered, Doc," was his answer. For some reason the owner smiled after he said it.

I looked at the rear view of the handsome dog and from my point of view he obviously wasn't neutered. Everything looked intact.

About to argue with the gentlemen, I caught a glimpse of mirth in his eyes. *Bingo.*

"Implants?" I asked him.

"The best that money could buy," he bragged while petting his dog.

In the corner, Mari fought to suppress a laugh. Testicular implants were available for dogs when owners, usually men, hated to see their pet without his natural equipment.

"Like breast implants," he proudly proclaimed.

This time Mari couldn't hold it in and let out a snort of a laugh, which made the owner laugh, too.

I could only imagine regaling Gramps with this topic of conversation.

Now that the atmosphere felt definitely more relaxed, I examined the dog and noted a cracked canine tooth. Most clients don't realize that veterinary medicine has board-certified doctors of dentistry who do root canals, crowns, extractions, and just about any other dental procedure.

"Hey, Doc," he asked me, "what can I do about that tooth? Can't have him looking bad for his lady friends."

I smiled and gave him a one-word solution. "Implant."

The next few hours galloped by as we admitted a dachshund with spinal trauma, a cat caught in a car motor, and a Dumbo rat whose tail tip had turned black. All these cases needed to be evaluated and given a treatment plan to discuss with the owner.

On days like this one, Mari and I ate lunch while working. Sometimes standing up. The adorable dachshund with the big pleading eyes was first. He was in obvious pain, and in need of immediate treatment with an anti-inflammatory. Because of his discomfort, we moved him by a towel sling under his belly. X-rays revealed arthritic abnormalities of the spinal column and a mild separation of two of the lumbar vertebrae. Ouch. He needed rest, he needed medications, and he needed time. This guy would be staying here at the hospital for the next day or two.

Our next patient, a smudgy striped kitty, had been trying to stay warm by climbing into the neighbor's car engine. Other than being greasy and sustaining a moderate lesion and loss of some fur from the fan belt when the car turned on, he miraculously escaped with just a few months shaved off his nine lives. Other cats I'd seen were not so lucky.

Our Dumbo rat, a "fancy" rat breed with large ears and a rounded face scampered up my arm to rest on my shoulder, his tail dragging. From up above, Mr. Katt, our hospital cat, stared down with inappropriate interest. Trauma of unknown origin had disrupted the blood flow and innervation to the rat's tail. That required an amputation.

"Did you know that in the 1880s, a scientist tried to prove that cutting tails off mice would result in tailless offspring?" I absently scratched along the rat's back.

"Really?" Mari opened a surgical pack and prepared for our short surgery. "That's like saying if a woman had her hand cut off, her babies would also have one hand."

"Basically," I agreed. "My genetics professor used to say Lamarck was off the mark. A funny mnemonic to remember who conducted this famous experiment."

Once our little Dumbo was under anesthesia, I dissected

the dead part of the tail from the healthy part, stitched it up with dissolvable sutures, and made a note to fit him with a tiny cone to stop him from gnawing on it.

"Make sure he is separated from their other pets for two weeks," I advised Mari. "No buddies nibbling on that surgical site. I don't want to keep chopping pieces of this tail off."

I looked up at the clock on the treatment room wall. My lunch hour was officially over. I'd gobbled down a banana, but my grumbling stomach remained unsated. A granola bar from a box Cindy bought and a large cup of coffee would have to do. For some reason, my thoughts drifted to Chief Garcia.

"Hey, Mari," I asked, taking a sip of coffee. "Have you heard any more about the murder-suicide of that couple in the woods?"

My assistant was busy scarfing down half a sandwich and some chips. She held up a hand as she finished chewing. "Nothing. If Cindy was here, we'd already have gotten a rundown."

"Absolutely, we'd have been updated by the lightning-fast sister-to-sister network. I don't suppose we could call Chief Garcia directly?"

"He was supposed to join his wife and kids in Florida. I think he flew down this morning."

"Not letting a couple of bodies prevent him from working on a tan," I commented. "Well, he deserves it. I'm sure the rest of the week will be stress-free."

"It better be," Mari said. "Honestly, I'm not in any hurry to be reminded about that day."

"I'm sorry," I told her. "Duly noted."

We turned as we heard shoes clumping toward us from the hallway. Babs opened the door, that familiar frown on her face.

"How's it going back here?" she asked.

"We're all caught up," I told her. "But I need to update some owners."

"Let's see," she began. "The dachshund is on cage rest for a few days, the car engine cat has to be observed overnight, and the rat can go home and the sutures will dissolve."

She stared at me, her eyes magnified behind the thick lens of her glasses.

"That's right," I said. "Remind me I need to make a cone for the rat."

"Done," she said. "I brought my vet assortment of odds and ends. A few months ago, I worked as a technician at an exotic practice. They bandaged all sorts of birds and lizards and rats. Oh, Mrs. Zelter called and wanted to talk to Dr. Kate about her bill."

"Oh, no," Mari said. "Not again. I've explained all her charges to her."

"Well," Babs said, puffing up a bit like a hen ruffling her feathers, "I put a stop to that. I believe Mrs. Zelter is lonely and needs to complain, but I explained the office staff takes care of billing, not the doctor."

"Really? And she accepted that?"

"Hurummph. I gave her no choice. The matter is settled, and she made a recheck appointment in two weeks."

Mari and I looked at each other. Cindy had been trying

to placate Mrs. Z all last week. I'd been dreading talking to her, and now—on the job for less than twelve hours, it seems that Babs had succeeded where all others had failed.

"Good job," I told her.

She adjusted her glasses and said, "Thank you. Afternoon appointments start in five minutes. Don't be late."

We listened again as the clumping sounds of her shoes faded away.

"That's a pleasant surprise," I said, snatching up my stethoscope and brushing granola bar crumbs off my coat. "Babs has gumption."

"Time will tell," Mari said cryptically, voicing her favorite saying. "Time will tell."

Chapter Seven

BY THE TIME I FINISHED CHECKING MY PATIENTS AND answering email, it was seven p.m. The last thing I remembered eating after the granola bar was a handful of Mari's tortilla chips around five thirty. My dog, Buddy, danced circles in front of me signaling how much he loved me and also how much he needed to go out. I'd snuck in a quick walk just before our working lunch, but he deserved my full attention.

Right outside my front door, which opened on to the side parking lot, Doc had built a fenced-in area for dog walking. Buddy favored certain trees and always looked for the resident squirrel. I'd shoveled a path and uncovered some frozen grass, but the rest was compacted snow. Buddy didn't care. As soon as he did his business, he checked out the oak tree, hoping to see his nemesis. The squirrel and the dog never got within ten feet of each other, but you'd never know that from the fuss Buddy made.

Near the pines that separated our property from our snowplowing person, Pinky, a crow cawed. Buddy answered the bird with a bark.

It was still bitter cold, but at least the wind had died down. Some brave bushes revealed tiny buds waiting for warmer weather to open. I scanned our small strip of green space and the surrounding forest for bright yellow forsythia, the harbinger of spring. Nothing. Spring had not sprung.

The motion detector light above my door popped on, reflecting only frozen ground and leafless bare branches.

It suddenly occurred to me that I didn't have to spend Valentine's Day alone.

———————

Once inside, I cleaned off Buddy's cold feet, gave him his dinner, and poured myself a cold glass of white wine. One was my limit. The inside of the refrigerator looked pretty bare. It contained an almost empty bottle of ketchup, a bag of limp salad greens, and one take-out container containing who knows what. A light fuzz of mold decorated the surface.

Better stick to the wine for now. It would be Ramen noodles from the pantry for dinner again.

A glance around the apartment didn't lift my spirits.

My renovated garage home came fully furnished, with a large lumpy sofa and a queen-sized lumpy bed. The round Formica-topped kitchen table must have dated from the seventies. All were serviceable, but not very cheery. I'd bought a thick mattress topper, some throw pillows, and a slew of soft colorful blankets to make the room seem like home, but it felt temporary.

Just like my job. My year's contract to run Oak Falls Animal Hospital would be up soon. I needed to email Doc Anderson, busy relaxing on his round-the-world cruise, and see if he planned to keep me on. One more thing to add on my growing to-do list.

Buddy jumped up next to me, licking his chops in

appreciation for his dinner. We curled up together, and after settling in I dialed the one constant man in my life, Gramps.

After the fifth ring I figured Gramps was out, but he answered just as I was about to hang up.

"Hello?"

In the background an oldies radio station played Ray Charles.

"Hi, Gramps," I said. "What are you up to?" Whenever my grandfather decided to cook, he always turned on the radio.

"Can't hear you. Let me turn this volume down," he said. I listened to him moving toward his kitchen, muttering something. Even though meals were provided in his independent living complex, he often preferred to cook his own dinner. "That's better. I had to stir the sauce."

No need for me to ask which sauce. Gramps only cooked one sauce, an Italian Bolognese red sauce one of his firemen buddies taught him to make.

"You have to give me that recipe sometime," I told him. "Except measure everything out the next time you make it." I'd watched him several times, and every time he did things slightly differently.

"How about we do a video call when I make the next batch?" he said.

"Great idea." Gramps had become increasingly tech savvy over the last few years, even taking several computer classes.

"Any news about that deceased couple you and Mari found by the lake?"

How many times had I asked that same question?

"No," I picked up my glass and took a sip. "Cindy is on vacation, so my local news updates have been temporarily canceled."

"Got to love her. I didn't see anything on her Facebook page today except a photo of some margaritas on the beach."

"I'm missing her already," I confessed, "although so far her replacement is doing a good job."

"Speaking of taking a mini vacation," Gramps said, "remind Cindy I told her to give you a Saturday off so you can come visit me in person. Not on Zoom."

During the COVID-19 pandemic, a large number of people adopted animals. The increased need for appointments had put a strain on veterinary facilities across the country. Some specialty practices were booked out for months. To help out my clients, I'd been working most Saturday mornings, seeing my last appointment at noon or one o'clock. According to Cindy, I averaged about fifty to sixty hours a week. It didn't give me much of a weekend.

"I'm using the extra money working Saturdays to pay down my student loans," I reminded him. Gramps had retired from the fire department and lived on his pension and Social Security. "Being fiscally responsible, just like you taught me."

"Maybe I'll win the lottery and we can live in luxury together," he joked. "Me and the boys buy ten tickets a week. We promised to share unless someone kicks the bucket."

"Which won't be anytime soon," I reminded him.

He laughed and coughed at the same time, finally catching his breath and saying, "Sorry to cut this short. The guys will be here any minute for our poker game. Say, why don't you come to our Valentine's Day party? I've got a date, but you can hang out with us. Come to think of it," he added, "I might have two dates."

"Two dates!" We both laughed again. "Aren't they going to fight over you?"

"Sweetie," he said. "This is senior assisted living, not high school. They're happy I'm still kicking."

The doorbell to his place rang; most likely his poker crew had arrived.

"Anyway, I'll talk to you later this week," he said. "And, Katie, try not to work so hard. Give yourself some downtime."

After we hung up, I felt canine eyes staring at me. "I know," I said to my dog. "Gramps wants me to take some downtime. And he's got two dates for Valentine's Day."

Buddy thumped his tail in sympathy.

Chapter Eight

IN THE NEXT FEW DAYS, MY LIFE RETURNED TO NORMAL. No more dreams about being trapped under the ice. But hoping that Chief Garcia had finished interrogating Mari and me turned out to be a big no-no.

As I left exam room two the following day with an ear swab destined for the microscope, Babs interrupted me. In a gloomy voice, she explained that Chief of Police Garcia wanted to speak to me on the phone—now. Her demeanor indicated she expected me to be arrested momentarily.

"Great," I answered as enthusiastically as I could. "Looking forward to it."

The disbelieving look she sent my way was worth the lie.

The chief spoke to Mari and me separately during lunchtime, basically once again going step-by-step over everything that led to the discovery of the bodies. No new information came to light.

"Aren't you in Florida?" I asked him. Cindy had said that her sister and Bobby and their kids and she and her kids were all taking a vacation together.

"Affirmative," he said in a voice that stopped me asking any more personal questions.

I thought it strange he brought up Bruce several times.

What he looked like when he flagged us down. His demeanor. Did he initiate any small talk? I wondered if Bruce was more involved than he appeared.

Good Samaritans who discovered bodies sometimes were the killers.

At least twice more I repeated exactly what happened, including the eerie discovery of the body under the lake ice. When it came my turn to ask a question, I heard an electronic wall of silence. Since the investigation was still under way, no public statements would be released.

But brick walls aren't as solid as one might think. They're only as strong as the mortar holding each brick together. Chip away at that, and the walls come tumbling down.

———

We were sitting together in the employee lounge finishing our lunches after our conversations with Chief Garcia when Mari randomly mentioned, "Marjorie loved to swim. Mom called her our own little mermaid. She'd wade into rivers, swim in the quarry—even when everyone else thought it was too cold to get in the water."

Babs nodded in remembrance.

I took it as a good sign that Mari initiated this conversation.

"Did you swim much when you were kids?" I asked her. "I swam on a team in middle school and high school."

"What was your best stroke?"

"The butterfly. You should have seen my shoulder

muscles." For emphasis I flexed my biceps. "One summer I worked as a part-time lifeguard at the Y."

"Which is why it's so unfortunate," Babs said.

"What's unfortunate?" I mumbled between bites of my sandwich.

"She was a swimmer, too."

"Who are you talking about?" Mari asked.

I'd noticed that sometimes stories from Babs didn't proceed in any obviously logical manner.

"Alicia. The young woman who died in that lake. She was a swimmer."

Babs knew the murdered woman? Why hadn't she told anyone? "How do you know her, if you don't mind my asking?"

Her grumpy stare indicated she might mind my asking. I took another bite of my sandwich and waited her out.

"I've done a lot of jobs since I retired, not all of them for veterinarians. A temp agency sent me to work at a law firm. That's where I met Alicia. Very organized, a lovely person."

I suspected Babs liked anyone who was organized.

"Was she engaged then?" Mari asked.

"No." Babs sipped from her iced tea for what seemed like hours before answering. "I knew the other boyfriend."

———

With plenty of prompts, Mari and I extracted the history of Alicia's love life from Babs, going back about five or six years. Babs doled out every syllable she spoke as though it was money she was losing at a casino. The fewer words spent the better.

After fifteen minutes we knew all the basics. Babs met Alicia when the young woman interned at Ramsey and Pratt, a mid-size legal firm located in Kingston. Only a year away from graduating law school, she worked there one summer. One of the married partners, James Ramsey, became infatuated with her. Their heavy-handed sneaking around embarrassed the rest of the staff, especially when his wife showed up unannounced looking for him. Alicia went back to school at the end of the summer, whereupon Mr. Ramsey separated from his wife prior to filing for divorce. Six months later, Alicia sported a diamond engagement ring and drove a Lexus convertible.

As soon as she graduated, Alicia went to work for Ramsey and Pratt, taking two-hour lunches with her boss/fiancé, James Ramsey, to the dismay of the staff and his business partner.

"Then what happened?" Mari asked.

"I have no idea." Babs got up from her chair. She glanced at her watch and reminded us that appointments started in twenty minutes.

"Do you think they got married?" Mari asked after Babs left. "She must have married because she took his last name."

"But something else must have happened because when she died, she was engaged to José," I added. "I suppose Alicia and James Ramsey could have married and divorced, or the first husband died." My brain went into overdrive. "What if the first husband was murdered?"

"Okay. I get the picture. Time to go back to work," Mari

said. "I wish Cindy was here. She'd straighten this out in a heartbeat."

Putting the remains of my lunch in the trash, I picked up my stethoscope, draped it around my neck, and took a quick look in the employee lounge mirror. Half my hair had slipped out of my hair band. I'd stashed a small hairbrush in the bathroom, so a few sweeps smoothed everything back to normal. My mirrored image showed pale blond hair framing an equally pale face with a longish nose.

"Ready?" I asked Mari.

"Ready as I'll ever be," she replied, then tossed her empty chip bag toward the garbage pail. It banked off the side of the lower cabinet and dropped into the basket.

"That's good luck," I predicted.

"I'm not counting on it." Mari started moving toward the front of the hospital. "Bad things come in threes. We're two bodies down and one to go."

———

After we finished our last appointment early and closed up the hospital, I persuaded Mari to join me at Judy's Café. Usually my assistant ran directly home to her dogs, but I shamelessly tempted her with visions of fresh baked brownies and blueberry scones.

"My treat," I added.

"Well," she began, "okay, but I can't stay very long."

"I've got an ulterior motive," I explained while we walked to our cars. "I'm hoping Judy knows something about Alicia and José and why they might have been hiking near the lake."

Mari ran a hand through her dark curls and said, "That's a long shot."

Pulling the front door of the truck open, I answered, "So? Worst case is no info, only a nice piece of pie."

―――――――

A village staple praised by weekenders and locals alike, Judy's Café welcomed its main customer volume for breakfast and lunch. She closed down just before seven on most weekdays. It was six forty-five when we strolled through the door.

"We're about to close," Judy said while cleaning off the counter.

"We'll be super quick," I promised her. "In fact, we'll take our meal to go if necessary."

"No worries," Judy said. She walked over to the front door and turned her sign from OPEN to CLOSED. "You two, I can handle. Lord save me from New York City millennials with crazy food requests. Hold the butter because it's not vegan, or is this fresh? What do they think I serve? Rotten food? The best was some guy wanted to know where the chicken in the chicken soup was raised."

Both of us sympathized with anyone working with the general public. Most people were great, but there were a few...

"We're easy. Soup of the day, toasted blueberry scone, and a piece of pecan pie with whipped cream," Mari told her with a smile.

"Sounds good," I said. "Me too."

"Easy peasy," Judy countered. "Anything to drink?"

"Earl Grey tea," Mari said.

"Just ice water," I told her. "I've had enough coffee today to raise the *Titanic*."

Judy laughed and said, "Be out in a few."

While we waited, Mari and I went over some of our patients today, once again laughing about testicular implants.

"I'm just saying," Mari began.

"Don't go there," I begged her, "or I'll be on the floor."

Within minutes Judy served us the soup of the day, Tuscan white bean, along with our beverages. When she hung around after delivering Mari our toasted scones, I asked, "Judy, do you know anything about Alicia Ramsey and José Florez, the victims we found up by the lake?"

Judy poured herself a cup of coffee and rested it on the counter in front of us. "So, what do you want to know?"

Paydirt! "Everything," I said.

It sounded like an episode of *Desperate Housewives*, except Alicia was much more refined than those ladies. Beautiful and sweet, she put out vibes like a guy magnet, and it didn't seem to matter if the guy was married or not. She did indeed marry James the lawyer, but only after she told him they were through if he didn't divorce his wife. Needless to say, the wife, Linda, didn't go quietly. A mom with three kids, she publicly denounced Alicia as a home breaker while fighting her husband for alimony and child support. His being a lawyer meant she was outgunned. Her former Prince Charming orchestrated a very contentious divorce to claim his prize, but two years after the wedding something went wrong. Amid claims of spousal mental abuse, Alicia filed for divorce and a split of the couple's assets.

"What did James say?"

"He protested. Unfortunately, before the divorce was finalized, James killed himself, leaving everything to Alicia."

"No," Mari exclaimed.

"Afraid so. It turned into a big scandal. His first wife was distraught, much more so than Alicia, I think because his death stopped her child support and alimony payments. That left survivor's benefits from Social Security. She had to sell her house and move back in with her mother."

"Sad," I said. "She must have hated Alicia."

"Hate is too mild a description," Judy said.

"How did Alicia hook up with José?" Mari asked.

Judy stopped to take a sip of coffee. "I'm not sure, but José was working as a physician assistant when they met. That was a couple of years ago."

"So no wife in the picture this time."

"No. José seemed like a nice guy, saving up for a down payment on a house for his bride. I'm not sure where they met, but once they did they became inseparable."

"How long were José and Alicia engaged?" Mari asked after taking a bite of her scone.

"That, I don't know," Judy admitted. "I do know José referred to Alicia as his beautiful Princess Bride."

"And the wedding was going to be held…"

"In June."

"Very traditional," I commented. I'd finished my soup

and began thinking of the two victims, spending their last moments on earth together in the snow. "So Judy, what do you think happened up there on the mountain?"

She shrugged her shoulders. "They seemed so much in love, but I guess you never know." Judy looked out the window at happy couples walking arm in arm along Main Street.

"I suppose somebody got pissed off."

Chapter Nine

I'd hoped to sleep in the next day, but that didn't happen. To my surprise, Mari knocked on my apartment door with two takeaway cups of coffee and a paper bag tucked under her elbow. Upon seeing his friend, Buddy gave one yip and then erupted into his happy dance.

"Did you see the paper this morning?" she asked as she bustled her way into the living room a good forty-five minutes before I intended to get up.

"Nope." This early in the day I considered standing upright in my bathrobe and pajamas a major accomplishment. A morning person I wasn't.

I followed her into the kitchen. The coffee she brought smelled exceptionally alluring. My nose became obsessed with figuring out what was in the paper bag.

Mari put the coffees down on the table and began pacing in my tiny kitchen. "That creep Bruce gave a reporter an interview about discovering the bodies. I read it when I stopped at the Circle K this morning."

"So?" If I were a dog I'd be salivating, drool trickling down my chin. My nose weighed in by sending visions of breakfast sandwiches to my brain.

She stared at me then said, "You're not really listening are you?" A folded-up newspaper smacked against the tabletop.

"Let's sit and eat, and you can tell me all about it." I lifted the lid of my coffee and put some plates on the table. "Come on. I know you're dying to tell me." I unfolded the paper, scanning the front page.

"Alright," she acquiesced. "One bite, then we discuss what Bruce said."

My face broke into a grin when I saw Mari had brought my favorite egg, bacon, and cheese on a biscuit. "You're the best."

"Yes, I am. But I'm so annoyed at that idiot Bruce, I could spit."

Rationing out my pleasure, I took a reasonable bite and then washed it down with some coffee. That bite made my world brighter. Then Mari trampled on it.

"First of all, Bruce makes himself into some kind of big hero and not the gigantic weenie he really is," she began. "Nothing about puking his guts up in the snow or running away from José's body without checking for vital signs."

"Well…" I began. "He's not used to medical stuff like we are."

Mari glowered at me like a giant raincloud bristling with thunderheads. "Don't make excuses for him, please."

"Ahhhh…"

"You didn't read what he said about us. How he held our hands because we were so afraid. And how he implied he single-handedly led the police chief to the woman in the lake."

"Bruce said that?" I cried out in disbelief.

"I'm paraphrasing. You come off worse than me," Mari added, checking her watch. "Much worse." She sipped her coffee and took a few bites of her breakfast biscuit.

I noticed the time. If I didn't hurry I'd be late.

"Sorry to load all of this on you so early in the day, but it's helping me feel better to talk it out. I'll clean up after breakfast while you get ready for work."

"What?" I yelled as I turned on the shower.

"Meet you in the clinic," she said whacking the sofa with the newspaper before hightailing it out into the animal hospital.

I should have stayed in the shower for the rest of the morning. At the first opportunity during a break, Mari updated me on the rest of Bruce's interview. I was "abrupt" and "antimale" in my encounter with him, not to mention dismissive.

"Why is he saying this stuff?" I wondered.

"Because he has nothing else to say. He ran away from a man lying facedown in the snow, then refused to show us exactly where the body was. Bruce didn't even use the emergency 911 function on his phone, which the police claim was available to him. He's trying not to look so bad by verbally attacking someone else."

Babs helpfully suggested I move out of the state.

All the justifications in the world didn't negate the fact that thousands of people who didn't know me were reading his lies, but since it was stated as his opinion—well, I didn't think I had much recourse. Chief Garcia's job didn't include taking the media to task.

My former boyfriend, Luke, texted me to forget the slurs and move on. That was his legal opinion. He was about to take his law boards for the second time. I hadn't heard from him for quite a while. After that sound advice, he asked me out for drinks. I declined.

I also declined Mari's invitation to meet her and some friends for karaoke at the Red Lion Pub. At this point, I preferred to be alone.

My phone pinged with texts throughout the evening, most of which I didn't answer. The majority expressed their support for me and wished me well. I appreciated it but didn't feel like talking to anyone.

One text I did answer.

Dr. Mike was free to perform piglet surgery tomorrow evening.

"He called you what?" Dr. Mike said as he repaired our mini potbellied pig's umbilical hernia under the hot surgical lights. We'd started as soon as he arrived, hoping to finish up by six thirty or seven.

"You must be the only person in the Hudson Valley who doesn't read the paper." Watching him was a pleasure. His surgical technique looked precise and fluid as he layered his sutures, swiftly completing the repair.

"Well," he said to me as we moved to the second already prepared surgical site, "I'm so busy at the moment, it's all I can do to finish the day and collapse into bed at night."

Remembering his newborn twins, I said, "Another reason to thank you so much for helping me. You'd be amazed how much my clients love this little guy."

"I hated to think of your patient becoming a surgical emergency. Besides, I like pigs."

"Me too." I'd noticed I felt very comfortable talking to this large-animal vet. It reminded me of countless conversations with my classmates.

"One of my roommates in school brought home a mini-pig one semester. It turned out to be smarter than our dogs and very friendly." He rapidly finished the inguinal ring closure and neuter, burying the sutures with the finesse of a plastic surgeon.

"I'm impressed," I commented while assisting in our postsurgical checks. Together we unhooked Porky from the anesthesia machine and waited to remove his breathing tube. All vitals were stable. We both sat down on the floor after moving him to his cage, me scratching Porky's speckled snout and Dr. Mike observing the bandaged surgical sites.

"Want a coffee?" I asked, standing up again. "It's a little late but our office manager, Cindy, brings in the most amazing coffee for us. Mocha Almond okay?"

"Perfect. Although I find it usually smells better than it tastes." He laughed then continued, "but that would never stop me from drinking it."

"Speaking of drinking, I think I saw a swallow reflex," I called out to him from across the room, the coffee filter in my hand.

Dr. Mike agreed, deflated the cuff, and removed the plastic endotracheal breathing tube. Porky took a few nice breaths for us and started to wake up.

"Our patient says he takes his coffee black."

"Coming right up," I joked.

I scrounged around for the tin of butter cookies one of our clients dropped off for Valentine's Day. With some fancy paper plates donated by Babs balanced under my coffee, I handed Mike the cookies and one of our extra mugs and sat down alongside him.

"Think of this as a picnic, veterinarian style."

He laughed. "During clinics at school, I think half my meals were eaten in one treatment room or another, sometimes in the hallways between classes."

"Same here," I said, hunting for one of the marble shortbread cookies. "How did you decide on veterinary medicine as a career?"

Mike leaned forward to check our patient's surgical sites for seepage one more time, then closed and latched the cage door. Porky lifted his head and shoulders to glance around the room. "My parents ran a dairy farm in Cayuga County. From the time I can remember I did chores in the barn, watching calves being born, hauling hay. Until I was about seven, I thought everyone's boots smelled like cow dung."

"But you didn't go into dairy medicine," I said.

"Nope. I'm not sure if I want to continue in large-animal practice, or go into teaching, or join the CDC." He wiped a few porcine bristles from his pants.

"I know what you mean. My year contract will be up soon, and then I need to decide what to do next. It's fun working small-animal medicine, but I've been feeling a little restless. Good thing there are plenty of jobs out there to choose from."

"True. How is Babs working out for you?" he asked me.

"So far, so good. Much better than I expected, to be frank." I ate the vanilla half of the cookie, saving the best for last.

"Nice to hear. She's worked for our clinic before, and someone mentioned Babs is scheduled to fill in for one of our receptionists going on maternity leave. Sometime in late March, early April, I think, for three months."

The chime of a text message sounded from inside his jacket pocket. He glanced at the message and texted back.

"Sorry, I've got to get going. Glad I could help out," he said. To my surprise, after he stood up he did a yoga stretch. "Helps with my stiff back," he noted.

"Remember I promised to help you out with those barn cats," I told him as he picked up his coat and looked around for his medical bag.

"Right. Keys, glasses, phone," he muttered the words like a mantra, patting his pockets. "Sorry, I've been known to forget things. My roommate in school was the same way and always talked to himself. I found this reminding sequence to be pretty successful."

I walked him out to the front of the hospital and unlocked the door. "Two human pig parents are now very happy," I said. "By the way, you've got an excellent surgical technique."

He smiled, his gray-blue eyes wide behind his glasses. "Thank you. I assisted at a surgical practice my last two years of vet school," he explained as he zipped up his coat. "I was lucky. My mentor turned out to be a masterful surgeon and a great teacher."

"Thanks again," I told him. Out on the main road that

ran past the animal hospital, a bevy of trucks passed by, rumbling around the corner before disappearing from sight.

"See you around," Mike called out before he stepped into his boxy Scion. The driver's side door had a sizable dent below the handle as if another car door had dinged it. With a quick wave goodbye, he backed up and headed out of the parking lot.

Hurrying along to the treatment room, I noticed Porky standing in his cage, clearly acting annoyed at the lightweight cone around his neck. I called Porky's owners and arranged for them to pick up their pet. He'd go home with a cone to make sure he didn't bother his surgical site.

———

After Porky left, it only took a few minutes to clean up the hospital surgical suite. After checking the anesthesia machine, one of two we used, and making sure all the anesthesia tanks were turned off, I wheeled it back into the corner of the room. As I scrubbed the surgery table and soaked the surgical instruments, I thought how pleasant it had been talking vet med with Mike, reminiscing about school and our professors. I'd found it comforting to know I wasn't the only practicing vet contemplating future career changes. Once finished with the cleanup, I walked through the hospital, checking the windows and doors before turning on the alarm. Passing my office I noticed the hospital cat, Mr. Katt, had bypassed his bed and was curled up asleep on my office chair.

Buddy yodeled a hello when I opened the connecting door to my place. Walk time, I realized, slipping on my coat. Fighting off the cold, I watched him frolic in the snow. I recalled again Mike discussing his future, not sure which path to take. I knew exactly how he felt. In a world of medical specialization, I loved my small-animal patients, but to the exclusion of exotics and large animals? I wasn't sure.

Socializing with a colleague made me miss my classmates. I'd found it hard keeping up friendships when I worked all the time. Gradually, I'd begun to feel emotionally isolated, socializing with people only at work. A vision of me growing old surrounded by a menagerie of creatures appeared to be a real possibility—perhaps morphing into a crazy cat lady with tangled hair. No husband. No children. Only animals.

Mike had his wife and twins to consider in his decisions. Not me. My year at the Oak Falls Animal Hospital would soon run out. Did I want to pack up and leave again? I put that disturbing thought aside.

Just when you start getting comfortable in a life, you have to go.

Chapter Ten

FOR SOME INEXPLICABLE REASON, I WOKE UP THE NEXT morning at five forty-five and, for the life of me, couldn't get back to sleep. Another light mist of snow had fallen overnight, but our plowing neighbor, Pinky, had already cleared our parking lot. He'd even brushed the flakes off my windshield. Accepting the inevitable, I went outside with Buddy, then fed him breakfast and offered him a chew bone. With nothing more to do, I decided to get into work early. Once inside the animal hospital, the aroma of coffee indicated I wasn't the only restless employee today. Looking forward to a little downtime chatting with Mari, I strolled into the employee lounge—then froze.

Babs had made coffee and was busy cleaning off the clean countertops. She grinned when she saw my startled expression.

"Come on in, Dr. Kate. My bite is just as bad as my bark." She gestured to one of our comfy albeit beat-up armchairs.

When I didn't respond, she added, "I'm kidding. Have some fresh coffee."

I realized I'd never been alone with Babs or had a one-on-one conversation with her that lasted more than a minute or so.

"I always come in early wherever I work," she explained, using a damp paper towel to wipe down the upper cabinets. "I like to keep things shipshape. Idle hands are the devil's playthings."

The coffee tasted rich and flavorful, a touch bitter, but much better than usual. "Thanks, Babs. What flavor is this?"

"It's a dark roasted Italian coffee," she said, holding up the colorful mug she'd brought in from home. "I'm particular about my coffee. One of the vets I once worked with went to school in Rome and recommended this to me." She pointed to a foreign-looking can. "There are bagels and cream cheese over by the fridge."

Bagels? This morning I had no complaints about Babs.

"I've been meaning to ask you," I said, slathering a sesame bagel with cream cheese. "Have you worked at many animal hospitals?"

"Yes."

We were back to one-word answers. I'd have to work harder to have Babs reveal a bit of herself to me.

With my coffee and breakfast in hand, I headed over to the employee table. "What part of the job do you like the best?"

She stopped fussing for a moment. "Trying to befriend the temporary employee, are we?"

I lifted my cup to her. "I like to know the person I'm working with."

Babs smiled at that and pulled out a chair near me. "Same here. Although I don't expect to learn that much in a few days."

"True," I agreed. "And Cindy is never sick. Mari and I swear she's bionic."

She laughed. "I worked with Cindy and Doc Anderson about five years ago for almost six weeks, after one of their vet techs was in a car accident."

My eyebrows went up at the surprising information.

"I'm a licensed veterinary technician as well as a receptionist and office manager," she confided. "These days I'm
not sure which pays more."

Babs continued to impress me. "How many years have
you worked in vet medicine?"

Her eyes drifted to the ceiling and her lips mumbled
some numbers. "It must be thirty-five years or so by now.
Old enough to remember when most vets were men."

I nodded. Many people don't realize today's veterinary
school graduates are over 60 percent women. In fact, my
team consisted of only women.

"Thirty-five years," she repeated. "A long time. I started
volunteering at the local animal hospital in high school, then
worked weekends while I took classes at the community
college."

"That's a coincidence. So did I. What was your major?"

"Biology and zoology. I wanted to go to veterinary school,
but it wasn't in the cards. Had to drop out of school to take
care of my father after his heart attack. He became bedridden
and required more and more professional care. Then my
mom passed suddenly, and I was the only one he had left.
Eventually, I had no time or money for anything else."

Her explanation sounded matter-of-fact, her voice
unemotional.

"Would you have gone into small- or large-animal work?"
I asked, curious now about our temporary receptionist.

"Neither," she said. "Exotics, or wildlife perhaps. Maybe
research. I've got an analytical mind."

So I was finding out. "That's interesting."

"I still take nonmatriculating classes online," she continued. "There are so many innovations in genetics and gene-splicing, advancements I never thought I'd witness in my lifetime." She folded her hands together and rested them primly on the table.

"That's so true," I said. "Even since I graduated, the field of neurobiology and production of vaccines have become more sophisticated."

"Yes. It truly is a brave new world we live in." She took a sip of coffee and looked across at Mr. Katt looming over us from his perch on top of the cages. "I understand you are a bit of a detective."

Embarrassed by her comment, I answered, "Yes. I guess so. I like seeing victims get justice."

She persisted. "Some friends told me you are very good at finding murderers."

"I've been lucky," I told her, taking another sip of coffee.

"You make your own luck," she answered. "Do you think José killed Alicia?"

Alarmed by the suggestion, I said, "What else could it be?"

"Alicia loved him very much. She wanted to marry him." Again she stared with those pale eyes. "The coroner hasn't released cause of death yet, and with the chief on vacation in Florida, I suppose we'll have to wait to find out."

Was she questioning the murder-suicide? I remembered that Alicia had been her friend.

Finished with her coffee, Babs walked over to the coffee station, washed out her cup, and put it away. "You know. If someone was about to kill me, I'd try to leave as many clues as possible."

"Me, too. That's if I had time," I stipulated. "I suppose we do have some things in common."

"I think we do."

While I watched, she cleaned behind the coffee machine, moving everything out then putting each item back in its place.

"Do you enjoy working part-time?" I wondered what her answer would be.

"Yes, I do. It keeps me current, and I get to meet new people," she said, "as well as keep in touch with the ones I know. Thanks to some lucky investments, I don't have to work, but I enjoy staying busy. Oak Falls suits me. I play bridge. I've joined the Hudson Valley Garden Club. I'm in a bowling league. It's a very satisfying life."

Strange. I'd made a cursory judgment and assumed Babs to be a lonely older woman, one a bit standoffish among strangers.

On an impulse, I asked what she was doing on Valentine's Day. Her answer surprised me.

"Well," she began a bit hesitantly, "I've got a secret admirer."

"What?" She might as well have confessed to being a serial killer.

"Not exactly a secret," Babs replied. "Just unexpected at this point in my life. I think he's reaching out more from loneliness than anything else. You see…"

"Hi, guys." Mari appeared at the door, her puffy coat

filling the doorframe. "You're both here bright and early. Especially you, Kate."

"True. Babs and I are comparing our lives in veterinary medicine."

"Let's see," Mari began as she hung her coat up and put away her things. "I started cleaning kennels at sixteen. I told them I was seventeen and never got caught. Washed show dogs and groomed for a while, too." She walked over to the coffee maker, picked up her cup decorated with her two dogs' pictures, and poured herself some coffee. After taking a tentative sip, she said, "Hey. This is nice. That must be your doing, Babs."

"Guilty," she said.

"You won't believe how much veterinary experience she has," I told Mari.

Babs leaned back and looked over my shoulder toward the far wall. "Now that I'm thinking about it, I've been working with vets for closer to forty years," she volunteered. "I remember taking X-rays without a radiation badge on and developing them in a darkroom with wet tanks. Chemicals dripping on your shoes. That's something I don't miss." She laughed at the memory. "For the most part, veterinary medicine has improved," she added. "But I think you younger vets should ask more questions because there's a lot to learn from a good history. At least that's what I've been told."

"Being able to take a detailed history is essential," I agreed. "It can narrow the focus and save some time."

"Or not," Mari commented, taking another sip of coffee. "There's always the owner who really doesn't notice much."

"I think I've met every kind of owner and veterinarian there is on the planet," Babs said, her words directed at me. "As long as someone stays on the straight and narrow, we'll be okay. If not…"

In an abrupt move, Babs gestured with her finger pantomiming a knife slitting her throat.

Chapter Eleven

IT WAS FRIDAY AFTERNOON, THE END OF A LONG WORK week, and we were winding up our house call appointments. Mari sat next to me in the hospital truck, her fingers clicking away on our office laptop in frustration. "I can't believe this. Babs sent us on a wild-goose chase, and we're the geese."

We'd been parked at the side of the road overlooking a large field for about ten minutes, trying to decipher the last message Babs texted to my phone. We'd spent the morning at the hospital seeing appointments and the whole afternoon on house calls. So far this was the only mix-up.

"Why doesn't she pick up?" Mari asked me, waving her cell in the air. A town dump truck swooshed by, our truck buffeted by a push of displaced air. I weighed the odds of us being hit while waiting on the side of the road and decided to find a store parking lot to pull into. Meanwhile, Mari kept talking to her computer and phone.

"Maybe she transposed the address numbers?" Many people have mild dyslexia and mix up numbers or letters in written messages.

"She sent us to an empty field." Mari's fingers tapped a staccato pattern on her passenger window. "What are you supposed to examine? Rocks?"

"There's a farmhouse over there," I said, pointing to a nearby driveway. "Perhaps that's our destination?"

"Who knows? We can't just show up at some random

house," she said. "Babs better have a good explanation for all this." Mari sounded angry, an infrequent state of affairs and one to be avoided.

After a truck full of firewood passed, leaving a shower of wood chips behind it, I eased onto the road and made a course back to the animal hospital.

By the time we returned to the office, Mari had called the hospital landline and called and texted Babs's cell phone number multiple times, with no answer. Twenty minutes had passed, and her anger morphed into concern, as did mine. Had our receptionist slipped and injured herself? Suffered a heart attack or stroke? Approaching our parking lot, I saw her car parked in its usual place near the hospital's main entrance.

As soon as I put the truck into park, Mari jumped out of the passenger seat, pulled out her keys, opened the front office door, and ran inside. I followed right behind her, calling out for Babs to answer us.

Reception was empty.

The employee lounge was empty.

The animal hospital was empty.

Babs had vanished.

Mari and I stared at each other in disbelief. "Maybe something is wrong with her car?" my assistant ventured.

"Then why isn't she answering our texts?" I asked.

Mari stared out the reception area picture window as if the answer lay somewhere in the gravel of our parking lot.

The office line rang and startled us both. After two rings, we heard it routed to our answering service. "She put the answering service on," I said. "Maybe she fell ill and took an Uber home instead of driving. Or went to the emergency room. I don't think you're supposed to use your cell phone inside the ER."

"I guess that's possible." Mari stared out the window again. "What would Cindy do if she were here?"

Immediately, I realized we had skipped the obvious. "She'd check the controlled drug log." Like most veterinary hospitals, we kept any potentially addictive drugs and anesthesia meds under lock and key. Any time they were used, the exact amount was written in the drug log. Babs knew exactly where it was.

"Come on." I took off down the hallway, my boots slipping on the floor. Past the exam rooms, through the treatment room, stopping at the double doors marked SURGERY, AUTHORIZED PERSONNEL ONLY.

I pushed open the doors.

Babs lay on the surgery table, an anesthesia mask over her blue-gray face, hands folded daintily at her waist.

Mari and I immediately went into emergency mode. My veterinary assistant quickly turned off the blue nitrous gas tank as I pulled the mask away from her nose.

"There's no oxygen on," Mari said. "Only nitrous."

I started chest compressions, bringing room air into her oxygen-deprived lungs while Mari called 911. She tossed me my stethoscope and took over while I listened for a heartbeat. No heartbeat. As Mari performed CPR, Babs's arms slipped down, dangling over the table. I pressed her darkened nail bed to search for any capillary refill. None.

"Anything?" Mari asked.

"No," I answered.

The body that had been Babs lay on the cold stainless-steel table. We covered her with a warming blanket and kept doing CPR. Within minutes, sirens sounded in the distance.

We stood aside when the EMTs arrived and assessed their patient. After a flurry of activity, they whisked her away, but not before one of them looked at me and shook his head.

Mari and I stood in our quiet surgery suite staring at each other in disbelief. Scattered on the floor around us lay medical debris left by the EMT team.

"How did that nitrous tank get hooked up?" I wondered.

"No idea. It was stored in the surgery closet behind the extra oxygen tanks," Mari said. She walked away toward the employee lounge, sat down in a chair, and pressed her forehead against the table.

I followed. I didn't want to stay in that room that smelled of death.

Seeing the nitrous hooked up made me think. In modern veterinary medicine, we rarely used nitrous, or laughing gas as people called it, anymore. That old blue tank had been buried behind the green oxygen tanks for as long as I'd been here. But something else felt wrong. Veterinarians deliver gas anesthesia to dogs and cats by endotracheal tube after intravenous induction. Safety procedures around gas anesthesia for human staff as well as our animal patients were extremely important. The older-style human masks often leaked around the rubber seal, potentially exposing everyone in the room. Modern two-step anesthesia reduced that.

I fought to clearly process what we'd just witnessed.

The emergency team had instructed us to wait. After a few minutes, I bounced back up and started taking pictures of the surgery room with my cell phone. Still attached to the anesthesia machine by a plastic hose was the mask that had covered Babs's nose and mouth. I'd never seen it before.

Where had that human anesthesia mask come from?

Chapter Twelve

OVERDOSES AND EVEN DEATHS OF EMPLOYEES FROM drugs are not unheard of in the medical world. Dentists, veterinarians, and medical doctors can unwittingly hire persons with addictive personalities or habits. Injectable medications were stolen at a practice I once worked at, and in veterinary school, a technician was fired for using ketamine, which she insisted was harmless.

There had been no oxygen flowing along with the nitrous oxide into Babs's lungs. She most likely died of anoxia, lack of oxygen, pure and simple, but the medical examiner would reveal the whole story. Perhaps she'd taken other medications or drugs? Had our formidable temporary receptionist been an addict?

When I pointed out the human mask to Mari, she shrugged and said maybe Babs brought it with her. When I looked in the reception desk drawer where Cindy usually kept her purse, I saw a smallish designer bag lying on its side.

For the second time in little over a week, Mari and I were embroiled through no fault of our own in a police investigation. The police officer who arrived to take our statements was a stranger to both of us. He seemed particularly young and nervous.

"Where's Chief Garcia?" Mari asked him.

"On vacation in Florida with family," the officer reminded her. "We're under orders not to disturb him. I'll be handling this investigation. Did the victim seem depressed or suicidal to you?"

"Suicide?" Mari repeated.

"Hold up," I said. "Who said it was suicide?"

He looked at me as though I was incredibly stupid. "This kind of thing happens all the time," he said. "Someone decides to have a little fun and accidentally overdoses. Or they're depressed and figure this is a painless way to die. We're taught in the police academy about the dangers of anesthetic drugs."

As he spoke with us, a forensic team passed by in booties. Our surgery area was cordoned off with tape. One of them glared at us.

"Should we move to my office?" I asked. "It's more private."

"Fine," he told me. "But don't touch anything."

―――――

There were several things that didn't add up here, but I didn't feel like arguing. Mari looked exhausted, her face pale and tight. For once I missed Chief Garcia.

One thing needed to be discussed, however. "Officer. You might want to recover our alarm system camera images from today. The system is completely digital and is hooked up to a Wi-Fi system. The outside cameras are motion activated."

"Good idea," he told me. "I'll tell the detective."

Mari and I obediently bobbed our heads in agreement. There wasn't much we didn't know about the animal hospital building, like which windowpane rattled in storms, how to unclog the tub table, and, more important in this case, the setup and peculiarities of the alarm system. Cameras had been placed both inside and outside the hospital. From my office desk, I could watch my patients in their cages in the treatment room. I could even access that specific feed from my phone if necessary. There was a camera over the reception desk and in the waiting room. For the life of me, I couldn't remember any cameras in surgery. There were no motion detectors in the treatment area and the rest of the hospital because of Mr. Katt, who often dive-bombed people or raced around the hospital for no reason. Cindy usually turned the system off in the morning, and I activated the system at night. Would Babs have turned the outside cameras on when sitting alone in the hospital?

As soon as we were released, Mari headed home.

"Sorry, Kate," she said as I walked her to her SUV. "This is too much to deal with. I'd invite you to come home with me, but it's gaming night with my friends. I know you're not a big fan."

"I'll be okay," I told her. My brain felt like mush. We'd worked with Babs for only five days and now…

"I told you bad things happen in three's," Mari said. She opened her driver's side door, threw her stuff on the passenger seat, and then leaned down to give me a hug.

"You alright?" she asked again.

"I'll survive."

"Talk to Gramps. He'll make you feel better." She climbed into the driver's seat and slammed the SUV's door closed.

As I watched her drive away, I knew I couldn't talk to Gramps yet. He'd insist I stay somewhere else tonight. I didn't have the energy to go anywhere. All I wanted was to not think for a while. That sense of isolation enveloped me again. Cindy would be back from Florida late Saturday night. Maybe she had better insight into the mystery that had been Babs. As for me—I felt numb.

Buddy followed me as I paced back and forth in my apartment thinking it was some kind of new game. I went over and over the horrible scene in our surgery suite. I knew the room intimately, having cleaned every inch of it, stocked it at night, and basically worked in it almost every day. I also knew the contents of each drawer by heart. There were no human anesthesia masks.

Something felt wrong. Something set off alarms in my brain, but I couldn't figure out what. It lay just beyond my conscious mind, tantalizingly close.

I tried all the usual ways to wind down. Hot bath. Lying in bed with a new book. An icy cold glass of wine. Meditating. Nothing worked.

Instead, I moved to the sofa and turned the television on to HGTV. Wrapped in a blanket and snuggled up with Buddy, I stared at the screen. My faithful dog blissfully stayed awake for five minutes before he started snoring.

I desperately wanted to talk to someone about Babs, but who else knew her? As I stared at the screen my text chime sounded.

Piggy okay?

It was Mike. Asking about Porky the Pig's hernia surgery. He knew Babs.

I texted back.

Porky's doing fine. Got a moment to talk?

He didn't answer right away. I'd almost given up when he texted back.

Sure. give me a few minutes. I'll call you if that's ok?
OK

For some reason I felt I could talk about today with him. Maybe because I wouldn't have to explain everything. He'd worked in our surgery suite. He knew the setup. And he was almost a stranger.

A new episode of *House Hunters* played. I watched another young couple with completely different tastes in homes battle it out over city versus country living—which seemed petty. Ridiculous, really. In frustration, I yelled at the television, waking up my dog.

I almost texted Mike to forget it, that I'd explain everything tomorrow. The poor guy and his wife were juggling twins. I felt guilty taking family time away from him. I chastised myself for even contacting him.

The phone rang as I beat myself up again.

"Hello," I answered.

"What's wrong?" Mike said immediately.

"What do you mean?" This wasn't going the way I'd planned.

"You sound upset. You don't strike me as a person who gets upset easily."

How could I blurt out someone died in my hospital today?

"Have you had dinner yet?" he asked me.

I looked at the empty glass of wine on the coffee table. "Nope."

"Neither have I. I'm on your side of town. I'll swing by and take you to Judy's if she's still open. You can tell me what's bothering you over a bowl of soup."

I started to protest, but he added, "Let's go over your schedule and set up a time when you're free to examine those barn cats for me. My client bugged me again about it today."

"Sure." I recognized how tired I was. Too tired to drive into town.

"See you in ten minutes?"

"Sure," I told him. At least I'd showered and changed after my interview with the police.

"See you soon."

"Sure," I said for the third time.

With Buddy already fed and walked, I again looked at my empty wineglass. *Heck*, I thought. Mike said he'd drive, so I poured another glass and pulled on my boots. The tension in my back and neck muscles started to ease. Talking about Babs and what Mari and I had been through today wouldn't be that hard, I tried to convince myself. Besides, if we ran out of subjects, we always had veterinary medicine chatter to fall back on.

When I saw the headlights turn into the parking lot, I slipped into my coat, picked up my backpack, and waited outside on the step. The motion detector light clicked on. Tonight he drove the older Scion with big snow tires, not the large-animal practice truck. As soon as he parked, I opened up the passenger door.

"Hey," I said. "Thanks. I needed a break tonight. I hope I'm not taking you away from anything important at home."

"Nope. No worries. I'm solo tonight," he said, with a worried face. "We've got to get going, though. Judy's going to close soon."

Buckling my seat belt I sighed, not sure this was a good idea after all.

Mike drove carefully, all the while telling me about an American paint horse with colic he saw today at the large-animal hospital. I got the feeling he was trying to keep my mind busy.

I mentioned that as a freshman in vet school I ended up walking a colicky horse around a paddock for six hours. Our professor had already passed a nasal tube and administered lubricants and pain medication, listening to gut sounds every half an hour. We students each took turns keeping this horse on his feet. After a rectal exam followed by an explosion of gas and poop, our professor said the prognosis just got better.

"Which professor did you have?"

"Lundquist," I told him.

"So did I," Mike admitted. "Great teacher."

"I agree."

To my surprise, I realized we'd reached Judy's place with fifteen minutes to spare. I hopped out of his vehicle, my backpack over my shoulder. Mike held the door open for me, and the café's warmth and delicious smells delivered a welcome slap in the face.

There were two tables available, one by the window and one in the back corner. Knowing the town's love of gossip, I decided poor Mike didn't need to get into trouble for helping me, so I hurried to the corner by the brick wall. Mike didn't seem to notice or care. We quickly divested ourselves of coats, hats, and sweaters, basking in the warmth of the café.

A new waiter I'd never seen came over with glasses of water and announced the café was about to close, and we should order immediately.

Mike took no offense and ordered the soup of the day, two blueberry scones, a brownie, and a glass of milk. "I'm getting the extra scones for breakfast," he confided to me.

"Good idea." I ordered the soup and two slices of banana bread. After those unaccustomed two glasses of wine, I stuck with only water to drink.

Our waiter scurried away, probably in a hurry to get off work. Judy's wait staff often consisted of out-of-work artists or musicians not planning on waiting tables for the rest of their lives.

"So," Mike said in a gentle voice, "is this about Babs?"

"You know?"

"Of course," he answered. "I didn't want to say anything over the phone. An employee death inside Oak Falls Animal Hospital? That's big news."

As he spoke, I caught several people surreptitiously observing us. Of course, the other animal hospitals would know. Mari probably told one of her many vet tech friends. How could I have been so stupid?

"I can't..." I began.

"Kate," he said briefly squeezing my hand, "did you ever consider you might be in shock?"

Shaking my head, I said, "Of course not. I've gone through a lot worse than this." His suggestion angered me. Of course I wasn't in shock. I could handle myself.

The waiter interrupted my thoughts by slamming the soup down in front of me. A tiny wave of fluid containing strands of tomato slid over the top of the bowl and onto the plate below. Looking down, I experienced a wave of nausea.

"Try this," Mike said, sliding a piece of scone on a napkin over to me.

The crumble of plain pastry lay benignly in front of me. With swallows of water, I finally got it down.

"Sorry," I said to Mike.

"Nothing to be sorry for." Then he regaled me with stories of his high school followed by his undergraduate years in vet school, all the while encouraging me to eat my buttered banana bread. The waiter came and went. Somehow the soups with their glistening slick of oil miraculously disappeared.

Distracted by his stories, I relaxed a bit and shoveled in the two pieces of banana bread and one of his blueberry scones. When I realized I'd eaten his intended breakfast, my cheeks turned red.

"Oh, Mike. I'm so sorry. I didn't realize how much I was eating," I began.

"Nonsense. I noticed the soup made you gag. Plain carbs go down easier, especially bakery carbs."

"Still…"

"Next time, maybe I'll pinch your dessert," he said in a teasing way.

Despite his effort, I didn't crack a smile.

The waiter came over and I dug up my credit card. "Please, let me pay. You've been so kind."

"The bill's already been taken care of," the fellow said as he cleared the plates.

Mike smiled. "Shall we go?"

I started fishing around for my sweater and backpack, which had slipped under the table. Mike helped rescue them and bumped his head.

"Sorry," I said.

"Stop saying sorry," he told me. "You've got nothing to be sorry about."

We walked toward the front of the restaurant, just as Judy came out of the kitchen, a dishrag in her hand.

"Hey, docs," she said. She glanced at me with concern, then immediately looked away. "Stay safe. Drive carefully." After a hesitation, she headed back through the swinging doors into the kitchen.

"How long have you been in the Hudson Valley?" I asked Mike as we walked to his car.

"I've worked at my current practice for two years. Great place."

The snow began falling again. Soft intermittent flakes floated in the night breeze.

"Winter is trying to remind us she's still got some tricks up her sleeve. It's only the beginning of February," he continued.

Mike clicked his fob and opened the doors. He'd walked with me over to the passenger side and held the door open while I climbed inside. I'd been afraid meeting him would be a mistake, but instead, I'd been able to relax somewhat and put my terrible day into some kind of perspective.

"Listen, before we go," I said as he turned the ignition, "what can you tell me about Babs?"

"So that's what this is about," he answered with a hint of a smile. "I figured you had an ulterior motive."

I was about to say "sorry" again but held my tongue.

"Babs worked at the equine clinic of our hospital about six months ago, when their receptionist was out on sick leave with a knee replacement. We got along fine. She had a sort of rough exterior, but once you knew her, you appreciated her organizational skills and business sense. And she always advocated for the animals. Babs was fierce in her opinions of what was right and what was wrong. No gray areas for her."

That brought back a memory of Babs sliding her hand across her own throat, mimicking slitting someone's throat.

Mike checked the rearview mirror and began to wind his way out of the parking lot. The streets were quiet. Most residents had settled in for the night.

We drove in silence while I digested what Mike said. "How much do you know about what happened today?" I asked him.

"Not much," he replied. "Someone at the hospital told me Babs had passed away suddenly while working at your place. What was it? A heart attack? Stroke?"

The windshield wipers moved back and forth sweeping lacy snowflakes off into the night.

That feeling of calm I'd had disappeared. I stared at the windshield wipers, my stomach churning. "No, it wasn't anything like that," I started to say, unsure of how much I should reveal. "I suppose you'll hear all about it soon." I glanced down at my hands clutched together. "Babs either accidentally overdosed on nitrous oxide or committed suicide. My vet assistant, Mari, and I found her hooked up to our anesthesia machine in the surgical suite."

I wasn't prepared for him to slam on the brakes. His small car skidded and came to an abrupt stop, blocking someone's plowed driveway.

"Impossible," he said. "That's impossible."

A truck flashed its bright lights at us as it sped down the road. When it passed us, the Scion shook.

Mike looked both ways and pulled back onto the highway. Just ahead, the Oak Falls Animal Hospital sign glowed, lit by spotlights embedded in the ground.

When he turned into the parking lot, he drove straight to the side of the hospital and the entrance to my apartment. He shifted his car into park and then turned toward me.

"You remember I told you there were no gray areas with Babs. Everything was black or white, right or wrong."

"I remember."

"Well, one of the things she hated the most was staff using drugs, especially any drugs needed for the animals. She'd even made a complaint about someone she'd worked with to the State Boards a few years ago."

"So you're saying…"

"In my opinion, it is highly unlikely she hooked herself up to your anesthesia machine. Totally out of character. Incomprehensible."

A rushing sound flooded my brain. I saw Babs lying still and cold on the surgery table. An image of Mari and me pulled over to the side of the road this afternoon intruded. We'd been trying to figure out why Babs sent us to a house call in the middle of a field.

Mike hit his steering wheel with the flat of his hand. The horn sounded and cut through the white stillness.

"I think Babs was murdered," he said.

Chapter Thirteen

BABS WAS MURDERED. BABS WAS MURDERED. THE WORDS stuck in my mind.

It was no wonder that for most of the night I sat bolt upright on the sofa, the television on, trying to digest Mike's statement—"I think Babs was murdered." I didn't want to contemplate the consequences. With every creak of the roof above I startled. Strong wind gusts had tree limbs swaying. The outdoor motion detector light switched on and off, on and off, visible through the curtains.

On the television screen the endless Valentine's Day commercials, all of which centered on buying something for the occasion, forced me to lower the volume. I watched couples nuzzling and kissing over diamond rings in silence. It was officially Saturday morning, although still dark outside. The office was closed until Monday, but I needed to check my client email and review any messages from the answering service. Cindy's flight from Florida was due in late today.

More thoughts intruded. *Babs's dead body lay on your surgical table in your surgery suite, where you will be working on Monday. Did her uneasy spirit stay behind to hover overhead?*

At seven a.m. I woke with a start, still scrunched up on the sofa with Buddy on the floor nestled between my feet. My text message chime had gone off. I wasn't ready to face this day or look at my phone.

One of the few constructive chores I'd accomplished

was preloading the coffee maker. A push of the button and coffee would be ready when I came back inside from walking Buddy. The lock on the doggy gate momentarily stuck to my fingers, reminding me it was still February. While my dog frolicked in the snow, I began the day by reading the early morning text.

WHAT HAPPENED??????? R YOU 2 OK??????

News travels fast even down to Florida. Cindy must have been contacted by a friend or family member, which means Police Chief Bobby Garcia, also currently in Florida and off duty, knew. A tsunami of questions was heading my way. My text chime sounded again. This time it was Mari.

Cindy knows

So, Mari must have received this same text. I sent back an emoji of a woman shrugging her shoulders. Mari sent me the image for a pile of poop.

The only bright spot in this crazy week was that I wasn't going through it alone. Like it or not, Mari and I were yoked together like a couple of reluctant draft horses. And like tired horses, we were expected to pull our load regardless.

———————

The morning crawled along as I did mindless chores, cleaning and laundry. I'd been planning to take a late afternoon nap, but instead, the answering service called around one o'clock.

"Doctor. One of your clients insisted I contact you," the annoyed woman on the phone began. "She gave her name as Daffy? Her Little Man is sick."

"That's it?" I asked. "No symptoms. No phone number?"

"Ms. Daffy said she couldn't discuss the problem with a stranger."

"Ahhhh. Okay. I'll take care of it."

"Weird." The woman from the answering service declared popping her gum in my ear. "People are getting weirder all the time. The world's flipping."

That sounded about right to me. Not knowing what else to say, I said, "Have a good day."

"It's flipping," she replied and hung up.

The truth was Daffy didn't need to leave any more information. I knew her dog Little Man's medical history as if it were my own. A nervous owner, Daffy could build a broken toenail into a catastrophe. The only problem? It took three people to handle her Chihuahua, Little Man—Mari to hold him, me to examine him, and Daffy to wring her hands, walk around in circles, and coo apologies to her pet.

Buddy had already had his breakfast and a treat. I wandered around the kitchen, searching the pantry for a can of soup for lunch, while I dialed Mari's number.

"Hi," she answered. "Are you as bummed out as I am?"

"Probably," I said. "Maybe more at the moment. Want to do a house call at Daffy's place?"

"Sure, anything but sit around here. What's wrong with Little Man?"

"No idea. The answering service didn't…"

Mari interrupted. "Let me call. She'll probably ask a zillion questions."

"Done. I'm going to hop in the shower. Text me in about fifteen or twenty minutes."

———————

By the time I got out of the shower and dried off I had five text messages. Two were from Mari, confirming an appointment this afternoon with Daffy and suggesting she meet me here at the office. The three others were from Gramps, Cindy, and Mike.

I texted all three that I was fine and would talk to them later.

A short honk outside my front door meant Mari had arrived. She suggested we take her giant SUV instead of the hospital truck because she needed to pick up dog food. I had zero desire to drive, and since the SUV seats were far more comfortable than the old F-150's, I readily agreed.

"Guard the house," I told Buddy before I walked out the door.

Mari waved when I appeared in front of her vehicle, putting the phone down in the charger console. I opened the passenger door and stashed my medical bag behind the seat.

"Ready?" I asked, settling into the soft leather.

"Strangely enough," she answered, "I'm looking forward

to being distracted by Daffy. I'm also hoping she'll feed us. My stomach's been wonky since—you know. I had problems getting my breakfast down this morning."

I knew exactly what she meant, having experienced that same problem.

"Daffy always feeds us," I said, buckling my seat belt and tossing my backpack into the back seat. I made a point to keep our conversation light. "Remind me not to eat any more chocolate, though. All this stress has been terrible for my diet. I figure I'm getting half my calories from sugar."

"Me, too," Mari said. "For dinner last night I had strawberry waffles and fudge ripple ice cream."

I laughed. "At least we're both eating some fruit."

She stopped at a red light and turned toward me. "I'm giving myself a pass this weekend to pig out. You should too. Monday starts my return to regular food."

The two of us had been to Daffy's home so many times in the last few months that there was no need to look up the address in the GPS.

"So, did she tell you what was wrong with the little guy?" I asked, trying to prepare myself for the visit.

"Problems down south."

Laughter literally exploded from my mouth. "How far south?"

"All the way," Mari answered with a giggle. It was the first time I'd heard her laugh since discovering Babs.

Always in perfect condition, Daffy's cottage looked like a brigade of fairies fluttered in overnight and magically cleaned every inch of it. Her sidewalk glistened with fresh rock salt, cleared of all snow. The paint on her clapboard and shutters might have been applied yesterday, while the white picket fence in front gave it a homey feeling. A cheery wisp of smoke rose from a nearby house, perfuming the outside air with a mild applewood smell. Everything appeared as normal as apple pie.

Moving along the walkway, I noticed the white dotted curtain in the living room twitch. Daffy knew our hospital truck. I wondered if she recognized Mari's SUV?

I got halfway to the front door when it abruptly opened, and Daffy and Little Man appeared. Even though my patient was "ill," he still had been dressed up—as a living Valentine's Day card. Daffy wore a plush velvety white dress with cupids and hearts on it, along with a hat topped with a naked cherub flourishing a bow and arrow. The absurd sight of them brought well-needed smiles to our faces.

At least someone we knew was having a good time.

With a perfectly straight face, Daffy told me her Chihuahua, Little Man, had been having problems down south.

Oh, what a stand-up comedian could do in this situation. Instead, also with a perfectly straight face, I asked, highway Exit Number 1 or Exit Number 2?

Her unexpected answer? Both.

Meanwhile, the subject of her concern growled at Mari and me in a robustly healthy fashion.

Mari ended up coaxing the real-world symptoms out of Daffy. It seems her pet was rubbing his butt on the rug and leaving some peculiar marks, along with a dribble of pee.

"If I remember correctly," I began, "I treated Little Man for anal gland disease a few months ago."

Our client gave a slight nod of the head. The reminder that Little Man was a dog was a bit distasteful.

"Well," I said. "Let's take a look."

Little Man revved up his growl to third gear, his eyes bulging and front fangs glistening like a doggy Dracula.

Mari glanced over at me. "Ready?" She held up her car keys.

"Ready," I answered. We weren't planning on taking this Chihuahua for a ride. The keys acted as a distraction while I snuck up behind him with a custom-made tiny gauze muzzle.

Practice makes perfect. We synchronized our movements like a pair of veteran ice skaters at the Olympics. Although Little Man put on a big show, I suspected he was a willing partner in our choreographed routine.

With the gauze securing his muzzle, the tiny eight-pound Chihuahua calmed down and let Mari hold him while I examined him. Periodically, he snarled for the benefit of Daffy, who nervously circled around us telling her pet, "Mommy loves you" and "Be a good boy," in a ridiculously high voice.

It quickly became apparent that our patient needed his anal glands cleaned out, followed by a treatment plan of warm compresses and medications. He'd tried to address the problem by scooting his tush on his mommy's living room rug.

Having worked this job before, everything moved quickly.

Once finished, we all breathed a sigh of relief. Mari and I rewound our synchronized routine, ending in Little Man all cleaned up and safely hugged in his mommy's arms. He rewarded us with a fierce rolling of his upper lip, exposing his fangs. In that ridiculous Valentine's Day costume, he'd become the anti-Cupid. After disposing of our medical waste in a separate bag, we washed up then followed our client's voice into the kitchen.

With Mari and me in our scrubs and our client and patient dressed like valentines, it felt as though we'd stepped into an alternative universe. Daffy plied us with fresh coffee and homemade pound cake. After checking that we had everything we needed, our hostess pulled up a chair, sat down, and said, "You two have been busy this week."

It was both cryptic and an understatement. My stomach sank.

"Three bodies in one week," she added shaking her head and clicking her teeth.

Mari reached for the strawberry jam. "Yep."

Daffy waited patiently for Mari to continue. When that didn't happen, she focused her laser sights on me.

"You know I don't get out much," she began, "but I do still hear things."

That was the understatement of the century. Daffy had contacts in the village like the FBI has confidential informants. Plus she spoke to everyone about everything, being the naturally curious person she was.

"Now that you've brought it up," I said, taking another sip

of coffee. "This has been a very rough time for both Mari and me. The worst, obviously, being Babs's sudden death."

Mari nodded and clenched her teeth, fidgeting in her chair.

"Did you know her?" I asked our host.

Daffy took a moment before replying. "Yes. I knew Babs through our bridge club. She joined after she retired and moved up here. Smart person, although a bit set in her ways and somewhat stubborn."

That description also fit Daffy.

"We don't know what to think," Mari blurted out, "and the police have no idea either. Was it an accidental overdose of nitrous? What do her friends say?"

I turned to observe Daffy. Her hand absentmindedly petted Little Man, her face deep in thought.

"That's a bit of a problem. Babs didn't have a lot of friends. Acquaintances, yes; friends, not so much. No family or children to speak of. Cared for her father for a long time, then married an older gentleman who passed away after only a few years."

"We barely knew her," Mari said. "She was filling in for one week while Cindy took her vacation."

"Yes. That sounds like just the kind of job she liked."

Exactly what Babs told me, I thought. I felt sadness creeping back inside my chest.

Daffy must have sensed how we felt. "Don't worry. Chief Garcia and Cindy will be back at work on Monday. Life will return to normal."

Normal. What's normal anymore?

"Daffy," I asked, "do you have any thoughts about why

Babs died? Plenty of people do nitrous for fun, but if they make a mistake, they can lose their lives." My usually bubbly assistant sat with her hands folded, staring at the floor.

Daffy frowned, signaling what she thought of having fun with nitrous.

"These deaths have been particularly hard on Mari and me," I continued.

Our client frowned. "I suspect Babs was murdered, and I assume I'm not the only one who thinks so."

With still no official decision on cause of death, I didn't answer.

"Murder. It's love or money, isn't it?" Daffy said. "It's always about love or money."

A simplistic statement but often true.

"I can definitely see love as a motive with the engaged couple," I pressed on. "Alicia decides to end the engagement, and José kills her. Men often kill women who reject them. But why Babs?"

"Fun for women our age is not huffing nitrous, Dr. Kate. That's a loss of control, which for many of us is the opposite of fun. And you can also probably rule out romantic love with Babs," Daffy added. "Although I suppose you never know."

"She once told me she had a secret admirer," I said.

"Really?" Mari suddenly came to life. "Did Babs say who it was?"

Thinking back on our conversation, I struggled a bit. "I'm not sure of the context, and I think we were interrupted…" A vague sense we'd been discussing the murder-suicide tap danced in my brain.

"So," Daffy continued, "that leaves money. Or her murder might have been damage control."

Mari and I looked at each other, horrified.

Daffy clapped her hands and said, "This conversation is becoming much too sad. How do you like our costumes?"

"Nice," Mari told her. "But Valentine's Day is a couple of weeks away."

That remark bounced right off our client's cupid hat. "Since we mentioned love as a motive, are you ladies aware that the Ancient Greeks classified love into eight distinctive categories?"

I covered my eyes with my hands, dreading some sort of bizarre story.

"There's romantic, platonic, selfless, family love, obsessive love, affectionate, mature, and narcissistic love," she recited. "Obsessive is the most dangerous, of course. The obsessive lover feels that if he can't have her, then no one will."

I sat up straight. Obsessive love. Once again, I pictured Alicia's pale face staring up at me from under the ice. "They kill the thing they love."

Chapter Fourteen

I FELT VERY FRUSTRATED AFTER LEAVING DAFFY'S PLACE. *What secrets might be lurking under the surface in our picturesque town?*

"The village of Oak Falls has had three suspicious deaths in one week. We sound like Detroit," I muttered.

Mari came alongside, her puffy coat undone and floating behind her. I was happy not to be driving. Daffy's Ancient Greek definitions of the eight types of love made a home in my brain. I detoured to the passenger side of the vehicle. Once inside, I continued speculating relentlessly.

"Is it alright if we walk through these three deaths again? So the first victims, Alicia and José, are thought to be a murder-suicide, plain and simple, don't you agree?" I asked Mari. "He killed her. Then shot himself."

"If murder-suicide can be simple," she answered me. We stayed parked outside Daffy's while Mari opened up our laptop and began updating our client's record.

Despite her less-than-interested answer, I persevered. "We can look at Babs's death in the same way. An easily explained isolated incident. A rigid older woman with a secret addictive nitrous habit. Maybe she usually snuck in a few puffs where she worked. But this time she forgot to turn the O_2 on and passed out. Simple."

"Whatever." My assistant frowned and closed down her computer. Once it was stowed away, she started the SUV.

Sensing a lack of response from Mari, I let her get on with the business of driving, wondering why I tried to tie all these deaths together—maybe to make some kind of sense of events that made no sense? Or perhaps because I secretly agreed with Mike that law-and-order Babs didn't seem the type to use the office drugs to try to kill herself.

Which made me curious about the deaths of the engaged couple, José and Alicia.

———————

Another early morning text the next day summoned Mari and me to the office. Our leader had returned. Sunday morning, and Cindy arrived like a tornado, sweeping up everything and everyone in her path.

She herded us into the employee lounge.

"Did you have a nice time in Florida?" Mari asked, trying to start the inevitable conversation on a positive note.

Cindy raised an eyebrow. "We had a fabulous time. Fresh fish, hot sand, and salt-rimmed, shivery-cold margaritas. Strangely enough—no dead bodies."

"You should have brought Kate with you," Mari said. "Wherever she goes, people turn up dead."

"Thanks, Mari," I replied. "You're a good friend."

Cindy ignored our banter, tossing her head back, eyes resting briefly on the closed surgery suite doors.

"How am I going to tell Doc Anderson that Babs died on our surgery table?" Cindy cried out. "That we had the police in here searching our hospital. Our hospital."

"Well, technically..." Mari started then stopped dead at the expression on Cindy's face.

"This is serious," Cindy continued. "Her passing is terrible for the hospital's reputation and a personal tragedy for everyone who knew her. Doc Anderson and I worked with Babs several times over the last few years. She was very professional. That's why I felt comfortable going on vacation and leaving her in charge of the front office."

Mari and I listened, our heads down. There wasn't much for us to do except let Cindy get everything she wanted to say off her mind.

Our receptionist paced back and forth, her sneakers scrunching against the floor in a menacing way. "I know the preliminary report is pointing toward accidental overdose, but I can't believe it. Babs was...formidable in her ideas of right and wrong. I can't see her using any of our hospital drugs at work, much less any other drug."

"What do you mean *hospital drugs*?" I asked. To my knowledge, Babs had died of nitrous oxide poisoning.

Despite her frustration, Cindy appeared well rested with a healthy light tan, her hair sprayed into submission. Mari and I looked like we'd been lost in the woods for a week. Maybe seeing us this way made her feel bad enough to share what she knew.

"The chief received a preliminary toxicology report. In addition to the nitrous, they found ketamine in her blood, as well as Xanax."

Ketamine, a veterinary anesthesia, had been getting a lot of press lately as a helpful tool for treating humans with

PTSD, among other things, when used under strict guidelines. It also had an illegal street use as a date rape drug. One of the older veterinary anesthetics often used in cats, ketamine can be unpredictable, as anyone working with it in surgery would attest to. With over thirty years of veterinary experience as a technician and receptionist, Babs knew all about the injectable drug we stocked.

"That doesn't sound likely to me," I said.

Cindy plopped down in one of the chairs, her left foot tapping on the floor. "I did know Babs. For that reason, and some I can't go into, the chief might change her death to suspicious."

Suspicious? What could Babs have done to get herself murdered?

That thought stayed stuck in my mind. Mari and Cindy needed to go over next week's schedule, so I ducked out to call Gramps like I'd promised. While I tried to eat a microwaved frozen pizza slice, I envisioned him hanging out with his firefighter buddies at Sunday brunch. At first, I hesitated to bother him, then realized he and Cindy most likely were heating up Facebook and Messenger with postings.

He picked his cell phone up after two rings.

"Sorry, Gramps. I don't have much time to chat. What do you think about Babs's death? Why would someone kill her at the Animal Hospital?"

"Not so fast, Katie."

I didn't realize I blurted out my questions without even a hello.

"First, how are you and Mari doing? You should be getting some kind of counseling, you know."

True statement. I'd already had one nightmare about death, but, like always, I tried to tough it out. "We're okay, but I'll mention it to Mari."

"Cindy is pretty upset," he added. "We talked for quite a while last night. I told her to take it easy with you and Mari because you're both victims too."

Cindy and Gramps had bonded over the last few months by using social media and keeping watch over me. He was easy to talk to. It didn't surprise me that our office manager would turn to him for impartial advice.

I snuck another bite of pizza and burned the roof of my mouth.

"I'll tell you what I told Cindy. Look for someone who cared about her," Gramps said. "The killer arranged her body neatly, hands folded, legs straight in a proper ladylike manner, or so I've been told."

While searching for ice to put in my glass of water, my memory pulled up that same vision of Babs lying still on the stainless-steel table.

"I see what you mean." No point in asking him where he got his information. "But why did someone kill her? And why pick the animal hospital to do it?"

"Good questions," he said, "and dangerous ones. Let me think about it and meanwhile please be extra careful, Katie. Keep that pepper spray handy at all times."

"I promise."

"One thing I can say is that from all indications, Babs let her killer into the hospital. You might, too."

I joined Cindy and Mari in the employee lounge. Given

the circumstances, we decided to keep appointments light over the coming week and close a half hour early. Personally, I would have preferred working every day until I dropped from exhaustion.

"Do you mind if I ask you both some questions?" Cindy sat upright in the least comfortable chair we owned.

"Go ahead," Mari said unenthusiastically. I waited, debating on zapping another slice of frozen pizza.

"So what kind of forensics work did the police do here?" Cindy asked.

"It was pretty chaotic," Mari began, "because when the EMTs arrived they inserted a line, started their protocol, and loaded her into the ambulance. From what I gather, things went badly quickly en route, and she was pronounced DOA at Kingston Hospital. The police arrived later, but we mostly stayed out of their way."

"Then what?" Cindy sipped some herbal tea, bypassing the potato chips Mari had poured onto a plate. The roof of my mouth started to blister from the lava-temperature pizza.

"We were escorted into Kate's office and told to wait. One of the newer deputies, Paulie, I think, spoke to us first. At that point, he mentioned accidental death or suicide."

As I listened, I experienced the same cold bewilderment I felt that day.

"But the police still investigated, didn't they?" Cindy said. "They closed off the surgery, you said?"

"Right. An officer put up caution tape and cordoned it off from the rest of the hospital. I think they searched reception, too. I assume the chief asked you about the controlled drug log and safe—and what they found?"

She twitched her lip. "Right. At first, all they were interested in were the anesthesia tanks. I don't think they knew about the propofol, or ketamine, or any of our other drugs. Most people don't understand that veterinarians use many of the same drugs as human hospitals."

Mari cleared her throat. "We don't have any Xanax in the safe, do we?"

"Nope," I answered. "Cindy, was Babs prescribed Xanax for anxiety?"

Her brow furrowed. "I don't know."

"If she wasn't prescribed it, the killer could have used it as the induction drug."

Cindy made a note in her phone. "I'll add it to the list of things for Bobby to check. He'll have to get around the HIPAA laws and interview her doctors."

So many things we still didn't know.

———————

Babs died on Friday while Mari and I were finishing our house calls, and since then, I'd stayed out of the surgical suite. With Cindy home from vacation, it reminded me that come Monday we'd be back at work. I floated the idea of Mari and me searching the treatment area, employee lounge, X-ray, and surgery, while Cindy searched reception, pharmacy, and the exam rooms. We should look for something…anything that didn't seem right. I reasoned that once our animal hospital went back to normal hours and scheduled surgeries, any remaining evidence would be wiped away.

Mari and I decided to start in the obvious spot, the surgical suite. We'd both avoided going inside and assumed it might be a bit disheveled from the forensic team. That didn't matter. We knew everything that belonged in this well-used room.

"Let's get the worst out of the way," I suggested to my assistant as we stood in front of the surgery suite double doors. Neither of us moved. I took a deep breath and opened the doors.

The room didn't look as bad as we thought after EMTs, police, and a forensic team had traipsed through it.

Our surgery table is stainless steel, with a foot-controlled raising and lowering feature. Although this is where we discovered Babs, I figured after the forensic team did their thing there would be little to find here.

We started at the bottom, searching underneath the table, taking care to check the pedestal all the way up from the tiled floor.

"It looks okay to me," Mari said, "but I need to clean the top. There are a million fingertip smudges from the investigation."

"Let's wait until we finish, then I'll help. The police and EMT crew sure left a mess." The metal waste paper bin was filled with medical debris, mostly packaging.

"Yep. I'll take this side of the room. Meet you in the middle."

Our surgical suite, where we performed all the sterile

surgeries like spays and neuters, was separated into two sides, with the surgery table located in the middle of the room. Doc Anderson owned two portable anesthesia machines, both stored in the same area as the metal gas cylinders. Everything necessary for anesthesia administration had been located on one side of the room. On the other side were stored surgical instruments and sterile surgical packs, pathology materials for the lab, and drawers of orthopedic instruments, bandage materials, etc.

"So far, I don't see anything unusual," Mari said. She counted our anesthesia gas canisters and checked the tubing and hoses. "I'm assuming the police confiscated that anesthesia mask she was wearing."

"Good assumption, but we should ask Cindy." All the drawers I inspected appeared normal. We both did a final look around then went out the surgery doors into the treatment area. This is where "dirty" surgery or "nonsterile" surgery was performed—procedures such as cat abscesses and some dental procedures, where everything needs to be clean but not necessarily sterile.

Sitting high on the top of a bank of cages, Mr. Katt glowered down at us.

"I wish you could tell us what you saw that day," I said to the kitty. "Anything would be appreciated."

In true feline fashion, he turned his back and started grooming himself.

The two of us methodically searched the cabinets and counters but noticed nothing out of place. We even went through everything in the employee refrigerator and our biologics refrigerator, with all the vaccines and medical items that needed to be kept cool. Nothing.

We'd just about finished when Cindy joined us. "The front office is almost exactly like I left it. There are a few more paperclips than usual, some assorted pens, and a drafting pencil. Everything was filed and the computer records appear to be up-to-date. The receipts tallied up, and the locked petty cash drawer is accurate."

"It's as though Babs wasn't even here. What happened to her coat and purse and boots?" I asked. "Do the police have them? I'm assuming so, but maybe you can find out, Cindy?"

"Will do."

Mari ran her fingers through her curly hair. "I need a break."

"Perfect timing," Cindy said. She pointed to a box in the corner labeled V-Day.

"Can you both help with the Valentine decorations?"

Cindy's request made no sense at first. "What do you mean?"

"It's almost Valentine's Day. I've put up decorations for every major holiday as long as I've been here, and I'm going to continue that tradition no matter what." Her voice steadily rose in volume. "Besides, Babs would have wanted me to."

Mari and I exchanged looks. I didn't think Babs much cared if we decorated the waiting room, but the frown on Cindy's face suggested I hold my tongue.

"You two go ahead. I'll clean up surgery and meet you up front," Mari said.

"Alright." I grabbed some scotch tape from our junk drawer. "Let's get this over with."

Cindy's sneakers made a low-level crunchy squeaking

sound on the floor as she walked ahead of me. I recalled the clomp of Babs's shoes walking down this same hallway.

"Kate?"

I turned toward Cindy's voice, realizing I'd been staring at nothing.

"Here's a box of garland with little red hearts on it," she said. "Go ahead and fasten it up along the chair railing."

"Okay." Doc Anderson had New England–style chair railings in the exam rooms and in reception, with a darker greenish blue painted below the rail and white above it. A combination of stickpins, scotch tape, and sticky putty stuff usually secured the seasonal decorations. My lack of enthusiasm felt patently obvious.

"Isn't this cute?" Cindy showed me a large heart-shaped greeting card. "It's from Pinky and his fiancé and their dogs Princess and Queenie. So sweet."

"Sweet," I repeated.

I watched Cindy attach the card with a clip to a cord strung below the animal hospital bulletin board. The large cupid on the front now pointed his arrow directly at me.

"I'm taking a picture for our website," she said. "We might as well try to get back to normal."

Cindy's plan was to soldier through our tragedy and to conduct business as usual. She motioned to me to continue decorating.

At the bottom of the box lay another garland with silver and red dogs and cats and tiny cupids. "Where should I put this?" The reception area was quickly filling up with sparkling crap.

"Go ahead and put that in the employee lounge," Cindy told me. "Then I release you from this torture."

"Sorry. It's hard to pretend everything is normal."

"I understand. But we can't think only of ourselves. We need to think about our clients and patients. It's not going to help them for us to sit here and cry."

"I suppose you're right," I replied begrudgingly. Draping the glittering garland around my neck in place of a stethoscope, I turned to my receptionist. "Is that better?" Almost crashing into one of the waiting room chairs, I twirled around as if in a fashion show.

Of course she laughed at me, and darned if my spirits didn't feel a speck lighter. Even the tiny animals and cupids danced a bit.

"You know," Cindy said as I began to leave, "in mythology, Cupid fired two types of arrows. One was tipped with gold and made you instantly fall in love. But the other was coated with lead and forced you to turn away from your suitor."

"I guess that explains it," I told her. "He's been getting the lead out with me."

As I moved down the hallway, I heard Mari banging something in the storage closet. A few more steps and I'd reached the employee lounge. Calling it a lounge was a compliment since it basically was a collection of well-used furniture plus a table and chairs for sitting and snacking. The garland around my neck ended up taped to yet another chair railing and sort of tucked behind one of the bulletin boards. This particular board held all the government declarations, EPA safety updates, and various veterinary news items.

Articles were two and three deep, as newer postings were pinned over older articles.

Taking a detour to the side-by-side refrigerator used to store our human snacks and foods, I searched around for an apple I'd left on one of the shelves. The banging noise stopped. As I took my first bite, Mari appeared.

"How's it going?" I asked her, sitting down at the table so I wouldn't make a mess everywhere.

"Okay." She scrunched her lips up.

I didn't need a dictionary to read that something was wrong. "Just okay?"

"This isn't much, but I found one of the spray cleaners for surgery stuck behind a bunch of regular cleaning products."

It didn't seem like a big deal, but it was. The hospital bought cleaning and sanitizing products in bulk then transferred the contents into smaller spray or squirt bottles. Each of those needed to be properly labeled with the product name, the date it was filled up, and where in the hospital it was assigned. Cindy had a system, of course, with each product designated for a specific place and task. That way there was no frantic hunting around for which bottle you needed.

And because it was Cindy, they were also color keyed.

"Did you touch it," I asked?

"No. I was so surprised to see it there that I froze."

"We need to get Cindy, ASAP."

The three of us stood in silence, staring at a clear plastic spray bottle half full of blue liquid. A red band of tape provided the product name, usage, strength, and date of refill.

"Where did you find it?" Cindy asked.

"Right here in the treatment room, shoved behind the autoclave." Mari pointed to a part of the countertop used for washing and sterilizing surgical instruments. "Almost out of sight."

Our office manager ran a tight, organized ship, as I knew Babs had.

"Any chance Babs forgot where it went?"

"No chance in hell," Cindy replied. "It says SURGERY right on the front, plus it's got a red identification band on it."

"So..." I began a thought, only to stop.

"Only one of two people put it there: Babs or the person who killed her." Cindy's perky voice took a dark turn. "I think it must have been Babs. She wanted to let us know something was wrong."

The hairs on the back of my neck stood up. In disbelief, I told both my friends about a conversation with Babs in which she mentioned if anyone tried to kill her she would leave clues.

Mari spoke up. "She sent us on a wild-goose chase the day she died. Her last text sent us to the wrong address."

"Could that have been a call for help? Maybe she started to feel threatened and knew you two would head back to the hospital."

"Cindy," I began, "I'm positive this is a clue from Babs,

but I'm not convinced the police would agree that an out-of-place spray bottle was deliberate."

Anger fueled her response to me. "I don't care what they think. She left us a message. I'm sure of it. Don't touch anything. I'm calling the chief."

Chapter Fifteen

ALTHOUGH IT WAS SUNDAY MORNING, ONE CALL FROM Cindy had a police car in front of the hospital in fifteen minutes. Mari and I peeked out the window, but the officers stayed in their vehicle until a large police SUV pulled in, and Bobby Garcia got out. His normal pallor had temporarily vanished thanks to his family vacation in Florida with both his and Cindy's families. I felt sorry for them coming back to this mess.

Cindy met her brother-in-law at the front door. He leaned down, and she whispered something in his ear. Meanwhile, Mari and I pretended to be busy.

"Let me show you," Cindy said before bringing him back into the treatment area. We noticed the other officers stayed put in the parking lot.

"What should we do?" Mari whispered to me. She noticed an unopened cardboard box stacked near the prescription diets and gestured to me to open it.

"Don't eavesdrop, for one thing," I whispered back. "I'd rather not see or hear anything I'd have to testify to."

The box contained one of the medical diets prescribed for urinary tract infections. While I helped unpack the cans, Mari entered the shipment into the computer inventory and placed the shipping order on Cindy's desk. By the time we finished stocking, Chief Garcia walked past us and opened the front door, a look of annoyance on his face. Cindy discreetly followed a moment later.

"Well, he's not happy, but I couldn't let it go," Cindy said. She picked up the shipping statement and gave it a cursory glance. Automatically, she filed it into the marked hanging folder in her desk drawer. "Mari, will you set aside six cans for Buttons McCavitt, please?"

"Sure," Mari said. "Anything else?"

"Yes. Sorry, ladies, but you've both got a date with the chief."

———

The chief interviewed each of us separately. Later, when Mari and I compared notes, we found his questions were simple and similar. He went over our daily routine, quizzed us about our cleaning rituals and who did what, and asked how our house calls work.

When it was my turn, he asked my opinion of Cindy's theory that the surgery spray bottle was out of place on purpose.

Although freshly back from his vacation, Chief Garcia still showed gray patches under his eyes. No wonder. Three people dead in Oak Falls while he'd been frolicking on the warm sand and drinking cold margaritas.

He waited for my answer, the jowls on his face giving him a hound-dog look.

"I'll try to explain. It's important for the treatment and surgery suite to be clean and organized," I began, "because we never know what kind of emergency might show up. When you're evaluating a critical trauma case in front of you, there's no time to waste searching for something."

Chief Garcia tilted his head and made notes in his pocket notebook. Cindy said he liked to gather his thoughts before typing them into his computer.

"If it helps," I continued, "we always clean up and put things back in place at the end of the day. Babs only worked here for five days, but the way she worked felt very similar to Cindy's. The reception desk was clear of paperwork when we closed up, and the hospital set up for the next day's appointments."

None of this seemed new to the chief.

"On Friday, you and Mari came back from your house calls," he said. "Was there anything out of place that you noticed when you came in?"

My mind slid back to that horrible afternoon. "Not at first. Mari couldn't reach Babs by text or phone, very unusual and upsetting. We thought she'd gone for the day—except her car was still parked out front."

"Did you normally turn the alarm system on during office hours?"

"No. I set it after we close each night."

"Does that include the indoor and outdoor cameras?"

"Yes, always."

Again the chief took his time and scribbled more notes. I stared out the window, curious about what else he wanted to know.

Outside, the sun played hide-and-seek with the growing gray clouds. Shadows danced across the parking lot.

"What did you think of Babs?"

He calmly watched as I tried to compose a cohesive reply.

Smart, I thought, *and organized, like Cindy.* It was hard to define someone in a few words, someone you didn't know that well. "One thing I can tell you," I said with more certainty, "She was nobody's fool."

After Chief Garcia and his officers left, taking multiple pictures and the infamous spray bottle with them, Cindy, Mari, and I closed up the hospital. My vet assistant and I doubled-checked the treatment room windows, kennels, and employee lounge, leaving Cindy to clean her reception area and the front storage/outpatient drug and food cabinets. I threw out an old cardboard pizza takeaway box. Only one other room to go. Surgery.

"I already cleaned it," Mari protested.

"But the police went back in there. We'll make it quick."

I figured Mari was thinking the same thing I was. Seared into both our brains, the sight of Babs lying still on the surgery table. Maybe Gramps had a point about PTSD.

"They probably made a mess," I said, referring to the police.

"Probably." Mari sounded unenthusiastic.

"We've got surgery scheduled for tomorrow," I told her. "I don't want any surprises, so let's get it over with."

"The only surprise would be if Babs jumped out and yelled April Fools!" my assistant said.

I hoped that image wouldn't visit me in my dreams tonight. "That would be a surprise, considering we're in the early days of February."

"Bad joke." She took a deep breath. "Okay. Let's get this done."

We pushed open the doors to find very little mess, just some powdery stuff near the storage cabinets. The countertops shone, and both anesthesia machines were stowed in place.

Seeing the cold impersonal sterility of the room felt like a closing in a way. Lying on the surgery table tomorrow would be a furry dog having a tumor removed under anesthesia. I'd be gloved up and gowned up, a surgery pack open on the portable instrument tray. As usual, Mari would be checking the anesthesia levels and watching a bag of saline slowly drip through the intravenous catheter taped to our patient's outstretched front leg.

The day would be noisy and slightly chaotic, and the two of us would be scrambling to get all our work done in time. We'd barely have time to think. Business as usual.

I wanted tomorrow to be loud and messy—anything except the icy sterility of our silent surgical suite.

Chapter Sixteen

As I went about my job the next day, I realized something. Usually, I am the one curious enough to investigate crimes in Oak Falls, but this time it was Cindy who was on the killer's trail. Before we opened up, she ambushed Mari and me while we poured our coffee.

"I've been thinking about this all night. Someone came into MY office where Babs was working and killed her in OUR surgery suite. No way are they ever going to get away with this."

I'd never heard Cindy so angry. Her cheeks began to flush, lips pressed together. "That's what I told the chief, and that's what I'll tell you both. This means scorched earth—no prisoners," she continued.

You didn't interrupt an angry Cindy.

"The police better find him before I do."

Is this coming from the person who always advised caution? But I understood her wrath. Every time we walked into surgery, in the back of our minds would be thoughts of Babs—our own group PTSD nightmare.

"You can't do it by yourself," I told her. "This should be a team effort, and I know that Mari and I will help all we can."

Mari said, "Agreed."

"Is there going to be a memorial service?" I asked Cindy.

Her face tightened. "Tomorrow night. It's been posted on the funeral home website, and an obituary will be in the paper today. So far, no one has claimed her body," she added, "but the service will proceed regardless."

"Still no relatives that showed up?"

"Nope." Cindy, uncharacteristically fidgety, pulled her sleeve.

"What's wrong?" Mari asked her.

"The police took her purse. There was an emergency list on Babs's phone. She'd listed a lawyer in Albany. When the chief called him, he discovered that Babs had made a will. The lawyer then contacted the identified trustee of her estate."

Strange. I'd forgotten Babs had a life away from the office.

"Who is it?" I asked. "Whoever gets the money could be the murderer."

Cindy's eyes met mine. "I'm the trustee."

Of course we had a million questions for Cindy, but they had to wait. Between morning appointments and afternoon surgeries, today had been completely booked. I, for one, was more than glad to be back to work.

My first appointment turned out to be an exam on an older cat whose owner had noticed her eyes looked "weird," according to Mari's brief triage history.

After knocking on the exam room door, I entered to see an elderly tabby cat struggling to get out of her owner's arms. On top of the woman's head sat a large faux fur hat, the same shade as her cat.

"This is Ms. Ryan," Mari said, placing our computer tablet on the exam room desk.

"She hates being held unless it's on her terms," the owner

explained after peeling the cat off her jacket and plunking her on the exam table.

"That's very common," I said, taking the opportunity to pet the thin kitty. "What's her name?"

"Jane Austin," the owner said. "I name all my cats after authors I admire."

"Well, I'm a fan, too," I admitted. Although it looked like I was simply petting her cat, in reality I had already started my exam. I could feel the bony protrusions of her vertebrae along the back and the subtle loss of fat from her ribcage.

"How is Jane's appetite?" I asked, taking my stethoscope and placing it above her heart.

The owner beamed. "She's got a great appetite. Not picky at all. Some of my friends have such problems getting their cats to eat, but not me."

After listening to the rapid pounding heartbeat and palpating Jane Austin's thyroid gland, located in her neck, I believed I knew the secret of a cat that ate everything but didn't gain weight.

We'd worked so long together, I could see Mari anticipating my next move.

"Ms. Ryan, I'd like to take Jane into our treatment room, so I can perform her eye exam, plus take some blood for lab tests, if that's alright."

Mari picked up the kitty and scratched her ears.

"Is it something serious?" the owner asked, a note of panic creeping into her question.

"Jane has tachycardia," I began, "which is a faster than normal heartbeat. It can be caused by several things, but I need to run some blood tests to confirm a diagnosis. For now, I'm thinking she has an overactive thyroid, which is causing high blood pressure, affecting her eyes along with a big appetite without weight gain."

"Oh, my gosh," the woman said and sank into one of the exam chairs. "Can you treat it?"

"That's the good news," I explained. "It can be treated, and the sooner the better."

Mari calmed the cat, who'd gotten tired of being held and was eyeing the room for hiding places. "Should I set everything up?"

"Yes, please," I answered. At this moment, the owner needed some attention. The woman in front of me looked like she was going to burst into tears. I rolled the office chair away from the small computer station and said, "Try not to worry. The best decision you've made for Jane is to bring her to the vet. I should have preliminary answers for you in about twenty or thirty minutes. Would you prefer to wait here or with Cindy in reception?"

"Reception, I guess," the owner said.

"We've got some veterinary literature I'd like you to read," I told her. "Cindy will bring it to you in the waiting room."

After escorting her to reception, I turned her over to Cindy, who gathered a packet of information about senior kitties and hyperthyroidism.

When I opened the treatment area door, it sounded like Jane Austin was dictating a new book to Mari. I hoped her deep yowls weren't carrying all the way to reception.

Mari laughed when she saw me, raising her hands up in the air. "I didn't do anything. She's talking up a storm."

"Look at the shape of her head," I commented while getting a rapid test for thyroid hormone ready. "Loudmouth, talkative Siamese genes are lurking in there somewhere."

Jane Austin stayed fairly cooperative but didn't stop yowling during any of her tests. She even continued in the darkened room during the eye exam. Meanwhile, her total T4 rapid in-house screening test was positive, indicating an overactive thyroid. We would send another, more sophisticated test out to the lab for confirmation, plus a metabolic panel that checked for kidney disease, diabetes, liver function, and a host of other issues. At least I had some preliminary happy news for this owner.

Mari prepared a cage for our senior kitty, while I made sure the lab requests were correct and set to go out tonight. I'd recommend that Jane Austin stay with us this evening and receive her first dose of medication.

Happily, the owner and Cindy had gone over the medical literature, and she felt relieved with her cat's preliminary diagnosis. She did have one question. "Was that Jane yowling?" Ms. Ryan asked.

"Yes," I answered truthfully.

"Good," she said. "Maybe you can cure that."

Chapter Seventeen

THE FUNERAL HOME IN OAK FALLS WAS LOCATED IN AN older, dignified building painted white with black shutters and doors. A modern addition held the meeting rooms where memorial services were held. The large parking lot had several cars parked near the entrance when Cindy, Mari, and I arrived the next day, carpooling from the office.

Inside, the atmosphere was hushed. A young woman sat in one of the lobby chairs, gently rocking a large baby carriage. Near her foot rested a gray diaper bag decorated with elephants. Farther down, an older man sat with his hat in his hands, staring at the wall.

Directly in front of us, overseeing everything, stood a funeral parlor employee, whose discreet name tag I couldn't read. A sign guided us toward a room on the right. There, a professional photograph of a much younger Babs devoid of glasses rested on a wooden table near a sign-in book. We each took our turn while I wondered how many people attending actually knew her.

Cindy walked ahead of us, choosing seats in the front row. Before we arrived, she mentioned that she'd arranged for tonight's memorial service. Almost as soon as we sat down, Cindy excused herself to speak to the funeral director, while I tried to casually check out the crowd. To my surprise, I noticed Dr. Mike sitting in an aisle seat and reading the card provided. Next to him a blond woman wearing a black hat blotted her eyes. Farther back, a familiar-looking man with close-cropped dark hair was texting on his phone. As I glanced around the room, several persons I recognized as clients acknowledged me with a head nod.

Of course, now I remembered that Babs said she'd worked as a temp for various companies and animal hospitals across the Hudson Valley. However fleetingly, she obviously touched many lives.

Mari leaned over and whispered, "I'm glad there are so many people here. I was having nightmares of the three of us being the only mourners." Before I could answer, Cindy made her way back to us and sat down.

Soft music spilled from the speakers placed around the room. The lighting gave off an indirect warm glow, creating as pleasant an atmosphere as possible. A podium stood off to the left next to another, larger photo of Babs. On a small table in front of that photo sat an urn.

I swallowed hard and looked away.

The room continued to fill, including a large group of older women who entered together. Most wore black.

"That's the bridge club," Cindy whispered.

A well-dressed family settled into the seats behind us. The children looked to be about ten and twelve, on the cusp of being teenagers. I heard chairs creak as they squirmed in their seats. The woman greeted Cindy by name, whispering how sad this entire situation was.

A funeral home employee I'd noticed in the lobby appeared at the door with another, older man holding a black folder in his hand. The younger one glanced at his watch and then said something to his associate. The six p.m. service was about to begin.

As the older man dressed in a black suit introduced himself, my mind wandered. I tried to recall all my conversations with Babs, realizing in the five days she'd been working for us, we'd barely spoken about anything but work. Instead of socializing, I'd been holed up in my office or seeing clients with Mari. There'd been so little time.

As the funeral director asked for remembrances, Cindy stood up. At the podium, our poised office manager/receptionist spoke of a longtime friend who enjoyed gardening. Someone responsible and trustworthy. Someone who liked an occasional beer at the Red Lion Pub after work.

Someone I didn't know at all.

More than enough people volunteered to speak of their friend, Babs. The bridge ladies joked about her insistence on being the scorekeeper and her uncanny winning streaks. Others told of a willing pet sitter, an animal lover grieving the death of her elderly terrier.

From the hallway outside, I heard the muffled cry of an infant.

The stories went on and on, including a lovely story from the couple who sat behind us. Babs lived on the same property, in what would have been the gatekeeper's cottage. Their two children called her Auntie Babs. Together they tended a large vegetable garden in the summer and harvested apples in the fall. She often babysat or created art projects with the kids.

It sounded as though Babs had a nice life.

Until an unknown someone decided to end it.

When the service finished, Cindy stood next to the funeral director, forming a sort of thank you line. Mari and I decided to wait in the lobby for her. As the participants filed out, many of our clients came over to express condolences. Dr. Mike stopped by briefly to tell me how sorry he was and how much his office staff missed Babs. Once more I appreciated his calm voice and kind eyes. He added that anytime I wanted to talk I should call him.

About twenty minutes later it was all over. The lobby emptied out, save for the funeral home employees. Cindy thanked them all again and walked over to us, her coat in her hand.

"I'm so glad you're here, guys," she said. "This was tougher than I thought."

Mari gave her a hug. "No problem. Wonderful that so many people came to say goodbye."

The younger employee wished us good night and began closing the meeting room doors. We slipped on our coats and headed toward the exit.

"I saw you speaking to Dr. Mike," Cindy said, wrapping her muffler around her neck. "He's a great guy. Maybe you should go out with him."

Mari's eyes widened. I laughed and answered, "What about his wife and the twins?"

"What twins?" she said, stopping abruptly, her hand resting on the exit door.

It wasn't like Cindy not to be current on the lives of everyone in Oak Falls and near vicinity—especially the surrounding animal hospital employees. "Cindy, he's married with two kids."

She looked puzzled then laughed, "You must have them mixed up."

"What? Who mixed up?" Mari asked her, pulling on red knit gloves.

"The Hudson Valley Animal Clinic and Equine Center hired two Dr. Mikes. The hospital staff refer to them as Dr. Mike C and Dr. Mike M, so no one gets confused. It's Mike C who has the twins. He sat in the back tonight, balding guy wearing a tan coat. Didn't you see his wife sitting in the lobby with the baby carriage, waiting for him?"

My mind blanked.

"So the Dr. Mike Kate met..." Mari paused midsentence.

Again Cindy laughed, only to blush with embarrassment as the funeral home attendant cleared his throat.

"Your Dr. Mike is available."

Considering we were coming from a funeral, there was way too much laughing in Mari's SUV, at my expense.

"You must be wrong, Cindy," I said, although she most often was right. "Even Judy asked him about the babies."

"Fur babies," she replied. "They're fostering some stray kittens, I think. The info is on the office website."

It never occurred to me to check out his bio on the office website.

"Hey, nothing ventured, nothing gained," Mari quoted. "Although I'm not quite sure what it means in this case."

Cindy turned toward me from the passenger side of Mari's SUV. "It means they can go out on a date. Finally, some good news."

I leaned against the aromatic fifty-pound bag of dog

food on the seat next to me. "He's a friend, guys. Just a friend."

"Valentine's Day is coming up," Mari reminded me. "Maybe Cupid's getting the good bow and arrow out for you." Cindy made a faint sound, like an edited giggle.

"So you haven't been flirting with him?" Mari added.

"Of course not," I said, slightly offended at the suggestion. "He's married. Or at least I thought he was married."

Again both of my friends dissolved into laughter.

"What about Babs?" I asked them, trying to change the subject. "We still don't know if her killer is wandering around Oak Falls."

Cindy turned around again. "I haven't forgotten. As the executor of her estate, I received the keys to her house from the lawyers. I'll be going through it tomorrow night, right after work. Does anyone want to join me? I'm cataloging and packing up some of her more valuable things. The estate lawyer suggested we store everything for six months or until an heir is found."

"I'm in," I told her.

"Can't," said Mari. "The Schutzhund club is meeting."

"I thought I read that competitive Schutzhund is now called IGP?" Another bit of information gleaned from my veterinary journals.

"It will always be Schutzhund for me," Mari answered. "I'm not competing anymore, anyway. This is more social." She slowed down to make the turn into the parking lot. Spotlights illuminated the animal hospital name but kept the rest of the property in a puddle of darkness.

The giant bag of dog food next to me was for Mari's two Rottweilers, who were both trained in Schutzhund, which highlights obedience and protection. Her one hundred-pound male was built like a doggy battering ram. Mari always bragged about how safe she felt with her dogs.

My dog, Buddy, only weighs twenty-five pounds. Not quite the same level of security.

"Home sweet home," I said, sounding more sarcastic than I meant to.

Cindy and I climbed down, our feet hitting a dry spot on the asphalt. The motion detector lights above clicked on. We wished Mari a good night before she sped away.

"It's only seven thirty," Cindy said. "How about a sneak preview of Babs's place? I'll get a quick idea of how much work there will be."

Although she'd never admit it, her voice sounded tremulous, a bit emotional. After all, she's suggesting entering the home of a dead friend at night. Cindy might uncover things best left hidden.

"Please?" Cindy asked again.

The thought of her facing this alone was too much. "Of course," I answered. "I'll drive my truck, though, so you don't have to bring me back."

"Good thinking. Thanks again. I'd hate to have to do this alone."

She smiled a soft grateful smile and started her truck. After I'd gotten into mine, she called out, "Follow me" and took off with a roar.

I had no expectations of how Babs lived. At the memorial service, a family with two children indicated she lived in the guesthouse on their property. Sure enough, what amounted to the gatekeeper's place was what Babs called home.

It's odd the things that strike you when you walk into a room. The quiet. A slightly musty smell. My eye immediately focused on the windowsill. In front of it sat some plants that desperately needed water.

"I'll water the plants," I told Cindy, taking in the spare decorating in what looked like a midcentury modern style. Gramps took me to an exhibit at the Museum of Modern Art in NYC that highlighted furniture from that period. Babs's sofa was a sort of purple-blue velvet and low-slung. An unusual six-foot-long coffee table with a lattice-pattern drawer was placed directly in front of it.

I carefully picked up the plants and moved them to the kitchen sink. "We can touch everything, right?" No way I wanted the police chief mad at me.

Cindy disappeared down the hallway. "Forensics has come and gone," she called out to me. "I'm checking her office."

Automatically, I removed the dead leaves from the geranium and carefully watered the purple African violet blooming happily in a small pot. The flowers on the geranium were beginning to fade. It had been lipstick red, a popular color that my own mom kept in a bumped-out garden window behind the sink. One of my chores when I was a kid was taking care of the plants.

I remember after my mom died, I brought her geranium into my room. It didn't like the change of light, despite my attention to it. After spending the weekend with Gramps, I returned to find our housekeeper had thrown it out.

The bright blooms weren't the only spots of color in Babs's house. Vivid orange throw pillows graced the two swivel chairs in front of the sofa. A sleek flat-screen television hung on the wall, while a door opened on to a bluestone courtyard. At the far end of the room, a fireplace loomed, built when fireplaces provided the only source of heat. This gatekeeper's cottage had been renovated with care, many of the original details kept intact. I found this mix of rough stone and modern furnishing pleasing, very minimalistic. It fit Babs in a way.

Cindy came around the corner as I placed the plants in the sink to drain.

"Do you want these plants?" I asked. "If not, I'll take them."

"Go ahead. I've got too many houseplants as it is."

"Find anything interesting?" I asked her. As soon as the plants finished draining, I'd pack them up for the quick trip home.

"I'm not sure," Cindy said in a distracted tone. She entered a note into her phone. "Babs had one of those blotter-style year calendars on her desk. I noticed she planned to attend a wedding in June."

"So?"

"José and Alicia's wedding."

"The same couple that died up by the lake?" I asked.

"Right. I knew Alicia and Babs had worked together, but I didn't know they kept in touch. The two of us used to have lunch about twice a month, but most of the afternoons we got together we talked about work. And the stock market."

That surprised me. "The stock market?"

Cindy headed into the living room, her answer trailing behind. "Her late husband worked as a stock market adviser," she said. "He passed away in his early seventies from a heart attack. There was about a twenty-year age difference between them. Babs told me he'd made some good investments. Like buying some of the first Apple Computer stock."

I looked around the modest rented home and figured her husband's advice didn't help that much. The gatekeeper's cottage appeared very up-to-date, but with two bedrooms, it still felt relatively small.

Wait, I thought. *This cottage is bigger than where I live.*

From the end of the hallway, I heard Cindy slamming kitchen cabinet doors.

The large stainless-steel refrigerator doors stood wide open. A big black garbage bag waited for any trash to be thrown out.

"I guess Babs liked ordering from Amazon," Cindy noted, pointing to a stack of flattened boxes near the mudroom door. "She must have been recycling the cardboard."

The modern stainless kitchen appliances glowed, the upper cabinets a sleek glossy white. Underneath the quartz countertop stood pale wooden cabinets. To the left of the gas cooktop protruded a faucet from the wall.

"What's this for?" I asked Cindy.

"Pot filler faucet," she quickly answered. "Those city folks did a fantastic job renovating this place."

"I guess Babs lucked out," I admitted with a little bit of envy. "There's also an enclosed porch that way," I pointed to my right, "and some kind of square greenhouse room past the master bedroom."

While I spoke, Cindy took canned goods and packaged goods out of the pantry and placed them on the countertop. "I've got to call the food bank tomorrow and donate all of this," she said. As she made a note in her phone, I looked around more closely.

The kitchen table was bright white with a long slender base nestled in the corner of a built-in L-shaped banquette. Brightly patterned upholstery covered the seats. I sat down. Very comfortable, and from where I sat, I could see the approach from the main road.

In a square Lucite box in front of me lay some brochures, junk mail, and a familiar-looking small notebook. Meant to fit comfortably in a jacket pocket, it reminded me of the one Babs carried during office hours or the one the chief used.

Out of curiosity, I opened it. Someone had ripped out the beginning pages. The metal rings held small paper fragments of discarded pages, leaving only the empty white ones behind.

I was about to point it out to Cindy, but she was preoccupied listening to a voicemail. Before I could say anything, she redialed the number. "Sorry. Emergency. Got to call the lawyer back."

Travel brochures made up about half of Babs's mail with fanciful full-color pamphlets advertising high-end cruises to almost every part of the world. I could picture Babs having a cup of tea and browsing through them. Periodically, I'd get one in the mail and do the same thing, looking at exotic Easter Island and the Galapagos and making a promise that someday...

"What?" Cindy spoke louder than normal into her phone. "I know you gave me a copy of the paperwork, but I didn't finish reading it yet."

A look of bewilderment on our receptionist's face caught my attention. She raised her hand in a wait gesture when I caught her eye.

"Are you sure about this?" She turned her back to me. "I'm going to need some help. In fact, tell your assistant to book me a video appointment with you ASAP. I want my husband to hear this."

Face flushed, she ended the call and sat down across from me at the kitchen table.

"Something wrong?" I asked. Maybe Babs owed credit card bills that the estate couldn't pay.

"Nothing wrong. Just unexpected." She continued placing foodstuffs into the cardboard box. Outside, traffic on the main road rolled past, headlights briefly illuminating the empty field flanking the house before moving out of sight. "Babs wasn't renting this place."

"She had a lease? Did she break her lease by dying?" I remembered when Luke was studying for his law exam there were crazy questions about leases and when they could be enforced. "Cindy, some states enforce a lease even after you pass away. Can you…"

"Babs was loaded, Kate. Rich. She owns this entire property, including the big rental house. She's worth millions."

Chapter Eighteen

MILLIONS OF DOLLARS PRESENTED A STRONG MOTIVE FOR murder, but Babs's estate turned out to be very complicated. There were over thirty monetary gifts, as Cindy explained the next day to Mari and me, serving as thirty motives for murder. The family currently living in the large home on her property was gifted their home, with all taxes paid. Her lawyer said Babs wanted to do something nice for this former military family.

"What else did the lawyer say?" Mari asked Cindy during our lunch break.

"The trust was drawn up by a big law firm in Albany that specializes in estate planning," she explained. "But she also had a local lawyer. To his knowledge, she didn't share the details of her estate with anyone. The family who rents the main house always paid a management corporation."

The microwave dinged. "So they didn't know."

"Right. They still don't know. Her estate lawyer is handling those kinds of details." Cindy carefully removed her soup. "Meanwhile, the chief is checking out the alibis of all the named beneficiaries. The remainder is split between any blood relatives located and several animal charities."

"You should be okay," I said to Cindy. "You were in Florida with your family and the police chief's family when Babs was killed. That's what I'd call an airtight alibi."

Mari added, "Kate and I were seeing house call clients. So

we're in the clear, too. Although I'm guessing no beneficiary money for us."

A completely new motive entered the murky picture of these murders. Relatives who benefited from Babs's death.

"Millions of dollars certainly changes everything," Cindy said, "and the chief is getting nowhere."

I sat there eating my lunch, many questions on my mind. How did Babs make so much money? Why did she anonymously give away chunks of money to so many people? But the thing that kept bothering me was—a June wedding invitation from Alicia and José. Maybe she planned to gift them something—like stock or cash.

Three people dead in a matter of a week.

All participants in a canceled June wedding.

Was there a connection?

———

The next day all three of us were dragging. Poor Cindy kept having to call or answer texts from both lawyers. After the office closed, in the stillness of an empty hospital, I thought about Babs having plenty of money yet choosing to continue to work.

If I were honest with myself, I'd probably do the same thing.

I also realized I knew next to nothing about Alicia and José except they died under unusual circumstances. Since Cindy was determined to find Babs's killer, I decided to do groundwork on the engaged couple. I wasn't sure if Judy knew them, but it couldn't hurt to ask her some questions. The best time to have a conversation with the owner of Judy's Café would be right before closing. The added benefit was that even if I learned nothing, I'd come home with some takeout for tomorrow.

Having lived in Oak Falls all her life, it seemed that Judy knew everyone and vice versa. I'd been told she'd enjoyed numerous romantic relationships in her younger days until she met up with a skilled carpenter and settled down. She painted and sculpted, but her art was not for sale. Her creations were given as gifts or donated to libraries or nursing homes. She once told me she didn't want the hassle or the judgment that came with commercial sales.

I'd have to move it to get there before she closed, so I finished up my emails, answered all the last-minute questions from clients, and reviewed outstanding lab results. Mr. Katt lay in my lap, a furry heating pad. Given his unique personality, I hated to remove him, but I needed to get going.

Although I gently put him on the ground, he looked up at me with such an expression of entitlement that I laughed. He swatted my ankle to show his displeasure. I'd have to corner him, with Mari helping, to trim those feline daggers. He had turned into a kitty tyrant.

On the other hand, Buddy danced and yipped and acted eternally grateful for his evening walk and feed.

I took a little longer than usual with my appearance, smoothing back my hair into a high ponytail then securing it with a velvet scrunchie. Searching through my closet, I rediscovered a fluffy pink sweater that reflected some color into my pale face. A little makeup and rosy lip gloss, and I was out the door.

Lingering in my subliminal mind was the hope I might run into Dr. Mike at Judy's tonight. The Dr. Mike with no wife.

———

A quick look at the few customers left in Judy's confirmed no Dr. Mike tonight. I felt a momentary twinge of regret before I sat at the countertop stool and waited for Judy to appear. At this time of night, most of her staff were heading home. Judy always closed her restaurant herself. She also rang up all the receipts and made the business bank deposits. It keeps people honest, she once joked to me.

My phone pinged with a text message, so I missed Judy's sudden appearance in front of me.

"Dr. Kate," she said in a pleased voice. "What can I get for you? We have one order of a truly outstanding chicken pot pie left."

"I'll take it to go. What else do you recommend?"

"Clam and shrimp chowder, New England style," she said quickly. "With a side of green beans, mushrooms, and bacon. Tea?"

"Perfect. I've never heard of clam and shrimp chowder," I said.

Judy laughed. "That's what happens when you run out of clams. Improvise, baby." She continued chuckling at her own joke before disappearing into the fragrant kitchen.

Judy always has fresh coffee, but she knew I rarely drank coffee this late at night. Being a regular somewhere means they get to know your likes and dislikes, and I qualified as a regular.

Waiting for my food, I glanced out the large front window that faced Main Street. The deserted sidewalk shone brightly under the streetlamps. Outside, the air temperature continued to drop. A thermometer attached to the restaurant window read thirty-six degrees. No wind, but still darned cold outside.

A foursome in the corner stood up and started putting on their coats amid much chatter. At the end of the counter sat an older man eating a burger. He briefly glanced at the remaining customers before going back to his meal. I noticed thin fingers with a gold wedding ring. His bony wrist stuck out past his shirt cuff. Was he a client? I knew I'd seen that face before.

As the foursome leaving brushed past, their puffy ski jackets bumped into my seat. From their sunburned faces, I deduced they recently had spent some time outdoors, maybe skiing?

I watched them open the door and step out into the cold. One made a fuss and wrapped her coat more tightly around herself, while her companion pulled his ski hat out of his pocket and pulled it low on his head, trying to cover his prominent ears. Their breath created puffs of white, warm air colliding with cold.

Judy walked toward me with a big bowl of soup and a coffee mug.

"Let me know if you like it," she said, placing it down on the counter.

"Perfect. Thanks, Judy." Steam rose from the chowder. If you ordered hot food, it always arrived piping hot. That gave me a perfect excuse to savor it slowly while asking the restaurant owner about the first two victims, Alicia and José. All I knew was what Babs and Daffy had told us. The short version was Alicia had an affair with a fellow lawyer, who left his wife for her. They married but it didn't end well. After Alicia threatened to leave her husband, he committed suicide.

About José, all I knew for certain was his profession: a physician's assistant. The steamy chowder felt too hot to eat, which made it a perfect time to gossip. I thought I'd start with José.

For once, I didn't have to randomly bring up murder to a town resident. Judy jumped into it with no prodding at all. "How's Cindy doing?" she began, sipping a coffee while checking out the remaining customer.

"She's doing okay," I managed to say midmouthful of the veggie side order. "Babs's death has been tough on all of us."

"They've known each other a long time." She paused to check again on the slim man at the end of the counter. From the empty plates in front of him, I could tell he was almost finished. "I'll be right back," Judy said.

Wiping her hands on the towel tucked into her apron, she asked if he wanted anything else. When he answered no, she wrote up his check and waited. He finally figured out she wanted payment, so he dug out a credit card and slapped it on the counter. "Thanks, Greg," Judy said. She processed his payment and brought back both the card and receipt. "Everyone," she announced, in a louder voice, "we're closing in five minutes. If you need a takeaway box, please let me know."

A well-dressed older couple made their way to the front with their check and cash in the gentleman's hand. Meanwhile, Greg put on his coat, called out a "good night, Judy," and started toward the exit. With his hand on the doorknob he hesitated, then glanced back my way, a thoughtful expression on his face.

Once all her customers had left, Judy walked over to the front door, turned her sign from *Open* to *Closed*, and locked the doors with a large set of keys.

"Who was that man? There's something familiar about him." I got up, ready to leave, figuring I'd talk to her another time.

"That's Greg Owens. Hey, where are you going?" Judy asked.

"Aren't you closing?" I asked.

"Yes." She drew the blinds in the window facing the street and turned some of her lights off. "But I'm pretty sure you didn't come here tonight only for my chowder. Let's sit back here." She pointed to a dimly lit far corner.

"Now first tell me about how Babs died."

Judy sat quietly while I described what Mari and I saw the day Babs died. Most importantly, I explained that Cindy didn't think Babs committed suicide.

"I'd have to agree with Cindy," the restaurant owner said. "Completely out of character, for one thing."

"What else?"

"She'd booked a high-end tour of Japan this spring when the cherry blossoms are in bloom. Said it was her dream vacation."

Someone rattled Judy's doorknob. She ignored it. "There's always one person who doesn't believe I'm closed."

I listened as it rattled again.

"They'll get tired and go away."

A low murmuring of voices that quickly faded away proved her correct.

"I'm also pretty sure she didn't use drugs. A glass of wine or a beer periodically, okay. But not anything like you described. Too...old-fashioned, I suppose."

I took a sip of rapidly cooling tea. "What do you mean by old-fashioned?"

"Someone with a strict moral code. Applied across the board. It was right or wrong, plain and simple. Not a lot of gray zones."

"You're the third person who's told me that. Sometimes it's not that simple," I said.

"Modern life presents plenty of gray zones," Judy replied. "Sometimes all your choices are dilutions of gray."

We spoke for almost an hour, with Judy staying on track, for the most part, only straying to inform me about a pop-up art installation to benefit a local women's shelter. Ten dollars at the door with snacks and a cash bar, as well as the artists speaking about their work. She urged me to attend, even if only for half an hour.

It was when I asked her about José and Alicia that she really let it rip.

Chapter Nineteen

"So now you have three open deaths in Oak Falls?" Gramps asked at the start of our phone conversation. It was a testament to our times that he didn't sound surprised. "I suppose it's useless for me to tell you again to leave the investigating to the police."

I wisely kept my mouth shut.

"Just promise me," he repeated, a little huskiness to his voice, "you'll be careful, and always keep that pepper spray in your pocket."

"I promise, Gramps. Try not to worry about me."

I'd called him to chat and get him up to speed with the investigation. Earlier Police Chief Garcia announced that José and Alicia's deaths were now considered to be suspicious. Forensic evidence revealed that José did not commit suicide.

"By the way, Babs knew Alicia well enough to be invited to her wedding," I told Gramps while opening the fridge.

"Let me get this straight," he said. "They all knew each other, and they all were murdered within a week of each other? I'm betting murdered by the same individual."

"But why?" The cool air from the refrigerator gave me a momentary chill.

"When you figure that out, you'll find the killer."

Between my late-night talk in the restaurant with Judy and a quick phone call to Cindy and Daffy, I better understood the dynamics of the engaged couple so brutally murdered. According to my notes, Alicia felt she was being harassed by her first husband's ex-wife and filed a lawsuit against her. The wife, Linda, blamed Alicia for ex-hubby's suicide and for the fact that she and her children were cut out of his will. She came close to wishing Alicia dead. The ex-mother-in-law, Crystal, the children's grandmother, also got into the act, posting pictures of Alicia's workplace and advising customers to boycott the law firm. The family wrote nasty reviews saying she was a terrible lawyer and uploaded unflattering pictures of her on Facebook.

José was not without his problems, too. A physician's assistant, José currently had a malpractice suit pending in the death of a woman from pancreatic cancer. He'd been treating her for a urinary tract infection on and off for several months, before referring her to a specialist. It took his patient another two months to get a CT scan. By then her highly malignant cancer had metastasized. Despite treatment by oncology specialists, she died within a year.

The woman's husband, Greg Owens, showed up at José's work and threatened him. A complaint was made but later dropped.

Wait, I thought. Didn't Judy say the client eating at the counter tonight was Greg Owens? He seemed familiar, but I didn't remember why. I made a note to find out more about Mr. Owens.

So far, there were no suspects or motive for Babs's

murder, but several suspects for the murder of the engaged couple. Where did all their lives intersect? Did they live near each other?

Tomorrow, we had a two-hour lunch break because of Cindy's meeting with the estate lawyer. I decided to do a little snooping.

———————

From my experience working house calls, I realized that mere distance between people's homes didn't always tell the true story. For example, I met more clients getting gas at the Circle K than at the grocery store or drugstore. Why? Because the Circle K was at the crossroads of two major roads and had a few unbeatable things going for it: cheap gas, lottery tickets, and a small grocery section open for business twenty-four hours a day.

Mari and I usually gassed up before we got back to the animal hospital, and always used Circle K instead of the Chevron, which is closer to the office. Humans are creatures of multiple predictable habits. Was there some place these three people regularly bumped into each other? A coffee joint? Chinese take-out? Or might it be way more complicated than that?

To my surprise, I discovered that both Alicia and José lived with roommates. José shared a house with a fellow physician's assistant, Rob Patterson, who worked at the Wellness Depot in town. Alicia had sold her home and moved in with Nora Etting, who rented out her second master suite for extra cash.

After confirming Alicia's home address, I decided to drive over and see how close her place was to Babs's. When I arrived, I noticed an athletic-looking woman watching her dog run around like a maniac in the front yard. The small black dog with a distinctive white splotch on his back was a patient of mine, I realized. This might be easier than I'd thought.

When I got out of the truck, the dog ran over and yapped a few times.

"Sparky, be quiet," the woman told her pet, who proceeded to ignore her. He took another look at me and approached the fence, not sure if I was friend or foe. The garage door stood open, revealing stacked boxes and a snowmobile. The car, of necessity, stayed parked in the driveway.

"Can I give Sparky a treat?" I asked. The deep pockets of my winter coat held a multitude of treats for all species. As I'd promised Gramps, the pepper spray was safe in my front pants pocket—so there was no chance of mixing them up.

"He'd love that," she said, thoughtfully gazing back at me.

My hair, ears, and forehead were covered by a knit hat so I wasn't sure I'd be recognized. I was wrong.

"You're Dr. Kate? From the animal hospital?" she asked enthusiastically. "We're clients of yours."

"Yes, I remember." By this time Sparky could smell the dog treat in my outstretched hand and started wagging his tail.

"What are you doing here?" she asked.

Since she recognized me, it was time for the truth. "I'm trying to find out if the death of our temporary receptionist, Babs Fields, is connected with your roommate Alicia's death."

Nora pushed a strand of hair behind her ear and said, "Sure thing. Come on in. Tell you what, I'll be happy to answer all your questions if you'll take a look at Sparky's tail."

It sounded like a perfect barter.

As we made our way inside, Nora began a running commentary on how she inherited her place from her parents free and clear. She grew up in this house and made a big mistake by taking out a small mortgage then spending all the equity from the transaction. Which is how she ended up with a roommate.

The older home had been updated to Nora's modern aesthetics. Her parents were probably turning in their graves. She'd painted all the original woodwork white, leaving only the ornate solid mahogany staircase alone. One wall in the living room, I noticed, was Day-Glo yellow, while another appeared to be painted a muddy maroon color. The furniture was modern but cheap, mostly gray.

"Let's go into the kitchen," she said as I followed along. Sparky's nails clicked on the floor. "Want some coffee? French press."

"Sure," I answered, and made a resolution to start cutting back on my caffeine intake after Valentine's Day.

She indicated that I should sit at a round, white lacquered table with four modern bucket-style seats. It reminded me of something out of the classic Jetsons cartoon.

"Alicia's death has put me in a bind," Nora began. "I need to rent out her room, but her sister hasn't arranged for pickup of her things yet. I've started carting the boxes of her stuff into the garage, which means I can't park my car inside."

I listened sympathetically, noting that Nora didn't appear overly sad at the brutal demise of her roommate.

"At least I don't have to get a new kitchen table," she commented as the smell of coffee began to spread across the room. "Her sister said I could keep Alicia's furniture if I would temporarily store all her personal belongings."

Again I nodded. So this very modern-looking table and chairs belonged to Alicia. I took another good look at it, noticing the tulip-like shape and graceful curves. I'd seen something similar not too long ago. But where? It came to me in a burst of clarity. Babs had a table in her house very similar to this one.

Did Babs and Alicia share a fondness for midcentury modern?

Nora chatted away, going on about the French press coffee and how she was addicted to it. My input proved unnecessary to the one-sided conversation. Just below me, Sparky waited, anxiously hoping for food.

"So, did Alicia talk about Babs at all?" I interrupted. "We know that Babs was invited to José and Alicia's wedding in June," I explained.

Nora took a sip of coffee and said, "Oh. They canceled the June ceremony. Alicia and José planned to elope on Valentine's Day. Then off to California."

"What?"

"Oh, the two kept it secret, but she had to tell me because she was going to move out early. Alicia swore me to secrecy. Very romantic, just the two of them and a minister."

"Any idea why they decided to move to California?"

"Her sister is out there, first of all," Nora said, her eyebrows scrunching together. "Maybe 'cause she'd become convinced that someone was following her? Alicia was pretty jumpy lately. Always insisted the curtains stay closed once she got home."

"You don't say."

"Or it might have had something to do with that crazy woman who was harassing her."

The wronged wife, I assumed. Hopefully, there weren't any other crazy women in her life. "Do you mean her husband's ex-wife, Linda?"

"Yeah. That's the one. Real Looney Tunes."

It was obvious there was no sympathy to spare.

"Anyway. Here's the strangest part. I couldn't tell anyone that she moved. She didn't even want to leave a forwarding address at the post office, so instead, she offered to pay me to mail everything to California once she got settled. Real cloak-and-dagger stuff. Plus I was supposed to drive into Kingston or Rhinebeck to mail her stuff. In person. Not dropped in the mailbox."

"That's pretty complicated."

"I didn't mind. She said she'd pay me in cash. Did you know Alicia had to get a restraining order on that bitch? Can you imagine?"

News to me. "Did that upset Alicia? I can't even imagine."

Nora excused herself to refresh her coffee. "Get this. She'd gotten to the point of driving around the parking lot checking for that bitch's car before she'd go into a store—to avoid confrontations. Hiding in booths in restaurants. Alicia confided to me that the decisions about the will were all her husband's idea. Maybe he felt some kind of vendetta against the first wife? The children each had trust funds set up. Why did that ex-wife hate her so much?"

She possessed a very cavalier attitude about the breakup of a family.

"Is that all you remember?" I asked, sipping the last of my coffee.

"Nope." Nora held up a dog treat for Sparky, who immediately came to attention. A calculating look came into her eyes. "Now can you look at Sparky's tail? The fur is falling out."

A bargain was a bargain. "Sure," I said. I bent down to see what she pointed to. A tuft of hair was missing at the end of his tail. "No lesion. No active bite wound. It looks fine. Maybe his tail suffered a mild trauma? Just keep an eye on it." I snapped a picture of it and sent it to my office email. "I'll put this in his file. Keep an eye on him and see if his tail whacks the walls or furniture. Repeated trauma can look like that."

"Great. I thought it might be bedbugs."

Bedbugs didn't ride around on dog tails, but I skipped that lecture. "You said there was something else?"

"Right. Alicia said the wife and mother-in-law both threatened to kill her."

———

José's home was in a modern community that preserved, for the most part, a farmhouse look. Many were rented out by investor-owners. The builder had elected to install black metal roofing, a boon during high snow loads. There were wide sidewalks and a small park with a gazebo. Prices for these homes had been going up and up, Mari told me. I wondered when José and his roommate had moved in. After passing by once again and seeing no one, I continued into town and parked at the Wellness and Rehabilitation Depot. I hoped to speak with Rob, José's roommate and friend, and perhaps find out about this malpractice lawsuit that had been pending when José died.

Wellness Depot oozed an ultramodern sensibility, with rows of pictures of athletic happy people hiking, running, and pushing their bodies to the max. Of course they showed good-looking fitness models exercising in fashionable workout gear. No real people with jiggly stomachs in baggy T-shirts. I felt tired being in the same room as them. Even the colors of their workout clothes coordinated with the waiting room colors. The staff I saw all dressed in black athletic-style pants or yoga gear with Wellness Depot logo scrub tops in sky-blue.

The receptionist sang out a good afternoon and asked, "Can I help you?" Whoever hired the trim blond woman at the desk had kept to the athletic corporate image.

"Hi. I'm Dr. Turner. Does Rob have a moment to speak with me?" I asked.

"I'll see," she answered, giving me a studied look. The name tag on her uniform top read Missy.

I immediately sucked in my stomach, even though it was invisible underneath my coat. Usually, I expected a receptionist to ask what my request was in reference to, but Missy fired off a text message instead, no questions asked.

"Lovely office," I told her.

She smiled with big bleached white teeth. "Thanks. We believe that a clean, bright space helps promote mental and physical wellness."

"Can't hurt," I commented and sat down in an uncomfortable black-and-chrome chair near the exit. Best not to quibble.

"I'll be right back." Before she disappeared, Missy stopped to check her lipstick in a small pocket mirror fished from her purse.

When the receptionist returned almost five minutes later, her expression reminded me of a cat who'd caught a mouse. Her cheeks flushed with pink and her neatly touched-up lipstick was smudged. Maybe a receptionist with benefits?

After another five minutes, I noticed a pair of Nike sneakers in front of me. When I looked up from my phone, I saw that they were attached to a buff guy, about six feet tall, in workout clothes and a white coat. His dirty blond hair spoke of snow skiing—hair bleached by the winter sun. I figured I'd met José's roommate Rob.

"Dr. Turner," he said, offering his hand, "I'm not familiar with your name. Are you here about the job opening?"

Job opening? I wondered who was being replaced.

I stood up, my five-foot-ten almost nose to nose with him. His eyes were an unusual vibrant green color. Tinted contacts? "I think there's been a misunderstanding," I explained.

"I don't need a job. It's about a personal matter involving your former roommate, José."

A bewildered expression was quickly replaced by a more questioning stare. "Let's talk privately in my office," he replied. "But I can only give you about ten minutes before my next appointment."

I spotted a lipstick smudge close to his left ear. "That's fine."

We traveled down a corridor with more pictures of skiing and hiking before I followed him into what I gathered was a consultation room.

"So, did José owe you money? Because I have nothing to do with that," he began as he sat behind the desk. "Best you contact his lawyer."

Vivid green eyes caught mine. No hesitation. No sign of distress. His demeanor made it two for two—neither Alicia's nor José's roommate seemed devastated by their passing.

"Actually, I'm interested in his friendship with a friend of mine who recently passed away. Babs Fields." I watched closely. Her name elicited no reaction.

"Listen," he began, "José and I met when I moved to Oak Falls, and we've been roommates for barely two years. We only had our jobs in common, but we worked in different places and in different specialties. Truthfully, I didn't see much of him this past year because he spent a lot of time over at Alicia's place—plus I've been working crazy long hours."

I signaled my understanding then tried a different tack. "My friend Babs was planning to attend their wedding in June."

"Oh?" He fiddled with a pen, writing something on a scratch pad. He appeared distracted.

"You mentioned they planned to be married this June? Correct?"

I noticed a slight hesitancy in his manner for the first time.

"Well, I suppose I'm no longer held to my promise since they've both passed." Another pause for a pen doodle. "They'd decided to cancel the wedding and simply elope. I thought it was a great idea." He looked down at his drawing. "But all that's moot now, isn't it? I still can't believe what happened."

"No one knows exactly what happened," I said.

Again a look of momentary bewilderment before saying, "José killed her. A murder-suicide. Just terrible. I suppose Alicia threatened to break off the engagement and the dude lost it."

Now it was my turn to be surprised. "Don't you know?"

"Know what?"

Where has this guy been the past forty-eight hours? "Police Chief Garcia declared both their deaths to be suspicious. José didn't kill himself and didn't murder Alicia."

This came as a shock. I saw it in his face, raw like a scab pulled off a wound. "When did all this happen?"

"The chief of police announced it yesterday, I believe. Your friend isn't a killer."

Rob's mouth twitched then broke into a smile. "Thank heavens."

"But, Rob," I said, "that means someone else is."

The brief meeting with Rob provided some clues to José's personality. As soon as I mentioned the police, Rob opened his laptop and searched for the chief's statement, to make sure I wasn't a wacko off the street spreading false rumors. Once confirmed, Rob said he never believed it to be a murder-suicide anyway because the couple seemed madly in love and rarely fought.

"They were great together," he said. "I envied José because he found his true love match."

"Did your roommate have any enemies?" I also wondered when Rob would tire of my questions and kick me out.

"I suppose I can talk about it now, but José was in the middle of a contentious lawsuit pertaining to one of his patients. An older gentleman whose wife died under José's care sued him. That's why I prefer sports medicine to internal medicine," Rob said. "My patients either get better or they get a referral to an orthopedic surgeon."

"So no one dies on your watch from torn ligaments or a sprained ankle. Must be nice."

"Exactly." He glanced at his sports watch and stood up. "It's been great talking to you, but I've got an appointment in a few minutes."

"Thank you for fitting me in." I rose and reached out my hand, but by that time he'd started walking out. "Can I ask you what you were doing the day of the murders?"

Rob stopped dead. "I'll be happy to release that information to the police. Are you accusing me of something?" His annoyance toward me flared instantaneously. "I think it's best that you leave."

We headed down the hallway to find two people in the waiting room. Rob addressed them by name and escorted them back toward the office. Before he disappeared he gave me a dirty look.

The receptionist smiled and asked if I needed to make a follow-up appointment. Her mouth had been redrawn with a peachy toned lipstick.

"What sort of wellness services do you provide?" I asked. She reached into one of her desk drawers and handed me a pamphlet similar to the ones you get from the beauty salon. Along with physical therapy, they offered massage, yoga, reflexology—all designed to enhance the wellness experience for a price.

Curious, I checked out the lists of services, to find none were covered by my health insurance. I figured most people had to pay out of pocket for those goodies.

No wonder the office was empty.

———

When I called Gramps that evening to tell him about the odd vibes I got from José's and Alicia's roommates, he merely uttered a noncommittal sound. "I used to see it all the time in the fire department when we confirmed a death," he said. "You'd expect loved ones to cry and sob, but sometimes they acted as if you told them they had a spot of food on their shirt."

"Why is that?"

I heard another noncommittal sound. "Wish I knew.

Some people aren't emotionally invested in their fellow man or woman."

"But…"

"It's also possible they're in denial, or the true reality hasn't sunk in yet."

That made more sense. "I'd expect that from José's roommate—they barely saw each other—but not Alicia's roommate. I suppose you never know a person or what they're really thinking."

"True. Most of us don't even know ourselves."

When we got off the phone I felt restless, no closer to understanding the victims or why they were targeted. I could see how Alicia and José might have been ambushed up there on the Lover's Lake—but Babs? She was smart, direct, and, as Cindy said, nobody's fool.

I lay down flat on the bed to think. Pushing the pillows to the side, I powered through some yoga stretches, ending in the final pose of most yoga classes—Savasana—or Corpse Pose. I forced my limbs to relax and closed my eyes.

Assuming the front door of the animal hospital had been closed and locked, then Babs must have let the killer in. Was it someone she knew? Going over the little I knew of our temporary receptionist, I didn't see her inviting a stranger into the hospital. With both Mari and me out on a house call, she wouldn't be admitting any patients either. Therefore, she recognized the person at the door. What next?

The answer shone in my face like a flashlight beam. We already figured out she'd do what she always did. Offer them some of her slightly bitter specialty coffee. Being a fastidious person, Babs drank from her own mug, the mug she'd brought from home.

And she'd pour her visitor a cup using one of the hospital's extra mugs.

I bounded out of bed, catching poor Buddy by surprise. He sat up in his doggy bed and whined.

"Go back to sleep," I told him. I'll be right back.

I hoped I wasn't too late.

Chapter Twenty

LIKE AT MANY OFFICES, EACH EMPLOYEE AT OAK FALLS Animal Hospital had their own coffee mug. Over the years, extra mugs had appeared. Joke gifts from clients, leftover mugs from old employees. None were thrown out. Many ended up in limbo on the shelf above the coffee maker.

Cindy used two mugs from home—one for tea and one for coffee. She swore she could taste the remnants of coffee, even if the cup was washed. We didn't dispute her claim.

I started by examining the mugs next to the coffee machine. There were five. Cindy's mugs had floral designs, one with daisies the other with irises. No BEST MOM or joke phrases for her. Mari's personalized mug displayed a posed picture of her two Rottweilers, Lucy and Ricky. My mug, a Christmas gift from Gramps, said, "Take time to smell the roses." This was the third mug I'd used, the first two being casualties on the ceramic tile floor.

The last of the five mugs on the countertop said, "Cats Rule, Dogs Drool," a Christmas gift from a client. It currently held two teaspoons, a pen, a Sharpie, and a few wooden tongue depressors, which we used as stirrers. As far as I remembered, no one used it for any beverage.

Where was Babs's mug?

Something rubbed against my legs. Mr. Katt demanded my attention. His cat eyes stared up at me. When I bent down to pet him he took off, bounding off the countertop and climbing to his favorite spot—six feet high on top of the bank of cages. From that kingly perch, he turned his back and ignored me.

I continued my search, this time on the shelf directly above the coffee maker. Just in case, I slipped on a pair of exam gloves. As I searched for Babs's lemon-yellow mug, the one I'd seen her use for coffee, I found it pushed behind another joke cup. Odd. I slid the cup toward me. Immediately I noticed about a half inch of old coffee in the bottom of the cup. A slight scum hovered on the top layer.

With my gloved hand lightly touching the bottom, I placed it back on the shelf, in the same position I found it.

I'd only worked with Babs for a week, but in that time I never saw her leave any mugs or utensils dirty. She rinsed her cup out right away like Cindy did.

Why would she hide a dirty cup?

———

As soon as Cindy arrived I told her about Babs's coffee mug.

"I'm going to call the chief, although he's probably sick of hearing from us," Cindy said. "Maybe it tasted funny, or she realized she'd been drugged."

Remembering Babs, I figured that was a good possibility.

I'd given this some thought. "I read that Xanax is bitter. Maybe the killer put it in her coffee. That dark roast she drank had a bitter aftertaste."

Cindy frowned. "Do you realize her murderer probably stood right where we are standing? Kate, please put the alarm system on when you're here alone," she said. "And make sure the new outdoor cameras are activated."

Our alarm system was a bit temperamental. None of the inside motion sensors could be used because of Mr. Katt and his gymnastic leaps. Doc Anderson didn't think an alarm necessary in my apartment, so the only safety features hooked up were the motion detector lights above the door leading to the side parking lot and the light over the front entrance. The connecting door to the animal hospital had a deadbolt, but the door itself was flimsy.

I didn't want to think about my personal danger at the moment, but I vowed not to take a cup of coffee from a stranger—or any other beverage. Or food. Or chocolate.

A bit of paranoia went a long way.

———

I met Linda, the wronged wife of Alicia's dead husband quite by accident. Mari and I stopped at the supermarket after our last house call that evening. Mari needed flour for a biscuits recipe, and I was following a resolution to eat healthier. My basket contained asparagus, a quick-cook jasmine rice, and boneless, skinless chicken breasts. It took all my willpower not to add some chips and ice cream.

"Let's get out of here," I told Mari, worried that the longer I stayed near the freezer section the worse my resolve would be.

"Almost ready," she said. "I need more baby wipes and cleaner."

"Puppy mess?"

"Yes. It's been a lot of fun and a big headache both at the same time. The puppy we kept from the litter doesn't like to go in the snow, so it's wee-wee pads and cleanup until spring."

We pushed both carts to the cleaning product aisle, where I picked up dish detergent and a sleeve of plastic scrubbies.

"Hey," Mari whispered, "don't stare, but I believe that's Linda Ramsey and her mother."

I casually turned my head. Standing in front of the spray disinfectants stood a tired-looking woman with two grumpy children. Next to her loomed a large older woman, built like a linebacker with frizzy gray hair, who scolded the kids and threatened them with no candy if they didn't behave.

The ex-wife and her angry mother? Could this be Crystal, the grandmother who, according to her roommate, had been harassing Alicia? We were about the same height, five-ten, but the granny had about eighty pounds on me. She must have felt my eyes on her because she stopped dead, turned, and glared at us.

Her eyes rested on me first, then took in Mari, who was busy putting wipes in her cart.

"Do you think that's enough?" I asked my vet assistant, deliberately turning my back to the family only a few feet away.

"I certainly hope so," she said. "Ready to check out?"

"Ready." I pointed the shopping cart toward the front of the store. Mari's cell phone chimed, and she stopped to reply with her own text. I took the opportunity to glance back over my shoulder.

The linebacker grandmother was still staring at me.

After saying goodbye to Mari, I carried my groceries into the apartment, trying to dodge Buddy, who was celebrating my return by yipping and twirling around. The only vehicle in the parking lot was mine. Cindy always put the alarm on if I was out, but with the way I was feeling, I needed to double-check it myself. Buddy went with me, a bit nervous about being in the same room as his nemesis, Mr. Katt. I'd never uncovered a reason for their ongoing feud, which was more a case of cat against the dog than vice versa.

Cindy had locked up, but I decided to double-check her.

I checked the hospital windows, doors, and even the bathrooms before going back into my place. An app on my phone allowed me to monitor the outdoor cameras, something I normally didn't do. The one over my door kept blinking on and off. Maybe the crows foraging around the dumpster set it off. I'd mention it to Cindy in the morning. Buddy was a good little watchdog and barked when a stranger came near the place, so I wasn't worried someone would creep up on me.

But what if the killer wasn't a stranger?

———————

After a very healthy dinner, I felt restless. The memory of Babs lying still on the surgery table kept intruding in my thoughts. To break that thought pattern, I decided to work on the computer and focused on a search of Linda Ramsey and her mom, Crystal. Place number one to look? Facebook.

Their profiles and picture walls were vastly different. It appeared that Linda posted infrequently, usually pictures of her kids doing cute things. Her mother, on the other hand, used social media in a completely different way.

Cindy was a mutual acquaintance of both women, which didn't surprise me. I called her up and asked if she'd mind me going on her page to do some snooping.

"Go ahead," she said. "I've been too busy to do much of anything. No posting as me, though."

"I promise." There had been a time in college when I'd been on Facebook a lot, but now I mostly used it as a forum to catch up with what my friends were doing.

"Let's rock and roll," I told Buddy, who was snuggled next to my feet. I didn't even get a wuff of approval back. Maybe he'd been talking to Gramps.

Facebook is an odd conglomeration of cat and dog photos, fun updates on what your friends and their families are doing, and rants, both personal and political. I am always amazed at what people will reveal to their Facebook friends, many of whom are essentially strangers. Revealing my thoughts in public didn't appeal to me since my personality tends toward the private and guarded, which I wouldn't necessarily recommend to anyone.

Like most of us, Cindy had a public page and a private page. Scrolling through the postings would be daunting and probably useless. Instead, I did a search for Linda and Crystal. I wondered how candid they'd be on social media about Alicia, the object of their mutual hatred.

Reading through their conversations, I noticed two

things. One was that Linda, the ex-wife, seemed exhausted, often depressed, and quick to ask her friends for help. She took joy in her children and their accomplishments. I found no mention of any boyfriends or date nights, no pictures of desserts at restaurants. No fun recipes. Maybe she'd learned to keep her private life private.

Her mom, Crystal, on the other hand, shot from the hip and didn't bother to censor herself in any way. She'd been in Facebook jail numerous times, she joked, and expected to wind up there again in the near future.

Not only did she berate Alicia for going after a married man and breaking up a "perfect" marriage, but she also posted pictures of Alicia's workplace, her work schedule, her home, and even a link to her Facebook page. She bragged that she may even have initiated a few "dirty tricks" to make her life miserable.

Buried in all the postings, I found something important. Crystal, the ex-mother-in-law, was a nurse, part of a surgical team. Someone who worked in a surgical suite every day.

The most revealing item turned out to be a post titled "Ten Ways to Get Even," which redirected the user to multiple websites. I had no idea these sites existed. Dedicated to making someone's life difficult, it included mild pranks— putting wet ink on the inside door handle of a car—to downright dangerous suggestions. It took a specific kind of personality to entertain trying even one of those things.

Someone with few boundaries.

Someone who might have no problem killing?

Reading all of the spewed hatred postings on page after

page of these revenge websites depressed me. I'd been through my share of difficult relationships, but I'd found the best thing is to cut your losses and move on. Obsessing about being wronged didn't help move your life forward. I closed down my computer and absently stared at the wall in front of me. Buddy stretched himself, groaned, and went back to sleep.

I thought about Alicia and José, madly in love, planning to leave Oak Falls and all the drama surrounding their lives behind. Did someone hate the couple so much that they murdered them both? Was Alicia the primary target? Or was the motive something different altogether?

And what about Babs, a smart resilient woman who curated her orderly life, devoid of a family but full of friends? Why did she have to die?

There was only one reason I could think of. She knew something about Alicia's and José's murder. With her strong sense of right and wrong, she wouldn't keep quiet. She'd tell the cops.

A thump on my door broke my concentration. Buddy raised his head, not barking, but interested. I peeked out into the parking lot. Empty, except for the hospital truck. Odd. By now Buddy was up and asking to go out. I slipped on my coat, checking to see if I had my pepper spray with me, and opened the door.

Lying on the step was a crow.

At first glance the crow looked dead, but as soon as I picked it up, glittering black eyes opened. The bird must have misjudged his flight or was escaping a predator when he flew into my door. I wrapped him in my coat and brought him inside. If he didn't recover quickly, I'd need to bring him to a wildlife rehabilitator.

Birds become stunned when they fly into things. The best treatment for now was for the crow to rest in a dark quiet space, as you'd do for a person with a concussion. A small cardboard Amazon box proved the right size. I lined it with paper, poked air holes in it, and placed the bird inside. My last glimpse showed it struggling to right itself, a good sign.

I wondered what had drawn it to my door? We did have all new outdoor cameras, thanks to Cindy, which looked bright and shiny instead of pitted and rusty. Crows are curious. Perhaps that was its focus, although I'd been taught in vet school that it was usually captive crows that craved metallic objects.

Then I had a thought. The Dr. Mike I'd met mentioned he'd worked for an exotic animal practice. Maybe he'd have some suggestions? Finally, I had a good excuse to contact him.

Especially since he didn't have a wife or twins to take care of.

Although I genuinely wanted his advice on the injured crow, I also found Mike easy to talk to. Surrounded by Valentine's Day stuff every day in the hospital, I was acutely aware of the holiday coming up.

I texted him before I could overthink this. I'd put him in the friend zone from the day I'd met him, thinking he was taken. Could I adjust my thinking now?

At least twenty minutes went by without a response. *Oh, well*, I thought and researched some additional information on crows on an ornithology website.

Crows were very social, able to recognize people, and particularly smart birds. Here in upstate New York, many flocks migrated, while others stayed put. They'd survive the winter by foraging wherever they could. The month of March, the article said, was their normal time to nest and mate. A baby crow often hung around till the following year to help raise the next year's brood.

My cell phone rang as I started reading about crows mating for life.

"Hello?" I already knew who it was from my caller ID.

"So how did you end up with a crow?" Mike asked.

"Short story. I heard a thump, opened my door, and saw him lying on my front step." Mike's straightforward question and caring voice was a relief to hear. Why had I been so nervous about contacting him?

He chuckled and said, "That is a short story. Want me to come over and take a look at him or her?"

A big grin he couldn't see signaled a yes. "That would be perfect. As you know I live in the luxuriously converted garage attached to the hospital."

"What a coincidence? I also live in a luxuriously converted garage rental. I gather that many locals convert garages into rental units for extra income up here."

"Really?"

"Sadly, yes. I keep telling myself it's temporary. See you soon."

After our call ended I took a look around. A quick cleaning and laundry systemization was definitely in order. Stat.

Mike looked exactly as I remembered. A little rumpled, although he had obviously put on a brand new shirt for our meeting. The crease marks from being folded up were distinctly present in the button-down blue shirt that complemented his eyes. A sizing tag, M, stuck to the sleeve.

When I peeled it off for him, he said, "Oops. All my shirts were in the dirty clothes hamper."

Buddy greeted him with a cautious bark and then a wag of the tail. Mike bent down to pet him and asked, "King Charles spaniel?"

I nodded. "Rescued."

"Heart issues?"

"Not yet."

We'd quickly fallen into a sort of shorthand veterinary speak. It proved a far cry from my usual dates, who asked dozens of questions about treating animals, then wanted you to check out their pet for free. I wondered if proctologists fielded the same problem?

"Where is he?"

"I've got him in a cardboard box for now. I'd feel more comfortable opening it up in one of our cages, so he doesn't escape." I had visions of us trying to catch a flying bird in my apartment, dodging bird poop—or worse—seeing a crow flying around in the hospital with Mr. Katt lunging, mouth open hoping to score big.

Mike obviously agreed. "Just a second." He went over to his coat and dug around in the pockets. "I've brought some peanuts, dry kitten kibble, and a few mealy worms, just in case he's hungry." He smiled and held up a plastic ziplock bag.

"Okay. See, I knew this box would come in handy." I'd placed the cardboard box on top of the sideboard table, wedged behind some canned goods, in case the crow started trying to break out.

"I always keep a couple of sizes of cardboard boxes around, in case I have to rescue a critter," he confessed. "Got some stashed in my car, too."

I was beginning to like Mike more and more.

Once we were inside the animal hospital, I placed the cardboard box in an upper cage.

"Let me get Mr. Katt out of here," I said, searching for our hospital cat.

A quick flash of fur over by the computer station signaled that our cat had found us. Unbidden, he leaped onto Mike's shoulder and gave him a head butt.

"Mr. Katt, I presume?" Mike rubbed under Mr. Katt's chin just the way he liked it.

"Come on, big guy," I said and carefully removed him. His long back nails tended to get stuck. "I'm going to put him in my office and bribe him with some wet food." I figured the crow would appreciate not having a big fluffy cat staring at him.

With our hospital kitty safely stowed away, Mike walked me through how to approach our wild visitor. It involved hanging two sheets in front of the cage, poking his head through, and carefully opening the box. I served as the backup catcher, armed with a towel in case of escape. All our fears were for naught. Although the crow appeared to have recovered from the head blow, he couldn't be released yet.

"Let's feed him, give him a water source, and cover the cage overnight. He's got no obvious leg or wing damage, although it looks like he injured one of his wings in the past. See the uneven feathers? My guess is he'll be good to be released in the morning when he can orient himself."

"Thanks so much for your help," I told him. "Want a quick hospital tour? Last time you had to hightail it out of here."

He smiled again. "Sure. Let me wash my hands first."

We started at the front of the hospital with the reception area and our in-house pharmacy. He asked some questions about what drugs we stocked and the length of our appointments. As we continued to stroll around. I noted his strong profile, with a firm chin and slightly bent nose, as though it had been broken. His hands were working hands, short nails, a healing scratch on his wrist. I assumed he'd been doing a similar inventory of me.

I suddenly became acutely aware of all the hearts and Valentine's Day stuff decorating the front office.

"This is a nice card." Mike had stopped to read one of our thank-you cards from a grateful client. "Very complimentary."

My face flushed a bit. "You've got to excuse the decorations," I said. "Cindy loves to celebrate all the holidays."

"Our staff celebrates every holiday too but goes all out for Halloween," he told me. "Everyone dresses in costumes. We even have twinkling orange lights with skeletons outside. Last year they made me wear a bloodhound mask."

"I'd like to have seen that," I laughed.

When we got back to the treatment room, I stopped in front of the surgery doors. He'd been inside already, when he performed the hernia repair on Porky the piglet. Did I want to revisit where Babs died? He must have noticed my hesitation.

"We can skip the rest," Mike said. "Let's go back to your place, and I'll give you some tips on our crow friend."

Very grateful our tour was cut short, I opened the connecting door, and Buddy immediately began his doggy dance.

"Want some coffee? Tea?" I asked him, not sure what snacks I had on hand. I'd been so careful about only putting healthy items in my cart I forgot to buy things to stick in the pantry. After pushing some big cans of tomatoes aside, I discovered a package of biscotti a friend had brought as a gift. Even better, they were individually wrapped.

"I'll take some tea," he said. "I'm trying to cut down on my coffee intake when I'm not working."

"Tell me about it," I said, placing a handful of the biscotti in a bowl before putting the kettle on.

He sat down at the kitchen table. Buddy, of course, sat next to him, eager for extra food. "I think you're out of luck, Buddy," he told the dog.

Once the water boiled I loaded the teapot and put it out with two cups. "Earl Grey okay?"

"Great." He glanced down at his phone after a text message pinged. "Sorry. One of our techs is worried about her horse."

"No problem." I joined him at the table and waited for the tea to brew.

After entering in a long text, he sighed and put his phone on the table. "She's got a sweet Appaloosa who's recuperating from a hoof injury and she's double-checking something. Tea ready?"

I poured some into my cup. The color looked perfect.

As we ate our biscotti and drank our tea, we swapped stories of vet school and discovered we had some mutual friends.

"Of course, I haven't seen most of them since graduation," he explained. "Too busy working and paying down my student debt."

"Same here. Not having to pay any rent here is a godsend. I do think I'll stick with a small-animal practice after all, though a mixed-animal job is a temptation."

He shifted his weight, making Buddy double up on his begging stare. "I'm still torn between academics and working at a mixed practice. I suppose I don't have to exclude one or the other at this point."

We chatted for a bit. He asked when Doc Anderson was coming back and what I was going to do.

After another long sip, I answered, "I'm not quite sure. Ask me in a few more months."

"Oh, there's another odd thing we have in common."

"What's that?"

"The couple that died, Alicia and José. They were my clients."

Of course, I wanted to hear every detail. It seems that José owned an older ferret named Hobo that developed lymphoma, a type of cancer. Unlike many pocket pet owners,

José elected to treat it, so he and Alicia would come into the hospital every week for injectable chemotherapy.

"This was at least six or eight months ago. Hobo did well for a while, but eventually went out of remission. I got to know them over that period of time fairly well."

"What was your impression?"

"I liked them. José worked as a physician's assistant, so he understood the chemotherapy protocol. He asked me about malpractice in vet medicine since he'd been agonizing over a lawsuit. I think they both wanted to relocate and get a fresh start."

"That's what I heard, too."

"They did tell me that they might elope. Get married outdoors just the two of them and a minister. Someone they knew had a license from an Internet church to perform weddings. It's sad to think their lives were cut short."

The whole situation was sad. Babs, José, and Alicia didn't deserve to die, and so far their killer or killers were getting away with murder.

"You know," I told him, "this is the second time you've helped me out. When can I return the favor and wrangle those barn cats for you?"

"Any weekend is good, preferably in the morning. The older couple whose barn cats need their vaccinations found bats in one of their outbuildings. Updating all the kitty's rabies shots is essential. Most of them, I might be able to do by myself, but you never know."

"Got it. I'll check my schedule with Cindy and get back to you."

"Looking forward to it." He chugged down the last of his tea, got up, and put the cup and saucer over by the sink. "Sorry, I've got to run. I told my tech I'd swing by and check out her horse."

"Alright. See you soon?" I realized how similar our lives were. Too similar perhaps?

When I opened the outside door, Buddy immediately ran to his outdoor run, intent on doing his business. Nearby, angry crows started cawing, one flying down and dive-bombing us.

"That's probably our crow's bird family," Mike said, staring up into the trees. "They're angry with you."

Images of Crystal glowering at me and Rob shooting me a dirty look made me think—*sorry, crows. You'll have to get in line.*

Chapter Twenty-One

THE NEXT MORNING BEFORE WORK, I LIFTED THE TOWEL from the front of the crow's cage after again securing Mr. Katt in my office. The crow had popped the top off the cardboard box and was standing upright, his eyes on mine. I noticed birdseed scattered around. He'd eaten most of the sunflower seeds, all the mealy worms, and all the shelled peanuts.

The bird tried to flap his wings. I quickly covered the cage back up and thought about the best way to get him outside. A combination of a metal strainer to keep me safe from his beak and another larger box did the trick.

Moving quickly with my now-agitated, wild friend, I glided through my apartment and out the side door, slamming it before Buddy could sneak out. Hoping for the best, I placed the box on my doorstep, turned it on its side, and opened it.

The bird stuck his head out, assessing his situation and getting his bearings. In no time he hopped out, looked around—then spread his midnight black wings and flew up into the nearby trees. A chorus of cawing ensued.

I still had a bit of the seed mixture left in my pocket that I'd intended on feeding him. Since he was recuperating, I didn't want to throw it in the snow. I bent down and pulled up the rubberized mat I usually wiped my wet boots on.

Walking over to the truck, I cleaned off the hood, placed the rubber mat on the level part, and then sprinkled the bird food mix on it. At least for the time being, the crow might be able to easily enjoy some food without digging in the garbage or foraging in the snow.

When I returned to my apartment, a confused Buddy greeted me with a woof. "Sorry, guy," I told my dog. "We'll go out in a minute. I promise."

From behind the living room curtain, I snuck a peek out my window into the parking lot and watched first one crow, then another, then another fly out of one of the pines and land on the truck hood. Within no time the three birds had finished up most of the food.

One of them was my patient. I could tell by the uneven wing feathers on one side. To avoid another flying accident, I planned to spray the shiny metal of the outdoor camera over my door with a matte finish paint, leaving the lens clean and functional.

It felt good to be able to help such a beautiful wild creature return to his natural life with his crow family.

I envied them.

———————

"You're not going to believe what they named this little dog." Mari was waiting in the treatment area for me as I prepared to meet my last patient of the day.

I'd fished out my lip balm and paused for a drink of water. "Don't make me guess."

"Their dog is having some behavioral issues they want to discuss with you. I'll meet you in exam room number 2."

"Come on. You're not going to tell me?" I begged to her disappearing back.

All I saw was the back of her head, shaking no, strolling down the hallway. Her curls bounced with each step.

People named their animals the strangest things. Besides the usual pet names, like Brownie or Mittens, we'd examined many named after famous people. Keanu, Clint Eastwood, Marilyn Monroe, and Cher had all been clients of mine. Types of liquor are favored, like Whiskey or Baileys, along with cities or towns or even countries. Movie and book characters remain popular as are the made-up names and descriptives, such as Pudgy, Fatso, Stinker, and Fluffy.

From Mari's reaction, the name my next clients picked for their pet must be a doozy.

After a short knock I opened the door to find a mixed-breed white dog on the exam table, with two outwardly normal owners. Mari approached and handed me the medical record with her mouth contorted into a grimace to stop from bursting into a grin or a laugh.

I glanced at the dog's name. Yep, it was a good one.

"So how is Booty Call doing today?" I asked with a perfectly straight face. I heard a concealed snicker escape from my tech.

"Booty boy is having some issues," his dog mom explained.

I placed my hand on the dog and started my exam. He immediately latched onto my arm and started humping away, a determined expression in his eyes.

"Stop that," the owners said in unison. Predictably, their saying "stop" didn't stop anything.

"He's driving Polly and me nuts. We have to lock him up before guests come. It's so embarrassing."

Mari came over and held the small dog while I extricated my arm. I was going to make a joke and say I guess this means we're engaged, but the wife looked too forlorn for humor. My first step would be a urine sample, which I asked Mari to try and collect.

"See if Cindy can help," I added as she walked the little white dog out of the exam room.

"Now, there's no need to be embarrassed," I began. "How old was Booty when he was neutered and did he hump things before his surgery?" This kind of behavior could have its origins in so many things, including medical problems. A good history was essential. The urine sample would be our first diagnostic step.

The husband and wife looked at each other. "We got him at a dog rescue event, already neutered," she stated.

"Okay. When did you first notice the behavior?"

Again the couple shared a look. "Maybe after the first week? We gave him several stuffed toys to play with, but he picked a teddy bear and..."

"Went to town on it?"

"You got it, Doc."

So far. So good. "What was your reaction?"

The wife stared at her shoes and the husband stared at the wife. "I'm afraid we thought it was funny. Sort of cute and funny."

"So you probably laughed and smiled at him."

The husband answered this time. "Wrong reaction?"

"Not the best choice. The dog took that as your approval of his behavior." I entered some notes into the computer.

"If that's all he ever did, it wouldn't be so bad," the wife commented. "But he goes after our guests and even children. Our niece is three, and she's afraid of him. He followed her down the hall, latched onto her leg, and pushed her onto the floor."

"How did you handle that?"

"Jason picked him up and locked him in the spare bedroom with his toys."

"Did you scold him?" I asked the husband.

"Sure," he said. "But he didn't mean to hurt her, so I didn't come down on him too hard."

His wife frowned and said, "What does that mean?"

"Uhhh. I gave him a few biscuits."

"You gave him treats after he scared my sister's only child so bad she was crying?" Her voice started going up as the sentence progressed until at the end it had morphed into a shriek.

It looked like I might have to step in and referee these two.

"A few biscuits at this point doesn't really matter," I explained. "If his behavior isn't caused by a medical issue, such as a urinary tract infection, then you might benefit from help with an animal behaviorist."

"A shrink for a dog? You've got to be kidding." The husband rubbed his forehead in amazement. "What's next? Prozac for puppies?"

His wife looked like she had chosen her side and come out fighting.

"I wouldn't mind," the wife admitted, frowning at her husband.

"That might be one option. First let me go check on that urine sample," I said making haste for the door. "I'll have Cindy stop in with literature on breaking bad dog habits. Believe it or not, there are plenty of worse things a dog can do." With those comforting words, I got out of there. The couple resumed their argument before I'd closed the door.

When I entered the treatment room, I heard the spinning of the autoclave, which meant we had a urine sample.

"Nice one, Mari," I told my technician.

"I thought you'd get a kick out of it," she answered.

"Did you get a chance to set up a slide for me?" I asked.

"I did."

"Where did you put Mr. Humpty Dumpty?" I said, almost ashamed of my lame joke but not enough to take it back.

Mari giggled and answered, "He's cooling his heels in an upper cage. I thought he was going to ask Mr. Katt out on a date."

"Let's stop, shall we?" I slid one of the chairs over and positioned it in front of the microscope. "Did you set up a full urine sample for the lab?"

"Ready to go."

"Can you add a culture and sensitivity to that? Also, I'd like to run a full blood panel on this little guy. Let's make sure his kidneys are okay." I turned my attention back to the sample of urine waiting under the microscope. It was packed with crystals.

Except for his behavior issues, Booty Call was a friendly

happy little dog who managed to hold still long enough for me to draw his blood tests.

"How clean is this urine sample?" I asked Mari.

"As clean as I could get, given the circumstances. There's no more up there though."

"Okay. This will have to do for now. We can get a sterile sample by urinary catheter on recheck."

There was a lot to explain to this dog's parents, and I hoped they'd listen instead of fight about it. Maybe the urinary tract infection and crystals precipitated his behavioral problem or vice versa. A burning sensation on urinating could be part of it. At this point, it didn't matter. We had to treat all the symptoms at the same time.

As I moved him down to the ground, he grabbed onto my leg so tight I felt his nails dig in. Booty continued doing his thing until Mari peeled him off me.

"Don't say it," I warned her to no avail.

"Happy almost Valentine's Day," she said with a laugh.

"Same to you," I retorted as Booty locked onto her shoe.

Preliminary tests indicated that the fluffy white dog's kidney and liver functions were normal. For now I felt comfortable sending him home with a special urinary tract diet while we waited for more laboratory results.

Even in reception they continued their fight.

Cindy texted us: I'm guessing no booty call for that husband tonight.

Booty Call and his owners were our last clients. When they finally left the animal hospital, Cindy locked the front door, pulled down the blinds, and turned off the lights. She'd already tidied up and was ready to leave.

"Sorry, I've got to run," she said. "Parent-teacher conferences at the high school, and I don't want to be late."

"Good luck," Mari said.

"I've got a teenage boy. I'm going to need it," she answered before walking out the door.

Mari and I cleaned the exam rooms and straightened up the treatment room. "I'll take care of the microscope and centrifuge if you put the samples out."

"Deal," she said. Because of the freezing temperatures outside, we couldn't put lab samples out early. Mari always texted our driver to see what time he was picking up.

"We've got fifteen minutes," she said. "I'll set the timer."

"Fine. I've got a few callbacks. You okay?"

"Sure. I'll poke my head into your office before I leave."

"Mari. Have you noticed a pattern in the problems of some of our dog patients lately?"

She scratched her head. "No."

Maybe I'd taken to heart Daffy's list of the eight types of love. "We've had a dog with fake testicles, one named Cupid, and now Booty Call. Doesn't that seem strange?"

"Nothing seems strange anymore," she concluded. "Not even that guy kissing his pig."

I always helped Mari at night, even though I didn't have to. She worked hard all day, just like I did, and this way she could get home a little earlier. Before going to vet school and even while I was in training, I worked as a veterinary technician. Cleaning was only one small part of the hard work technicians did. Being a doctor didn't stop me from helping straighten up and making things easier for us all.

Cindy had left a list of callbacks for me to make on my desk. I also needed to check the incoming lab reports, update the results in the client records, and discuss a treatment plan based on what the lab tests said. My job didn't end once the last client left the building.

No wonder I felt so tired at the end of the day.

Mari left while I was still in front of the computer. Then Mr. Katt decided to join me in my office and sit on my lap, trapping me in my seat. Anyone who lives with a feline knows how psychologically difficult it is to disturb a sleeping cat, so I resigned myself to being a kitty accessory for a while.

The news sites were so depressing that I found myself scrolling through the celebrity news instead. I took a break from rational thought to peruse those rich and richer individuals and their lives. A text message from Cindy saved me from ordering a very expensive moisturizer used by a gorgeous actress guaranteed to make my skin appear dewy.

FORENSIC LAB FOUND XANAX IN BABS COFFEE MUG.

LOTS OF IT.

I closed the celebrity page and looked up Xanax and how quickly it was absorbed into the body. An antianxiety medication, it worked rather quickly, with most people falling into a relaxed or sleepy state within thirty to forty-five minutes, or sooner.

Leaning back in my office chair, I closed my eyes and thought back to the day Babs died. Mari and I were out of the office all afternoon, doing house calls. We usually left around twelve thirty. Mari typically loaded all our medical notes into the office laptop we brought with us, which then updated into our main computer. I reviewed and added my notes once we were back in the office. Only at the end of the day did Mari usually contact the office manager with our return time and to see if any cases needed a follow-up phone call.

Our regular routine had been disrupted by Cindy going on vacation. That Friday, if I remembered correctly, Mari only became worried after she couldn't find the address Babs sent us to. That gave the killer at least a four- to five-hour window when only Babs would be in the building.

Friday had been split between hospital appointments in the morning and house calls and/or emergencies in the afternoon, a fairly common end to the week. Cindy usually kept the *Open* sign on the front door of the hospital while we were gone, but the door locked. Our clients were welcome to call the office for refills of medications, to schedule a recheck, or just schmooze.

Did Babs do the same thing?

I texted Cindy and asked her. Her reply was not what I wanted to hear.

Left it up to her.

Back to square one. When I bent forward to reach for my

water bottle Mr. Katt stretched, opened his eyes briefly, and gifted me with a loud purr.

Trapped for a while with a purring cat on my lap, I closed my eyes again and thought through a possible scenario.

Babs looks up from her desk, surprised to see the visitor at the front door. A friend or close acquaintance—someone she felt comfortable letting into the building. Did she unlock the front door, turn the sign to *Closed* and escort him or her back to the employee lounge? Was she fearful at that point? I didn't think so. That must have come later.

Whoever this visitor was, they most likely came ready to kill her, bringing the human anesthesia mask and Xanax with them.

What about the ketamine? Because it's a controlled substance, our injectable ketamine was always locked up. Like all modern drugs, it carried the possibility of abuse, in this case being well known as Special K. It induced a dissociative state. When combined with an opiate, it can cause a fatal overdose.

According to a manufacturer, ketamine was now available in a nasal spray and in lozenges, both of which needed a doctor's prescription. Cindy performed a drug inventory when she got back and found all our controlled drugs accounted for. How did the murderer have access to it?

Once again I shut my eyes and thought about Babs inviting her killer to have some coffee with her. Babs unapologetically brewed a very strong coffee. Even I occasionally added milk to cut some of the bitterness. At home, she explained, she only drank espresso.

It was likely her killer knew that, too. Distracting Babs for a moment he or she slid the powdered Xanax in her coffee, stirring it with one of our stirrers or a spoon.

Babs must have figured something was wrong as soon as the drug began to kick in. Before it knocked her out, she'd experience a wave of tiredness or dizziness. I admired her quick thinking and leaving her coffee cup for us as evidence. Did she offer to wash out the killer's cup along with hers, before surreptitiously storing it in the cabinet unwashed?

I'd forgotten something important. We'd all forgotten.

What cup did the murderer use?

I catapulted out of my chair. Poor Mr. Katt shot me an evil glare from the floor, hissing his anger. Rushing into the treatment room, I tried to remember how many mugs in total we had. No dice. In desperation, I called Mari.

"Can you remember how many coffee mugs we have?" I asked as soon as she answered the phone.

"Hello to you, too. I take it this is important." The tone in her voice sounded doubtful.

"I think Babs's murderer used one of our cups."

Barking noises began to dominate our conversation. "Wait a minute," she said, and then I heard footsteps and a door slamming. "Someone took someone else's toy," she explained.

"Did you rehome all the puppies?" I knew every one of her puppies had homes, many with Mari's relatives.

"The last one left with my cousin a few days ago. I'm glad we're keeping one. I have to say I got emotional."

Mari assisted with their birthing and had been there every day of their lives. It was always sad to say goodbye to babies, even if you knew it was coming.

"Okay. Sorry for the interruption," she said. "You asked how many mugs we have? Is this a trick question?"

"Well, it's more like how many mugs do we really use. Including coffee for visitors. It's important."

"Can you send me a picture?" she asked. "It's easier to visualize."

"Sure." I placed a glove on my hand and carefully lined up all the mugs side by side on the countertop. The police already had Babs's coffee mug, and I easily recognized mine, Mari's, and Cindy's.

"There's one that's badly chipped. The one with the horse. I'm not sure why we keep it, but you can eliminate that."

"You sure?"

"Babs told me no one should be forced to drink from it."

"Okay. One down. Next?"

The remaining assorted mugs were left by various former employees or had been gifts from clients.

"I think we can also get rid of the Santa Claus as a golden retriever mug and the GREATEST MOM cup. Not her style."

"Agreed."

"That leaves the solid blue cup and the raining cats and dogs one." There was a silence before Mari started debating out loud. "The raining mug is whimsical, very appropriate for an animal hospital. The blue mug is sturdy, the shape of the mugs you used to get in old diners. Kate, which do you think Babs might offer a visitor?"

"The blue one?" The plain no-nonsense cup seemed the obvious choice.

"I agree." Mari waited for me to say something else, but I was lost in thought. Had anyone used that mug since Babs was murdered?

As if reading my mind, Mari said, "I don't think anyone has used either of those cups. Certainly not Cindy or me. What about you?"

A memory of someone else drinking coffee in the treatment area circled in my consciousness. "Nope. I can't think of anyone specific. Okay, I'm going to hang up and call the chief." I didn't want to disturb Cindy again and felt I needed to speak to the chief directly this time.

I decided not to bag the mugs in question but instead waited for the police to arrive. The more I thought about it, the more I convinced myself we were on the right track.

It took Police Chief Bobby Garcia an hour to get to the animal hospital. I gave up waiting in the treatment area and went back to my place. Buddy and I were enjoying a snack when he knocked on the door. My dog sprang up and started barking ferociously at the stranger in the parking lot.

After a quick look I let him in.

Our chief of police always had dark circles under his eyes, but they'd gotten more pronounced since I'd last seen him— that Florida vacation tan a faded memory. Trying to solve three murders had taken its toll.

"Dr. Kate," he said as he knocked some snow off his boots.

"Chief Garcia," I answered, handing him a towel. Without a mudroom to keep mud and snow confined, I had to rely on two doormats and several towels to keep things clean.

The chief and I often ended up sparring with each other, but today felt different. Not only was the chief tired, but he also seemed…preoccupied.

"Good idea about the coffee mugs," he told me as he followed me into the hospital, with Buddy trailing along. "We should have thought of it."

I kept my remarks to myself. Everyone I knew connected with these crimes was under pressure from their friends, relatives, and the general public to solve them. He didn't need any added criticism from me.

"Is that it?" he asked, seeing the blue mug sitting on the countertop.

"It's either that one or the one that says 'Raining cats and dogs'. Mari and I eliminated all the others."

He didn't bother to ask how. Instead, he sat on one of the office chairs and asked, "How is Mari doing? I'm worried about her."

"She seems better. A bit thrown by everything, but so are all of us. We're trying to carry on as best we can. Work helps. But it's still tough walking into the surgery suite."

"I can imagine." He sat slumped over and rubbed his face with his hands. "I just came from a domestic abuse call. Had to turn three kids over to Child Protective Services. The kids were begging us to please let them stay with their mom, who was on her way to the hospital. Dad is in custody for assault. Couldn't reach any relatives."

As I listened I realized I'd forgotten what police have to deal with on a daily basis.

"Do you ever get the feeling the bad guys are winning?"

the chief asked. "Never mind, don't answer that." He got up and walked over to the mugs. "So, just these two?"

I watched him bring out two separate evidence bags, glove up, and then take them into his custody for forensic testing.

"I'd check the cup handle and rim specifically. I think Babs tried to save what evidence she could," I said.

As soon as he turned toward me, I regretted telling him what to do. I expected a sarcastic retort, but instead he laughed. "Anything else?"

"Take care of yourself," I answered. "You look tired."

"I am tired, but that comes with the job. When the shit hits the fan this many times, the whole office feels it. Add these crimes to our usual caseload, and you can see where these bags under my eyes come from."

"Can't you ask for help?" Like most local police departments, the Oak Falls Police Department hated calling in the Feds.

"It might come to that," he admitted. "We've got some irons in the fire."

He left it up to me to interpret what that meant.

After the chief left, I pondered my choices: Sit back and let the overworked police force do their job, or do a little snooping on the side?

Buddy came and put his chin on my knee in sympathy. "Need to go out?"

The word "out" was celebrated by my dog like it was his birthday. He twirled and danced and yipped as I slid on my coat to face the winter weather. First, I made sure there were no more birds on my doorstep, then opened the door wide for Buddy to rush out. He made straight for his exercise area, probably hoping the squirrels had stopped their hibernating and were ready to play.

Instead of squirrels, we did have a visitor who stayed far away from Buddy—a single crow flew out of the trees and landed on the truck hood.

The feather sticking out on one wing identified him as my patient from the other night. He cawed at me then stared as if expecting me to caw back. Food, I guessed, was both the question and the answer.

"Just a minute," I told him and dashed inside. I made a mix of dried cat food, birdseed, and peanuts. No mealy worms today. If he kept showing up, I'd have to be a bit more prepared.

I placed the used mat on the truck hood again. There was no snow for me to push off, but I expected the crow to fly away. He didn't. Instead, he intently stared at the ziplock bag in my hand.

"Want a snack?" I asked. I wouldn't have been surprised if he'd answered, "Yes, please."

Buddy was busy with a toy he'd abandoned and found, so I poured out the bird dinner and stood back. The crow cawed and scratched at the mat with his pointed beak. From one of the trees near the dumpster I heard a noise, as first one then another crow flew down, landing as far away from me as they could get and still eat.

"I suppose I'll be feeding you three until springtime," I said. "You still have to forage for yourselves, though. This is a bonus snack."

The crows looked up and then went back to work on what was left. Their feathers shone a blue-black, their ebony beaks as shiny as their eyes. The Internet was full of firsthand reports of how clever these birds were. I knew they could imitate sounds and other birds, but I didn't want this crew getting too used to humans.

"Come on, Buddy," I called to my dog. "Let's leave these fellows to eat in peace."

Once inside, I fed Buddy his biscuit, cleaned his feet, and poured myself a glass of white wine. Did I want to get on the computer and spend the night investigating the three murders? No.

Or think about the chief's comment about the bad guys winning? No again.

What I'd have liked to do is relax and daydream about flying unencumbered high into the sky, catching a contrail with the tips of my black wings, and gliding over the earth below.

Chapter Twenty-Two

MARI AND I WERE BETWEEN APPOINTMENTS WHEN MY phone's text message alert chimed.

> How did our crow friend do? Text me back when you can. About to go into surgery

I'd been thinking about texting Mike but had gotten sidetracked by a difficult case that came in, a radiologist needed to call me back on a consult, and seeing a ton of appointments.

"Anything I have to know?" Mari asked, assuming it was Cindy texting.

"It's Mike. Checking on the crow I found." There were no secrets between Mari and me. She nudged me out of my comfort zone to share events going on in my life.

"That's Mike, as in Dr. Mike who isn't married with twins?"

This had become a sort of running joke between us, Mari not letting me forget my first wrong impression of the large-animal vet. "Yes. No Twins Dr. Mike."

She laughed and promised not to refer to him in that way again. "You two should go out. On a date."

The thought had crossed my mind.

"Don't you owe him a barn cat house call?"

"Yes."

She took her computer tablet out and just before opening the exam room door said, "I'd get on that if I were you."

Good advice.

The day passed in a blur. With the increase in pet adoptions nationwide due to COVID-19, veterinary offices across the country were swamped with calls for appointments. Staffing shortages meant there were only a finite number of clients we could see. Diagnosing and treating a patient properly took time, which you didn't have if there was a new appointment every ten minutes.

I met Mike after work, and we commiserated on the subject. We were eating at Lucky Gardens, an Asian fusion restaurant at the far edge of town. There were no Valentine's Day decorations here, just a white porcelain Happy Cat statue next to the stack of menus, waving hello and wishing us good fortune. Our table looked out over a fast-moving stream, which ran into the Esopus Creek, eventually finding its way to the wide waters of the Hudson River.

To clear the air, I told him about the Dr. Mike With Twins mix-up.

"That explains it," he said with a laugh. "You'd put me in the married friend zone."

"Yes." I admitted, completely embarrassed.

Mike reached across and took my hand. "Does this mean I've had an upgrade into a different zone?"

"I believe so," I replied. "You're now in the zone of infinite possibilities."

"Infinite possibilities. I like that."

When our double order of dumplings came out, we pounced on them. I'd ordered shrimp, and Mike had ordered chicken.

"I'm thinking we ordered too much food," I told him between bites.

"That statement does not compute. It is impossible to order too much Chinese food. This will make fantastic leftovers and next-day lunch."

"Or breakfast."

"Guilty as charged," he said and plucked a dumpling out of the dish.

I looked at him sitting across from me and noticed a slight dimple in his right cheek. It made him appear more boyish, as if the dimple only surfaced when he relaxed.

"What?" he asked. "Do I have dirt on my face? Because that is a possibility."

His joke made me laugh. "No. I never noticed you had a dimple."

"I get it from my mom. Hopefully, I've inherited her hair too. My dad went bald in his forties."

He continued to work on his dumplings, almost beating me. Almost. "What do your parents do?" I sandwiched the question in between bites.

"Mom is a teacher, and my dad works for IBM. They live in the same town they grew up in, near the dairy farm."

We were interrupted by a waiter carrying the rest of our

order, who thoughtfully brought a refill on our jasmine tea.

"Is that what made you go into veterinary medicine?" The food smelled heavenly. I started to roll a mu shu pancake.

Mike was busy scooping velvet chicken with broccoli onto his plate but answered my question. "From the time I was little, I helped out my grandparents. They owned a small family dairy that has been in our family for over seventy years. My sisters and I had fun doing chores like collecting eggs and feeding the calves. Idyllic for a child, but tough to make a living at it in modern America."

"That's what I've read."

"Yep. Backbreaking work," he said. "To modernize takes a lot of capital, and with no one stepping up to run the place, my grandparents sold to a local dairy farmer cooperative. We kept a hundred acres for our family to use. All for the best, I suppose." He didn't sound happy about it.

The death of the small family farm was well documented, with the small producer unable to compete with corporate dairies. One or two bad years in a row with milk prices down could wipe out profits.

"My grandma kept her favorite cows, and now she and Gramps live on a small organic farm with a few horses, goats, and chickens. They sell their butter and eggs to a local restaurant where they know the chef. One of those farm-to-table places." He went back to working on some leftover spicy eggplant.

"You call your grandfather Gramps? So do I." I paused with my empty chopsticks in the air. "Gramps is the only family I have left. Well, that's not exactly true," I explained. "But I'm not close to my dad or stepmom."

He looked up but didn't ask me why.

So I explained how my mom and my brother, Jimmy, went out for ice cream and were killed by a drunk driver when I was fifteen. Instead of grieving, my surgeon dad moved on quickly with his surgical nurse, who became pregnant only a few months later. I was furious and showed it. Gramps offered to take me in, and my father was more than willing to get rid of me. I'd basically lost two parents.

"It must have been a terrible emotional blow, especially at that age. It's bad enough being a teenager without those kinds of complications." His eyes caught mine and he smiled. "But you came out the other side."

"Thanks to Gramps and veterinary medicine. My work is a big part of my life."

"As it should be," he replied. "We have a fascinating profession that demands a certain amount of sacrifice on our parts. I feel it's a calling, not only a job."

I knew exactly what he meant. We were kindred spirits who had bumped into each other on our way somewhere else.

"Agreed, it is a calling. But we still have our own lives to live."

Mike said, "I have to confess. Balancing my private life with my professional life hasn't been very successful so far."

I looked down at the black river water rushing below our window. Swirls of white broke over the rocks and boulders on the way. Our two reflections were captured in the glass, shadows superimposed over the roughly flowing stream.

"Balancing my job and personal life has been difficult for me too," I also confessed. "I've just about given up."

He reached over for the second time and gently squeezed my hand. "Don't give up. You should never give up."

"Never give up. Never surrender," I quoted.

"*Galaxy Quest*, right?"

I smiled at him and said, "Yes."

"Loved that movie."

We both had to work in the morning, so we parted ways after dinner and a cautious kiss. Going slowly suited me. I'd mooned over guys, been swept off my feet, and been cheated on more times than I cared to remember.

If it was meant to be, it was meant to be.

But I hoped I'd have a date on Valentine's Day after all.

Chapter Twenty-Three

THE LAB RESULTS CAME BACK FOR OUR DOGGY PATIENT Booty Call. He had a urinary tract infection and crystals in his urine. This would be a complex case combining a medical issue and a behavioral problem that were intertwined. His bad habit of humping further irritated his urinary infection. And this couldn't be solved overnight, or by a pill, as most clients wanted.

After I spoke to his owners, I had them set up a recheck appointment in ten days, when his medication would be finished. Meanwhile, Cindy sent them a list of animal behavior specialists plus information on urinary tract problems.

"Do you think they'll follow your advice?" Mari asked. As someone who showed and trained her two Rottweiler dogs, she knew the importance of consistency.

We were on our lunch break, so I answered her between bites of my leftover Chinese food. "Reward good behavior and discourage bad habits. Easy to say, hard to follow through on."

Mari agreed. "People think their dogs are little humans covered with fur instead of animals. Booty Call isn't going to grow up and enroll in animal studies at Harvard."

I laughed and took another bite of shrimp.

"On the other hand," Mari continued. "He'd be pretty popular with the ladies. And guys. And inanimate objects."

Our giggles were dying down when Cindy joined us at

the employee table. As always, she'd brought her lunch. This time she carried some homemade soup and a healthy salad. She eyed Mari's bag of chips and corn dogs with the usual disapproval.

"All that junk food is going to catch up with you," Cindy told Mari.

"I think I've heard that before. Care for a chip?"

"No thanks."

Cindy's soup smelled delicious but so did my Chinese food. Mike and I had ordered an extra plate of stir-fried vegetables, and I'd taken half home. As I virtuously lifted a pea pod into my mouth, Cindy asked me which restaurant I got my takeout from.

"Lucky Gardens," I told her, deliberately skipping over the not-takeout part before I realized she'd been there when I'd taken Mike's call.

"So, how did it go last night?"

I knew I'd end up telling my friends everything, but I wanted to make them work for it.

"Fine."

Mari handed me a couple of chips and winked at me.

"What did you and Mike talk about, if you don't mind me asking?" This time Cindy gave me the famous *you must tell me* glare.

"Work."

Mari broke out in laughter.

I decided to put Cindy out of her misery and said, "It went well. We have a lot in common, but it's too early to say that we're anything but friends."

"Well, it's a start."

"Guys," I said, "I don't need a man to be happy."

Cindy seemed to be in agreement. "Tell me about it. Half the time I want to hit my hubby over the head and bury him in the backyard."

"Can I quote you on that?" Mari asked.

"That's the problem with relationships," Cindy reiterated. "Don't mind me. I need to blow off some steam. The rest of the time I love him to pieces and don't want to live without him." She paused to take another spoonful of soup. "Sorry, but I've been pretty up and down lately. My hubby knows how much Babs's death upset me, upset us all."

At the mention of Babs, the room turned silent.

Cindy was right. We were all joking and laughing, but barely ten feet away was our surgery room—where a friend was murdered.

We were all traumatized, the three of us, something I shouldn't forget. No wonder Cindy wanted to talk about something else, in this case, my love life. Anything but the fact that someone murdered our temporary receptionist in our surgery suite.

After lunch, Cindy pulled me aside. I thought she was going to ask me more questions about Mike, but she wanted to update me on the coffee mugs.

"The forensic guys found Babs's full handprint on her mug, the one with the traces of Xanax. The only other prints were smeared. The results on that other mug that the killer might have used are still pending. The chief decided to send some samples out to some kind of specialized DNA lab to see if they can capture anything else. But don't tell anyone. Not even Mari. Promise?"

"Of course, I promise. What about Alicia and José? Any luck there?"

"Nothing. José was killed with his own gun. He bought it legally only a few weeks ago. No trace evidence could be found on either body. They think the killer wore gloves and probably ski clothes, goggles, and a hat."

I remembered that Bruce, the fellow who flagged down our truck, wore a ski jacket, so I asked her if he was considered a suspect.

She frowned and shook her head. "I'm not sure. The chief's interviewed him several times, but so far they haven't uncovered any evidence to tie him to the murders. His record is clean, no arrests."

"Maybe I should check up on Bruce myself."

"Go ahead. I'll help you any way I can, but I'm so busy with my kids and the house and being the executor of Babs's estate right now that I've got no time left over. I feel bad, but I'm sure you can understand." Cindy, who always appeared upbeat, looked anything but.

"Don't worry," I told her. "Between all of us we'll figure it out."

"I certainly hope so," she answered before telling me to get back to work.

———————

From my initial searches on the Internet, I thought Bruce appeared pretty good on paper. He'd relocated from New York

City a few years ago and made his living as an accountant. I remember how condescending he sounded and wondered if he acted that way with his clients. Just because he was an a-hole didn't mean he was guilty of murder. A local search revealed an office number, as well as an address. Where should I start? Dare I book an appointment with him? Taxes weren't due until April 15, and this was the beginning of February.

Unsure how to proceed, I logged on to Facebook again. I'd read it was the first thing an employer looks at when hiring someone—and you could peruse it from the comfort of your home. My friend request to Bruce was immediately approved. I wondered if Bruce even recognized my name. The two "girls" who called the police and waited with him in the snow were probably off his radar by now. He'd really spoken more to Mari than to me.

What I discovered was a shock.

Bruce had been Alicia and José's accountant.

What? Why hadn't the chief of police released this information?

Granted, Oak Falls was a pretty small town. Bruce worked for an accounting firm with offices in Oak Falls, Kingston, and Rhinebeck, so he might have been handed the couple as clients of the firm.

That made me wonder if Bruce mentioned finding José. I scrolled back through his pages and sure enough, Bruce posted this.

SO I CAN'T BELIEVE IT BUT I FOUND A BODY TODAY IN THE WOODS. NO LIE. I DECIDED TO DO SOME ICE

FISHING AND STUMBLED ACROSS THIS GUY IN SKI CLOTHES LYING FACE DOWN IN THE SNOW.

Scrolling forward he posted this:

UPDATE ON THE BODY IN THE WOODS. NOW IT'S TWO BODIES AND I KNOW BOTH OF THEM. THEY WERE CLIENTS. AND NO—I DIDN"T KILL THEM WHEN I GAVE THEM MY BILL. LOL

His final post regarding José and Alicia was:

SORRY IF ANYONE TOOK OFFENSE WITH MY POST. I DIDN"T MEAN TO BE INSENSITIVE. SOME OF YOU GUYS ON FACEBOOK NEED TO LIGHTEN UP. PEACE. OUT.

Ice fishing? I didn't remember him having a fishing pole, but his gear could have been in the trunk of his SUV. Another question to ask Cindy.

What about a motive?

We knew that José had a wrongful death suit pending against him, possibly for several million dollars. Many doctors, dentists, and veterinarians carried their own malpractice insurance, or the company they worked for paid it. American medical facilities long ago figured out they'd save money by hiring doctors as "subcontractors" not directly employed by the hospital. Corporate medicine was all about the money and profit. Perhaps José and Alicia wanted an accountant's opinion on the lawsuit. But what did that have to do with murder?

When I realized I didn't remember who was suing José, I shot Cindy a message. She immediately answered.

> Greg Owens, Doris Owen's husband. Doris died of pancreatic cancer that he says José completely missed.
>
> Pancreatic cancer can present with vague symptoms. That's why it's usually diagnosed so late in the course of the disease.
>
> It appears Greg doesn't think that way. It took months before José referred her to a specialist. I'm not sure if the lawsuit will continue with both parties dead.

Me either. But my cynical side bet it would.

As I scanned Bruce's Facebook pages, I noticed plenty of angry posts about dating and women. He believed most women lied about their #MeToo accusations to get back at guys. Pretty girls were only after your money. Women trapped men into marrying them so they could have a free ride. Skipping down, I saw he posted his likes as superhero movies, weed, and some popular conspiracy theories.

I assumed Police Chief Garcia knew all this. Bruce's Facebook page revealed no obvious motive for murder, but it was interesting he knew both the victims.

That ice fishing alibi sounded fishy, too.

Trying to be efficient, I looked up the ice-fishing season in New York state parks. You would think it would be simple, but there were several schedules depending on what type of fish you wanted to catch. Most ice fishing takes place on a solidly frozen large lake. The fisherman cuts a hole in the ice and usually brings a chair or small shelter to fish from. Lover's Lake, where Alicia's body was found, was fairly small, maybe three Olympic-size pools large? *Not a classic ice fishing spot.*

Bruce bore further investigating. But first I needed to pump Cindy for anything else she knew about our not-so-Good Samaritan.

This time Cindy answered her phone after five rings. In the background, it sounded like a war was raging.

"Just the guys watching some disaster movie. Let me move into the other room so we can talk," she said.

The explosive noises faded and stopped after a door closed.

"That's better," I told her. "Sorry to bother you again, but do you have time to talk about Bruce, the guy who hailed us down and found José's body?"

"Ahh." A grunt of contentment was followed by, "I'll tell you what I know. Then I'm taking a nap in this recliner."

"I'm ready."

"My sister told me that Bruce is a piece of work. He's dabbled in that male supremacy thing, banning books, survivalist stuff, and a bunch of other things I can't remember at the moment."

"Did the chief find any fishing equipment in his car?"

"Not that I recall. Was that his excuse for being up there?"

My notes were in front of me. I turned a page to my "Bruce Suspect?" column to make certain I remembered correctly. "He mentioned on Facebook he was doing some ice fishing."

Cindy laughed. "Lover's Lake isn't stocked by the state. It's pretty small as far as lakes go. We locals use it mostly in the summer."

Not a fishing destination.

"What does the chief think?"

"Well, he's pretty sure Bruce wasn't ice fishing. They found him in possession of two sets of powerful binoculars and one portable telescope."

"That sounds like equipment a voyeur might have. Maybe he likes to catch glimpses of women in their underwear."

"Ick."

I remembered Bruce's face that day. He gave us all kinds of excuses why he couldn't call 911. His phone was out of charge. He didn't have any reception. I remember he refused to even show us where the body was. When Mari and I asked if he'd checked for a pulse, he hadn't seemed to care. Like he knew it wouldn't do any good.

"Kate. Are you there?"

"Sorry, I was going over what happened that day. So is he a suspect?"

"Yes, he is. Here's something else. The coroner is waffling on the time of death because both bodies were frozen."

"When was the last time anyone saw them?"

"At work, on Wednesday. They each took Thursday and Friday off for a long weekend."

"Bruce hailed Mari and me down when we were coming back from our last house call on Friday, just before you went to Florida. That means…"

"Possibly a two-day window. And here's another thing."

I'd been taking notes about days and times and paused. "What's that?"

"The parks department maintains a one-lane road that comes pretty close to that spot, but you approach it from the other side. In the summer we locals use it. We pull off and park our cars in among the trees. There are a couple of places that you can't see from the road. That's how Lover's Lake got its nickname. From horny teenagers."

"Funny."

"Lover's Lake. I confess to going up there a few times my junior and senior year in high school."

"Cindy, you naughty girl," I mock scolded her.

"Don't knock it till you've tried it," she answered.

We'd gotten a bit off track, and I had one more question for her.

"Why did Bruce leave the main highway and drive across the field? It makes no sense. As it was, his SUV got stuck in a gully coming back down."

"That's what the chief wanted to know."

———

After we hung up, I pondered all this new information. I recalled very clearly following the set of tire tracks Bruce had left as his SUV dug in and climbed to the tree line. If called to testify, I had to say I only saw one set of tire tracks. I tried to remember if it snowed on Thursday or Friday morning, or both.

Maybe Bruce kidnapped the couple and forced them to walk to where José's body was found shot to death. But why wouldn't Alicia try to break free? Her cause of death was strangulation. The lack of forensic evidence suggested that the murderer wore gloves, and in the case of Alicia, the lake water washed away any evidence.

José was shot at close range. Then that same gun was placed in his hand and fired, so he would be positive for trace evidence. Was the plan to shoot Alicia first? Things didn't add up.

Another issue presented itself. *Whoever killed José put the gun in the wrong hand. Would a person who knew him make that mistake?*

So many unanswered questions. We didn't know at this point whether Alicia was alive and restrained when José was shot or already dead. Both victims, the chief assumed, were killed in a short period of time, which meant the killer had their work cut out for them.

Unless there were two separate killers?

When I called up Gramps, he didn't think much of my two-killers theory.

"Keep things simple, Katie," he said after hearing me out. "Don't think you're hearing the thunder of zebra hooves when it's only a mule strolling by."

Gramps's riff on that old zebra saying was pretty funny, and I told him so.

"Thanks. Remember, most crimes aren't planned by master criminals. That's only in the movies. There's usually a pretty clear-cut reason someone murders someone else, unless we are talking psycho serial killer, which I don't think is the case here. This crime appears to be planned but only up to a point."

"I agree. Whoever did this was sloppy with a lot of the details. José's and Alicia's deaths feel personal, but Babs's murder might be a crime of opportunity. Thankfully, the forensic guys caught a lot of discrepancies with all three killings."

"Exactly." Speaking to Gramps clarified my ideas.

"Whoever killed the couple wanted the police to believe it was a murder-suicide. That's why they tried to do a better job with Babs. They learned from their mistakes."

That made sense. Babs's murder was almost too specific, too staged—unlike the violence directed at José and Alicia.

"What the killer didn't count on was how resourceful Babs was," Gramps added. "I admire the way she left you clues in the short time she had before the Xanax kicked in."

"If we had only gotten back earlier…"

"Stop that," Gramps told me. "You and Mari did everything you could. The blame is on the person who committed these crimes, not on the innocent."

I knew Gramps was right, but it helped to hear him say it out loud.

"One last thing, Katie. This murderer. It takes a certain amount of strength to overpower two people. Keep that in mind when you talk to any suspects."

My mind was racing through all the names in my notes. Bruce was a big guy, at least six feet. A bit bulky, a little out of shape but in the larger man category. The victims' room-mates, Nora and Rob, seemed pretty fit. When I visited Nora at her home, I remembered seeing a snowmobile and snow-shoes in her garage as well as a ten-speed bicycle hanging on the wall.

"That probably rules out Linda, the ex-wife. She's fairly thin and frail-looking."

"Promise me you'll keep that pepper spray on you."

I patted my jacket pocket. "I promise, Gramps. Keep you posted. Love you."

"Back at you, Katie."

After I hung up, I felt more focused. With this information and a new way to look at the crime, I could concentrate on those people closest to the couple who fit the right physical profile. I made a mental note to find out what Greg Owens looked like, the man who filed the lawsuit against José.

A few sips of water refreshed me enough to think about having a snack. Thanks to Gramps, I'd concentrate now on the male suspects.

Then I remembered Crystal, the two hundred-plus-pound former mother-in-law with those linebacker shoul-ders. Crystal, who worked as a surgical nurse and would do anything to protect her daughter and grandchildren. Surgical nurses work in surgical suites.

Like the one Babs was killed in.

Chapter Twenty-Four

IN MY DREAM, ALICIA BANGED ON THE ICE ABOVE HER with her fists, screaming my name. I woke with a start. Someone outside yelled my name, but it wasn't a ghost.

Bright lights flooded through the curtains into my one-room apartment. Buddy was already awake, whining by the side of the bed.

I put on my bathrobe and cautiously snuck a look outside. A giant of a man stood on my front step, tears rolling down his face. In his arms he held something wrapped in a blanket. Was his beloved older dog in trouble?

"Pinky," I opened the door for my next-door neighbor. "Is there a problem with Princess?"

He came inside, being sure to rub his boots on the mat. His mother had trained him well.

"It's not Princess, Dr. Kate. She's in the truck. I found this doggie tonight while I was plowing one of the weekenders out. I think it's a doggie."

"Bring it into the treatment room," I told him. He followed behind, still choking back tears.

I prepared myself for the worst.

He placed the blanket down on the treatment table and stood back.

Gently I removed the first layer of blanket to uncover what looked like an alien creature. The dog was a young female, completely hairless, skin a gray color, like elephant skin. A fishhook penetrated her top lip, snagging the side of the bottom lip.

I understood his tears.

"It's not as bad as it looks, Pinky. Hold her on the table and don't let her fall."

"Why is she gray and all crusty? Was she burned or something?" Fresh tears started streaming down his face.

I'd been searching our hospital junk drawer for some special tools, a pair of pliers and a wire cutter. "It looks like she has mange."

"Mange?" Pinky gasped. "Am I going to get it?"

I shut the drawer and went back to the treatment table. "I'll have to take a skin scraping, but I think this is demodectic mange and that's not contagious. Now, can you keep her steady while I get this fishhook out?"

Pinky bit down on his own lip and said, "Yes."

I'd removed fishhooks before. After carefully advancing the barb, I cut it with the wire cutter and removed the rest of the hook. After I put pressure on the wounds, the bleeding quickly stopped.

Blue doggy eyes looked at me with gratitude. While Pinky held on, I performed a quick exam, confirming this was a young female dog in urgent need of a meal.

"What kind of doggie is she?" Pinky asked as I made up a meal of prescription dog food for gastrointestinal issues. Not knowing when she'd eaten last, I didn't want to overload her GI tract with too much fat or calories. It would be small, frequent feedings and constant weigh-ins for her until I got a handle on her condition.

"I have no idea," I told him. "We'll have to wait until her hair starts growing in and her body fills out."

"Princess is the one who saved her," Pinky said. "I was about to leave when she started barking and wouldn't stop. That's when I saw this doggie standing over by the woodpile. If it wasn't for Princess, I would have driven away." Telling his story elicited another round of tears.

Princess, Pinky's elderly poodle, rode everywhere with him.

"You need to give Princess a special treat tonight," I told him. "She saved this baby's life."

His round pink face remained incredibly sad.

"Come on. Let's give her a name," I said in an attempt to cheer him up as we both watched her lap up her food. "What do you want to call her?"

"You name her, Dr. Kate. I'm not so good at names."

"Alright. I think we should call her…Bella, because in about four or five months she'll be a beautiful dog."

"Bella. I like that. Are you going to keep her here until she is all better?"

Bella's sweet trusting eyes held the answer. "Yes. I think Buddy needs a friend."

I noticed Pinky seemed embarrassed, keeping his eyes to the floor.

"You're wearing your bathrobe, Dr. Kate. Do you want to put on your doctor coat?"

"That's a good idea," I replied, knowing that Pinky needed me to put it on. I'd left it on my office chair, where a sleepy Mr. Katt refused to move. Pinky had been raised by his mom and held back by the local school district. He was shy and kind, over six feet tall and three hundred pounds, and I counted him as a friend.

"You said Princess is in the truck? Don't you think she needs to go home now?" The office clock read three a.m. With any luck I might get a few more hours of sleep.

His eyes lit up. "She's probably wondering where I am. I left the truck running and the heat on so she wouldn't get cold."

While he was talking, I started herding him out the connecting hospital door, through my apartment and toward his plow truck idling outside in the parking lot. He bent down to pet Buddy before walking to my front door.

"I'm sorry I woke you up, Dr. Kate. I didn't know where else to go."

"You did the right thing, Pinky. Please try not to worry. Why don't you call us tomorrow, and Cindy will tell you how Bella is doing."

Still not looking me in the eyes, he said his goodbye and softly closed the door.

After hearing Pinky drive off, I locked my door and went back into the treatment room to see if Bella had held down her meal. I'd put her in a dog run with a nice soft bed. Free of the fishhook, she'd emptied her food bowl and half the water bowl.

When I greeted her, she thumped her tail. I wrote a note to Mari on the treatment board briefly explaining who Bella was and setting up a treatment plan for the morning.

"Let's give you a nice toy to keep you company," I told

the young dog. We kept a bin of toys just for this purpose. She needed something very soft, since her mouth was still tender. Near the bottom I found the perfect toy—a plush koala bear.

"Bella," I said, "this is for you."

She came over to the front of the cage. I very carefully patted her crusty head and handed her the toy. I wanted her to know she was safe—that we'd be here when she woke in the morning. Her blue eyes held mine, then she plucked the toy from my hand, walked over to her bed, and curled up.

"Good night, Bella." I decided to leave one of the lights on so she wouldn't be frightened.

At the sound of my voice, she lifted her sleepy head, then laid back down, the koala bear tucked under her paw.

Chapter Twenty-Five

As I slid my damp coat on to walk Buddy and Bella, I realized how sick I was of the cold. To my mind, February is a far crueler month than April, despite what T. S. Eliot says, because it feels like winter will never end. Spring flowers were still hiding from view in the frozen ground.

Buddy had been tentative at first meeting this new funny-looking dog, but he asked her to play. Bella stayed put, the koala bear in her mouth.

"Give her a few days, Buddy," I told my dog, handing him a chew bone. "She needs time to adjust."

———————

"What a little sweetie pie," Mari commented after handling Bella for her blood tests. "I wonder what color fur she'll have?"

We'd finished up our Saturday appointments and were concentrating on our newest arrival. Mari and I reviewed all the new treatments for demodectic mange available as we started Bella's medications. The cigar-shaped microscopic mite was a normal inhabitant of canine skin, but the combination of an immature immune system and stress had overwhelmed her body's defenses and let them go wild.

"I worked for a vet one summer my junior year of high school and had to assist with a lime-sulfur bath," I said while looking at Bella's feet.

"Yuck. That stuff smelled like rotten eggs," Mari answered. "Or funky garbage. I'm glad we've got other options now."

"Bella, did you hear that?" We'd finished a medicated bath to sooth her skin and were gently drying her on the treatment table. "You smell like you came from the beauty parlor."

By checking her teeth, I'd determined that Bella was still a puppy of about five or six months old. As a young, otherwise healthy dog, her prognosis was excellent.

Cindy walked in while we had Bella up on the table. "I've checked the lost and found notices. Nothing there."

"I'm not surprised. Her skin didn't get like this overnight. I bet she was searching for food and got snagged by the hook because it smelled like fish." I pet Bella's nose and continued examining her footpads. They were thickened and crusty from hard use and mange.

"Sit," Mari said.

There was no response, only a bewildered look.

"That's the first thing most dogs learn. I bet her mom was a stray."

"Oh, Kate," Cindy interrupted, "Pinky called. He still sounded frightened from last night."

I lifted Bella up and placed her on the floor. "Of me in my nightgown, or the dog's plight?"

Cindy laughed. "I'd guess the nightgown."

———

That afternoon turned out to be payback day. I'd promised to meet Mike at his client's place and wrangle their barn cats. We needed to vaccinate them, especially for rabies.

Also on my mind was Mike, who didn't have a wife or twins and had gone from a friend to perhaps—I wasn't sure.

I'd thrown the office Have-A-Heart animal trap in the back of the truck in case the kitties were feral, along with a cooler case full of vaccines, antibiotics, and a veterinary first aid kit. A barn cat can be perfectly fine one day and in need of help the next. They dealt with coyotes, foxes, raccoons, and dogs, to name a few common predators of cats, who might come sniffing around the barn.

Unfamiliar with the address, I let the truck's GPS guide me. Always wary of a mistake in the programming, I made sure it didn't send me up a logging road or a road closed for the winter. I'd read horror stories of people stranded in the snow in places they were sent by their GPS.

One thing I did know was that this destination was closer to Rhinebeck than my usual Oak Falls house calls—more in true horse country. Most horse people liked having barn cats, since they cut down on the rodent population, keeping expensive animal feed from being gnawed on. While I was in vet school doing farm calls, I often found barn cats perched on the backs of horses, cows, and even goats. They liked the warmth and the height. Trust a cat to figure out how to be comfortable under any circumstances.

The scenery rolled by, still covered with snow except for some brown patches that caught direct sun. The weather report said cold today, but with no snow or crazy winds expected. I'd packed some hand warmers anyway, the kind skiers used. I'd have to stick them in my pockets since I needed full use of my hands. They'd serve to keep me warm and thaw out any frozen digits in case the weather turned.

Before I left, I texted Mike. He was finishing up an appointment and would meet me at the barn. The owners knew I was coming.

Handling a barn cat can be tricky. Some barn cats are like house cats, often living an indoor/outdoor life. Others were truly feral or wild—okay with the people they knew but frightened by the rest of humanity. I had no idea what I was in for but hoped for a tame population of kitties. Uncooperative felines turn into a twisty bundle of claws and teeth. I'd seen plenty of cat bites over the years and wanted to avoid that.

The GPS sent me down a road that paralleled the Hudson River. The next turn at a mailbox must be their driveway, since it led toward a large farmhouse with a red barn. As I drove the F-150 toward the house, I noticed three dogs running on the driveway determined not to let me proceed. Weaving in and out, scooting in front of the truck barking, I slowed down considerably as I drove along so as not to hit them.

The ruckus they raised brought a woman out onto the porch, her long, gray hair cascading down her back in a loose French braid. While I watched she called the dogs, then signaled for me to park near the house. As I drew closer, I noticed a cane in her right hand. She deliberately remained on the porch, not attempting to navigate the stairs.

My pockets were stuffed with cat treats, but the dogs sniffed them out right away, resulting in wagging tails and happy faces. Wading into the pack of canines, I asked each mixed shepherd to sit, and when they obliged they got a yummy snack.

After the barking died down, I called up, "Hi, there. I'm Dr. Kate Turner, here to take care of your barn cats." The dogs followed close by up the stairs. If the homeowner had any doubt, the sign on the side of the truck read Oak Falls Animal Hospital. No sense taking any chances. Mari and I once were greeted by a shotgun-toting property owner.

This barn call posed no threat.

"Welcome. Eunice DeVries," the woman said. "Let's go inside and get out of the cold."

When we entered the house, I was surprised to see a long, slim space running the width of the house that served as a mudroom. One of the older dogs broke away, grabbed a worn toy from the tiled floor, and retired to a dog bed in the corner. A comfortable pet space, complete with plenty of toys, beds, food, and water, muddy dogs could bed down in this heated area till they dried off.

"That's ingenious. Is it original to the house?" I asked her.

"Yes. My great-grandfather was an architect and dog lover. They considered this mudroom very innovative for his time."

She opened the double doors into the house, and I followed her inside. Stuffy and overheated, it was chock full of huge mahogany furniture, many pieces oversized for a small farmhouse.

Eunice must have noticed my surprise. "The furniture comes from our former place in Rhinebeck. When my parents passed, I kept several pieces that I knew and loved. They're too big, I know, but I grew up with them. They're family."

I didn't know about family pieces. After my mom and brother died, my dad sold our house and all the furniture. "Too many memories," he'd told Gramps.

My text chime sounded as I followed her slow progress into the living room.

Be there in 5 minutes

"Is that Dr. Mike?" Eunice asked.

"Yes. He's almost here." The heat inside felt practically unbearable. I wanted to rip off my coat and peel down to my undies, but instead I made do with unzipping my coat and draping it over my arm. Sweat beaded up on my forehead.

To take my mind off the sweat rolling down my back, I asked, "How feral are your barn cats?" I wanted to know what I was in for. Casually, I wiped my brow with the back of my hand.

Eunice didn't notice.

"All of them are pretty tame and friendly. They usually follow me around. The mommy cat wandered in about twelve years ago, scrawny and scared. The next year before we could get her spayed, she became obviously pregnant. After the kittens were born everyone got neutered. We lost one to a coyote, so now they get locked up at night in the barn."

"Good idea. Would you like to come out with us?" I fanned my face in a futile attempt to attract cool air.

"No, thanks. This arthritis is bothering me something fierce today. Unless you need me, I'll stay here with the dogs. They'll recognize Dr. Mike's truck. He treats our horses."

"Alright. I hope you feel better. I'll let myself out." As I left, she was rubbing her knee. On my way down the hallway, I passed a half-open door where an elderly man hooked up to oxygen dozed in a wheelchair.

After going back through the mudroom, I snuck out, making sure no dogs broke past me. The cold outside air felt fantastic. As I walked down the stairs, I saw a truck come lumbering up the driveway.

Mike climbed out, then removed two bags from the back seat.

"Let me guess," I said. "A capture net."

That made him laugh. "Our lunch. Two turkey sandwiches with a side of fruit and two coffees to go," he answered. "It's a late lunch."

"I'm sure that turkey will be a hit with the kitties." I walked beside him, my house call bag in my hand.

"Who says I'm going to share?" His steps matched mine as we made our way to the barn. He lifted the latch then pulled the door opened to reveal large stalls and two that immediately whinnied at us.

"Eunice wants me to float some teeth," he said. "Can you stick around to help?"

I'd filed the points off equine teeth in school, referred to as "floating" by most horse owners. "Sure," I answered. The pungent smell of horse and hay tickled my nose. To the right of the door stood a square wooden table and four chairs. The barn looked neat and tidy.

"Let's eat first. I'm starving." From the first bag, he took out a container of wipes and proceeded to clean the table. Then Mike put the second bag and the coffees, some paper plates and napkins, and packets of mustard and mayo in front of us. "I wasn't sure what you liked, so I got a little of everything."

A broom hung on the nearby wall. He lifted it off and used it to clear our chairs of straw and dust.

"You've done this before," I said after I sat down. "Dining alfresco in the barn."

"Yep. Before her knee started acting up, Eunice would bring me cookies or a sandwich while I worked."

We unwrapped the very generous turkey sandwiches. Before I could take a bite, a pitiful meow sounded down by my feet. There sat a striped tabby cat, more interested in the turkey than in me.

Mike took a piece of meat from his sandwich. "Here you are, Tiger."

This might be easier than I thought. "How many cats are there?"

"The mommy cat, Tiger, and her four kittens. Let me see if I get their names right. Tootsie, Tommy, Taffy, and Tiny. Tiny is the big one."

By now cats began appearing from all directions. They mewed and purred and bumped against our legs. I tried to pet each one to familiarize them with my smell. Again, they were more interested in the turkey.

"Why don't we see if we can get the vaccines done now?" he suggested. "I'll hold while you do the shots."

Mike took a package of turkey breast out of the bag and laid it out on the table. When he scooped up Tiger, she spotted the meat immediately. While she nibbled, I checked her lymph nodes then gave her a yearly feline distemper multishot and a rabies booster. She didn't even flinch.

Once finished, we put her down and lifted up another one. They were all vaccinated in less than twenty minutes. I began to suspect Mike could have done this all by himself. *Could this be sort of a date?*

Mike took the remaining crumbs, brushed them on a paper plate and the family of felines all dug in.

"Take half of my sandwich," I told him, noticing he'd sacrificed some of his lunch to the cats. "I ate before I got here."

He took another bite of sandwich and washed it down with coffee. Today, in this light, his eyes were a deep shade of blue-gray. "Thanks, I'll take you up on that."

We sat there comfortably, the cats circling the table just in case. Despite the cold outside, the barn stayed comfortable, a tribute to horse body heat.

"By the way," he said, finishing his sandwich and removing the lid from the coffee. "My staff says you're sort of famous for solving crimes."

I felt my face begin to flush as I admitted my luck in catching murderers. "I suppose I got the habit from watching my Gramps go over evidence files. He investigated arsons for the NYC fire department."

"An unusual hobby for a young girl." One of the cats jumped into his lap, checking for scraps.

"So I found out."

"I thought I'd try to help you." He absentmindedly stroked Tiger, who started purring up a feline storm. "So I asked the staff about Alicia and José to see if they had any ideas about who killed them. One of our part-time technicians lives in Oak Falls, and she had quite a bit to say."

I leaned forward. "What did you find out?"

"Gossip says Alicia was a world-class flirter. Guys fell for her all the time. She acted like a very merry widow until she hooked up with José."

"How did that happen?"

"I believe she met him at the medical practice he worked for. Some kind of nervous stomach issue, my source said."

"A doctor or PA dating a patient? Isn't that a big no-no?" One of the kitties with sharp claws tried to climb up my leg, which I discouraged.

"In principle, I suppose, yes. It's a little murky if he transferred her care to someone else."

"What about José? What was he like?"

"Studious. Serious. Nice guy. Supposedly he adored Alicia. He even went over to Crystal's place to tell her to stop harassing his fiancée."

"The ex-mother-in-law, Crystal? He threatened to take legal action?"

"Yes. Oh, and José gave notice at work since the couple planned to move to California."

I didn't reveal to Mike that I already knew the couple's plans.

He checked his watch. "We need to get started on floating those teeth."

We threw our garbage in the waste can and secured the lid. Mike checked his bag to make sure he had a rasp and restraint twitch if needed. We made our way over to one of the stalls. A big chestnut with a white stripe stuck his head all the way out and nuzzled Mike, searching for treats. "After we finish, dude," he told the horse.

He opened the stall door and clicked a lead onto the horse's halter.

"Oh, I almost forgot," he said, turning toward me. The horse stomped his rear leg and shook his head. "Some guy kept sending Alicia love notes after she was nice to him. He became quite a pest. That's why she developed a stomach problem—from anxiety. My technician didn't know the name of the guy, but it had been going on for years."

He took out the long rasp file then added, "Also, Alicia thought someone was watching her."

Chapter Twenty-Six

MIKE AND I HAD FUN WORKING AS VETERINARY DENTISTS on the horses, who didn't enjoy having their teeth filed at all. Copious amounts of foamy horse slobber went flying everywhere, as Mike slid his fingers along the cheek side of the chestnut's teeth.

"We're done," he told me. "This guy deserves an apple wafer." From his jacket pocket he brought out several chewy treats and held them out on his flattened hand.

I scratched the horse's long nose as he chomped away. We moved to the next horse, a placid older bay gelding with perfect manners. His floating didn't take long, only a few irritating places on the back teeth to fix.

While we worked, I noticed Mike's efficient and compassionate way with his patients, always stopping and comforting them if they spooked. He genuinely enjoyed animals, of all shapes and sizes. He also was a nice guy, working on his own time to help out this elderly couple who had mobility issues.

I tried to casually check him out. Taller than me, he appeared more muscular than I remembered, but large-animal work can do that to you.

What I didn't feel? That zing you get sometimes when you meet a stranger, that crazy attraction that made no sense. Cupid's golden arrow didn't hit any target today but instead shot past me to disappear in the air. I was attracted to Mike, yes, but in a quiet way.

That didn't worry me. So far all the guys I'd "zinged" with had led to short bumpy relationships, and ultimately heartbreak.

"What are you thinking about?" Mike asked. "You were staring into space."

Embarrassed, I said the first thing that popped into my head. "Cupid."

"Ah, Valentine's Day, which is coming up soon. If you aren't busy maybe we can go out to dinner? That is, if you don't have plans." The bay pawed with his front hoof, waiting for more apple wafers.

When he looked at me, his gaze steady, I felt a warm feeling, a sense of peace. "I'd love to, Mike."

"I'll book a restaurant. Are there any types of food you hate?" he asked, "because I don't care. I've been told I have an unrefined palate."

"So you'll eat anything."

"Basically."

"Me too. Do you want me do some research? There are a few new restaurants in Kingston."

"Nope. I've got it covered." He leaned toward me. I expected a kiss but instead he lifted something out of my hair. "Big horse goober," he said and flicked it onto the hay.

I appreciated the grooming fix, but I felt a bit disappointed Mike didn't make a move on me.

His phone chime pinged then rang again. "Work," he explained.

"Isn't it your day off?" I questioned.

"Yes, but you know how that goes."

"I do indeed." We straightened up our mess and made sure the horses and cats were fine. When the kitties noticed we were leaving, they began a pitiful mewing, hoping more food would miraculously appear. "Should we turn the horses out?" I asked, ready to let them out of their stalls and into the outside corral.

"No. Eunice said her stable help is coming over and to leave everyone in their stalls for now."

"So, I'll see you...?" I knew we had a Valentine's Day date, but not much else.

He carefully waded through the pool of cats at our feet. "Whenever you want, Kate. I've got to warn you, though, I'm kind of a serious guy. I'll tell you right up front, if you want someone flashy, that isn't me."

"What do you mean?"

"I'm coming off a two-year relationship," he explained. "We broke up because she couldn't stand the number of late nights I worked, being on call. Scrubs that smelled like a barn. I haven't dated since."

His eyes reflected a pain I recognized.

"I don't know what to say." My mind went blank while the horses stomped and whinnied behind us and the cats curled round our legs.

So he kissed me. Really kissed me.

And somewhere Cupid fired another golden arrow in an attempt to pierce my frozen heart.

Chapter Twenty-Seven

ONLY PROFESSIONAL DECORUM AND THE GREEN LIGHT ON the barn camera deterred us from a roll in the hay. From the sparks that flew between us, I was surprised we didn't singe our clothes or set the straw on fire. Our kiss goodbye held a promise I hoped would come true.

So much for not feeling the zing.

The drive back to the clinic passed quickly, as though I were on autopilot. I wanted to keep our budding relationship secret for now. I loved my friends, but sometimes they wanted to share too much.

The parking lot looked freshly plowed, with our landscaping guy Pinky thoughtfully breaking down the piles of dirty snow on our property line. Cindy told me Pinky had vowed to keep our parking lot the cleanest in town for helping little Bella. After I pulled in close to my apartment door, I got out and unloaded the back of the truck. A loud cawing caught my attention. Our recovered crow patient flew over and landed on the truck roof.

"Were you waiting for me? Here you go," I said, knowing I was getting the bird into a bad habit. There were still a few apple treats in my coat pocket, so I removed them and tossed them on the roof. When I headed toward my door, the other crows fluttered out of the trees and landed on the truck beside him. Their very sharp beaks stabbed each treat, breaking them into pieces.

"Enjoy yourselves," I said. "It's on the house." Buddy barked a welcome from behind the door, but the crows barely looked up. They must be used to our goings in and out by now.

Once settled in the apartment, I decided to straighten up, full of restless energy. With her first round of treatments finished, I'd brought Bella over from the hospital along with her bed. Both dogs nailed their potty walk. I noticed the puppy watched him, copying some of the things he did. But she still hadn't barked.

Despite wanting my privacy, I fought an irresistible urge to tell someone about Mike, and Gramps was first on that tell list.

"Hi, sweetie," Gramps answered, music playing in the background on his end.

"I've got some news," I blurted out.

"From the tone of your voice, I'd say it was good news. Wait a minute. Let me turn this down. Alexa. Stop."

The music stopped. "Gramps, I'm getting worried about you and Alexa. You're spending a lot of time together."

He laughed. "Very funny, Katie. To tell you the truth I'm finding more and more things to use her for, such as reminding me about appointments. Or timing the asparagus."

"I'm glad my Christmas present is useful."

"She's much better than a sweater."

"I'll remember that." While we chatted, I went over to the refrigerator and poured myself an iced tea.

"So tell me some good news. They caught Babs's killer?"

His voice sounded enthusiastic. I knew how worried he'd been about my safety.

"Nope. But the chief is working as hard as he can to solve all three murders. No, the good news is much closer to home. My home."

"You've won the lottery and we're rich," he joked. "Or maybe…you've met somebody?"

"Yes." He astonished me with our psychic connection. "How did you guess?"

Once again he chuckled. "It's about time. So you've got a date for Valentine's Day?"

"Yes, I've got a date for Valentine's Day. I'm as surprised as you are."

"Tell me a little about him, Katie. What does he do for a living?"

Gramps always cut to the chase. "Mike's a mixed-animal veterinarian based near Rhinebeck. That means he works on large and small animals. We met at one of my farm calls. He was delivering triplet goats, and I was examining a litter of puppies."

"Very romantic so far," he said with a chuckle.

"I got him confused with someone else and thought he was married, so we started off as friends."

"Best way to begin a relationship. Your partner should be your friend, too."

"Some partners of mine should have stayed in the friend zone," I commented, thinking of Luke. We'd been great friends, but there'd been plenty of warning signs I chose to ignore.

"So, tell me more."

"He graduated from Cornell ahead of me, and his

grandparents ran a dairy farm. He's kind and thoughtful and gentle and a very good veterinarian who cares about his clients and patients."

"Just like you, sweetie. He sounds cut from the same cloth. This one I'd love to meet."

"Only one thing, Gramps," I said. "He's not sure about continuing to practice or heading back to school and going into research or teaching."

"In other words, he's trying private practice for now to see if it's a good fit. That sounds like a practical plan."

"I'm hoping to spend more time with him, but I'm feeling guilty. Cindy wanted help in solving Babs's murder, but I've learned very little. The chief and the rest of the police aren't getting much further either. No witnesses, no clues, except for the coffee cup."

"What coffee cup?" he asked.

After I told him what we suspected, he agreed with our premise.

"We older people develop pretty set habits," he explained. "If she always washed out her cup and dishes, she wouldn't suddenly put a dirty cup away. I'd consider it a deliberate act on her part. Babs sounds like a pretty smart woman."

"She was."

"Then, if she served her killer coffee, she must have known them, or felt comfortable being alone with them in the hospital. Now you have to figure out who. I'd rule out anyone who showed antagonism to her. I doubt she'd want to have coffee with someone like that."

"I agree. Unless they wanted to make up with her."

"You've got a point," he said. "You might want to check out her other acquaintances."

What he said made sense. I took another sip of tea and wrote myself a note.

"It's important that the victims get justice, Gramps. That someone is punished for these crimes, however many people are involved."

"Meaning?"

"Meaning we might be looking at two murderers. The car thing doesn't add up. They found José's car pulled off a forestry road, with Alicia's purse but only José's phone inside with no charge. Alicia's phone hasn't been found. That stumps me. In case of an emergency, I would have expected one of them to keep their cell phones with them."

Gramps thought a moment before saying, "One thing I've noticed. You kids are never without your cell phones."

"That's true. Plus Alicia loved to take selfies. They're all over her media sites. If they were planning a wedding, wouldn't they want pictures?"

Gramps coughed then cleared his throat. "That's supposition, but anything's possible. Perhaps her phone is at the bottom of the lake? Can't they track her phone with one of those apps?"

"Listen to you talking apps."

Gramps ignored my technology comment. "If you discover something, turn it over to the police right away. Don't keep any information to yourself. That makes you less of a target."

"Okay."

He cleared his throat. "Remember, kiddo, you're a veterinarian, not a detective."

I'd heard that line before but not paid it much heed. "Gramps, I'm going to blame you for my crime-solving curiosity. Who brought home his investigations and taught me how to proceed in a logical fashion?"

"That must have been me. What was I thinking?" he laughed.

"Thinking about your cases removed me from my real-life problems, helped me climb out of the gigantic hole I'd dug for myself after Mom and Jimmy died. Did you know for a while I wanted to become a fire investigator like you?"

"I'm glad you didn't. Working cases with you helped me too," he confessed.

"Don't worry about me so much," I told him. "I'm sitting here in my office at the hospital with my pepper spray in my pocket, an upgraded alarm system, new outdoor cameras, and one dog who barks at anything—birds, squirrels, leaves..."

"Alright, I know when to stop. Keep me posted, Katie, and if I can help out, I will. I trust your instincts."

"Which one of your lady friends will be your Valentine date this year?" I asked him, with a valiant attempt to change the subject. "Vicki? Or the widow you do ballroom dancing with?"

"Some things must remain a mystery to my granddaughter," he said. "But I'll send you pictures of the big V-Day celebrations."

"Sounds good."

"Then, Dr. Detective. See if you can figure it out."

Chapter Twenty-Eight

I FORCED MYSELF BACK INTO DETECTIVE MODE. WHAT Gramps said made me think. *Did I know much about Babs and her friends? Or enemies?* I decided to ask Cindy how the cleanup of Babs's home was going.

"Why don't you come over and find out?" she said in a slightly exasperated voice.

"You okay?" I asked her.

"Sorry, but this is sort of rough. I'm thinking about my kids going through my stuff when I'm dead. A great way to spend Saturday night." It was unusual for Cindy to be so morose.

"Want some help?"

"I'd love it," she answered. "Maybe bring a healthy snack over? No chips, please."

"Define healthy."

"Anything Mari doesn't eat. Just joking. I caught her eating some grapes the other day." Cindy had been trying to get Mari to improve her diet since I've known them.

"Okay. See you soon."

Driving into town I debated where to pick up Cindy's snack. A veggie/vegan place had opened up that specialized in salads and sandwiches to go. I figured it should be perfect.

The parking lot of The Green Revolution was surprisingly full. After pulling in, I reached for my backpack then stopped. Two people exited the store holding hands, quickly walking toward a newer-looking SUV. After hopping inside, they paused for a quick embrace and kiss.

The affectionate couple were Rob and Nora, the roommates of the murdered couple José and Alicia. *Interesting.* I'd suspected Rob had a flirting thing going with his receptionist, but now he'd added another woman into the mix. Unlike Mike and me, he didn't seem to care who saw him. It also suggested Rob wasn't overwhelmed with grief.

Nora also appeared to have recovered quickly from her roommate Alicia's death. Maybe they simply found solace together. *Or something like that.*

———————

When Cindy opened the door at Babs's place, she'd been crying. I followed her inside into the living room packed with neatly labeled cardboard boxes—the graceful midcentury modern furniture almost hidden behind stacks of stuff.

"Thanks for coming over," Cindy said, blotting her eyes. She sat down on the sleek sofa, a box of tissues nearby.

I decided to give her a few moments to herself, so I brought the food into the kitchen and looked around for some plates.

"What did you end up getting?" Cindy called out.

"Some sort of veggie quinoa and chickpea thing for you and Caesar salad with grilled chicken for me."

"Thanks. Sounds good," she said with little enthusiasm.

"What's upsetting you so much?" I asked when she joined me at the kitchen table.

She popped open the plastic lid of the premade salad. "I

found her day planner Babs had two trips booked. One trip to Japan and another to Southern Italy and France."

"Was she traveling with anyone?" I hoped Cindy had come up with another name we could contact.

"Doesn't look like it. They're tours. She paid as a single traveler."

It felt wrong eating lunch at Babs's kitchen table while… Once again that image of her lying still on the surgery table overwhelmed me. It must have shown in my face because Cindy admitted, "I'm having a tough time today. Plus, so far we have nothing. Nothing! Only the Xanax in her coffee cup. No clues, no suspects, no one to inherit her stuff. I feel like a big failure."

Cindy hated loose ends. If she saw a problem, she fixed it. This must be an added frustration.

"What can I do to help?" I asked, finishing the final bite of grilled chicken on my salad.

Cindy picked up a notebook and glanced down at one of the pages. "Could you take a look in her office and go through the paperwork in her file cabinet? Don't worry. I removed all the legal stuff. Then tackle her day planner from last year. She's got a stack of old ones, but that's as far as I got. See if you uncover any notations or correspondence about family."

"Okay." After disposing of my trash and recyclables, I made my way down the hallway to the door Cindy had indicated. I didn't expect what was behind her office door.

The room was large, probably five times bigger than my small double-closet-sized office. Someone must have taken down a wall to make this space. Custom off-white wooden bookshelves lined one side, with a built-in wine cooler and bar sink. She'd opted for bright white walls and ceiling, which made the space feel even bigger. Double French doors led to a patio, with stems of slumbering espaliered roses waiting to burst into bloom in spring.

A comfy office chair upholstered in pale gray leather sat in front of two short filing cabinets.

Now I try to store everything on one or more of my electronic devices, but Babs, like Gramps, grew up in a paperwork world. I decided to get an overview of her filing system first, then concentrate on each section individually.

As I expected, both filing cabinets were neat and well organized alphabetically. I passed by the Auto and Garden files, but stopped at Health records. The HIPAA laws didn't matter now. Death cancels privacy, at least in this instance with Cindy as acting executor. I removed the thick file and placed it on the desk.

The file dated back almost fifteen years, with mostly routine visits to a women's health clinic in Kingston. Quickly scanning forward, I came across a record of gall bladder surgery seven years ago and a visit to an internal medicine clinic. So far her only chronic condition seemed to be mild hypertension. The next few years were all routine with once-a-year visits to the women's health center and her primary care physician. Then, I hit pay dirt.

Two years ago, Babs slipped and fell outside the CVS in town on a patch of ice in front of their door. She tore several ligaments in her left knee and suffered a hairline fracture of her kneecap. A lawsuit was filed on her behalf by our victim, Alicia. *Bingo!* Backtracking through the paperwork, I noted that Babs was first seen in the emergency room, then transferred to an orthopedic group that included José. *Bingo again!* For rehab, she went to Rob's Wellness Depot clinic in Oak Falls. *A third Bingo!*

So, two years ago, Babs was in contact with both of the victims and one of the roommates. But the money trail petered out with all of their deaths, or did it? I couldn't see CVS hiring a hit man to wipe everyone out because of a slipping lawsuit.

Nor did I believe a twisted twin sister waited in the wings.

After putting away the medical file, I opened up her investment portfolio. It was complicated, with multiple investments shared by Vanguard and Fidelity, an active e-trade brokerage account, and several dividend statements. I couldn't make sense out of it, but I did come across a familiar name and business card paper-clipped to the top of an investment proposal.

When I told Cindy, she wasn't surprised about the injury, but she was surprised to hear Bruce's name.

"You mean Bruce drew up some kind of investment plan for her? Can you tell if she acted on it or not?"

"Beats me."

"I'll have to copy this and turn it all over to the detectives investigating the murders. Plus notify the estate lawyer."

"Cindy. This is getting weird."

"Very weird." Cindy sat back and stared at the ceiling. "I remember that whole tripping incident," she said, pausing in her inventory and packing. "I visited her in the hospital and a few times in town. But I didn't ask the name of the lawyer or her physical therapist or anything like that. She could still drive herself to her appointments because the injury was to her left knee, so I wasn't that concerned. I know it seems odd that everyone feels interconnected, but Oak Falls is a small town. We shouldn't jump to conclusions."

The headlights moving on the road below flashed and faded.

Cindy didn't think much of this coincidence, but I did.

"You know, you never told me the terms of Babs's will or who the beneficiaries are. I think we were so overwhelmed…"

"I don't think I even read the whole will until a week ago. There was so much else to do as far as identifying her property and protecting it while the lawyer searched for heirs. Plus my regular work at the animal hospital, plus the house, plus the kids."

"You have a very full plate."

Cindy ran a tight ship. Even tight ships can founder. She stood up, stretching her neck and back.

"Honestly, it's overwhelming. There is a large list of beneficiaries, mostly with gifts of jewelry or furniture. The estate is divided in half with close blood relatives receiving one portion and the rest going to animal charities. I suppose I could copy it and go over it with you. I'm probably not supposed to do it, but at this point, I don't care."

Cindy took a few cleansing breaths. "Okay. Feeling better. Back to work."

Working your way through a dead friend's possessions

made you face the inevitable. I thought of Babs planning her vacations, expecting years of comfortable living ahead of her.

"If you want, I'll keep sifting through the paperwork. But there's an additional task to do. I'm going to talk to Bruce."

Chapter Twenty-Nine

A SURPRISE EMAIL POPPED UP IN MY INBOX THE FOLLOW-
ing day. Beginning immediately, Cindy expanded our lunch
hour at the animal hospital to a leisurely two hours. With all
the estate documents and added responsibilities, she desperately needed time to catch up.

"You and Mari deserve a bit of extra time too," she
explained between clients. "Do whatever you want. Get a
massage. Speak to a therapist. Whatever. Just don't expect
this to go on past mid-February."

Pronouncement over, Cindy hurried back to her desk.

That gave us shy of two weeks to "relax."

"I might stay right here and take a nap on the sofa," Mari
told me.

"Take one for me," I quipped. "I'm in detective mode."

During my extended lunch hour, I intended to drop in
on the accounting firm Bruce worked for and scope it out. I
arrived a little before noon. On the off chance he was there,
I'd changed, put on makeup and a nice dress, and brushed
my hair out. When I opened the front door, I immediately
noticed Bruce leaning on the check-in desk, chatting someone up. Dark wood coupled with dark paint cast a gloomy
vibe.

The receptionist, a pleasant-looking blond in her late
thirties, didn't appear to be thrilled with his attention. As I
approached the desk, she said, "Bruce, I'm sorry but I've got

a load of messages to get through. I'll speak to you later." She picked up the landline phone, dialed a number, and turned her back to him.

He moved away, almost running into me. No recognition in his eyes. When I last saw him, I wore a fuzzy hat jammed on my head and a bulky winter jacket with a muffler wrapped around my lower face. Most of his short conversations with us were with Mari. *Did he not remember who I was?*

"Can I help you?" he asked, smoothing his hair.

"I don't have an appointment," I began. The receptionist still had her back to us, working the phones.

"That's okay. Why don't we go into my office so we don't bother anyone?"

There was no one waiting, but I quickly agreed.

"I'm Bruce Ormnis, certified public accountant. And you are…?"

"Kate."

"So, Kate," Bruce didn't bother asking for my last name. He held his office door for me. "What can I help you with today?"

"Ah," I lied, "my grandfather needs to speak to someone about investing his retirement income. Right now, he's relying on some Internet site."

Bruce spluttered away at hearing Internet. "I always recommend that a personal accountant oversee investments, preferably one with asset management training such as I have. Investments should be tailored to his specific needs as an older American."

"Well, he does have a bunch of money market accounts, some stocks, and various items of value."

He picked up a notebook and jotted something down. "Many seniors have complicated portfolios. But, Kate, speed is of the essence. I remember drawing up a proposal for a senior, not too long ago, and before we could implement it, she died."

Bruce looked pretty smug. *Was he talking about Babs?*

"You might have heard about a series of unexpected deaths here in Oak Falls." He continued. "Very unusual, but it proves that you never know when your time will be up." He punctuated this statement with an oddly happy smile.

"That's interesting." I smiled back. "Does my grandfather need copies of his investments to show you?"

"That's probably best. I'll make duplicates for his file. If he forgets any, we can always download them from the Internet. By the way, does he have a current will in place?"

"I'm not sure." I wrinkled my brow as though deep in thought.

"I see. Now, what is your grandfather's name?" Bruce lifted his pen, ready to jot down any information on his notepad. That was my cue to leave.

Glancing at my watch I stood up. "Oh, my. Look how late it is. I've got to go. Thanks so much for your help." I'd already opened his office door by the time he reacted. "I'll call your receptionist and make an appointment if my grandfather decides to pursue this. He's pretty stubborn."

I practically sprinted down the hallway and almost made it out the door before he called after me. "Kate. Perhaps we could discuss this over a drink? I've got the rest of the afternoon free."

Yikes. Bruce didn't care about the ethical dilemma of dating your clients either.

"Sorry. I'm working."

As I sped along the sidewalk I wondered if he tried to date many of his clients. So far, that's two men with wandering eyes, Rob and Bruce, mixed up in the three murders. Maybe this flirting and office romance thing is more common than I knew.

Halfway to the truck, I realized I knew one more person who had recent contact with all three victims. *Mike.*

No. No. No. I thought. *Okay. Get it out of your system. Mike knew Babs very well. Both Alicia and José were his veterinary clients. So what. He probably worked on the days they were murdered. He works all the time.*

Wait. I recalled that Mike texted me from work on the Friday of Babs's death. We went to Judy's. That momentary relief faded when I remembered the rest of what he said. *He was nearby.*

Babs would immediately let him into the hospital. We knew the killer had at least a four-hour window. As a veterinarian, he easily could have staged her murder.

Now I felt like I was going crazy. What sort of motive would he have? Was he Babs's long-lost son adopted out at birth? Such a soap opera plot.

With a huge effort, I moved the idea of Mike being involved out of my mind. Oak Falls is a small town like everyone said. Everybody knows everyone.

A car behind me flashed its lights. I was moving too slowly for his liking.

Enough. I could probably tie everyone in town to the three murder victims. *Just concentrate on facts and stop worrying about the impossible,* I told myself. Still, a little voice whispered, "Please be careful."

═══════════════

Mari and Cindy scurried away as soon as our work finished. Someone mentioned a storm. With the sky overhead appearing more ominous, I decided to swing by the grocery store and stock up on both dog and people food. The packed parking lot meant everyone else had the same idea.

Wandering through the aisles, I concentrated on pantry items, canned goods and plenty of soup and chili. If we got socked in by another storm, Buddy and I wouldn't go hungry. When I pushed my cart down the animal food aisle, I ran into a client staring at the cat food. I remembered the elderly but healthy feline she doted on. The owner held a list of canned foods her kitty would and would not eat.

"Oh, hi, Dr. Kate."

"Hello. Buying cat food?" That wasn't a hard guess.

"Our fur baby is so picky," my client complained. "One day she loves the fancy tuna feast, and the next day she turns up her nose at it."

A common complaint with some cats, I told her. I suggested she try some of the flavor enhancers available on many pet websites. Or she could cook up some of her own. A little roast beef gravy or turkey gravy went a long way toward making canned food taste really delicious. Finally, if she wanted to cook for her pet, our office provided lists of healthy pet food recipes.

I only needed a few cans for Buddy. Bella would be on a special diet for a while. As I loaded my cart with Buddy's favorite food and some treats, my client decided to follow me around, still discussing her cat. I was slightly embarrassed by my detour into the liquor section but shouldn't have worried. She scooped up two jumbo-sized bottles of vodka to my modest bottle of white wine.

"Stocking up in case we get snowed in," she said in a virtuous voice. "You should get another bottle of wine, just in case."

After a side-eye glance, I picked another bottle of wine and deposited it in my cart.

"Good for you," she said and with a wave moved her cart toward the dairy section.

I had the craziest vision of my client and her cat sitting at their kitchen table drinking martinis together while the snowflakes fell.

I'd spent too much time in the grocery store and found myself starving. I decided to stop for takeout, buying two meals so I could eat one immediately and freeze the second. Unable to order while I was driving, I parked toward the back of the Lucky Gardens parking lot. My plan was to call the order in, swing by the pharmacy for a few items, then return to pick up my food. To my surprise, my go-to Chinese restaurant had posted a brand new menu on its web page. I turned off the truck and searched around for something exciting or different. Customers pulled in and out of the parking lot, most dashing in to grab a takeout order.

Trying to decide if I wanted to try the new shrimp with cashews and orange peel, I noticed yet another couple making out in their vehicle. *Better get the kissing in before your breath smells like garlic,* I thought. Still debating, I watched the driver open his door.

To my surprise it was Bruce. Wow. He'd asked me out for drinks only a few hours ago. Dying to know who he'd hooked up with, I stared at the passenger side window. The woman blotting her lips and putting on fresh lipstick looked like Linda Ramsey. As in Linda, who hated Alicia's guts for stealing her husband away.

What the heck? I needed a scorecard to keep all these couples straight.

It felt like playing a game of Six Degrees of Kevin Bacon or Bacon's Law, where you try to prove that every actor in Hollywood has some kind of connection with the award-winning actor. Only the Oak Falls version substituted Alicia for Kevin Bacon. *Poor Alicia, it looks like everyone either loved or hated you—or killed you.*

Not wanting to be seen by Linda or Bruce, I shifted gears and drove to the healthy eating store I'd ordered from the other day. The takeout line had ten people in it, most of them preoccupied with their phones. Since I needed food now, I opted for the fresh packaged meals in the large cooler. In keeping with the green profile, someone had painted all the surfaces green. Even the employees wore multiple shades of green.

Off to the side I saw Missy, Rob's receptionist, perusing the shelves. She held some prepackaged breakfast granola and was squinting, trying to read the label. I maneuvered myself over to a nearby shelf and pretended to be surprised at seeing her.

"Do you mind if I ask you a question?" Stretching the truth, I confessed that Rob had flirted with me and I didn't know how to take it. Was he serious or not? That's all the prompting she needed.

"Rob is into the conquest," his receptionist confided to me. "I can't tell you the number of clients he's been involved with. He's careful, though, to romance them toward the end of their therapy weeks. He can't afford to lose any more clients."

"Why's that?" I asked.

"Our office is a franchise," Missy explained. "The main company sets you up with equipment, advertising, price sheets, etc. Rob has to pay a monthly fee, which he's behind on. We might have to close. Not enough business volume."

"Why are you telling me all this?" I asked as we moved forward in the line with our purchases.

She tilted her head, as though thinking something through. "Because I fell for lover boy's line right after I got the job. I'm trying to save you the trouble."

"Oh." That didn't surprise me at all. I did wonder why she stayed, however.

As if reading my mind, she continued, "I really love my job. The salary is good and the benefits are great. I'm an exercise fanatic, and I get to use all our equipment free of charge, any time I want. Even if the Oak Falls office closes, I'm corporate. They've already offered me a job at the Kingston location."

"I'm happy for you," I said.

"As far as Rob is concerned, I really don't care," she said. "Our relationship was short and mostly sweet. I knew it was a mistake early on, so I suggested we remain friends, to his vast relief. We still flirt with each other and stuff, but mostly out of habit."

That tied in with what I'd witnessed in the rehab/spa reception area the day I dropped in on Rob.

"Let me be honest with you," I said, lowering my voice. "My coworker was murdered, along with a woman named Alicia and her fiancé, José. Rob knew all of them. Do you think he is capable of murder?"

Missy moved in closer. "Not only is he capable, but I really think he's already murdered someone."

What followed turned out to be a convoluted story of a woman patient that Rob started dating while she received physical therapy for a shoulder injury. He'd book out to give her a "private session" in her home. When he ended the affair, she committed suicide by an overdose of barbiturates and alcohol.

"Why do you think he had anything to do with her suicide?" I asked, knowing that overdoses were more common than people realized.

Missy took out a credit card as the line moved along. "I'm not sure. I think she loaned him money or gave him money, too. A sugar mommy, I suppose. Anyway, I've got a whole folder dedicated to Rob."

That made me pause. *She keeps a "folder" of incriminating information on her boss?* Obviously, this woman was no fool. I'd hate to make her mad at me.

"That's interesting." I tried to keep my voice noncommittal.

"He'd also transfer away patients whom he'd become a little too close to, if you get my meaning. That way Rob got rid of them before they'd run into another of his special handling patients. You know," she explained to me as if I didn't catch on, "the other ones he was screwing."

So much for subtlety. "Fascinating. Do you plan on staying at your job?" I asked her.

"Definitely," she answered with a whiter than white smile. "My hiring anniversary is almost here. Corporate has promised to bump up my salary and begin cross-training me in therapeutic massage. Really super opportunity. You get tons of tips with the right sort of massage."

She followed that statement with a raised eyebrow.

Too bad she had dumped Rob. It sounded like they were really made for each other. *Really.*

Driving back home, I was lost in thought when I received a text. I pulled over to the side of the road and read what Mike wrote.

How's your day going? Mine sucks.

My day had also been frustrating. Witnesses and possible suspects were dating each other. Leads petered out for lack of evidence. I'd listened to plenty of gossip but few facts. I felt like the murders of Babs, Alicia, and José would never be solved and that no one cared, except the chief, Cindy, Mari, and me.

Now I found myself viewing Mike with a tinge of caution. Until the chief arrested the murderer, I vowed not to give my heart away.

Another text: Spinning my wheels. Want to meet for coffee?

I might as well meet him. In case he did become a valid suspect. What kind of logic that was I didn't know. But talking to him made me feel better.

Sure. Meet you at judy's in 30 min?
K. See you then.

With not much time, I turned into the animal hospital parking lot and ran inside. I put away the groceries, and because I was starving, I stood over the sink and ate half my takeout. After changing my clothes and walking Buddy and Bella, I brushed my hair and put on a touch of lipstick.

"Be good," I told the dogs before I left. Buddy picked up his new chew bone and seemed to ask *what's your hurry*?

When I reached the truck, I was startled to see a crow sitting on the hood. For warmth, I wondered? Or simply to say hello?

Deep in my coat pocket I found one stray treat, so I called to the bird and held it up for him to see. As soon as I caught his attention, I put it down.

The crow quickly flew over, cawing all the way. That's when I noticed he'd left me a present. A silver bottle cap sat on the truck hood.

When I drove out of the parking lot, I saw out of my rearview mirror all three crows sharing their snack.

Mike waved to me when I walked into Judy's Café. He'd scored a table by the window, toward the back of the room. He stood up when I reached the table and helped me off with my coat.

"How is your day going?" he asked when I sat down.

"Obviously better than yours," I answered.

"Well," he began, "I had one of those depressing mornings when I had to tell several clients in a row some bad news about their pets."

Clients don't think about how their vets feel when they diagnose kidney failure or cancer in one of their animal patients. It hurts us too. Then, when you have back-to-back bad news to share, upset clients crying in the exam rooms, their sadness becomes your sadness. Maybe that contributes to the high suicide rate in veterinarians.

To make him feel better, I said, "One of my mentors in vet school used to tell us over and over that we have to embrace all aspects of life, from birth to death. We're lucky in a way that in veterinary medicine we don't have to let our pets suffer."

Mike nodded. "It doesn't make it easier."

"No, it doesn't." I reached over and took his hand. *How could I have ever suspected this kind man of murder?*

We stayed there holding hands until the waiter interrupted us.

"Can I get you some coffee?" he asked.

"Yes. And what are your specials today?" Judy usually

wrote them on her blackboard behind the bar, but it was too far away for me to read.

"We've got a mushroom quiche with salad and the desert is apple-peach pie from the Oak Falls Diner."

"Do you need more time?" I asked Mike. By then we'd discreetly stopped holding hands and focused on the menu.

"I'll have the special," Mike said, "with a piece of pie."

"Just the pie for me," I told the waiter, who wrote down our order and scurried away.

"For a change of pace," I said. "Let me tell you about my day." I tried to create a synopsis of what I'd been doing, but Mike interrupted.

"You're working at the animal hospital and trying to solve three murders on your lunch hour?" he asked.

"Sounds crazy when someone else says it," I replied.

Mike laughed. "That's not what I meant. Solving puzzles is what we do as doctors. I think it's natural your curiosity spills over into solving a crime. Especially if the deceased is a friend and the police aren't making much headway."

His answer made complete sense. "I'm so glad you said that."

"Of course," he added. "I don't want you to get hurt."

"I always keep my pepper spray close. My Gramps insisted on it," I told him.

"Your Gramps is a smart man," Mike said. "I better watch my step around you."

We chatted away, eager to learn more about each other and quickly discovered we'd taken many of the same courses, often taught by the same professor during vet school. Mike also needed to pay down his student debt, which is why he drove an old car. I didn't even own a vehicle. Part of my contract gave me the right to use the hospital's old F-150 work truck, covered by their insurance. When Doc Anderson came back, that would stop, and I'd have the expense of buying a car and finding a place to live.

"One thing for sure is that this job has reinforced my confidence in running a practice, of course with a great support team in place." I thought of how dependent I'd become on Cindy and Mari to make things run smoothly.

Mike nodded in agreement. "Here are my dilemmas. To concentrate on private practice or retreat to academia? Or continue in a mixed- or large-animal practice? Or try my hand with exotics again?"

That debate would have to wait since our food arrived, along with a freshening of our coffee. "Anything else?" our server asked.

"Not for me," I said.

"We're good," said Mike. "Which reminds me. We got way off our subject, and I know this investigation is bothering you."

"It is," I told him. What I didn't share was my running around town in my free time speaking to roommates, friends, and enemies of the victims.

"I've been mulling over what you said," Mike continued. "And I think the key to this whole thing is Babs."

"Why would you say that?"

He leaned back and took a sip of coffee. "Let's start from the assumption that Babs didn't kill Alicia or José."

"Right."

"So why was she murdered? It must be because she knew or suspected who did it. Track Babs's coming and going in the days between the couple's death and her death. I bet you'll find something that doesn't add up."

That was a good suggestion, but during most of that time frame Babs had worked at Oak Falls Animal Hospital. After I told Mike of my misgivings, he asked an obvious question.

"Have you spoken to the family who lives behind her?"

I had to admit they were on my list. Then something else occurred to me. "That means I need to go over our list of patients we saw during those last couple of days. Could the murderer be one of our clients?"

"Anything's possible," Mike said.

Before we paid our checks, I shared a picture of Bella.

"That looks like demodex," he said. "I remember in vet school treating a rescue puppy like her in clinics. One of the students adopted her, and in six months you'd never have known she'd been ill."

"That's what I'm hoping."

"She's a pretty little thing," he added.

Trust Mike to look past the bad and see the good.

Our farewells at Judy's were sedate, with a mild peck on the cheek—considering it felt like everyone in the café was observing us, including Judy. Between his office and my office, we counted many residents as clients. Call me old-fashioned, but it didn't seem professional for their local veterinarians to be making out in public.

In private was another matter.

The threatening storm clouds rolled past Oak Falls pushed along by an unexpectedly fast-moving arctic wind. I'd enjoyed being with Mike. I felt guilty putting him on the suspect list. *Could someone so kind be so cruel?*

Chapter Thirty

AFTER MEETING MIKE, I MADE A LIST OF THE PEOPLE I
needed to contact. I felt as though the sluggish cloud of
shock over Babs's death was lifting. My usual organizational
skills had taken a hit investigating a tragedy this personal.
After watering the houseplants and playing with Buddy and
Bella, I strode into the clinic the following morning with a
newfound enthusiasm.

No one's mood matched mine.

Over the usual breakfast coffee, I tried to rope Mari and
Cindy into my sleuthing plans, but this time the idea hit a
wall. Mari shared that she'd just climbed out of the "blues"
and didn't want to be pulled back under by even thinking
of murderers among us. Cindy informed me that the paperwork and time commitment serving as the executor of Babs's
estate took up most of her free time.

An unexpected gloom hung in the air.

"The lawyers sent out letters to all the beneficiaries
mentioned in the will and used public records to try and
find a next of kin," she said while staring at her computer.
"I'm still going through her files and boxing things up.
My hubby protested, so I can only devote a few hours
of my time on the weekend. It's going very slowly. We're
trying to hire someone to help, but the money needs to be
approved."

"Let me help. Just tell me when and where," I said. For

some reason all the Valentine decorations in the reception area seemed cheery today. "I'll do it for free."

"Thanks, Kate." Cindy walked over to one of the computer screens. "But you don't have much free time either. Everything must be meticulously documented for the court. At first I thought my family could help, but it's certainly not a job for my teenager. Or most people I know. It's also more emotionally draining than I realized."

I waited for her to finish.

"Look. I'm behind on the hospital monthly supplies order. I'll talk to you later." Her focus shifted away as she began typing vigorously on the computer keypad. Through the office picture window, I noticed snow beginning to fall.

I snuck back to my office without her noticing.

My Gramps always said to cut the people around you some slack. I'd found human behavior to be less predictable than animal behavior. Very rarely did I get tricked, scratched, or bitten by my furry patients. Most people I've met over the years turned out to be great; however, a select few were devious, self-serving, or downright liars.

And some were killers.

Chapter Thirty-One

"YOUR CAT HAS FELINE ACNE," I TOLD THE YOUNG COUPLE in front of me holding a wide-eyed orange tabby.

"He's got what?" the boyfriend said, leaning back on the exam room wall.

"Fela-what?" his girlfriend asked. "Is it cancer? Is he going to die?"

All three stared at me the same panic in their eyes. I decided to use nonmedical terms. "Your cat has zits. Blackheads on his chin."

"Cats can get zits? But he's a year old."

Mari pried Gingersnap off his owner's shoulder and placed him on the exam table. The handsome housecat sized up the situation quickly, his yellow eyes checking me out. I put my hands on him, petting him while examining his musculature. I immediately felt him relax.

Cats can feel the people who know and love them.

He purred so loudly I couldn't hear his heart, so I blew in his face. Startled, he stopped long enough for me to listen. In general, there is a higher prevalence of heart disease in male cats than females, especially purebred Maine Coon, Persians, Cornish and Devon Rex, and the hairless Sphynx. Nonpurebred Gingersnap's heart sounded strong and healthy.

We got down to his obvious problem. I'd noticed from experience that most orange cats have dark freckles on their lips and nose pads. Those are normal. The inflamed black-heads on his chin were not.

Some cats are more prone to getting acne, I explained. We start by advising owners to stop using plastic bowls, and instead switch to metal or ceramic and clean them often in the dishwasher. I suggested buying multiple water and food dishes, so there's always a clean one. If you feed your kitty wet food, you need to clean his chin after eating—like you would a toddler. Some kitties tolerate an astringent cleaning pad, while others prefer a hypoallergenic baby wipe. Once the problem is resolved, it often comes back. Checking your pet's chin periodically is a good idea.

The couple bobbed their heads like they understood, but I'd have Mari demonstrate the cleaning technique for them later. As always, we'd send the client home with a printout on their cat's problem.

"I'd like to give Gingersnap's chin a good cleaning," I told them. "Can you leave him here with us for a while?"

Their faces burst out in grins. "Sure. We've got errands to run and haven't eaten lunch yet."

Mari piped up. "You can pick him up any time after three. We close at five tonight," she warned them. Since we rarely got out before five thirty or six p.m., this extra half hour to forty-five minutes was our built-in buffer time for clients who might be running late.

Under the bright adjustable surgical light over the treatment table, I took a close look at Gingersnap's chin.

"Are you going to pop them like that pimple doctor on TV?" Mari asked with a little too much enthusiasm, her bad mood gone.

"Some need to be expressed," I replied, sticking to medical terminology. "We'll see as we go along."

Gingersnap stared at us with intelligent yellow eyes. He knew something was up. With only a slight tensing of his back legs as a warning, he catapulted into the air in full escape mode.

Mari played defense and caught him like a football with claws. She pressed him into her chest while I opened a top cage door. My assistant planted the cat behind the bars for a touchdown, while I sealed the point by closing and locking the cage.

"He's an escape artist," I warned Mari, flicking the stainless-steel lever that double-locked the door.

Every vet and vet assistant has a story about a pet that escaped. Most often it is a cat. Cat escape tales abound when people in the animal care profession get together.

My favorite story starred a small semiferal cat that knocked out a suspended ceiling panel and spent two weeks living in the crawl space above the animal hospital. Every day the staff put out food in a Have-A-Heart trap, and every morning they'd come in to no food and no cat. Finally, an intricate baited tunnel system did the trick. Cats will take advantage of any opening, like holes in the drywall around pipes left by plumbers or behind banks of cages. Eventually, all kitties are caught, to the relief of everyone concerned.

Gingersnap didn't know it, but he was up against a formidable team consisting of Mari, Cindy, and me. Now that we knew he wasn't going to play nice, we brought out the dreaded towel.

Since his chin acne was the target, the plan involved wrapping him up like a burrito in a towel, thus limiting his movement. At least, that was the plan.

Placing the towel on the stainless-steel treatment table, we held Gingersnap firmly and deposited him on the towel. After a few minutes of calm petting, we started to slowly wrap him up, making sure he was in a comfortable position—similar to swaddling a newborn covered with fur. Mari finished in under a minute.

"Duct tape?"

"Why not?"

She secured the towel with the tape no one should be without, attaching the towel to itself, being careful not to catch any kitty fur. To relax our patient, we stroked the cat's head and ears and made nice. A thoughtful look shone in Gingersnap's yellow eyes. He focused on the top of the cages.

"Keep hugging him to you," I advised my assistant. "He's casing the joint."

Cat chin fur is very short. I didn't want to upset our patient any more by shaving it off. Between the noise and smell and feel, I know if I were a cat I would try to bolt. Most of his zits were clustered on one side, so before we started, I checked his teeth. With tooth or mouth pain, an animal gets in the habit of chewing on the side that doesn't hurt. His teeth appeared fine, so I ruled that out as a contributing cause.

"Mari," I said, "can you scratch the top of his head?" This move was to divert sensation away from his chin while I worked on it.

Since I had a fondness for dermatology, getting rid of blackheads and cleaning the area with a mild astringent suited me just fine. A barrier protected the cat's eyes and nose from the fumes. Once confined, Gingersnap lay perfectly still in stoic silence broken periodically by a plaintive high-pitched meow.

"Good work," Mari said. "Maybe next time I have a pimple…"

"No dice. If you've got no fur, it won't occur."

"Funny."

Since one of the zits was infected and swollen, I administered a shot of antibiotics. The owners would have their hands full cleaning Gingersnap's chin each day, without also having to force a pill into him twice a day.

Once in his cage and free of the towel, Gingersnap bore no grudge, but brushed against the cage bars, demanding to be petted. His loud purrs and loving demeanor said *I would never do anything bad, Doc, I promise. Trust me.* We still double-locked the cage door.

That afternoon on my long lunch hour, I sat on the sofa with both dogs, unwinding from the morning appointments. I thought about Cindy, working her way through her friend's possessions, Bruce finding the first bodies, and Mari's trauma seeing another body trapped under the ice.

I began to write down random thoughts in my notebook. Why was Bruce up there in the woods? Did Alicia's mother-in-law back off her Facebook posts now that her target was dead? Who benefits from these murders? Is there a money trail somewhere? What about Alicia's stalker? Could Greg Owens, who filed a lawsuit against José for the death of his wife, have taken justice into his own hands?

And why was Mike so sure that Babs's murder was the key to everything? I texted Mike for an answer but didn't get a text back.

Unable to relax, I opened my laptop, cleared the kitchen table, and stared at the notes I'd jotted down. I'd started a file on the investigation but hadn't opened it recently.

The file began well enough, with a column of facts on each victim. A spreadsheet attempted to cross-reference jobs, friends, loved ones, etc. Other pages held random notations that catalogued rumors and interviews with acquaintances of the victims. I'd even written down ten reasons why Bruce must be the killer. The reasons sounded lame even to me, but I highlighted his name in yellow anyway.

After going through the entire notebook, I came up short.

I didn't want to add to Cindy's stress, but I had some specific questions she and/or the chief probably knew the answers to. After making yet another list, I called her cell.

"I'm so sorry to bother you," I began before she interrupted.

"No worries. I really need a break." Cindy groaned a bit then continued, "What's up?"

"I'm trying to prepare some sort of a time line and connections chart on Babs, José, and Alicia, and I have to ask a few questions, if you don't mind."

"Fire away."

"Ah, okay. Did Bruce tell the police what he was doing up in the forest?"

She thought a moment. "He said he was thinking of ice fishing and went to check out the lake. After he found the body, he insisted to the chief he panicked because of a case of severe shock."

Right. Listening carefully, I wrote down the official story Bruce gave the police. It brought back recollections of his panicked voice and clear evidence of vomiting in the snow. Was he simply a jerk in the wrong place at the wrong time?

"What about Rob, José's roommate?" I asked her.

"What about him?"

"Did the police check his alibi?"

There was a rustle of papers, then she answered. "Sorry. Doing two things at the same time. Yes, I believe he was cleared by his girlfriend."

"Which one?" I quipped. Rob had an active social life.

"That I don't know. I'll have to get back to you."

Another thought bothered me. "What will happen if a blood relative of Babs's can't be found? And why aren't they using DNA to find them?"

"Babs refused to have her DNA on any of those geneal-ogy sites. That's what's taking so long. If no close relative is found, all of her assets go to animal-based charities."

The idea of an enthusiastic animal lover wiping out three people for the money sounded ludicrous. I sensed Cindy fading, so I asked her one last question. "Did you know Alicia? What did you think of her?"

This time there was a longer pause. "I only saw her one time. Alicia was the most beautiful woman I've ever met. Every man in the room stared at her as well as most of the women. In her pictures she's lovely, but in person—she was exceptionally gorgeous. Like a model in a magazine."

That made me think. I'd seen two photos of José and Alicia together, one close-up with both in profile gazing at each other, and one long, full-length hugging. Neither showed her face completely. In person, I'd only seen Alicia staring up at me with wide frozen eyes.

My text chime pinged. Mike told me he'd been suturing up a large laceration on a rambunctious foal. A second chime contained photos of the wound, before and after. I sent back a close-up of Gingersnap's chin.

Who knew enough about Alicia to fill in the blanks? I decided to start with her sister, Ursula.

"Thank you so much for taking my call," I said over the phone after introducing myself. "I'm not with the police..."

"Good. They haven't made much progress." She cleared her throat and asked, "Why are you investigating then? Are you some kind of Internet troll?" Her strong angry voice resonated in my ear. "I'm hanging up unless you immediately tell me who you are."

Quickly, I briefly explained who I was. No reaction—until I mentioned Babs.

"Babs worked with you at the animal hospital?" Ursula asked. "Alicia admired her."

Finally, someone who connected Babs and Alicia.

Sliding the journal over, I began to take notes. "Yes, we

worked together. Babs worked relief jobs all over the valley. In fact, before she died, she mentioned Alicia and José."

The sound of someone blowing their nose exploded in my ear. I waited, pen in hand, until she gathered her thoughts.

"José was crazy in love with my sister. But then that's the effect she had on men. They flew out over Christmas and stayed with me here in Santa Barbara. Both were miserable and wanted to leave New York, so I told them I'd help." She choked back a sob, muffling the receiver.

Listening to someone's raw pain made me feel helpless.

"Sorry," she said. "It hits me at random moments that I'm not going to see my baby sister again."

Her remark resonated because it was the first time I'd heard someone express sadness on the couple's passing in such a horrific way. I wondered why.

"Ursula," I began. "I never met Alicia. Can you tell me about your sister?"

That was all she needed. A sea of remembrance poured out, the story of a beloved younger sister who'd been spoiled by the entire family. Alicia growing from a charming, beautiful child into a popular teenager. Prom queen, head cheerleader, on the swim team…

"Wait," I said. "Alicia was on the swim team in high school?" Babs mentioned this too.

"Yes," replied Ursula. "She also made the swim team in college, but she quit after freshman year. It took too much time, and the chlorine ruined her hair."

Now was not the time to discuss the irony of her sister's body being found in a frozen lake. A horrible thought struck me. Had Alicia been conscious for part of her murder, submerged in the ice? Swimmers are trained to hold their breath. The cause of death was strangulation, but did consciousness leave before or after she went into the lake?

To spare Ursula pain, I concentrated on Alicia's past.

"Babs once told me that Alicia had problems with a boy in high school. Do you know anything about that?"

"Yeah. A nerdy guy in one of her classes. Math, I think. They ate pizza after class, and he thought it was a date. When she set him straight, he stalked her. She confronted him. Said she'd report him to the police when he suddenly apologized and asked if they could remain friends."

"Did he keep his promise?" I asked her.

"I think so. She didn't have any other problems with him that I heard about. One of her boyfriends died in a car accident, senior year of high school," Ursula added. "A one-car, late-night thing. His vehicle went into a lake. Truthfully, I didn't pay that much attention because I had a job scouting film locations. My mom would know, but she's in a care facility for dementia."

"I'm sorry," I told her. "You and Alicia were the only children?"

"Yes. Mom and Dad adopted me first from China. I was more than three years old by the time they brought me back to the States. About a year later they got pregnant with Alicia. They called her their miracle baby."

"How did she end up in Oak Falls?" I asked.

"Our dad grew up near Rhinebeck and we used to visit our grandparents out there most summers. After high school

Alice applied to a fast-track college law program in Albany. She wanted to see seasons and snow and get a fresh start after her boyfriend died. Later she applied for an internship at the law firm in Kingston. There she met James, and you know the rest."

I didn't know all the details, but Ursula filled me in.

For the next ten minutes Alicia's big sister told a story of a young woman who rebounded from the death of her boyfriend into the arms of an older married man—a man who lied and told her he had separated from his wife. By then, madly in love, she insisted he get a divorce. The day after the divorce decree was finalized they eloped and flew away on an expensive honeymoon in Paris.

But the romance quickly faded, Ursula said. Alicia was hounded on social media. James's kids all hated him and needed therapy. His income dropped, as more and more clients learned of the divorce drama. The couple fought and eventually separated. Alicia flew out to California to visit her sister and mother and said she'd been thinking of trying to save her marriage. Before she talked to James, he committed suicide.

"That's a lot of tragedy for one person to deal with."

"It was," Ursula agreed. "I was so happy when she met José. They decided to make a clean start, elope, and move to California. I've got a separate guesthouse that they were welcome to use until they got settled."

"It sounds idyllic."

"It was perfect. Everything was perfect. What the hell happened? It feels like a nightmare I never wake up from."

There was no answer I could give her.

"Listen," Ursula said, "I've got plenty of money. Maybe I should hire a private investigator? What do you think?"

"That's a good idea. Can your PI do some deep background checking on a few people I'm curious about?"

"Of course. Send me their names. And Kate, I'm so glad you called me. It's hard waiting for the police to contact me every week only to tell me nothing. At least now I feel I'm doing something."

I knew exactly how she felt.

With the unexpected help from Alicia's sister, I became more optimistic. Maybe something unexpected would turn up. Small towns are funny. Most of the people who lived in Oak Falls had lived here their entire lives, but there were plenty of temporary residents and new residents, either seasonal or work related. Their pasts unknown. *Like me. And Mike.*

———

Cindy kept her head down when she returned to the employee lounge. For once she carried no packed lunch from home. Instead she held a professionally wrapped sandwich, coupled with a diet soda.

Mari almost exploded in her chair. "What are you eating?"

"I had a fight with the hubby last night," she told us. Cindy folded herself into one of our more comfortable chairs and slid it up to the table. As we watched she popped open the soda can and took a swig directly from the can.

Now I was shocked. Cindy never ever drank from the can and hadn't drunk a soda in all the time I'd been working at the animal hospital. She swore they tasted of metal.

A tiny belch escaped from her mouth. "Bubbles," she explained. "They give me gas."

"Technically bubbles are gas," I said, still in a state of shock. I'd sat through endless lectures about healthy eating from our receptionist. It felt bizarre—like watching Mahatma Gandhi chow down on a hamburger.

Mari's reaction focused on the practical. "What's in that sandwich?"

"It's the deli special—the works."

"The works?" I repeated. A strong smell of pickles and pepperoni wafted from the sandwich wrapper. This from a person who railed against processed foods and too much salt in most American diets.

"He wants me to have the lawyers hire someone to help catalog all of Babs's stuff. I've cut back on my weekend work, but he complains he never sees me." A large bite of sandwich emphasized her statement.

"Maybe that's not a bad idea," I told her.

Mari swiveled her head away from the sandwich back to Cindy, mesmerized. "Chip?" she asked holding out a large bag of Fritos.

Our receptionist paused for another gulp of soda then said, "Sure. Might as well lose all credibility."

I decided not to share with my friends right now the lengthy conversation with Alicia's sister, Ursula. Instead, we laughed and joked while the planet Earth spun under our

feet and Cindy belched. I thought we still had plenty of time
to catch a killer.

The calendar inched toward Valentine's Day. Mike texted
me about dinner plans. We'd left planning things a little too
late. Most restaurants had only very early reservations left or
super late ones. Although I'm not terribly fussy about those
things, I didn't want to eat dinner at four fifteen in the afternoon or ten thirty at night.

"Let's keep trying," I advised him, "and take any reasonable time available."

"Too bad Valentine's Day is in February. If it were in
springtime, we could have a picnic. The only things we can
eat outside now are popsicles and ice cream."

The idea of sharing popsicles in the snow made me smile.
"I'll take a Popsicle-sharing rain check."

"You're on." The sound of Mike's beeper interrupted us.
"Sorry, got to go. I'll call you tonight."

After we hung up, I realized Mike's picnic in the snow image
brought me back to a fundamental question that kept bothering me. What were José and Alicia doing at Lover's Lake?

After making a list of questions, I decided to call Alicia's
roommate, Nora. I have to admit I was also curious as to
why she was smooching Rob, José's roommate, in a Chinese
restaurant parking lot. She picked up on the fourth ring.

"Hi, Nora? This is Dr. Turner over at the Oak Falls
Animal Hospital."

"Dr. Kate. Thanks so much for following up with Sparky. He's doing great."

"You're welcome." This was going pretty well so far. "Do you mind me asking a few more questions about Alicia and José?"

"Sure," she said. "Anything to help find their killer."

"Do you have any idea what they were doing in the woods up by Lover's Lake?"

"That's easy. They got engaged there last June. José and Alicia used to picnic up there and swim during the summer."

"They swam in the lake?" That surprised me, though I'm not sure why.

"Yuck, I know. There are fish and plants and who knows what in that water, but they didn't mind. I prefer to swim in the rock quarry by High Falls or a pool, someplace where I don't have to worry about stepping on squishy stuff."

Nora's focus tended to shift. I needed to move along. "So they knew that area pretty well."

"It was one of their favorite spots. José in particular liked it because of the quiet. They both had pretty hectic jobs and liked to chill on the weekends." In the background I heard Sparky barking.

"Is that where they wanted to get married?"

Over the phone I heard her begin to respond then stop. "Let me think a moment," she replied. I waited while she thought things over. I hoped she wasn't taking the extra time to conjure up a lie.

"Alicia didn't tell me exactly, but my impression was that they were going to elope. I suppose they might have used Lover's Lake as their venue, but I'm not sure."

If that was true, then I needed to find out if Alicia and

José had applied for a wedding license. Were they planning to have the ceremony when they were killed?

"Thanks, Nora." I tried to phrase my next question as casually as possible. "By the way, I saw you and Rob outside the Chinese restaurant the other night. I didn't know you two were dating."

"It's recent. We got thrown together so much after the murders that one thing led to another…and you know."

I didn't know. But I wanted to find out.

———

The next morning before appointments started, I let slip that Rob and Nora were dating.

"Old news," Cindy commented while taking a small bite of her breakfast bar. "My hubby and I saw them making out in front of the grocery store about a week ago, right near the entrance. What do you kids call it? PDA? Public display of affection? They were pretty into it."

"Yuck," Mari said and took another bite of her jelly doughnut. "You'd think they'd have a little more…"

"Sensitivity?"

Cindy jumped in with a change of subject. "That reminds me of the kissing booth the football coach set up one year in my high school. The cheerleaders and the football players sold kisses for two bucks."

"Gross," said Mari. "Did you do it?"

"Yep. It was a different time then. No one objected, but the experiences were very uneven."

"What do you mean?" I asked.

"Well the jocks all got sweet kisses and giggles from the girls lining up, but the cheerleaders got guys trying to play tonsil hockey and cop a feel."

"Double gross," Mari stated in disbelief.

"Afterward we ratted to our parents, and that pretty much ended the kissing booth situation. To be replaced by the high school car wash to raise money for the team."

"Right," Mari said. "Guys in regular clothes and cheerleaders in tight tops and short skirts. Women grow up thinking that kind of stuff is normal. Football, football, football. Did anyone hold fundraisers for the girls' teams? Don't get me started."

As we finished cleaning up and getting ready for our first appointment, Mari's observation sparked a thought. Alicia was painted as a home-wrecker and flirt, but it took two to do that kind of cheating tango.

Chapter Thirty-Two

IT WAS THE START OF A BRAND NEW DAY, AND MY FIRST appointment began in a normal fashion. The young couple, Caleb and Portia, were in their twenties and had brought their fluffy Pomeranian dog Cutie-Pie in for her annual physical and shots.

We chatted a bit about their pet's history. While we talked, Cutie-Pie snuggled sweetly on her mommy's chest. When the boyfriend came near his girlfriend, the Pomeranian snarled.

That's not good, I thought.

I asked Mari to put Cutie-Pie on the stainless-steel exam table. She seemed fine with Mari and me, even allowing us to check her teeth with no resistance. Caleb and Portia had just become engaged, they confided. Everyone was pleased for them except the dog.

"Why don't you tell me about it?" I asked.

"Cutie-Pie poops in Caleb's shoes whenever she can," Phoebe began in a hesitant voice, "and on his side of the bed. She also chewed up his wallet and peed on his bath towel."

Caleb's face registered his disgust. "She's taking her revenge on me."

"But I love this smooshy baby so much." Phoebe held the dog up to her cheek and proceeded to cover her dog's face with kisses. Caleb reached over to pet her and, like a snapping turtle, this ball of fluff came close to biting off his fingers.

"Mari," I said, "why don't you take Cutie-Pie into the treatment area for her blood test? I'll be there in a few minutes." She nodded, slid the little orange fluff-ball into her arms, and hightailed it out before the Pomeranian could protest.

With Cutie-Pie safely out of the exam room, the couple moved closer, his arm around her waist. Time for Dog Psychology 101.

"Phoebe, can you tell me how you got Cutie-Pie and at what age?" The easy questions would come first.

"Well," she smiled at her boyfriend then continued, "a friend from work said her next-door neighbor's Pomeranian had had puppies. She knew I wanted a small dog, so she told me and I went over and completely fell in love with her. I've never had a dog before. She's my little baby."

"What about you?" I asked Caleb. "Did you have dogs growing up?"

A wide grin relaxed his handsome face. "Always. But mostly golden retrievers and lab mixes. I've got four brothers. Lots of rough and tumble in our house. We'd go hiking and camping with our dogs. They loved to play Frisbee."

Cutie-Pie was about the size of a Frisbee.

"It sounds like your pets were part of the family," I noted. "So you're used to handling dogs."

"Right. Which makes me so frustrated that Cutie-Pie hates me."

"She doesn't hate you," protested Phoebe.

"Oh, yes she does," countered the fiancé.

Oops. Trouble in paradise.

"I'm going to give you the names of some animal behavioral specialists and links to some literature."

"Is there anything we can do in the meantime?" Caleb asked.

"Of course. Think of this situation from the dog's point of view. She's always had her mommy, that's you, Phoebe, in her life. Everything was fine until Caleb showed up and you stopped paying as much attention to your Pomeranian. She sees no reason to share her mommy with you, Caleb. So, I would suggest you change things up. First, Caleb should be the only one feeding her dinner and giving her treats. Every day he needs to go through basic commands and reward her. Phoebe, you can buckle her harness on and attach the leash, but then let Caleb take her for a walk. Alone. What we're trying to do is establish Caleb as another source of good things, like food. Does Cutie-Pie like other dogs? You might consider some play dates with another small dog."

"She adores playing with that Jack Russell terrier at the park." They both nodded in agreement.

"You have to remember that Pomeranians are an ancient dog breed descended from the Spitz. They were guard dogs and companions to the wealthy, especially the British aristocracy."

"Are you writing this down, honey?" Caleb said to Phoebe, who had an astonished look on her face.

"Ah,…"

"Don't worry. Our receptionist will supply you with all this information, and I'll include it in my treatment notes. Now, let me draw the blood for her blood panel, and we'll have the three of you out of here as soon as we can."

Following me out to reception, I handed them over to Cindy.

In the treatment room Mari had set up for the blood draw, she had Cutie-Pie stashed under her arm.

"How's she been with you?" I walked over and let Cutie-Pie sniff then lick my fingers.

"A perfect little doll."

"She's got a bad case of 'Don't Touch My Mommy'. It helps that she's naturally sweet tempered. Behavior therapy should work well—if they follow the guidelines. The weakest link is going to be Phoebe."

"Cutie-Pie is her baby."

"And her baby has very sharp teeth."

It only took a moment to draw blood from the tiny, fluffy leg while Mari distracted her.

"See if they brought a harness and leash," I told Mari. "We might as well start now."

If the couple didn't have a harness, I would strongly recommend one. Little dogs are prone to collapsed tracheas, which makes them have a honking cough sound after straining at their collar. Constant pressure on and trauma to the trachea may lead to difficulty breathing and, worst case scenario for an older dog, heart failure.

A harness also makes it harder for these tiny dogs to slip out of their collar and leash and go AWOL.

Mari came back with a pink harness studded with rhinestones and a matching lead. After slipping the ten-pound Pomeranian into it, I commanded her to sit and stay and shake hands with me, all of which she dutifully complied with. I rewarded her with a tiny piece of dog treat.

When I arrived back in reception, Phoebe raced over to be with her beloved pet. "Tell you what," I said. "You go ahead and pet her, but I'm going to hand the leash to Caleb."

With that I placed the dog on the floor and handed him the leash and bag of dog treats. Both man and beast appeared astonished.

"Tell her to sit and then give her a small treat with a big fuss. Continue that several times today. Remember, Phoebe, Caleb feeds Cutie-Pie her meals and does the walking. She must learn to associate him with fun. And she needs to sleep in her own bed for now, not with you two."

Phoebe stared in amazement, watching Cutie-Pie sit like a champ and take her treat nicely.

"Please call or email me if you have any questions. It's been very nice meeting you. I'll let you settle up with Cindy."

"Thanks so much, Dr. Kate. We just got engaged, and Cutie-Pie was the only bump in the road." Phoebe held her ring up so we could admire it. "Everyone, have a Happy Valentine's Day."

Another engagement, another happy couple. If they followed the advice of the animal behaviorist, I believed they could solve this problem.

Obsessive love. Jealous vindictive love. You see it in people and in animals that fixate on one person. That one being is all they want, all they need. And when they can't have them—they show their teeth.

Sitting in front of my computer answering my email I realized I now knew quite a lot about Alicia and Babs, but next to nothing about the lawsuit brought against José by

Greg Owen. I thought back to my conversation with Rob, that José was being sued. I went on to the Internet and, sure enough, his Instagram account, Facebook, and professional profile were still up and running. He had worked at an orthopedic practice in Kingston.

Even the dead keep an online presence.

I went back to finishing up my paperwork, feeling a little frustrated. I couldn't show up at a medical practice asking personal questions. Access to the doctors were limited to patients.

My search for Greg Owens, the grieving widower, revealed his wife's obituary and the lawsuit. As far as the Internet knew, Greg Owens had no past.

———

Lunchtime offered me the perfect opportunity to snoop closer to home. I fetched my lunch from the employee fridge and sat down. Cindy and Mari were in yet another heated conversation about uniform colors, their heads deep in a veterinary apparel catalog.

"I hate yellow," Mari told Cindy. "It makes me look jaundiced."

Cindy smiled, knowing this was the beginning of decision-making.

"Kate. What color is a no for you?" she asked.

"Pink. Or any neon colors. You two can decide, just make sure there are a lot of pockets." Although I wore a deep-pocketed white coat over my scrubs, at the end of the day

I still had scraps of paper, sticky notes, and packs of gum in various pockets, not to mention my stethoscope, tongue depressors, tape, and assorted debris.

"I'm not sure if that makes it easier," Mari said, taking a bite of her sandwich.

"Tell you what. You guys choose your favorites, then I'll be the tiebreaker. Okay?"

Cindy reluctantly agreed to delegate some of her control.

With peace temporarily in place, I jumped right in with questions about José.

"I thought you were looking for the murderer," Cindy said. "José was a victim. Why are you asking us about him?"

"It's because I know nothing about him. Maybe the murders involve something in his past. Or his recent life in Oak Falls."

Mari began. "I know someone who saw him for a back sprain, and they liked him very much. He treated the immediate pain problem and gave them referrals for a pain clinic and a spinal specialist."

That sounded like standard care, nothing odd about it. "Anything more personal?"

After another bite of sandwich, Mari shook her head. "I did glimpse Alicia and José having lunch at Judy's. They were sitting in front of the picture window when I walked by. I only remember because I noticed how lovely she was. Really eye-catching natural beauty."

Not much help, unfortunately. "What about you, Cindy? Did you know José?"

Cindy answered with a shake of her head. "I mean he

was familiar in town. I think he grew up in High Falls, or Saugerties, or somewhere nearby. I'm pretty sure he was a bowler, because my hubby and I saw him several times on our league bowling night. We didn't know him very well, just enough to say 'hi' and 'how's it going.'"

So far, our conversations had been a bust. I was thinking about how I would approach his coworkers at the orthopedic clinic he'd worked at when Cindy added, "Maybe you should talk to Freddy."

"Who's Freddy?"

"Freddy Lassitor. He's on José's bowling team. He might be able to help, but I doubt it. Not a big talker, if you know what I mean. Once you finish discussing the weather, that's it for him."

"Great," I said. "This is so frustrating."

"You might try talking to Harriet, though," she suggested.

"Who's Harriet?"

"Freddy's girlfriend. She isn't a bowler, but she sticks to him like glue. She's jealous Freddy might meet someone else during bowling, so she goes with him to every game. And this ought to cheer you up, Kate. Harriet never stops talking."

"That's all well and good, but how do I meet her?"

Cindy squinted her eyes and looked me up and down. "Can you bowl?"

———

There was only one bowling alley in Oak Falls. It looked a bit run-down on the outside, but when I drove into the parking lot to meet Cindy and her husband, I was surprised by the number of cars. On the other hand, I suppose it became a good source of exercise and socializing during the Hudson Valley's brutal winters.

I actually knew how to bowl. After my mom and brother died, I was a very angry teenager. Gramps gave me bowling lessons every week, probably to force me out of the house and take my aggression out on the pins. It helped. I'd envision my dad's face on the pins and get pleasure knocking them down. Gramps also played on a league, so after my lesson, I'd have to hang out with his fireman buddies, who always offered to buy me pizza or sodas and never asked any personal questions.

I didn't remember how long ago I'd last picked up a bowling ball, but I figured my moderate skills would kick in after a few throws.

When I opened the bowling alley glass doors, the first thing that hit me was the noise level. Computerized programs blared on every lane, as the scores were posted electronically. Some lanes lit up with flashing lights that changed colors. Stunned at first, I didn't see Cindy until she tapped my shoulder.

"So I'm on a ladies team, but we bowl on another night. I try to practice while the hubby bowls. We've booked the lane right next to him, and guess what? Both Freddy and Harriet are here. Lucky you."

She surreptitiously pointed out Freddy, whose bright red-orange hair glowed nearly fluorescent in the artificial lights. He was very tall and skinny, and his eyelashes and eyebrows were so pale they vanished from his face, giving him a surprised look. I checked out my target, Harriet, who was sitting on the bench and wore a lot more makeup than most of the women there. When she stood up, I couldn't help but notice a large shelf of bosom proudly displayed in a skin-tight sweater. I also realized she often talked to Freddy's back.

"Let's do this," Cindy said with a surprising amount of enthusiasm, her hair in a high ponytail.

My friend brought her own bowling ball and shoes, but I was forced to use the everyday rentals. I decided not to think about how many feet had been in the size nine shoes before mine. Just before they handed me the shoes, an employee sprayed some sort of perfumed disinfectant spray inside. The strong pine odor made me sneeze. I didn't see how spraying a disinfectant for three seconds would thoroughly protect anyone's feet from the stuff that grew in bowling shoes—but I shoved them on over my socks and hoped for the best.

When I reached our lane, Cindy had already made contact with Harriet. They sat side by side, chatting away like old friends.

"Oh, Harriet, this is Dr. Kate Turner. We work together at the animal hospital. Kate, this is Harriet Wilder."

"I'm so glad to meet you," she said speaking loudly over the noise. "My friends say I'm wilder than my last name!"

Since it looked like she expected me to laugh, I did.

"Are you joining us?" I asked Harriet, hefting the ball up with two hands to feel its weight and balance.

"Oh, no," she protested. "I'm a little top heavy for bowling. The girls would keep getting in the way."

Stumped for a response, I said, "Okay."

Over the next hour, the three of us chatted away about everything under the sun—the price of groceries, which salon in town gives the best pedicures, and Harriet's favorite binge-worthy streaming shows. Once we felt comfortable, I snuck in a question about the murdered couple, Alicia and José. As predicted, Harriet expressed many opinions on the subject.

With wide eyes, she explained that she and her boy-friend knew José pretty well, and they were horrified by his murder. She said José had been so caring and dedicated to his profession—that it was a loss to the community. As she continued to chatter on about going out to dinner and how her hubby and José played a guys-only poker game every Tuesday night, I realized she hadn't said a word about Alicia.

After my next turn, which ended in a lucky spare, I brought up José's fiancée.

"Hum," was her response.

I waited, knowing she would not be able to stop herself from talking about Alicia.

"Well, I hate to speak ill of the dead," she began, "but Freddy and I were not happy when those two got engaged. She was…a stuck-up little bitch. Always thinking every guy was crazy in love with her."

So much for not speaking ill of the dead.

"I never met her…" I began, but Harriet interrupted.

"The first time José brought her over to meet us, I knew she was trouble," Harriet continued. "Sure, Alicia was okay to look at, but she never warmed up to either of us. Never. And I think she became paranoid or something."

"Why do you say that?" I asked before I had to get up and take my turn. Cindy was beating me, of course, but preoccupied by what Harriet said, I must have freed up my unconscious mind long enough to bowl a strike.

"Yes!" I yelled out and performed a little victory dance. Lights flashed and an electronic voice called out "STRIKE!"

Cindy must have realized I needed some extra time to talk to Harriet because she paused our game to buy an iced tea.

As soon as I sat down, Harriet continued to explain why Alicia seemed paranoid.

"For one thing," she said, moving closer to me, "she thought someone was watching her in college. In Albany, New York, of all places? José thought it was one reason she got married so fast to that lawyer, James Ramsey. For protection."

A tremor of alarm went off in my gut. "Did she…"

"José told Alicia that she was simply reacting to people staring at her because she was so beautiful." Harriet made a barfing gesture. "I mean she was cute, but there are a lot of attractive women in the world." Harriet adjusted her sweater then added, "And she always lost stuff, but she blamed it on a stalker. Such drama. Like there is a stalker here in Oak Falls."

From the expression on her face, I figured Harriet thought that an impossibility. "She even said someone was stealing her underwear."

"Her underwear?" I asked.

"Nutty, right? Those two traveled back and forth to each other's places so much she probably lost track of them. I lose panties all the time," Harriet stated.

Another wild statement, but she expected me to comment, so I said, "Me, too. Lose them all the time in the dryer along with my socks."

My answer didn't slow her down. "That lawsuit talk and the stalker stuff started getting José jittery, which is why they decided to move to California."

"José told you this?" I asked her.

She laughed and said, "Of course not. José told my Freddy, and then Freddy told me after I forced him to talk. I guess you could say I'm a teensy bit nosy."

Thank goodness someone is, I thought. Harriet turned out to be an overflowing fountain of information. As Cindy and I signed up to play one more game, I resolved to drain her gossip fountain dry.

Harriet's opinions revealed someone much more clever than people gave her credit for. She confessed she realized she was an average person in every way except her bra size, so in high school she decided to make the most of what she had. I told her in all honesty, she had plenty more going for her, which made her beam.

I asked her to try and remember any other details about José and Alicia, which might lead to their killer.

She came up with several. José came over to their house to say goodbye the week of the murder and indicated that he and Alicia were getting married that week. He didn't tell them where. They'd bought plane tickets to California for their honeymoon. He'd decided to sell his big truck now and buy a smaller vehicle when they got to LA. They'd both been saving money by having roommates, which allowed them to put aside a nice nest egg for their first home.

"Why didn't they move in together and save on rent?" Out of the corner of my eye I caught Cindy's throw knocking down nine pins.

Harriet shrugged. "For the sake of romance. If you can believe that." She made it obvious she didn't.

"Who did they hire to perform the ceremony?" I wondered, while Cindy picked up a spare.

"Freddy didn't say. My sweetie pie isn't very talkative. Sometimes I have to pry information out of him with a crowbar." Harriet looked over at her boyfriend bowling in the next lane and yelled out "Go, Freddy. Go!"

He turned his head and gave her a giant smile and a thumbs-up before bowling a strike with a series of fluid movements. I hadn't thought of bowling as graceful, but Freddy Lassitor proved me wrong. I, on the other hand, looked neither graceful nor skilled. I'd been trailing Cindy except for a few lucky strikes, and our final scores were separated by at least fifty points. After our final frame, Harriet said goodbye and switched lanes to sit next to her guy. I noticed several men surreptitiously sneaking looks at her assets.

Cindy's hubby was busy bowling with his team. Now I realized why my receptionist drove her own car tonight.

As we picked our way through the parking lot, Cindy asked if I learned anything interesting.

"Alicia had a stalker," I answered. "In fact, there are three people who corroborate her stalking fears at three different times in her life: high school, college, and in Oak Falls. Her sister told me about the high school stalker; José mentioned a college stalker to Freddy; and both Harriet and Alicia's roommate Nora remembered some odd occurrences here. Does the chief know about this?"

Cindy opened her truck door. "If he does, he hasn't shared it with his wife. My sister knows how upset we've been, and she immediately tells me anything to do with the three murders. But Bobby isn't saying much."

"I guess we'll have to keep plugging away. This is the first new bit of information I've found."

"Could Alicia and José have been killed by a stalker? Isn't that mostly in movies?" Doubt sounded in Cindy's voice.

"From everything I've read about stalking, I would say that it is a definite possibility."

With an admonishment to be careful, Cindy climbed into her car and waited for me to open my truck door. After a quick wave, she took off for home and family, while I headed back to the animal hospital alone, stalking scenarios playing in my head.

Jealousy was another possible motive added to the pile of motives.

Chapter Thirty-Three

THAT NIGHT I LEARNED IT'S NOT A GOOD IDEA TO DO AN Internet search on stalkers before you go to sleep. There were hundreds of postings, most of them from women whose former boyfriends wouldn't let go or family members remembering victims of murder/suicide brought on by jealousy. A recurrent theme was, "If I can't have you, no one can." It's a terrible outcome for everyone when a person prefers to kill their object of affection rather than let go.

I checked twice that night to make sure the alarm system was on and functioning. Reading these creepy cases made me jittery. I held my pepper spray in my hand when I walked Buddy and Bella, and when we came back inside, I made sure to double-lock the door. Then I poured a glass of white wine and headed for the couch.

"Hey, guys," I told my dogs, "let's watch some HGTV." The nice thing about having a dog as a TV partner is you always get to watch your show and control the remote.

As we all settled in with a few soft blankets, the text tone pinged.

How's your day been?

I texted back to Mike:

Interesting

About two minutes later, Mike called, and I explained about my bowling adventure.

"I haven't been bowling in ages," he told me. "Was it fun?"

How to admit I went bowling so I could talk about murder? At first I was tempted to simply say bowling was fun, but if Mike and I had any future together, he needed to know I'd been investigating the murders.

I hemmed and hawed before laying it on the line. "I went bowling with Cindy to find out more about José and Alicia, the murder victims Mari and I found up by the lake."

"Good idea," he said. "Did you find out anything?"

His interest in what I was doing surprised me. All my other relationships consisted of men telling me to be careful or to back off. "You're not going to say I'm out of my league. Or crazy?"

"Was that a pun?" Laughter rolled through the receiver, coming right from the heart. "Long ago I stopped trying to orchestrate everyone's lives, including my own. Life is messy and unpredictable. Maybe you're meant to help solve this crime. The Babs I knew would have encouraged you— perhaps even joined you."

"But look what happened to her."

My statement met with silence. Then Mike reminded me of something everyone knows, a basic fact pushed to the back corner of our consciousness.

"Everyone is going to die, but murder changes the natural course of events. Her death came as a surprise. Babs probably didn't suspect anything until she started to feel the effects of the Xanax in her coffee. Once she knew she'd been drugged, she did everything she could to help point the way for you. I miss her. She didn't have to die this way."

"No, she didn't."

"This is my motto. Live each day to the fullest and do what is right."

Of course, what he said was true. But I couldn't live with myself if I didn't keep trying to find the person who killed my friend.

"What made you so smart?" I asked in a joking voice. I didn't expect a real answer.

"When I turned fourteen, I was on my grandparents' farm plowing a field with a tractor..."

"At fourteen you ran a tractor by yourself?"

"You'd be surprised at the things farm kids do. I also gathered eggs and fed the chickens and cows and horses at four years old."

I could picture a serious blue-eyed little boy diligently going through his chores.

"Anyway, it was after some heavy rains and everything was fine until the tractor hit a soft spot, that turned into a sinkhole, and tumbled about twenty feet into a pit, pinning me underneath. We weren't visible at all. I shouted until I couldn't shout anymore and figured they'd miss me soon enough. What I didn't know was I was bleeding internally."

"When did they find out you were missing?"

"That's the bad part. I often helped my grandparents on Saturday, and sometimes stayed over until Sunday. Then we'd all meet up at church. That Saturday my grandma went to bed early with a migraine. Because of some miscommunication, each family thought I stayed at the other one's house."

"So you spent the night trapped under the tractor. In a sinkhole?" The idea of anyone suffering that kind of accident was horrific, but especially for a young teenager.

"Yep. I could see the stars above me. By then I felt numb below the waist, and I figured my spine had been broken. You hear people talking about their lives flashing past them, but for me, it was a realization that I was dying and there was nothing I could do about it. Just before I blacked out, I experienced an out-of-body experience. I was floating in the air looking down at myself trapped under the tractor. There were no feelings of pain or anger; it just was what it was. After taking one last look at the stars, I blacked out. I woke up in a hospital bed."

"That's some story. How bad were your injuries?"

"Broken femur, liver laceration, cracked pelvis, broken collarbone, and a bunch of minor injuries. But after that experience, I changed. I stopped trying to control everything in my life because—I'd surrendered to my fate. Looking up at the stars and nearly bleeding to death put everything in perspective."

"So the moral of the story is…"

"Go get him, Kate. Track down whoever committed these crimes. Take precautions, but don't let a bit of danger deter you."

If he'd been sitting on the sofa next to me, I would have hugged him. Unlike my other boyfriends, he sounded calm, focused, and much more mature. Seasoned, my Gramps would say.

The big question in this romance equation was me. What if this was it? If he was the one? As much as I bitched about the state of my love life, was I ready? To be honest—I was afraid to commit again, to get hurt again.

By the time we hung up, I'd forgotten all about stalkers. Mike suggested we spend more time together, so we compared schedules—the height of a modern romantic gesture, as far as I was concerned.

"I've got to be on call every other weekend because we're short-staffed," he began.

"I've got clinics every other Saturday, so our clients who have tight schedules can get in to see us. If I admit a patient, I have to be available on Sunday, too."

Since he lived and worked almost an hour away, near Rhinebeck, synchronizing our schedules was imperative.

"Tell you what," I offered. "I'll adjust to your schedule. I have a lot more flexibility than you do." I had no doubt when I told Cindy I wanted to try and spend more time with Mike, she'd figure things out.

"Maybe one Sunday I can come over to your place and cook you dinner," he offered. I felt as if I'd been struck by lightning. "You cook?"

"Yep. As the oldest in a big farm family, I learned plenty of homemaking skills."

Being who I was, I demanded clarification. "You're talking about really cooking dinner from scratch? Not heating up a frozen meal or microwaving takeout?"

Once more his warm laughter oozed out of my cell phone.

"Cooking from scratch, of course. And as long as we are

sharing, the other strange thing I have to confess is I like to do laundry. I find it soothing. My mom and I used to do at least four or five loads every weekend, so the younger kids would have clean clothes for school."

Be still my heart. "Okay, but I insist on doing the dishes," I said in a determined self-righteous voice. *Had I hit the jackpot with Mike? Was the universe finally going to give me a break?* I felt like dancing.

"Send me your schedule," I told him, trying to be extremely practical, "and I'll work it out with my office manager."

"Great," he answered.

"It's getting late. We should probably call it a night," I told him reluctantly. "I've got two surgeries tomorrow and a full day of appointments."

"My day is packed, too. Sometimes I think I should just sleep in my scrubs."

We laughed together and then said good night.

Before he hung up, Mike said, "I miss you already."

And I found to my surprise I felt the same.

So I told him.

Chapter Thirty-Four

WHEN I WOKE UP, I THOUGHT ABOUT MIKE AND OUR CONversation the night before. With former boyfriends, my schedule always proved an issue. When Luke moved away for law school, he barely came back to visit, not wanting to travel just to find out I was on call. Dating another veterinarian, who knew what I dealt with, felt like a big relief. Plus we could hang out even when one of us was working. I knew plenty of classmates who got married to each other during school, and all of them were still together. I let myself feel optimistic as I tied my robe tightly and took the dogs for their walk.

While Buddy sniffed his favorite tree, first one, then the other two crows flew down and perched on my truck. Bella stood stock still in astonishment. I'd already stashed a ziplock bag of food for the crows above the clothes rack, so I dug into my pocket and put their food as usual on the small rubber mat on the truck hood. That way they wouldn't be fishing food out of the snow and getting colder while trying to eat.

My former patient lifted his beak in my direction. Once again I noted glittering black eyes and shiny feathers. I said good morning to them and called for Buddy and Bella to finish up.

Since it was still early, I went into the hospital and was greeted by that delicious coffee smell. Cindy was there. She enjoyed being the first person in, making the coffee, and going over the day's schedule. I picked up my coffee mug and the memories started flooding back: Alicia being stalked, José buying a gun a week before he died, and discovering Babs's body in our surgery suite.

The coffee tasted bitter.

Cindy received a text from her son, so I went into my office to check incoming lab reports and client email. In my private account, I found an email from Alicia's sister, Ursula. Her private investigator had traced the high school boy who had stalked Alicia and enclosed a photo of David "Scooter" Hayes. He tried running down the guy's Social Security number, but it ended up a dead end—no information for the past five years. In the investigator's report, he mentioned Scooter had a close buddy, but that person had never been in trouble. On a side note, Scooter applied and was accepted at the same college in New York that Alicia went to but dropped out after his first year. A coincidence? I didn't think so.

The photo captured an obese teenager with pitting acne and crooked teeth. His dark hair was long and greasy. Large tinted glasses hid his eyes and upper face. A thin scraggly beard obscured his mouth and chin. I'd be hard-pressed to pick him out in a lineup but was quite sure I'd never seen him before. Although women often changed their faces and bodies with plastic surgery, it wasn't as common with men, especially young men. But to be thorough, I printed the photo and taped it to the wall near my desk.

Alicia must have filed a complaint against a boy in college, because the PI included it in his report. Her Albany college stalker also dropped out of school only to enlist in the army. He was killed in Afghanistan.

I leaned back into my desk chair and realized the men in Alicia's life hadn't profited by knowing her. A high school boyfriend who died. Her first husband's suicide, and now, the murder of fiancé José. *Are some people magnets for violence?*

Ursula closed her email by asking if there were any new findings in the investigation. On my part, no, I replied. But I told her to be sure to contact Chief Garcia every week and to tell him everything she'd told me.

Then I had a thought. *What if the Oak Falls stalker had been one of Alicia's clients?* After all, a lawyer works very closely with the people who hire them. *Maybe the killer was a former or current client or an employee? How could I get my hands on that type of highly confidential information?*

Just then Cindy poked her head in. "What did you think of Harriet?" she asked, walking in and making herself comfortable in one of the chairs in front of my desk. The other seat was occupied by Mr. Katt, who'd decided to spread some of his cat hair around and was lounging upside down in the other upholstered chair.

"I thought Harriet was a hoot, and I liked her. Very blunt and straightforward."

"That she is. Did she tell you anything important?" Cindy's eyes went to the picture of Scooter Hayes taped on the wall by my desk.

"She confirmed that both José and Alicia were jittery in that last week. José took Alicia's fears to heart and bought a gun for protection. What I'm curious about is who was going to marry them? Maybe he or she was the killer."

"She?" Cindy didn't sound very convinced that the murderer might be female. "Are there any indications that a woman killed them? And who is that?" She pointed to Scooter's picture.

"Someone from Alicia's high school. Probably a dead end," I admitted. "As far as a woman being the killer, I have no idea. There's no evidence either way."

"Wouldn't it take a lot of strength to kill them both?" she asked.

"We're not talking weightlifter-like strong. Gramps thought the suspect would have to be *fairly* strong, so that rules out some suspects, like Linda, the ex-wife. José was shot at close range, and Alicia was strangled. A larger woman might easily have caught José off guard and overpowered Alicia, who was quite slim and petite. I'm just not ready to eliminate that possibility."

"So Alicia might have had a female admirer?"

"Not necessarily an admirer. Maybe it was a wife who didn't like how her husband felt about another woman or one of José's former girlfriends. Maybe José was the real target, not Alicia. I'm eliminating nothing and no one at the moment."

Cindy rose and checked her cell phone. "This is too much for me to think about. Did I tell you we found a closet full of midcentury modern ceramics off the kitchen at Babs's place? Every piece has to be identified, wrapped, and assigned an approximate value."

"Did an heir come forward yet?"

"No one. I wish they would, because I'm beat."

"Sorry," I answered. Cindy shrugged her shoulders and headed for reception.

I realized I'd been saying "sorry" quite often these last few weeks.

Mr. Katt yawned and promptly stretched to his full length and then some, before curling back into a warm ball and closing his eyes.

———————

"I'm thinking of taking down that picture of Scooter in my office," I mentioned to Mari as I put on my white coat to see hospital appointments. "There is something about him that gives me the creeps."

"Agreed," she said, rummaging through her scrub top pockets as we got ready for our next appointment.

"Lose something?" I asked.

"No, just seeing if I have my favorite pen with me."

Like me, Mari often wrote herself quick notes during the day. Everything else was entered into our laptop or electronic tablets. A very efficient system, but at least once or twice a day I needed to write myself a quick note about something or other.

"So, what's the issue with this client?" I asked Mari.

"Routine exam and shots," she said, "and they also want to talk about cloning their dog."

"Oh, crap."

Speaking to owners about cloning their pets is a difficult topic, not to mention one fraught with ethical and moral roadblocks. With so many animals needing homes, it was a controversial topic. As I prepared to see these clients, I updated myself on the latest news from that field. Yes, there are companies that specialized in cloning pets, mostly dogs and cats. The cost is significant but the success rate, to read the advertising statistics, is pretty impressive. But reports have surfaced with concerns about all aspects of the procedure. This isn't only a debate for family pets; horses, sheep, and other food animals have all been cloned.

I let Mari do a quick triage before knocking on the door.

A well-dressed couple in their forties stood next to the exam table, where a happy mixed-breed dog was wagging its tail, just pleased to be out of the house.

"Want your stuffy?" the doggy mom said.

Immediately the dog sat down and put out its paw. The reward was a beat-up gray squirrel, rat, or rabbit, depending on your interpretation.

"Hi, I'm Dr. Kate Turner," I said, introducing myself.

"Ellen and Jeff Walden," the woman replied. "And this is Liz Tailer."

The dog's head swiveled on hearing her name. Not sure if she was being addressed directly, she glanced back at her owners, eager to please.

"Hi, Liz," I told the sweet little dog. Liz looked like a shih tzu-poodle mix. A shihtz-doodle. My exam uncovered no specific health problem with this seven-year-old girl, and the owners stated she'd been very healthy.

The couple seemed a bit nervous. I decided to make it easier for them.

"My veterinary assistant, Mari, says you had some questions about cloning Liz Tailer?"

"Yes," Ellen said, nervously cuddling her pet. "I hope you don't think we're horrible because all our friends think we're being selfish."

"And nuts," her husband kicked in.

I'd been to several CE seminars that touched on the pet cloning debate. Emotions triumphed over logic in most cases. Many of these pet owners had extremely strong emotional attachments to their particular pet and couldn't imagine a life without them.

"She's our baby. We don't have any children," the wife continued, tears springing into her eyes. "We adopted her when she was a tiny puppy."

"Have you researched the animal cloning companies?" I asked. "The largest in the USA, I believe, is located in Texas."

Ellen took her husband's hand for support. "Yes, they sent us their literature."

"They do offer," I began, "storage of your pet's DNA until you decide if you want to proceed. I noticed some tartar on Liz's teeth that we should remove within the next year or so, and that is a perfect time for me to collect the genetic sample while she is under anesthesia."

"So it won't hurt?" Ellen asked, squeezing her husband's hand.

"It won't hurt," I assured her. "The company will send me a collection kit. All they require is a punch biopsy, similar to how your dermatologist does a skin biopsy, and our hospital will send the sample directly to them. I think that eliminates being forced to make an immediate decision. As for being selfish—this is your decision. If it is important to your mental health, then it doesn't matter what anyone else says. By the way, there are thousands of genetic samples of pets currently being stored in advance of cloning."

"Thousands?"

"That's what the company says. Owners like you, who haven't decided what to do, can confidently store their dogs' genetic material."

Jeff still looked uneasy, as if he had another question for me.

"Do you have any other questions?" I asked.

Jeff blurted out his concern. "Who supplies the surrogate mom and egg? I'm not sure I understand."

"It is a bit complicated," I explained. "The company supplies both the eggs and surrogate mom. When it is time to clone, the donor egg's genetic material is removed and your dog's DNA is inserted. That egg is grown in the lab, and when it is viable and duplicating, it is placed into the fallopian tubes of the mother dog. After she gives birth, the puppy or puppies stay with her until they are eight weeks old. A company veterinarian will examine your puppy and make sure it is healthy before you receive it."

"How do we get our new puppy?"

"It won't be by Amazon Prime delivery," I joked. "There are several options available, but that's something to discuss with them. Let us know when or if you want to proceed, because I'll call and go over their protocol beforehand."

Ellen's husband picked up Liz Tailer and gave her a kiss.

"Thanks for the explanation. We've both read it a bunch of times, but it didn't make any sense. At least now we know we don't have to make a decision right away."

"No problem. Mari will take you to reception, where Cindy has a packet prepared for you on the dentistry. You can email me any time if you have questions. We included some Internet sites run by other families who have cloned their pets. Remember, the cloned puppy will be genetically identical to your dog but may not look or act identically. I also urge you to read about the negative aspects of cloning. Specifically the business of cloning and the lives of the surrogate mommy dogs."

Mari escorted them down the hallway, and I went into my office to touch up my notes. I also sent an email to a colleague of mine who had firsthand experience with cloning a pet for one of his clients.

I'd never had a client who cloned their pet.

———

By the time we finished for the day at around six p.m., Mari and I were exhausted. I'd admitted one of our scheduled surgeries early, so his owners wouldn't have to deny him breakfast tomorrow. His pleading eyes, they told us, forced them to cave and feed him a forbidden breakfast on surgery day. Having gone through two last-minute cancellations, I suggested our easy solution. This evening he'd board overnight and eat dinner at the hospital; I'd handle the rest. An NPO sign, nothing by mouth, would be posted on his cage, and as the surgeon, I'd make sure he didn't eat.

Cindy poked her head into the office to say good night. I should have asked her a million questions about the murder investigation, but seriously, I could barely keep my eyes open. I'm not sure how she felt, but I felt like I was on a treadmill that kept speeding up while I already was walking as fast as I could.

"Were you able to follow my link and give those clients the cloning information?" I asked our receptionist.

"Yes, thanks for the heads-up. That's one subject I don't have a lot of current information on. I also don't know how I feel about it, to tell you the truth."

"Me either. In the CE class I took, the speaker asked if your three-year-old child had an accident and you had the opportunity to clone them, would you?"

Cindy's eyes grew distant. "That's a rough one."

"Be nonjudgmental was the advice he gave. In a way, I think people hope to achieve a kind of immortality for their animal. But life is change. You can never replace one pet, and all your shared experiences, with another. It's better, I feel, to hold the memories of your loved one close and expand your heart to welcome another."

Cindy smiled, "That's something your Gramps would say."

"Maybe he did. Go home and get some rest. Mari and I will finish anything left to do."

About twenty minutes later, I'd done all my callbacks and records and went out front to check on Mari. I found her in surgery. My incredibly strong and dedicated assistant was crying.

She dried her eyes and blew her nose. "Sorry you had to see this. Every time I come in here before closing, I end up reliving the day we found her."

I gave Mari a hug. "You're grieving, plus Gramps cautioned we might have PTSD. Have you spoken to anyone about this?"

She broke away. "Who has time to talk to a shrink?"

"Please try to make time," I told her as I followed her out into the treatment area. "Check our insurance coverage with Cindy. You and I suffered tremendous psychological trauma over a period of a week. First José, then locating Alicia's body in the lake, followed by finding Babs right here in the animal hospital. I'm surprised we're still standing."

"I'm standing," she joked, "but barely."

We took out the countertop cleaner and put stray objects away where they belonged. Working was therapeutic for me, and I told her so. "I also think investigating is my way of dealing with these deaths. I can distance myself while trying to solve them intellectually. Gramps always talked about that, because he saw a lot of gruesome things during his firefighting career."

"You're probably right. One of my cousins is married to a psychiatric social worker. Maybe I'll see if I can get a little free advice."

"It's a start," I told her. "Let's finish up and get you back to your fur babies."

"Sounds good."

"Are most of your puppies gone?" I asked. She'd had one litter of Rottweiler puppies by her show-quality dog, Lucy.

All the puppies had homes, many with her family members. Mari and her partner intended on keeping only one.

"Yes, the chaos is over, and we're back to normal. The adults tolerate the little one, but occasionally I see them playing. They all sleep in a big pile."

"Send me a picture." I took my phone out and placed it on the countertop. Mari yawned. "Come on," I said. "I'll walk you to the door."

"How's it going with Mike?" she asked.

"We're taking it slow. Maybe planning a weekend together sometime soon."

She smiled. "Slow is good. As long as you don't stay locked in first gear."

Mari usually parked closer to my apartment door than the main entrance so we zipped though my place, pausing to pick up Buddy and Bella.

"How is our little girl doing?" Mari asked the dog in a doggy voice. "Look, I got a wag." Bella had only recently started vigorously wagging her tail, one of the many dog behaviors she'd learned from Buddy.

"Her skin is doing great," I said. "I'm still waiting for a bark, though."

As Mari walked over to her truck, loud cawing interrupted us. As usual first one crow, then the others landed on top of my truck. They'd come to expect treats, and I didn't disappoint them.

"Looks like you have some fans," Mari said as she climbed into her huge SUV.

"Only until the spring. Then they'll have to forage on their own." I didn't want to tame any of these guys. They needed to live as Nature intended, but winter was hard on everyone, human and beast, so I felt justified in supplementing their diet.

As Mari backed out of the parking spot, I waved goodbye. One of the crows followed everything I did, his alert eyes brimming with intelligence.

"See you later, alligator," I told my former crow patient.

I half expected him to caw back "after a while, crocodile."

———

I now had another reason to find this killer who had destroyed so many lives. It was affecting the people I loved and worked with. My best friend, Mari, was trying to hide her tears while cleaning the surgery. Cindy, a friend as well as a colleague, was barely holding it together, fighting with her husband, and going through Babs's estate as best she could.

And my own memories and nightmares reminded me of that terrible day.

Despite all I'd learned, I kept coming back to Alicia. Of all the victims, only her background included deaths, suicide, stalking, and harassment. The old saying that lightning never strikes twice in the same place is scientifically inaccurate. There are trees in the forest that have had multiple strikes. *Why? Are the electrons in the soil surrounding them particularly attractive?* Most people didn't realize that electrical charges rise from the ground and meet the electrical charges coming down from the sky—joining in a fiery lightning kiss.

Was Alicia a trigger point without knowing it?

Chapter Thirty-Five

THE IDEA THAT ALICIA MIGHT BE A TRIGGER POINT MADE sense to me. I'd been meaning to question the people in the law office who worked with her, but today was my first opportunity to do so. Cindy had yet another lunchtime meeting with the estate lawyer, which gave Mari and me time for a nice long lunch.

When I told Mari of my plans, she didn't seem enthusiastic. "I think I'll pass on that," she stated. "If you don't mind, I'll hang out with Buddy and Bella. Maybe try some basic obedience training with your little girl. Watch some television."

"I'm sure they'd both love that." Mari identified as a dog person. In fact, I was almost convinced by her abundant black curls that she'd been reincarnated from a Portuguese water dog. Canines of all shapes and sizes were immediately drawn to her, and she had her dog command voice down pat.

With the extra time available, I'd changed out of my scrubs into clean pants and a sweater. If the lawyers mistook me for a potential client, so much the better.

The office Alicia had worked in was in Kingston, thirty minutes away. Located in a newer building in a professional complex, it gave off a no-nonsense vibe. I hoped to speak to a few of the lawyers, but instead I was met with a brick wall of legalese. None of the those who ventured out to the lobby to speak to me would say anything except that Alicia was a lovely person and what a tragedy it was.

After being stymied by every lawyer available, I complained to the secretary filing her nails while waiting for her phone to ring.

"A woman who worked with me was also murdered," I told April, checking her name tag to make sure I had her name correctly.

A kind-looking woman in her fifties, her gray-tinged hair pulled back in a bun, her demeanor changed when I explained about Babs. "I'm so sorry," she said. "I think about Alicia every day. She didn't deserve to die so young."

"It would help if I could speak to someone who worked with her," I explained. "The police don't have a suspect yet. Maybe Alicia confided her fears to someone or mentioned she thought she'd been followed."

"Well…" She indicated with her fingers that I come closer. "You could ask Hughie. He's our law clerk, and I know he was very fond of her."

Finally, a break. "Where can I find him?" I asked.

"Go straight down the hallway. His office is the last door on the left." She pointed the way. "But be quick before anyone sees you."

"You're a lifesaver," I whispered.

I speed-walked down the hallway, zipping past every door until I found one that read "Hugh Finton." A quick knock, and I barged in.

Bent over his computer sat a pale pudgy guy in a white shirt and tie. His sleeves were rolled up, exposing mats of dark hair. A high forehead ended with dark buzzed hair. Startled by my sudden appearance, he glanced up through glasses that were anchored halfway down his nose. A winter jacket and muffler hung off a coatrack in the corner.

On his desk rested a picture in an ornate silver frame of Alicia and him smiling into the camera. A single red rose stood in a crystal bud vase next to the photo.

"Can I help you?" he asked, while shrinking the document he was working on so I couldn't see it.

"Are you Mr. Finton? Hughie Finton?" Although the receptionist called him Hughie, that smacked to me of someone under the age of ten.

"That's correct," Hughie answered in a throaty voice, as if battling a sore throat. He used a thick finger to push his glasses higher on his nose.

Without being invited, I settled in a nearby chair. "I'd like to talk to you about Alicia Ramsey. Do you know anyone who might have wanted to harm her?"

His eyes glistened behind thick lenses. The sound of his breathing became audible, harsher. On his desk sat an unopened bottle of water. With a certain delicacy he opened the twist top and drank freely, spoiling the effect by wiping his mouth with the side of his hand. Fine black hairs sprouted from his knuckles.

"Alicia was an angel. The most beautiful woman I've ever seen." He picked up the framed picture, kissed his index finger and transferred the kiss to her lips. A deep aching sadness reflected in his face and the photo's glass. "May she rest in peace."

I added, "May they rest in peace together, Alicia and José."

His face changed like a suddenly dark cloud. "I don't have anything to say about José, other than he can rot in hell."

That statement confirmed everything I needed to know. Hughie had been in love with Alicia. He cared little about her fiancé.

"Do you have any idea who killed her?" I was surprised Hughie had asked me no questions—such as who I was and what was I doing in his office.

His dark eyes were revealed as the glasses slipped again. "Everyone knows José killed her because she wanted to break off their engagement." His tone turned belligerent, somewhat petulant, as though he would gladly have shot José himself.

I reminded him of the truth. "The Oak Falls chief of police stated that José did not kill Alicia. Both of them were murdered."

"I don't believe it." He picked the photo up and pressed it to his chest.

This was someone who didn't want the truth. Who wouldn't believe the truth. He preferred his version of the events. I tried anyway. "Forensic evidence has proven it."

"What do they know?" he retorted.

Our conversation was going nowhere. *Time for a different approach.* "I'm sure you want to see justice for Alicia," I began, "and as a close friend, her death must be very hard."

He jerked his head and turned away from me.

"Before she died was anyone making her upset?"

"Other than José?"

"Other than José."

"Maybeeee," he said slyly. "But…I don't want to talk about it." He put the photo back in place, adjusting the rose in the bud vase slightly. Once satisfied, he opened the document on his computer and began typing. "If that's all, I'm rather busy. You can see yourself out. Now."

As I studied his face I remembered the photo of Alicia's stalker from high school, Scooter A big guy. Dark greasy hair and acne. Just visible on Hughie's cheeks were slight depressions that could be old acne scars. Was this Scooter? Would Alicia have recognized him?

I tried to recall exactly what her sister, Ursula, had written in her email. Scooter had apologized for harassing her, and they had become friends. The private investigator noted that he tracked Scooter until his first year of college, the same college Alicia went to, then lost him. There had been no online evidence of him for the last five years.

What wild coincidence would have them working at the same law office so many years later? Even with that old picture locked in my memory, I had no idea if this was Scooter Hayes.

Had her old stalker found an ingenious way to be close to his personal angel?

Two people were waiting in the lobby when I left. The accommodating receptionist was busy scheduling an appointment on the phone. I rushed outside, the cold air a welcome change from the rose-scented air in Hughie's office shrine to Alicia.

What do I actually know? I asked myself, hurrying to my truck. A light coating of snow covered the sidewalk.

Behind me I heard footsteps, determined footsteps, speeding up. I stopped and pretended to look in one of the shop windows. With people walking by, I wasn't afraid. It might be someone in a hurry to get home, the same as me.

"Excuse me."

An older man's face reflected back at me from the shop window.

"May I help you?" I asked.

The man appeared thin but wiry. His body looked tense, fists closed tightly by his sides.

"Are you Dr. Kate Turner?" he asked.

"Yes." I expected a veterinary question, this same scenario having happened before. "Do you have a question?"

"Yes," his jaw clenched in a nervous twitch. "Why can't you leave the dead alone?"

His words registered slowly and made no sense. But I sensed danger, like the danger building in an angry animal.

A couple passed by, so I started to walk behind them. He followed.

"I'm sorry, but I don't know what you mean," I told the man. "You know who I am. Can I ask your name?" All the while I moved deeper toward the shops, still surrounded by people shopping or visiting a favored restaurant. My left hand felt for the pepper spray I'd tucked into my pocket before leaving the animal hospital. If this stranger attacked me, I'd go down fighting.

"I'm Greg Owens."

The man suing José Florez. *Why is he angry at me?*

"Mr. Owens. My friend, Cindy, told me about the loss of your wife. I'm so sorry."

"Don't say that," he sneered. "You didn't know my Doris. Saying you're sorry is horse manure."

This man was hurting, and I couldn't help him.

"What do you want from me?" I turned and confronted him. He didn't flinch or back off but stared back at me.

"Stop investigating the murders. They got what they deserved."

"Babs didn't. I know Babs didn't deserve to die."

He broke eye contact, jaw twitching again. "Babs did what she had to do," he said cryptically. "Now if you know what's good for you, you'll stay out of what don't concern you."

Greg Owens must have followed me into Kingston. I'd seen him, I realized, sitting on a stool at the counter of Judy's Café, his thin wrist exposed under his shirt cuff.

Before I thought to ask any more questions, he crossed the street and disappeared into an alley. I had no desire to follow him. This encounter I would mention to the chief.

By the time I returned to the truck, another soft layer of snow had fallen, but I could still decipher the words scrawled on my windshield:

STOP OR BE SORRY

There was no doubt Greg Owens had threatened me. A man torn up inside with grief after the tragic death of his wife. Someone happy that José was dead and didn't care how many others had to die, too.

He was warning me.

I didn't think he would warn me again.

Chapter Thirty-Six

"WHAT!" CINDY YELLED INTO HER CELL PHONE. "HE SAID what?"

I was sitting in my office, after releasing a surgery to his waiting family. They'd called our office line in a panic, having incorrectly written down the hospital closing time as eight p.m., and since I didn't mind the brief company, I'd told them to come over.

Not sure how to handle Greg Owens, I decided to call Cindy. She knew Greg. Perhaps she had an insight into his strange encounter with me.

"I've got a photo of the windshield," I mentioned. "He's a very angry man."

"Yes, he is," she agreed. "Do you suspect him of killing everyone? Even Babs? They knew each other, you know. Doris was a bridge club member. Greg played too."

I didn't think knowing someone was a deterrent to murder. Gramps said whoever killed Babs liked her. She'd been respectfully laid out on our surgery table, hands folded over her chest.

"I need to tell the chief what happened."

"Of course. Did you feel threatened? You can come and stay here if you want."

In the background, another loud action movie played. It sounded as though buildings were exploding. I already had the beginnings of a headache just listening over the phone.

"Maybe the chief can call him tonight. Give him a warning," I suggested.

"Forget about the chief. I'm calling Greg right now and giving him a piece of my mind." The calm office manager I knew had morphed into Cindy the Avenger.

"That's probably not a great idea," I told her. "Besides, he did give me a warning. Maybe he thinks I'll listen."

"Hah," she said. "He obviously doesn't know you."

As we continued to debate my next move, I went back into the hospital and double-checked all the windows and doors. In addition, I opened the screen on my office computer and stared at the feed from the outside cameras. Nothing. No tire tracks other than mine in the parking lot, only the quickly fading coming and going tracks of the surgery release owners.

With the zoom feature, I enlarged the image, peering behind the plantings along the side of the building. Nothing.

My head started pounding for real. I honestly didn't think Greg Owens would pop up tonight. I took off my white coat and draped it over the office chair. The sweater I wore underneath was hot enough.

"Are you listening?" Cindy asked.

"Yes," I lied. The pounding in my head continued.

"Then what did I say?"

Between the heat and the headache, I didn't much care. Tucking the phone under my chin, I washed down some ibuprofen.

"Call the chief tomorrow and tell him everything you told me," she ordered. "He can have a patrol car swing by your place at night."

"I'd rather have Pinky on duty with his shotgun," I replied shutting my eyes.

Cindy laughed. "Yeah, one patrol car making the rounds every three hours doesn't cut it. But at least it's something. What about borrowing a Rottie from Mari?"

I stifled a yawn. "Sure."

"Okay. Get some sleep and keep your phone on your nightstand. I'll see you in the morning and we can sort this out."

"Okay." I went to turn off the lights then decided to keep them on. *It might look like the hospital is busy*, I thought. After making my way through the connecting door into my apartment, I realized that ruse wouldn't work.

The only vehicle in the parking lot was mine.

Chapter Thirty-Seven

ONCE INSIDE MY APARTMENT, I STRETCHED OUT ON THE sofa, pulled a blanket over my head, and closed my eyes. My brain and body needed to reboot like my laptop.

When Buddy started to bark, I awoke from my short nap. Nine p.m., but it felt like midnight. The barking continued—barking a not uncommon occurrence. To my surprise, Bella joined in with her first soft *wuff*.

"Was that a bark, Bella? Good for you."

She wagged her tail and picked up the koala toy. Every day I saw improvement in my undemanding patient.

Buddy walked stiff-legged, stopping at the front door. He continued to bark.

"What's got you spooked?" Still groggy from my sleep, I lifted a corner of the front curtain and looked outside. At the top of the driveway someone in a pickup truck had made a U-turn and was waiting to pull back onto the highway, signal light blinking. The rest of the parking lot stood empty except for the hospital truck.

Time to settle back on the sofa, except Buddy kept staring up at me and barking. It was a little early for the last walk of the night, but he seemed determined.

"Come on," I called to the dogs, picking their leashes off the coat rack. "You too, Bella. Let's get some of that energy out of you before we get ready for bed." I gently slipped a harness over Bella's gray wrinkled skin and clicked on her lead.

"Wait," I said. "I see some hair growing." Sure enough, in a random spot behind her shoulder was a thin short tuft of light brown fur. "Celebration time! First bark and first new hair growth." On an impulse, I sent both Mike and Mari a quick text and photo of Bella's shoulder.

Mike texted back immediately.

Congrats to Bella. I'd like to confirm that hair growth in person.

Anytime, I answered.

The ibuprofen must have kicked in because my headache hadn't gotten worse. I expected a quiet solo evening, which was fine with me.

As soon as I opened the door, Buddy bolted in the wrong direction, barking full throttle.

Bella remained glued to my side. A strange chemical smell lingered in the air.

An apparition appeared out of a clump of evergreens and moved toward me. The figure wore a full-length reflective garment with the pant legs tucked into high, black rubber boots. Face and hair were hidden under a grimacing Halloween mask. Plastic wraparound safety glasses covered both eyes. Something dark and dangerous hung down along its right side—gunmetal reflected in the pale light.

"Get inside," a male voice said. His left leg kicked out at Buddy who had lunged at him.

"Listen. We don't keep any money in the cash register..."

"Shut up and get inside," he repeated, this time raising the gun and pointing it at my heart. "I don't want that crazy giant next door to get curious."

How does he know about Pinky?

I froze.

"Get going or I'll shoot your dog. I swear it."

By now I'd recognized the voice. Rob had lied about most things, but he wasn't lying now. Over the barking the faint caw of a crow floated in the air.

Maybe Pinky would turn the corner in his plowing truck and see us. Pinky with his loaded shotgun.

"Move it," Rob snarled almost landing his boot on my twenty-five-pound dog. Bella began to shake.

No vehicles passed by. Pinky's home was dark and still. No witnesses to see me open the door and let a killer in.

"You first," he said gesturing with the gun.

I opened the apartment door, glancing up at the motion detector camera. The lens seemed dirty. Rob followed behind, his jumpsuit swishing when he walked.

"If you're thinking your outdoor cameras will help you, forget it. I spray-painted the lenses fifteen minutes ago. Cut your outdoor wires, too. So kind of Babs to explain your security system to me."

Buddy kept on barking, circling in closer.

"Shut him up, or I swear I'll kill him."

I bent down to pick up his leash while Bella continued to shake.

"What the hell is that?" Rob asked, pointing to her elephant like skin, crusted and bare of fur.

"She's a sweet dog with mange that I'm treating. Don't go

near her. It's contagious." That was a lie, but I didn't want Rob to get any ideas.

Buddy kept barking, running back and forth in front of me.

"Shut up," Rob screamed.

"What do you want me to do?" I asked, trying to sound as annoyed as possible. "I can leave him in here or put him in a cage in the animal hospital. Your choice."

He stared at me. "What do you usually do?"

"He's been a bit of a pest lately," I lied. "So at night I leave both dogs in the animal hospital." That of course was a complete fabrication. My friends knew both dogs slept in the apartment with me. I realized I'd started thinking like Babs, trying to leave clues for my friends in case...

"All right. Let's go into the hospital. No tricks now, Dr. Kate."

Under the bright fluorescent hospital lights, Rob appeared more like a bad nightmare. His voice sounded muffled under the mask. Close up, I realized exam gloves covered both hands. The wraparound plastic safety glasses ensured no stray eyelash would contaminate the scene.

He'd come prepared.

The treatment room smelled of disinfectant. Buddy continued barking, upsetting Mr. Katt, who looked down at him with hatred from his lofty perch on top of the cages.

Gramps made me promise to keep the pepper spray in

my pocket. I'd kept that promise. It was in the pocket of my white coat draped on the back of my office chair, about twelve feet away.

I opened a bottom cage, and Buddy scampered in. With a quick gesture I tied his leash to the cage bars. Another clue. Buddy chews his leash. My friends would catch that anomaly immediately.

Bella still shivered, reacting to the violence she sensed nearby. I placed her gently in a cage then walked over toward the treatment whiteboard.

"What do you think you're doing?" Rob said.

"Putting her treatment on the board for tomorrow. I do that every night."

He looked skeptical, but I swiftly wrote Roberta, skin scraping and lime-sulfur bath. Another clue. I wrote in cursive, my note deliberately sloppy instead of my usual clear printing. There was no Roberta in the hospital. I hoped they would connect Roberta with Rob.

"Is that it?"

"The dogs need beds, water and food bowls, and toys." I stood still not moving. *How could I catch him off guard?*

"Go get them. We don't have all night."

Still standing my ground, I asked, "What are you going to do to me?"

"Don't worry. You're going to take an overdose and die in your sleep. A tear-jerking suicide note will be on your night-stand. Babs's death was too much for you."

"No one will believe it," I told him.

"I don't care," he said.

I made a big deal out of getting the bowls and filling them with food and water. Then I glanced around as though searching for something. "My dog's bed and favorite toy are in my office," I lied. The only bed and toy in there belonged to Mr. Katt.

This time his answer sounded agitated. "Well, go get them."

"Alright." I bent down to pick the round pet bed off the floor. "I've got to get his toy or he won't shut up." Using the pet bed in my arms as a cover, I plucked the pepper spray from my coat pocket, camouflaging it behind Mr. Katt's squeaky mouse.

"Shove that stuff in the cages and let's go."

With the pepper spray safely in my pants pocket, I opened Buddy's cage and placed Mr. Katt's bed and stuffed toy inside. Buddy appeared confused, and Mr. Katt looked homicidal.

Gramps's voice whispered in my mind, *Good job, Katie. Remember what I taught you.*

I gave Bella a hospital bed and toy and closed her cage. When I stood up, Rob didn't seem so scary. Instead he looked like a pathetic pile of plastic.

He hadn't shot me yet. That wasn't his plan. I deliberately walked over to one of the lab chairs and sat down. "So tell me, why did you kill them?"

"Stand up!" he yelled.

"You had a great life in Oak Falls. Plenty of women, a good job. What happened?"

"What happened?" Rob said in a quiet voice. "Alicia happened. It was always Alicia."

Alicia. Her high school boyfriend died in a one-car crash.
Alicia. Her husband committed suicide. Alicia. Feeling
stalked for years. Her sister, Ursula, said bad luck seemed to
follow her golden baby sister.

"I didn't recognize you, Scooter," I told him. "You've
changed a lot since high school."

"Very good, Dr. Kate," Rob answered with a fake bow.
"That's precisely why you've become too dangerous. Why
would you recognize me? I've had gastric bypass surgery.
Laser resurfacing to get rid of acne scars—by the way, that
laser feels like your face is on fire."

"Rough," I replied, searching the room for another weapon.

"Plastic surgery on my nose, ear pinning, capped teeth,
and a new identity. I'm handsome now. I have to fight the
women off."

Narcissistic love. Scooter's obsessive love destroyed so
many lives.

"How did you pay for it?" I had to keep him talking.
Behind me, the ping of a text message sounded on my phone.

"Don't answer it," Rob yelled.

"Greg Owens threatened me today," I said. "You could
have pinned the murders on him."

Rob laughed. "Who do you think made him believe
José screwed up his wife's diagnosis? I kept hoping the idiot
would do my work for me and kill José, but instead he moped
around and cried."

"But if you loved Alicia, why did you kill her?" I began to
plot how to knock those glasses off his face. "Why did you
kill the woman you loved?"

"That was the one thing that didn't go as planned," Rob admitted. "José wanted to elope and say their vows at Lover's Lake. We drove up in his car to scout out the perfect location. The fool wanted it to be a surprise."

"You parked on the forest road on the lake side." That explained the lack of tire tracks.

"My plan was to make it look like an accident. Have him slip and fall into the lake. Hit his head, maybe. Then Alicia would turn to me for comfort."

"But instead…"

"She saw his car turn off the highway. Alicia knew how much José loved that stupid lake and guessed where we were going. I suppose she thought she'd surprise us. What I didn't know was José had his gun with him. We argued. There was a struggle. I grabbed his gun, pulled him close and shot him in the chest."

"Alicia saw it?" Now things made sense.

"She screamed at me. I told her it was an accident. I told her how much I loved her—and something I said—frightened her. She started running back to her car but tripped in the snow. When I picked her up and held her in my arms, she stomped on my foot and dove into the lake."

A fatal mistake, even for a strong swimmer.

"She didn't get far. Her clothes and boots pulled her down."

His words turned cold and clinical. No hint of regret in his voice.

"She struggled. Legs caught among the reeds. I promised not to hurt her. When she came close enough, I lifted her out of the water. Her lips turned blue but she still fought me. I saved her, and she still fought me."

Before I could comment, he added, "I kissed her while I strangled her."

The vision of Alicia's wide frozen eyes floated up into my consciousness.

"Afterward, I couldn't hold her any longer. She slipped from my arms and fell backward into the water. I watched her sink. I watched until the bubbles died away."

"And José?"

"I put the gun into his hand and fired off another shot— left him facedown in the snow to rot."

Nice guy.

Rob continued in a bragging voice. "My biggest problem was returning Alicia's car, so I took that one first. Nora was at a concert in the city, so I parked Alicia's car in the driveway as the snow started to fall, borrowed the snowmobile, and went back for José's truck. Stashed that at our place. Then I drove my car back to that stupid lake, put the snowmobile in the flatbed like I've done plenty of times, and had everything stored away before midnight. By the time Nora got home, I was asleep in her bed. Ingenious, right?"

"Not really. You should have left José's truck parked near the lake. You created a lot of questions leaving them without transportation." I used my most sarcastic tone. "Big mistake. Does Nora know?" I asked.

"Nora? Dumb as a rock." He shifted his weight. "Do you know how I felt after I killed Alicia?"

"No idea."

"Like a cancerous tumor had been ripped from my heart." The mask failed to filter out the note of exhilaration.

My text chime pinged again. Rob turned his head.

I needed to get his attention off my phone. "What about Babs?"

His head swiveled back toward me. Buddy put his paw on Mr. Katt's toy, making it squeak.

"Babs was too curious, like you, Dr. Kate. After you found the bodies, she asked me a butt load of questions. First she focused on Bruce as the murderer, but I suspected she'd eventually turn that focus on me. Killing her here in your animal hospital was a stroke of genius."

"Yeah, you're a real genius," I said as sarcastically as possible. "Except Babs left us clues. She figured out you were going to kill her."

"Liar. We had coffee. We talked. Then she went to sleep. Perfect."

Buddy squeaked Mr. Katt's toy again.

"Did anyone else help you? What about that friend from high school? You guys were inseparable."

"Funny you should ask." I had the feeling that under his latex mask he was smiling.

"Who is it? Bruce? Hughie?"

Rob lifted the gun up and pointed it at my head. "It's a surprise."

"Tell me."

"I think we're done here, Dr. Kate. I'm going to follow you into your apartment now. Walk slowly and keep your hands in the air or I'll kill both those mutts."

I stood up. So did Buddy, flipping the cat toy in the air as it squeaked over and over.

Mr. Katt had had enough. The hated dog had his toy and bed and an invader in his hospital smelled like danger. With a yowling screech, he hurled himself at Rob, landing in the middle of his back, claws extended and began ripping his latex mask into shreds.

"What the hell?" Rob tried in vain to grab the angry cat. Embedded back claws hung on tight.

I scooped my cell phone from the countertop, jammed it in my pocket, and ran toward the apartment door, slamming it behind me. Not stopping for a coat, I tore out the front door, Rob screaming obscenities behind me. Another car pulled into the hospital parking lot.

Mike. I recognized his old Scion and made a beeline toward it.

The car barely stopped before Mike opened his door. "Kate. You never answered my texts. What's going on?"

Rob burst through my door, his latex mask hanging down in bloody strips. "Hi, Mike," he said. "Fancy meeting you here."

Mike?

No. Not Mike.

Was he the second killer?

"Kate," Mike yelled out, brandishing a screwdriver in his hand, "run!"

Rob laughed and dodged the thrown tool that skittered across the snow. "My turn," he said and fired. A bloom of red appeared on Mike's coat.

"Change of plan," Rob said, sighting the weapon on me. "One down and one to go. So long, Dr. Kate."

I dove to the frozen ground as a shot fired, my hands and cheek scraping gravel and dirt. A black shape appeared out of nowhere. The angry crow dive-bombed Rob's face. Sharp talons and a deadly pointed beak went straight for his eyes, knocking the safety glasses to the ground. Another crow joined, and yet another flew at him, landing on Rob's head, attacking his forehead, his eyes.

He screamed, pinwheeling his arms to fight off the crows. Drops of blood painted the snow.

The diversion was enough for me to use the pepper spray. I showed no mercy. One hand shooed away the crows, and the other sprayed the pepper spray directly into his fake green eyes. Rob dropped the gun and screamed again, clawing his own face. I kicked him in the groin just like Gramps taught me.

"Special delivery from Babs."

Then I kicked him again.

When I ran over to Mike's car, I expected the worst. Instead, he stood up, grimacing in pain.

"We need to restrain that maniac. Right now," he said.

"But your shoulder?"

"I've had worse. Got any duct tape in that truck?"

"Doesn't everyone?" I threw open the cab door while Mike opened his trunk and removed some rope.

Rob lay writhing and moaning on the ground. I didn't expect him to stay there for long.

"You're still bleeding," I told Mike as I wrapped first one then the other of Rob's flailing gloved hands with tape.

Mike went to town with the rope, hog-tying Rob, securing his legs and arms.

"You've done this before," I said.

"Rodeo and 4-H," Mike admitted. When he stood up he said, "I feel odd."

I guided Mike back to his car and sat him down in the passenger seat, motor running and heat blasting. When I slid off his jacket, I saw a swelling circle of blood high up on his shoulder. "We need to apply pressure."

A gray sweater lay in the back seat, so I balled it up and pressed it hard against the gunshot wound. I called 911 and told them to hurry.

"Ouch," he said. "I think I overdid it tying him up." His teeth started to chatter, despite the warm air pouring out of the car vents. "Am I going into shock?"

His beautiful blue-gray eyes were the only color in a deathly pale face.

"Not yet," I said. "Keep holding my hand. Don't let go." In the distance I heard sirens. The sweater pressed under my fingers became slick and heavy with blood.

"I can't see the stars this time," he said, eyelids fluttering.

"Don't worry. We'll see them together."

Chapter Thirty-Eight

THE SURGERY WAITING ROOM AT THE HOSPITAL IN Kingston was meant to be a comfortable place for families waiting for news of their loved one's operation. It was painted in subdued natural colors, and clusters of separate seats gave an illusion of privacy. About ten other individuals waited with us. All glanced up periodically at the electronic board listing patients undergoing procedures.

I wouldn't know. I'd been pacing up and down for almost an hour, reviewing the anatomy of the shoulder in my mind—the arteries, the nerves, and everything that could go wrong.

Mari watched with dark solemn eyes.

"Shouldn't they be finished by now?" I asked. My cheek burned from gravel cuts.

"Sit down, Kate. You're wearing yourself out." She patted the chair next to her.

"Thanks for taking care of the dogs," I told her, trying to stay calm while feeling like I was jumping out of my skin.

From the depths of her purse, she pulled out a banana. "Take a bite," she said, "and tell me about Rob. I never would have picked him as a killer."

Where to begin? "Well, first of all, he isn't Rob. He's Scooter Evans, who stalked Alicia for at least a decade. He was obsessed with her. In his warped mind he figured if he changed his looks, she'd fall in love with him. When she didn't—he decided to kill the competition."

"Even though José was a friend?"

"No such thing as a friend in Rob's twisted "Scooter," mind. He may have killed Alicia's high school boyfriend and her lawyer husband, James."

"No kidding," Mari said. "So the husband may have been a murder, not a suicide?"

"It looks like it." I forced a morsel of banana in my mouth before jumping back up again.

"Was there a second killer, like you thought?"

"Nope," I answered. "Only Rob."

"The chief is going to have his hands full sorting all this out."

The surgery waiting room door swung open, and Cindy marched in. She carried two small duffle bags as well as her purse.

"Thanks for coming," I told her, hugging her close. With both my friends here, my anxiety level dropped a few notches. A flicker of change on the board indicated one of the surgical patients had been moved to recovery.

"I take it Mike's still in surgery," she said, claiming a seat next to Mari. "I contacted a few people at his work, so they're taking care of things on that end."

Mike's work? I was ashamed to say the thought didn't cross my mind. "What about his parents?" I asked.

"Kendra, their office manager, spoke to them briefly and will keep them updated. From what the surgeon said, it was a pretty straightforward repair."

"You spoke to the surgeon?"

Several people in the waiting room glanced my way. I didn't realize how much I'd raised my voice.

"Sit down, Kate," she whispered. "The chief talked to the surgeon, and I talked to the chief. The surgical team is finishing up and will move him to recovery soon. Then you'll be able to see him."

That hard lump in my throat and stomach melted. I reached over and smooched Cindy on the cheek. "Thank you so much. I've been thinking the worst."

"You're welcome." She dug out a bottle of water from one of the duffel bags. "Drink this. You've got to stay hydrated. Those cuts on your hands look painful."

"Yes, sir, General Cindy." I'd taken another big bite from my banana, which suddenly tasted fantastic. "Don't worry. They look worse than they feel."

"What's in the duffel bag?" asked Mari.

"Toothpaste, toothbrushes, comb, underwear, and clothes for Mike, change of clothes for you, Kate, your phone charger…everything I thought you'd need for an overnight stay."

There was no point asking Cindy how she knew sizes, etc. She was super-efficient and organized and a national treasure in my eyes.

From her purse she removed a computer tablet and powered it up.

"You're working now?" I asked in disbelief.

"No." Despite the circumstances, she appeared fresh and ready for anything, with makeup and hair perfect. "I've heard from Doc Anderson."

Mari and I exchanged glances. We'd been following the owner of Oak Falls Animal Hospital on his around-the-world-cruise from his postings on Facebook. In the last few months, they'd tapered off. We'd been so busy I hadn't noticed, but now I started to worry.

"Did he have another heart attack?" Mari blurted out, concern on her face.

"No," Cindy said. "He's getting married."

"Married!" Now it was Mari's turn to be stared at by everyone in the room. "He's on a cruise with his sister. Who did he meet? A mermaid?"

"Apparently not." She slid her electronic device over so Mari and I could view the picture he'd posted. There stood Doc Anderson on the deck of a ship looking healthy and happy, his arm around a woman about his age. She looked a lot like Cindy.

"I can't believe it either," Cindy told us. "Doc and his sister both play bridge, and I guess they were paired with two ladies from Virginia."

"Virginia? So Southern ladies."

"I suppose so because according to Doc, they started talking after the game ended—which led to a friendly drink."

"And…"

"Her name is Charlene, and she's a widow."

"That's perfect," Mari interjected. "Doc is a widower."

Cindy raised her eyebrows then continued. "For the past three months they've been inseparable. She owns a stud farm in Virginia horse country and has a place on the beach in Hilton Head, South Carolina—along with three grown children and seven grandchildren."

"An instant family for Doc."

I knew that Doc and his wife had been unable to conceive during their long marriage. His wife's health declined dramatically ten years ago after being diagnosed with brain cancer. Surgery proved unsuccessful.

"I'm so happy for him," Cindy said. "He'll make a fantastic grandfather."

This was all moving too quickly for me. Mike in the hospital—Doc getting married—and me out of a job.

"So they'll move back here to Oak Falls after they get married?" I asked.

"Hell, no." Cindy looked around to make sure no one else in the waiting room heard her. "Charlene wants to be near her children and grandchildren, so Doc is moving to her place in Virginia. She's putting him to work with her horses."

That still didn't solve my problem.

"Kate, Doc wants to know if you want to buy the Oak Falls Animal Hospital."

Buy a veterinary practice? My head began to ring.

I could barely afford to buy a car. Disbelief numbed my brain. *He wants to sell his practice?* Doc Anderson was only sixty-five years old. I remembered seeing a picture of his birthday cake. He'd practiced veterinary medicine in Oak Falls for over thirty years. How could he sell everything and move to Virginia after knowing someone for three months? It sounded crazy.

And brave.

Chapter Thirty-Nine

MIKE'S RECOVERY PROVED UNEVENTFUL, IF PAINFUL. THE bullet tore through skin and muscles, nicking a bone. His orthopedic doctor stabilized the wounded arm with a sling, but even a slight jolt made him wince. He'd gone back to work with some modifications, paired with a veterinary technician skilled in mixed-animal techniques and restraint. Each night after leaving work, he retreated to his own place, exhausted.

Not a situation conducive to romance.

A genealogist working for the estate lawyer found a distant cousin of Babs's, who was astonished at her good fortune. An animal lover, she wished she had met her second cousin once removed sooner. As a single mom with a preteen who currently rented, she planned to move into the gatekeeper's home, free of debt.

And she adored midcentury modern.

Rob "Scooter" Evans faced more charges when his personal computer revealed links to fake identities, ghost guns, and plenty of disturbing dark websites. People he knew had a bad habit of turning up dead. The chief brought in the FBI. Alicia's law firm, spearheaded by Hughie, watched and listened as the case against Rob took shape. They intended to help convict the man who killed their colleague, any way they could.

Winter hinted of the spring to follow in the Hudson

Valley. Snow periodically turned into rain, and the first golden forsythia flowers burst into bloom. My wild crow family spent more time away—scouting nesting sites—our cawing adventures over.

I missed them.

———————

Doc Anderson called from an Internet café in Europe early one morning before office hours and clarified his intention to sell the practice.

"I've got so many memories tied up there in Oak Falls," he told me over a static-filled phone connection. "But I realized during my travels I needed to create new ones. Things change. You only live your life once."

That, I agreed with. When I brought up money, he proposed a solution. He'd hold a private note for me at a reasonable rate, provided I came up with a suitable down payment.

"I won't sell my hospital to a corporate buyer," he stated, referencing the many large companies investing in animal hospitals. "If possible I'd like to help out a young vet like you. But you have to keep Cindy on," he stipulated. "And Mari."

"No problem," I answered. "I'd be lost without them."

"Take your time and think about it," he said, sounding oddly like Gramps. "But don't call me tomorrow. Tomorrow is Valentine's Day, and my fiancée, Charlene, and I are going dancing."

That night I found out dancing on Valentine's Day was a no for Mike and me. The same for dinner and drinks.

"One of the vets who covered for me while I was out sick wants Valentine's Day off. She's been so helpful working my shifts—I didn't feel right saying no." Mike's voice over the phone sounded both disappointed and apologetic. "However, I've got an alternative plan."

"I'm listening."

"February 15. That can be our Valentine's Day. I've even got the 16th off, in case our dinner runs late."

"Runs late? How late?"

"Into breakfast, hopefully."

"It sounds like this time you planned ahead," I joked, wishing he was sitting next to me. "So where is all this going to happen? My place or yours?"

Mike laughed. "It doesn't matter, as long as I'm with you."

A perfect answer.

"I feel the same."

Buddy groaned and twitched at my feet dreaming an energetic doggy dream. Bella slumbered next to him, tiny new hairs all over her body visible when the light struck just right.

"We can still hang out at my large-animal clinic on Valentine's Day, if you want," Mike suggested. "Just us, our receptionist, two techs, and a few sick horses. It might get messy."

"Thanks," I said, "but I think I'm needed somewhere else."

Alone on my sofa, dogs at my feet, I thought about love and sacrifice. I'd met clients willing to spend thousands to never say goodbye to their fur babies. Pets who mirrored their owners, and a dog named Booty Call.

Only one thing left to do. I called the most constant man in my life, my forever and ever valentine. When Gramps answered, I asked him an important question.

"Hey, Gramps, how would you feel about having three dates on Valentine's Day? I could referee if your two lady friends get frisky."

His belly laugh made me grin. "Thought you'd never ask, Katie."

I could almost smell his famous pasta sauce cooking on the stove.

THE END

If you enjoyed
Murders of a Feather, don't miss
the following excerpt from
Last But Not Leashed,
another Dr. Kate Vet Mystery
available from Poisoned Pen Press.

Chapter One

"KEANU. STOP KISSING ME."

Despite my pleas, Keanu drew closer, his soulful, dark eyes begging for more.

"You're being a bad, bad boy."

The friendly Labrador retriever mix, named after the famous actor, made a valiant effort to obey. I'd almost finished his final bandage change. The outside layer was lime-green vet wrap, and in about a minute I'd be done if my handsome patient would stop wiggling around. Keanu had cut his paw from catapulting himself in the air after a Frisbee; on descent, the athletic dog landed on a sharp wire fence but kept the disc firmly in his mouth.

Thanks to quick action by my staff at the Oak Falls Animal Hospital, the cut pad had healed nicely, but keeping a foot bandage dry in two feet of snow in New York's Hudson Valley presented a challenge.

"Okay, good-looking. We're done." With that, the dog stood up on the stainless steel table and looked around the treatment room. A bank of cages lined the far wall, punctuated by IV stands and infusion pumps. Most of our Christmas decorations were gone, but someone had left a card depicting Santa Claus as a water buffalo taped to the wall. Above the oxygen cage, perched on the highest point, sat our hospital cat, Mr. Katt, looking down in supreme feline disdain. A stealthy ninja, he sometimes jumped on our shoulders from on high with no warning.

My veterinary tech, Mari, waterproofed our work with some plastic wrap while I kept our star distracted.

"Ready?" I asked her.

"Ready, Doc," she replied.

The two of us lifted Keanu in our arms and gently placed him on the treatment room floor. We both received more doggie kisses for our work.

His thick tail kept whacking me in the knees as I walked him back to reception. As soon as he saw his family, the wags reached a crescendo. That tail felt like someone playing a drum solo on my legs.

The happy family reunion in our reception area quickly turned into chaos. Keanu jumped up on everyone, acting as though he hadn't seen them in years, instead of a mere twenty minutes. Trying to be heard above the ten-year-old twin boys' enthusiastic chatter, I reminded the adults to take the plastic covering off as soon as they got home, and to keep this new bandage clean and dry. Since dogs love to lick, Keanu had several types of anti-licking collars at home to wear, from stiff plastic to sturdy fabric.

"And no Frisbee playing until he's completely healed," I yelled as they walked out the door. "Promise?" At every bandage change I said the same thing, at the same time.

"Promise. Thanks, Dr. Kate. Happy almost New Year." We watched as the family of four piled into their SUV parked in front of our entrance, the mischievous twins sliding over to make room in the back for Keanu. Before the door slammed shut, I saw one of the boys hand the shiny black dog a bright red Frisbee.

My receptionist, Cindy, started laughing. "We should make up some 'No Frisbee' signs for those guys."

I sank into one of the reception chairs and asked, "Are we done for the morning?"

Mari slumped into the chair opposite me, her brown eyes glazed. "Please tell me we can eat lunch now. It's twelve thirty-two."

"Surprise." Cindy got up from her desk, purse and coat in hand. We watched as she flipped our office sign to CLOSED. Dangling her car keys in the air, she said, "Our next appointment isn't until two. The answering service is picking up our calls, so you both can relax. I've got to get to the bank and shop for some office supplies, but I'll be back to open up by one thirty."

The last time we'd had such a long lunch was when one of our house-call clients got murdered.

"Don't get into trouble while I'm gone." Cindy gave me a look like she'd read my mind. Then with a blazing white cheerleader smile she let herself out the front door, locked us in, and hurried over to her truck. Despite the wind, her hair remained undaunted, as unmoving as a steel helmet, stiff with spray.

We didn't wait around to watch her leave.

"This feels like I'm on vacation." Mari laughed as she hurried toward the employee break room to get her food.

"Don't jinx it," I said.

With so much extra time, I suggested we eat lunch at my place. It wasn't a long commute. One of the perks of the job, if you could call it that, was living in the attached converted garage apartment. It consisted of a bedroom alcove, a bathroom, small kitchen, living room, and not much more. With a student loan debt of over a hundred and fifty thousand dollars after graduating from Cornell University School of Veterinary Medicine, not having to pay rent made living in a converted garage more palatable.

My rescue dog, Buddy, barked and twirled with pleasure as we opened the apartment door. He loved company but also knew that Mari sometimes dropped delicious things on the floor that I allowed him to gobble up. Vacuuming up stray food was Buddy's contribution to housekeeping.

Usually when Mari comes into the apartment she says, "Looking good." This time she simply shook her head.

"I know. I know." The last week had been particularly frenzied. Piles of stuff were scattered all over the place. My boyfriend, Luke Gianetti, was finishing up his first semester in law school, living and working near the school, so I had no motivation to tidy up. At least that was my rationale. On the kitchen table, Mari found my list of things to do before he joined me for New Year's.

While munching on her sandwich, she eyeballed it.

The microwave pinged, signaling my canned soup was ready.

"You've got way too much on this list," she commented between bites.

"Welcome to my life." When I opened the microwave, I

heard my soup bubbling. I'd punched in the wrong number of minutes and turned my tomato bisque into lava.

"No, that's not what I mean." She ripped open a bag of chips and started munching. "If your list is too long, it can be discouraging. Professional organizers say you should break your chores up into manageable units."

"Units?" I also misjudged the temperature of the blue ceramic soup bowl and yelled, "Ouch!" while racing for the kitchen table.

Mari noticed my dilemma but stayed focused on her advice. "Yes, units. That's what they call them, Kate. Like a math problem, I suppose."

"Okay." I blew on my soup a few times before trying it once more. "How do you know all this?"

She held a finger up to indicate a full mouth.

Seeing her occupied, I stole a couple of chips.

"Well, my sister-in-law, Barbara, signed up for this lecture series on home organization at the community center. I'm going with her tonight." Her dark eyebrows arched as she turned and asked, "Want to join us?"

I did a slow pan around the room. Stacks of stuff were everywhere, multiple single socks lay scattered on the floor in no discernable pattern, and dirty clothes draped over the furniture. After clearing my throat, I managed a sarcastic "You think I need to?"

"Hey, I've got a roomie to help me. You're all by yourself, plus half the time you work on the weekends, what with treatments and emergencies. I'm surprised it looks this good in here."

"Thanks." Mari always had my back. "I have to admit I've been feeling overwhelmed lately."

She finished off the last of the chips and crumpled the bag. "So, the lecture starts at six, followed by a short Q and A. It's over by eight. Why don't you meet us there? Count it toward your New Year's resolutions."

I was about to protest that I had too much to do but then realized that most nights I simply sacked out on the sofa with my dog, poured a glass of wine, and watched HGTV.

"Okay," I promised her. "It's a date."

Chapter Two

I GOT TO THE COMMUNITY CENTER A LITTLE LATE, THANKS to a last-minute email from a client confused about his kitty's insulin dosage. I'd been to the center a few times, once to cheer on a client with a performing parrot. The large, paved lot next to the center, one of the newer buildings in town, was filled with cars tonight, forcing me to park at the far end.

Despite our recent December snowstorm, the main entrance was newly shoveled, with fresh sand spread about for added traction. Once inside the double glass doors, I followed the signs for the home-organizing lecture. The designated room proved easy to find and held a much larger audience than I expected. At the podium, a speaker discussed wood versus laminate cabinets. Mari had promised to save me a place, so once I caught a glimpse of her curly Afro in the front row, I attempted to join her. No such luck. The speaker paused, frowned at me, then pointed to the few empty seats near the back. I chose the closest aisle, slipped off my backpack and winter coat, and piled them on the seat next to me.

Behind me a man with a pink muffler around his neck scribbled in a pocket notebook.

The topic seemed to be drawers. I didn't know the speaker's name, but she'd dressed very professionally in a black pantsuit and white shirt. A striking green necklace made of large beads in differing shades drew attention to her attractive face. Her abundant brown hair with salon-bleached blond streaks was sleekly contained in a French braid. She radiated confidence.

As I tried to concentrate on her presentation, my body temperature went from comfortably warm to boiling hot. The room air smelled stuffy, full of people. Someone must have turned the heat up because my forehead quickly beaded up with sweat. In a hurry to leave my apartment, I'd neglected to layer, so I had nothing on under my heavy wool sweater except underwear. With sweat rolling down my back and sliding down my front, it became hard to concentrate on organizing your drawers.

While the lecturer continued discussing different drawer liner options, I scanned the room. Along the right wall was a beverage area. My salvation, in the form of a large iced-water dispenser, beckoned. As quietly as possible I stood up, reminding myself to grab a few extra napkins for damage control. Maybe I could casually stuff them down my bra?

"And we have a volunteer," the lecturer said loudly. "The blond woman in the back. Let's give her a hand."

I frantically searched for another blond but soon realized the applause was for me.

Dabbing delicately at my face with my sleeve, I slowly walked down the center aisle and stood next to her.

"So tell us," the lecturer said, pausing and raising her palm toward me like I was a game show prize. "What is your name?"

"Kate," I answered.

"Tell us, Kate, what do you use to line your dresser drawers?"

Instead of making something up, I told the truth. "I'm not sure. Some kind of wrapping paper, I think? It was in the drawers when I moved in."

The look of disgust on her face could have earned an Academy Award. "You put your clean clothes on top of someone else's…used…drawer liner? Did you wipe it off first?"

This time I lied and said, "Yes."

I don't think she believed me. When I searched for a bit of sympathy from the audience, only Mari managed a smile.

The presenter paused dramatically, then sighed. "I think Kate here needs our help." A ripple of laughter rose from the mostly female audience, some of whom I recognized as my clients. I tried to slink away, but the organizer said, "Just a moment, Kate."

She took a step toward me, then picked something off my shoulder and held it up like a dead bug. "What is this?"

Trapped with the evidence dangling in front of me, I straightened my back, stared her in the eye, and replied in a loud voice, "Dog hair."

More peals of merriment from the audience. Someone with a braying laugh sounded particularly amused.

With a cluck of her tongue, she wrapped the fur in a Kleenex fished out of her jacket pocket and announced, "You, my dear, don't just need help; you need an intervention."

Acknowledgments

This writing year turned out to have many unexpected adventures for Dr. Kate and me. Instead of looking out at the desert while working, I found myself gazing at a lake. Ospreys flew by, fishing with deadly precision. Ducks performed stylized mating rituals, and sleek otters swam past at sunset each night. An industrious crow and his friends caught my attention one afternoon as I stared out the window hoping for plot inspiration—and were incorporated into this book. Is it simply a coincidence that a cluster of crows is called "a murder"?

Thanks are due to my editors, Diane DiBiase and Beth Deveny, and the staff at Sourcebooks for all their hard work. My critique group, as always, was invaluable with their suggestions—Betty Webb, Arthur Kerns, Charlie Pyeatte, Sharon Magee, Ruth Barmore, and Donis Casey. As always, the help and moral support from my husband, Dr. Jonathan Grant, has been immeasurable. Living with a writer can be a challenge.

About the Author

A practicing veterinarian for more than twenty years, Eileen Brady lives in Arizona with her husband, two daughters, and an assortment of furry friends.

She can be reached at eileenbradymysteries@gmail.com.